The Illegitimate Duke

"I know it seems unreasonable, but you must trust me in this. There are things you do not know about me that you would surely find distasteful."

"Such as?" When Florian failed to respond she crossed her arms tightly over her chest and asked, "Are you a highway robber by night?"

He shook his head. "Don't be ridiculous."

She ignored his comment. "Have you committed a heinous crime?"

"Of course not. Juliette, this questioning will lead us nowhere."

"Hmm . . ."

He stared at her. "You don't believe me?"

"I might if you were to kiss me."

Crossing his legs, Florian pulled his bag onto his lap and met her gaze. Undeniable heat loomed there, the fire stoked inside him by that simple statement as blatant as her own. It sparked and sizzled in the air between them until the carriage drew to an unfortunate stop, signaling their arrival.

"I will not kiss you," he murmured as he opened the door and alit so he could help her down.

Juliette clasped the hand he offered and stepped down onto the pavement with a smile. "We shall see," she told him slyly.

By Sophie Barnes

Novels

THE ILLEGITIMATE DUKE
THE DUKE OF HER DESIRE
A MOST UNLIKELY DUKE
HIS SCANDALOUS KISS
THE EARL'S COMPLETE SURRENDER
LADY SARAH'S SINFUL DESIRES
THE DANGER IN TEMPTING AN EARL
THE SCANDAL IN KISSING AN HEIR
THE TROUBLE WITH BEING A DUKE
THE SECRET LIFE OF LADY LUCINDA
THERE'S SOMETHING ABOUT LADY MARY
LADY ALEXANDRA'S EXCELLENT ADVENTURE
HOW MISS RUTHERFORD GOT HER GROOVE BACK

Novellas

MISTLETOE MAGIC (FROM FIVE GOLDEN RINGS:
A CHRISTMAS COLLECTION)

Coming Soon

THE INFAMOUS DUCHESS

SOPHIE BARNES

The Illegitimate Duke

Diamonds
in the Rough

AVONBOOKS

An Imprint of HarperCollins*Publishers*

THE ILLEGITIMATE DUKE. Copyright © 2018 by Sophie Barnes. All rights reserved. Printed in the United States of America. No part of this book may be used or reproduced in any manner whatsoever without written permission except in the case of brief quotations embodied in critical articles and reviews. For information, address HarperCollins Publishers, 195 Broadway, New York, NY 10007.

First Avon Books mass market printing: September 2018

Print Edition ISBN: 978-0-06-284972-4
Digital Edition ISBN: 978-0-06-284973-1

Cover design and art direction by Guido Caroti
Cover art by Chris Cocozza

Avon, Avon & logo, and Avon Books & logo are registered trademarks of HarperCollins Publishers in the United States of America and other countries.
HarperCollins is a registered trademark of HarperCollins Publishers in the United States of America and other countries.

FIRST EDITION

18 19 20 21 22 QGM 10 9 8 7 6 5 4 3 2 1

To my ambassadors
Thank you for your constant support!

Chapter 1

Stepping forward in time to the music, Juliette Matthews held her dance partner's hand as delicately as she'd been instructed. Overhead, two massive chandeliers cast a brilliant glow across the Hawthorne House ballroom, the light from a thousand candles bouncing off gemstones and beadwork. It was a crush, the first ball of the Season, with footmen balancing trays of champagne and little iced cakes that looked a lot better than they actually tasted.

Ladies paraded about like birds showing off their colorful plumage while gentlemen stood in small groups discussing political issues or whatever it was men liked to talk about. Juliette wasn't entirely sure, except for the fact that this appeared to be the subject of recent conversations between her brother, Raphe, the Duke of Huntley, and her sister Amelia's husband, the Duke of Coventry.

Skipping along the line of dancers while executing the complicated steps she'd been taught, Juliette considered how different her life was now from what it had been only one year earlier. Having spent most of her life in the slums of St. Giles, she wondered if she appreciated her good fortune more than her peers. After all, she knew what it was to go hungry, to live in squalor with not enough money for firewood in the winter or to pay a physician's fee whenever she'd been sick.

"You look enchanting this evening," the Earl of Yates declared while leading her in a series of tight little circles. His eyes sparkled with deep appreciation.

Juliette liked him and always enjoyed his company, so she smiled at him warmly while saying, "And you look as dashing as usual, my lord."

His hand closed more firmly around hers and his gaze dropped ever so slightly. Enough to replace the contentment she found in his company with something she instantly recognized as deep discomfort.

"Perhaps we ought to discuss how wonderful we both look while taking a tour of the room," he said when the music was over and he was leading her away from the dance floor. His smile hadn't changed, and yet, the brief consideration he'd given her mouth, the tightening of his hand and the way his gaze had seemed to darken, urged Juliette to decline the invitation.

Because as much as she favored his company, she didn't want more than friendship from him, and she was becoming increasingly worried he might not feel the same way.

"You are always so attentive toward me, which I appreciate," she began, hoping to let him down easy, "but I would like to visit the ladies' retiring room. If you don't mind."

His smile faded and the glow in his eyes dimmed. "Of course not." He guided her toward the periphery of the room, stepped back and gave a curt, yet respectful bow. "I thank you for the dance, Lady

Juliette." Glancing over her shoulder, he said with a touch of dry humor, "It looks as though your friend is here to save you."

Turning, Juliette looked in the direction Yates indicated and found her good friend, Miss Vivien Saunders, coming toward them.

"Did I chase his lordship away?" Vivien asked when she was within speaking distance. Her aunt's marriage to a baron was what ensured her entry into Society, even though said baron had long since died and his widow was in financial straits. As for Vivien herself, she had few prospects and little hope of marrying a man with a title.

Juliette returned her attention to Yates only to see his retreating back disappearing into the crowd. She sighed as she linked her arm with Vivien's. Together, they headed toward the door leading out into the hallway where the ladies' retiring room was located. "I'm afraid I upset him."

"I sincerely doubt that, Julie. You're always kind and considerate toward others."

Juliette scrunched her nose. "I may have made up an excuse not to walk with him after our dance."

"Oh."

"Oh?" Juliette glanced across at her friend. "What on earth does that mean?"

"Well . . . the man obviously likes you. A lot. And you do seem to like him as well, considering how much you smile and laugh when you are together."

Juliette thought about that for a second. "Am I supposed to pretend not to like dancing with a gentleman simply to avoid making him think I might be encouraging a courtship?"

Vivien squeezed the right side of her face together

as if it required great effort to answer that question. "Pretty much. I think. Although I'm really no expert."

They entered the retiring room where two other young women were fixing their hair in front of a mirror. "Why can't a man and a woman be friends without either expecting more?" Juliette whispered to Vivien while one of the other women in the room giggled in response to something her friend had said.

"Perhaps because it's called the *marriage* mart," Vivien suggested, moving to a screened-off seating area and lowering herself to a comfy-looking settee.

Juliette remained standing, too agitated to stay still. She crossed her arms and eyed her friend. "Well, it's a shame." She held Vivien's gaze before throwing up her hands and dropping onto the vacant spot beside her. "Not only did I fabricate an excuse to avoid spending time with a man whom I genuinely like, but now I have to sit in here for a good ten minutes or more so it doesn't look like I lied to him. Even though he probably knows I did."

"Don't worry." Vivien patted her hand. "It will all work itself out in the end."

"Will it?" Juliette wasn't so sure. She'd suffered the hurtful remarks other young ladies had whispered behind her back, endured the most exasperating lessons in etiquette and tried to fit in as best as she could, but there were days when she wondered about the point of it all.

"—I mean, to think we could be so lucky is almost too much," one of the women on the other side of the screen was saying. "Our debuts looked positively dismal with no chance to snatch up a duke."

"Until now, that is," the other woman said in a

dreamy voice that made Juliette roll her eyes. She glanced at Vivien and had to force down a laugh.

"Can you believe our good fortune?" the first woman said.

"Well, he's not a duke yet. Is he?"

Juliette straightened and tilted her head. They were obviously talking about Florian Lowell, the physician Raphe had sent for when she'd been sick with the measles the previous year. News of his recent change in status had been the subject of great discussion at Huntley House the previous evening when Raphe had returned home with the announcement.

Juliette still wasn't sure she understood how the title or the inheritance had come about, but it did look as though Florian would one day outrank his older brother, Mr. Lowell, who was set to become Viscount Armswell one day.

"Either way, I could easily get used to the idea of marrying Florian," one of the women was saying. "He's ever so handsome."

Both women burst into giggles. Muted whispers followed and then the sound of the door opening and closing plunged the room into silence. Juliette looked at Vivien and grinned. "Well, I wish them luck. In truth I don't believe I've ever met a man more unapproachable than Florian."

"He does look rather starched," Vivien muttered. She stood and adjusted her gown. "Mind you, I've only seen him once or twice, so I could be wrong."

"No. I don't believe you are. In fact, my impression of him is not much different. He's an excellent physician who seems to take his work very seriously. One cannot fault him for that, though I do wonder what it might be like to see him smile."

"Do you now?" Vivien asked with a smirk as the two returned to the hallway and started making their way back toward the ballroom.

Juliette nudged her friend with her shoulder. "Oh, you know what I mean, Viv!"

"All I know is that you wondering what it might be like to see him smile will likely pester you until you find a way to make it happen." They entered the ballroom. "Of all the people I have ever known, none are as determined as you when you set your mind to something."

"Well I—" A wave of chatter cut Juliette's thought process short. She glanced around, aware of the agitation rolling through the ballroom like tremors threatening to toss all the guests up into the air. "What on earth is going on?"

"Look," someone said as Juliette pushed her way between a few people, pulling Vivien along by her hand.

"There he is," another voice muttered.

Shouldering her way past a cluster of women who craned their heads and stared toward the ballroom entrance, Juliette caught a sudden and very unexpected glimpse of the man she and Vivien had just been discussing.

Florian.

Her breath caught and her heart slammed hard against her chest. Because there he was and dear God if he didn't look superb! Dressed in evening black, his copper streaked hair was neatly combed, though a single stray lock slashed roguishly across his brow. She'd never seen him like this before. The last time they'd met at a ball he'd been wearing an unremarkable suit cut from brown wool, if memory served. Now, however, he looked like the dukely title would fit him as well as the perfectly tailored jacket and trousers he wore. They seemed to accentuate his masculine physique in a way she'd never considered. It was almost as if his shoulders were broader, his build a little taller and . . .

Juliette blinked. *No.* She would not be like all the other silly girls swarming toward him and vying for his attention. He was just a man, after all, even if he was capable of saving the sick and putting a broken body back together again, which was admittedly something to be admired. But that didn't mean she would ever be able to look past his stern demeanor or want anything from him besides medical advice and possibly friendship.

And yet, while she thought of all this, Florian's head turned in her direction and his gaze locked with hers. Juliette's pulse leapt and an unfamiliar flutter filled her stomach.

She sucked in a breath and deliberately turned away. Fresh air was what she needed, that was all. The stuffy heat in the ballroom had obviously affected her senses. So with this in mind, she maneuvered her way toward the French doors and slipped out onto the terrace, breathing a sigh of relief as the cool night air cleared her head.

Florian stared at the spot where Lady Juliette had just been. A strange sense of relief had driven its way through his limbs the moment he'd seen her. Because she'd been a welcome excuse, a means for him to escape the clamoring attention he'd faced when he'd entered the ballroom. But rather than come and greet him, she'd turned away, leaving him to his attackers.

"My daughter would love to dance the waltz with

you," an overeager mama insisted while shoving a dance card under his nose.

"Would she really?" He frowned at the woman who merely returned an expectant stare. "I do not waltz, Madam."

His dry tone had little effect. "The cotillion then?"

Florian knew that *he* would be labeled inconsiderate if he denied her request. So he reached for the pencil and reluctantly scribbled his name, which only encouraged others to be equally persistent.

"Would you like me to save you?" his brother, Henry, popularly known as Mr. Lowell, asked as he sidled up next to him.

Florian cut him a look. "I doubt even you can accomplish such a feat."

"Nonsense. All you need is a little charm, which I happen to have in ample supply." He waggled his brows which prompted a lady or two to snicker while Florian himself rolled his eyes. "Ladies," Henry proceeded, "my brother has had such a trying day. Please take pity on him and allow him a moment to get his bearings. The Season has only just begun, after all, so there will be ample opportunity for all of you to secure the dances you want."

Florian gave his brother a scowl. He wanted to nip this developing disaster in the bud before one of them started expecting more than he was prepared to deliver.

And yet, his brother's words must have struck some feminine chord, because the sea of expectant faces waiting before him became one of sympathetic understanding. Miraculously, they even began dispersing, allowing Florian the freedom to move further into the ballroom. He turned to Henry. "I have to admit I underestimated your skills."

Henry shrugged one shoulder. "What can I say? It's just a natural way I have with the ladies."

Florian snorted and snatched a glass of champagne from a passing tray. "I shouldn't have come here."

"Of course you should have," his brother insisted. "Your new position demands your attendance at such events."

Which was part of the reason why he'd done his best to dissuade his uncle, the Duke of Redding, from petitioning the Crown and making him his heir. A title was the last thing Florian wanted.

Taking a sip of his drink, he tried to forget the dance he now had to endure. He glanced about, instinctively looking for Lady Juliette's pretty face. The last time he'd seen her she'd seemed self-conscious and timid, which was likely to be expected considering all the challenges she'd faced. Enduring the aristocracy's censure was difficult even for him.

The cotillion was announced sooner than Florian had expected and Florian glanced about. "I suppose I ought to find my dance partner." He moved forward, weaving his way through the crowd in search of a woman whose appearance he could not recall.

"I think she's over there," Henry said, catching up with him.

"Which one is she?" He really should have paid more attention.

"The one with the lilac gloves."

"Right." Florian marched toward her and sketched a bow. "I believe our cotillion is about to begin." She stared up at him and batted her lashes. Unimpressed, he offered her his arm and resolved to do his duty while cursing the fact that this awful evening was only the first of many.

"You seem distracted, my lord," his dance partner said, scattering his most recent thought.

He made an effort to focus on her face and realized he didn't even know her name. "I was just thinking of one of my patients," he lied, because sharing his real contemplation was out of the question. "She came in this afternoon with a kidney stone, so—"

"Oh. I see. How delightful."

Florian scowled. There was hardly anything delightful about it. But his remark had had the desired effect, dissuading his partner from saying anything else to him for the rest of the dance.

To his shock and dismay, he found himself more irritated about this than he'd been with her comment. It would be nice to meet a girl who didn't cringe when he referenced his work. One who actually showed some interest?

But such rare creatures were apparently hard to come by. So far, the only one he knew was Viola Cartwright, the Dowager Duchess of Tremaine and St. Agatha Hospital's patroness. He had great respect for her, not only as her employee, but because he admired the purpose with which she lived her life.

"You survived the dance," Henry said, materializing by his side once more. This time, he'd brought the Duke and Duchess of Huntley with him.

"I'm as shocked as you are," Florian muttered. Smoothing his features so as not to glare at the duchess, he executed his very best bow and shook hands with her husband.

"I take it you're not fond of dancing," the duchess said.

"No, but I was ambushed, so I was left with no choice."

"You could have made an excuse," Huntley said.

Florian met the other man's gaze, aware he would likely have done precisely that if he'd been in Florian's shoes. "Unfortunately I don't have your advantage."

"And what would that be?" Huntley asked with a tilt of his lips.

"To not give a damn about any of this." Florian expelled a breath. "I grew up in Society. Expectations and proper manners were spoon-fed to me since infancy. So dismissing a lady isn't something I can just do, no matter how much I might secretly want to."

"Well, your sense of duty is certainly commendable," the duchess said.

"He is the very epitome of what one might consider heroic," Henry added wryly.

Florian glared at him. "Your sarcasm isn't helping." He glanced about. "Honestly, I find all of this so trivial. The expense is exorbitant! Just think of all the good we could have done if the money had gone to feeding the hungry or helping the ailing? I swear . . ."

"Well, in that case there is one advantage to gaining that title you're so opposed to," Henry said. His expression had sobered to an uncharacteristic degree of seriousness. "Once you inherit, you can spend your fortune on the causes that matter the most to you."

A comforting thought to be sure and definitely one he'd already begun considering, but to say as much would not be well done since it did involve the death of his uncle. An event he did not look forward to in the least. So rather than comment, he decided to change the subject entirely, by asking Huntley the first thing that came to mind. "I don't suppose your sisters are in attendance this evening, Your Grace?"

"Amelia won't be venturing back into Society until

she's delivered her baby, but her husband is just over there." Huntley nodded toward the other side of the room. "As for Juliette . . ." He glanced about. "I'm not sure where she's gotten to."

"Well, perhaps I should go and greet Coventry then." Florian stepped back. "It's been a while since I saw him last and I would like to know how his wife is faring." He took his leave while his brother said something about heading off to the game room.

Following the periphery of the ballroom, Florian made his way toward a spot where he would be able to cross the floor without too many people blocking his way. But when he reached the French doors leading out to the terrace, he paused. All thought of reaching Coventry fled his mind the moment he spotted a lonely figure staring out at the garden below.

Juliette.

He reached for the handle and pushed the door open, drawn to her in a way he couldn't begin to explain. All he knew was that she was there, a welcome reprieve from all his responsibilities and the chance he needed to simply get away and take a moment for himself.

Chapter 2

Juliette heard him coming before he reached her side, the slow tread of approaching footsteps clicking against the stone tiles. Inhaling deeply, she turned toward him, ready to take her leave if it was an unwelcome intruder. But it wasn't. It was the very same man who'd prompted her to flee the ballroom.

Florian, the new heir to the Duke of Redding.

Steeling herself, she waited for her nerves to respond in the same riotous way they had earlier and was thankful to find them completely calm and collected.

"My lord," she said by way of greeting, then pushed out a breath and shrugged one shoulder. "Forgive me, but I've no clue about how to address you."

He gazed down at her with all the solemnity in the world. "Florian will do. I have no title yet."

"I see." He came to stand beside her, his hip leaning firmly against the balustrade in a way that highlighted the length of his legs. Juliette forced her gaze away from that part of his body and looked him in the eye. "How did it all come about? If you don't mind my asking, that is."

A pause followed and she felt his stare, the unflinching mask of gravity he wore, not revealing a single thought. And then the edge of his mouth twitched and he moved so he could look out across the garden. "My mother's brother has no children, so with no one to inherit, he asked the king to elevate him to duke. As a favor."

"And this made it possible for him to name his successor?"

"Precisely." He glanced her way. "A Special Remainder has been put in place to allow for it."

She nodded, considered him a moment and finally asked, "Then why the glum expression?"

He lifted an eyebrow. "Perhaps because of the burdens attached to it, the plural estates I shall have to manage and the attendance expected of me in Parliament. Or maybe it's because becoming duke means the loss of my uncle."

Juliette's heart stuttered a little in response to the fierceness with which he spoke. "I'm sorry," she said, not knowing how else to respond.

She'd never expected Florian to offer a glimpse of his heart. The idea of him mourning anyone had never entered her head. He just didn't seem like the sort who would be too bothered, one way or the other, which of course was a very harsh judgment of character on her part. Fleetingly, she thought about reaching out, of offering some means of comfort if only with the touch of her hand. But then she decided against it, aware of the impropriety and the fact he would likely demand to know what on earth she was doing.

"It is what it is," he said as if speaking to himself more than to her. His features eased a little on a slow exhalation and his eyes seemed to focus more fully on her face. "You look more"—he hesitated as if searching for the right word—"at home amidst the *ton* than when I last saw you."

"Really?"

"There's no doubt you've adjusted to your new way of life. It suits you."

She couldn't help but smile. "Is that a compliment?"

"Perhaps."

"And here I was, convinced you couldn't be charming."

His lips moved ever so slightly, but he did not smile. "Let's not get ahead of ourselves, my lady. I merely made an observation."

"And consequently ruined the moment," she said with a sigh that was meant to convey exasperation.

He tilted his head, regarding her as though she belonged on display in some strange museum for rare artifacts. "You also seem bolder." His eyes pinned her in place, and she suddenly felt it again, that fluttery pulse and shortness of breath. "In fact, I dare say you're quite transformed from the girl I met last Season. You've bloomed, Lady Juliette." The barest hint of a smile did tug at his lips just then and she found herself transfixed. "I'm sure you have your fair share of admirers already."

Of all the conversations she'd ever expected to have with this man, this was certainly not one of them. In fact, to her dismay, it almost felt as though he was flirting with her, which couldn't possibly be true. Could it?

Swallowing, she tried to ignore the twisting of her stomach and the weakening of her knees. "The Earl of Yates has shown some interest," she said and immediately wondered if that was actually true since he hadn't really suggested a courtship.

"He would make an excellent match." A shadow crossed Florian's face, concealing his features.

"I disagree," Juliette said without thinking. She caught herself, but it was too late. The comment was already out there. "I mean . . . he's a likeable man, enjoyable company and—"

"Always polite."

"Hmmm. . . ." Juliette considered the way he spoke. "As much as I appreciate politeness, I think blatant honesty has its merits as well." Heavens, now she was flirting with him!

"An interesting notion." He leaned forward slightly, just enough for her to catch a flicker of intrigue in his eyes. "So then, if I were to launch into an in-depth explanation of a surgical procedure I plan on conducting tomorrow, would you honestly tell me to change the subject and spare you the boredom?"

"No. Probably not."

His eyes held hers until she was forced to look away for fear of revealing the blush she could feel creeping over her skin, in spite of the darkness. He huffed out a breath and leaned back. "I must confess I'm disappointed to hear it."

"Why?" When he looked at her again, she said, "Did it ever occur to you that I might find such conversation appealing?"

His lips parted and she allowed herself a moment to savor his astonishment.

The door opened behind them and voices filled the air. A group of people spilled out onto the terrace with Florian's brother, Mr. Lowell, bringing up the rear. He came toward them at a brisk pace, inclining his head to acknowledge her presence.

"Lady Juliette," he said and reached for her hand. Kissing the air above her knuckles, he straightened himself and smiled. "I see my brother is keeping excellent company this evening."

"Thank you, Lowell. It's a pleasure to see you again." She'd gotten to know the well-renowned rake through Amelia and Coventry, with whom he maintained a tight friendship.

"Oh, indeed, the pleasure is all mine," Lowell said, at which point it sounded as though Florian might have muttered something beneath his breath. Whether or not that was true, Lowell glanced his way. "Supper is about to be served." He returned his attention to Juliette and smiled broadly while offering her his arm. "Shall we go in together?"

Florian scowled at his brother. His jaw tightened, allowing shadows to play across the contours of his cheekbones. A second passed and then he gave a tight nod. "By all means. After you."

Juliette linked her arm with Lowell's and allowed him to guide her back into the sparkling light. He was just as handsome as Florian and definitely more charismatic. And yet, he didn't provoke the slightest emotion in her whereas Florian . . . his absence by her side made her feel slightly empty inside.

It didn't make any sense.

Chapter 3

A tingly sensation assailed Juliette when Florian took his seat beside her. Especially when he leaned to his left and their shoulders brushed against each other. Destabilized, she sucked in a breath and tried to force her bouncing heart into a steadier rhythm. He was just her physician; for her to respond to him in any other capacity than as his patient and possibly his acquaintance was beyond illogical.

"Is it just me, or does Lady Gilbrecht appear to be courting Mr. Haywood?" Lowell whispered close to her ear, prompting Juliette to choke on the spoonful of soup she'd just taken.

Florian leaned closer and patted her back. "Have some wine," he suggested.

She drank half a glass, thanked Florian for his help and turned to Lowell. "I didn't realize a lady could court a gentleman."

Lowell gave her a look—the sort that seemed to sympathize with her naïveté. "She's a widow and he's a rake. Of course she can, and is, if those batting eyelashes are any indication."

"But, they're in public," Juliette muttered, a little

appalled by the thought of such blatant flirtation going on around them.

Lowell grinned. "That won't stop a seduction if the couple's determined enough. I'm sure there are several feet toeing their way up various legs underneath all these tables." He lowered his voice. "Or hands straying to places they shouldn't be straying."

Having just taken another spoonful of soup, Juliette coughed again, and Florian patted her back, handing her the wine. He leaned past her and spoke to his brother. "What are you telling her, Henry?"

"Nothing too outrageous," Lowell replied.

"Judging from her shocked reaction, I very much doubt that." Florian patted Juliette's back once more for good measure. "I must apologize for my brother, my lady. I believe he has an unfortunate inclination for impropriety."

At Juliette's left, she heard Lowell say, "There's something to be said for knowing how to have a bit of fun, Florian. You needn't be so stuffy all the time."

"Have some more wine," Florian said.

"There's no need," Juliette told him. Her throat had cleared and she was able to breathe again without choking. "Really, I am not as delicate as most people think."

Florian knitted his brow. "I wasn't suggesting you were, but there are subjects one does not discuss with an innocent young lady such as yourself. Lowell crossed a line, I believe."

Juliette knew he was right and yet she didn't want his domineering righteousness to win over his brother's easygoing joie de vivre. Because it was like two opposing forces, each needing the other for the sake of creating perfect harmony. "It was a joke. You could try it one day," she said, not knowing where on earth her words were coming from.

His frown deepened and he removed his gaze from hers, seemingly concentrating on the soup before him. "Jokes aren't really my forte."

The gravity with which he said it was like a stab to her chest. "I'm sorry," she hastened to say, "I did not mean to offend or imply anything, I just . . ." She struggled to find the right words without making things worse. "You don't look happy."

His head turned slowly toward hers, catching her gaze in a riotous blend of emotion. "Happy?" The word sounded silly when he said it. "If only I had time for such frivolity, but the truth of it is that every time I catch a glimmer of it, life interferes and snuffs it out." His jaw tightened, as did his voice. "Most days bring pain and suffering to my doorstep, my lady. My efforts to fight death are often futile, many of my patients poor and destitute. The things I have seen have led to despair and anger. It troubles me to see how easily the class to which I belong wastes its money on meaningless and ridiculous things when it could be put to much better use by helping those in need."

It took Juliette a moment to process his cynical tone and the frank response he'd delivered. But rather than shy away from it as she might have done last year when she was still getting used to her new circumstances, she straightened her spine and prepared for battle.

"You have good reason to be frustrated, and yet I think you should count your blessings instead of complaining." His expression hardened and he looked ready to disagree, but she didn't give him the chance.

"Whenever you want a reprieve, you can have it. My siblings and I did not have that kind of luxury. Every day was an ongoing struggle for survival. We starved, as did our friends, leaving my brother with no choice but to accept help from Carlton Guthrie." Her voice quivered at the memory of what that had meant for Raphe. "That man owned him, Florian. He ruled his life, insisting he fight to pay back his debt, and still we barely had enough to make ends meet.

"When my youngest sister, Bethany, got sick, we couldn't afford a physician or medicine. I watched her die, her body carried away on a cart to God knows where because we had no money to spend on a funeral." She heaved a shuddering breath as the memories came flooding back. "Do you have any idea how often I wished to be whisked away from it all? To be someone else for simply one hour?"

"Lady Juliette, I—"

"This opulence you hate so much is a welcome escape from the hardships of life, Florian. It doesn't mean the people here are ignorant or that they don't care. It simply means they choose not to do so tonight, because life will be hard enough again tomorrow when this is all over." Her annoyance with him had increased, pouring through her in waves and demanding she speak her mind. "You have an advantage, the rare opportunity to do more than most and to make an actual difference and yet you choose to cast a shadow over everyone else's enjoyment with your brooding scowls and lack of enthusiasm."

A nerve ticked at the edge of his jaw and Juliette finally ceased with her lecture. Blinking, she considered the manner in which she'd just cut him down to size and immediately thought of apologizing, but then she decided against it. He'd said he valued honesty rather than empty platitudes, so there he had it. She'd served it to him on a platter.

"Were you serious when you said you'd be interested in hearing about my work?"

Caught off guard by his question and how he'd apparently chosen to ignore everything she'd just said, she gave him an absent nod. "It's certainly better than having to talk about who each debutante hopes to marry or which young lady might face potential ruin."

He snorted in a way that hinted at a grin. "You don't like gossip?"

"No," she told him without even having to think. "I despise it." When he arched a brow she said, "It's usually malicious. Additionally, it's hardly any business of mine what other people choose to do with their lives."

Dropping his gaze, he ate another mouthful of soup, appearing to hide the beginnings of a smile behind the spoon. Encouraged, Juliette chuckled lightly to herself and ate some more soup as well. This conversation between them had probably been the most unpredictable one she'd ever had, and something about that thrilled her. She set her spoon aside and dabbed her mouth with her napkin while trying to think of a way to engage him further. It wouldn't be easy since he was now discussing something with the man who was seated to his right.

Biding her time, Juliette decided to address the subject Florian had brought up twice already this evening. The moment she got her chance, she asked, "Did you see a lot of patients today before coming here?"

His glass faltered on its way to his mouth, the note of surprise widening his eyes as he darted a look in her direction, impossible to deny. He took a quick sip of his wine. "I um . . ." He cleared his throat and proceeded with greater certainty. "There were a few. One will require the removal of a kidney stone."

"Really?" She tried to think of what might be involved. "So you will have to cut this person open and extract it?"

"No, no. Nothing that drastic." He stared at her for a long hard moment before continuing. "There's a way for me to do it without having to use a scalpel."

Juliette pondered that comment and the vagueness of it while thinking back on some of the medical texts she'd managed to read in the past and the diagrams she'd seen of the human body. Realization suddenly hit. "Oh! You can go in through . . . there . . ." She felt her cheeks flush but refused to let it deter her. "And . . ." She couldn't quite figure out the rest.

"There's a special tool I use for crushing the stones," Florian explained. "It allows the patient to eliminate smaller pieces on their own and without excessive amounts of pain. Especially with the recent discovery of morphine."

"Morphine?"

He nodded. "It's not officially on the market yet, but when a German colleague of mine informed me of his development of it a couple of years ago, I knew I had to try it. The results are truly incredible."

"Better than laudanum?"

"Without a doubt, even though they're both derived from opium."

"Really?"

"The difference is in the way they're produced. And with morphine, I can operate on my patients without them feeling pain."

Fascinated, Juliette turned her face more fully toward his, allowing her to catch a glimpse of excitement in Florian's deep blue eyes. "That's astonishing," she murmured, momentarily lost in the depth of his gaze and the passion with which he was speaking. "It's amazing to think of the discoveries being made. The tool you mentioned for extracting the kidney stones is remarkable. I wonder who invented such a thing."

"I can tell you." Hesitance crept its way along his voice and he carefully added, "If you like."

Genuinely riveted by the extent of his knowledge and eager for him to share it with her, Juliette quickly nodded. "When we were living in St. Giles, my brother was determined to ensure our education. He always felt that if we were well-read, we stood a better chance at improving our prospects."

"That was very farsighted and wise of him. Considering how young he was at the time."

Juliette nodded. "He was only eight years old when we lost our parents." They shared a moment of silence before she continued. "When the debt collectors came, we fled our home to avoid being placed in different orphanages or, God forbid, workhouses.

"Raphe took a couple of books with him, never selling them no matter how desperate we were. Instead, he traded them for new books and continued doing so until we'd learned about all sorts of subjects. Maybe it was my need to understand why I was often sick that fueled my interest in the medical texts he occasionally procured, or maybe they simply appealed to me because they were interesting. Either way, I would love to hear whatever you have to say on the subject, so by all means, please go on."

Florian's face lit up, not with a smile or anything close to humor, but with the sort of enthusiasm a child might display when encountering a puppy for the very first time. His shoulders even seemed to relax and his voice eased into something much smoother than she'd ever heard before as he told her the history behind not only the lithotrite but other medical instruments as well.

It wasn't until he finished telling her about René Laennec's invention of the stethoscope three years earlier that Juliette realized the other guests had returned to the ballroom. Perhaps she ought to look for Vivien and see if she wanted company? She'd left her alone for quite some time already and . . . Florian glanced around, apparently noticing the same thing as her. Dismay crossed his face and then he blinked, focusing back on her.

Juliette's heart leapt and her stomach rolled over, the look in his eyes revealing a deeper respect than he'd ever shown her before. "I was wondering," he said, speaking as though he hadn't expected to say something more. "Would you like to dance the next set with me?"

"I um . . ."

"Unless you're already engaged of course, in which case—"

"Yes." He frowned and she realized she hadn't been clear with her answer. "I'd love to dance the next set with you."

His eyes held hers, drawing her in and holding her

captive. Whatever his thoughts, he hid them well. "Good." The word stirred the air, propelling them both into action as he pushed back his chair, stood and offered his hand.

Her palm connected with his, and even through the silk fabric of her gloves she could feel his heat and his strength rousing her senses. Confused by her curious response, which was unlike any she'd experienced before, she inhaled deeply and deliberately tried to concentrate on her posture and walk. The last thing she wanted to do was fall over and she feared she might do so at any moment.

It didn't help that he kept quiet while guiding her through to the ballroom, his silence settling between them like a heavy block of awkwardness. Juliette tried to think of something to say, but nothing seemed right or compelling enough in the wake of their recent discussion.

Entering the ballroom, her attention was momentarily drawn to Vivien, who was laughing at something Gabriella was saying. She caught Juliette's gaze for a second and gave her a cheeky smile after acknowledging who she was with. Juliette responded with a reprimanding frown—the sort that was meant to suggest there was nothing between herself and Florian and no need for Vivien to try and imply otherwise.

They reached the dance floor and Juliette became increasingly aware that they were being watched. By everyone. "Your new position has certainly caused some attention," she said as he slid his arm out from under hers and led her forward by the hand.

"An unfortunate consequence indeed," he said as he took his position across from her.

She glanced around. "What are we dancing?" She'd been so distracted by her thoughts and by the crowd and perhaps a little by Florian as well, she hadn't had time to consider the steps she would soon have to make.

"The waltz," he said.

A flutter rose up from Juliette's stomach to beat more rapidly inside her chest. In other words, she was about to be pulled into his arms, to have him daringly close. She wasn't sure why she found the prospect both troubling and enticing or why she felt the need to both run from him and to stay.

"There's no need for alarm," he added with impassive detachment. "It's only a dance."

"Of course it is," she said, aiming for her most nonchalant tone of voice and sounding breathless instead. She swallowed, chided herself for her silliness and squared her shoulders. This was Florian after all, the sternest man she'd ever met. Waltzing with him would likely be an unflappable experience.

But then the music started and he stepped toward her. His hand closed over hers while the other settled firmly against her lower back, pulling her closer. Juliette's heart tripped over, her feet moving of their own accord, thank heaven, because her mind was in no position to make sure she got the steps right. Not when all she could think of was the precision with which he moved. His posture was stiffer than any of the other dance partners she'd had and yet, in spite of that, he seemed to possess a greater degree of elegance.

Not to mention, the way he held her. It suggested dedication toward her—as though he meant to ensure she did not falter. The thought of him being so considerate warmed her heart and it struck her that she shouldn't have been surprised to discover he cared beneath his otherwise blunt and growly manner. Because what other man would dedicate his life to helping the sick than the sort of man capable of deep compassion?

"Your sister-in-law has worked a miracle with you and your siblings," Florian said as he led her around the edge of the dance floor. "You dance much better than I expected."

Trust him to crush her romanticized thoughts of him with a dose of unrefined candor. "What you're experiencing now is the result of several months' practice." It had been hard and grueling, especially in the beginning. She met his gaze and arched a brow, intent on giving as good as he gave. "You dance much better than I expected as well, by the way. In fact, I never thought you were the dancing sort."

"I'm not."

When he failed to elaborate, she simply had to ask, "Then why on earth would you choose to dance two sets in the course of one evening?"

"It wasn't by choice," he said. His brow knit and he suddenly added, "Except with you. I invited you to dance because I wanted to. The other dance was an obligation."

Juliette tilted her head back and gazed up into his face, at the firm outline of his jaw and the hard shape of his lower lip. Except, it wasn't really hard at all, was it? It was smooth and supple and only looked hard because of the way it was set. His eyes were difficult to see as they stared out over the top of her head, but she noticed for the very first time that his lashes were long and black, beautiful even, if such a word could be used to describe them.

He must have realized she was staring, for he dropped his gaze and locked it with hers while twirling her between two other couples. His fingertips pressed slightly harder against her back, producing a buzzing sensation at the base of her spine.

"I see," she said because she felt the need to say something in order to distract herself from the way she had started responding to him. "Then I am flattered."

He puffed out a breath. "Indeed, it is I who ought to be flattered by your willingness to listen while I went on about surgical tools."

"I would have found an excuse to extricate myself from that discussion if I had wanted to do so," she said, needing him to understand that she'd genuinely enjoyed hearing what he'd had to say on the subject.

"Hmph. You are a bit of an oddity, my lady." The edge of his mouth hitched just a little while the rest of his features transformed into something that almost resembled a look of admiration. "I mean that as a compliment," he added. "In case you were wondering."

Not knowing what to say besides thanking him, Juliette focused her attention on completing the rest of the dance while wondering why she'd never taken the time to get to know him better. The answer was simple really. For one thing, he hadn't been present at more than a couple of social functions she'd attended in the past. She'd been new to Society back then and he had been very standoffish. Then the Season had ended and she had gone to spend the autumn and winter at Raphe's estate in Gloucester. So the opportunity to improve her acquaintance with Florian hadn't really been there. Until now. And considering how much she'd enjoyed his company this evening, she had every intention of improving it even further during the course of the coming weeks.

Chapter 4

⁓

The dance came to an end and Florian reluctantly released his hold on Lady Juliette. He'd been honest with the woman who'd begged a dance from him upon his arrival. He didn't waltz, but somehow with Lady Juliette, he'd wanted to. Stepping back, he bowed while she curtseyed, after which he escorted her from the dance floor. "Would you like a refreshment?" he asked, hoping to keep her by his side just a little while longer.

The effect she had on him was curious. Whereas he always counted the seconds until he could leave a social event without being rude, he had no desire to be anywhere else right now than here, with her. The attention and depth of concentration she'd shown when he'd spoken about his work was not only unusual but strangely intoxicating.

And then when she'd clasped his hand and a surge of heat had swept through him, he'd felt momentarily unmoored, which should have alarmed him. After all, he was, if anything, the sort of man who thrived on certainty and fact, not at all the type who took to flights of fancy or succumbed to endless romantic ponderings. But Lady Juliette's effect on him had been a refreshing change, offering him a welcome reprieve from all his concerns. And the way she'd put him back in his place during supper had been strangely arousing.

"Florian?"

"Hmm?" He realized she'd been talking to him and that he had not been listening. Which again contradicted his character. Focusing on people was never a problem, and yet his mind had allowed itself to wander . . .

"You asked if I would like a refreshment."

"Would you?" He saw to his surprise that they'd crossed the room and were presently standing before the refreshment table.

"A glass of lemonade would be nice." Her eyes sparkled, her lips trembling as if she fought to suppress a smile, and Florian wondered if she knew the extent to which she distracted him.

He reached for a glass, grateful for a task he could anchor himself to, and filled it. Handing it to her, he watched as she took a sip. Her upper lip carefully settled against the edge of the glass, and something inside him tightened into a straining ball of fire. Reaching for another glass, he snatched it up and filled it, the lemonade sloshing slightly over the side because of his shaking hands.

Bloody hell!

No woman had ever affected him so. He was a physician, accustomed to the human body in ways few people could even imagine. There was no mystery there for him. Lips and breasts had never stood apart from hands and feet. Until now, when the smooth skin rising above the neckline of Lady Juliette's

bodice and the sudden urge to claim her mouth overcame him with the force of a charging carriage. It
threw his entire world off balance and challenged his
composure.

"Are you all right?" She asked the question with
innocent eyes while he did his best to bury some very
inappropriate thoughts.

A cold sip of lemonade helped, as did his deliberate effort to think about the procedure he'd be performing in the morning. He took a deep breath, and
a second later, he knew he'd managed to school his
features and calm his nerves successfully.

"Fine," he said, in answer to her question. "I was
merely experiencing a little discomfort. On account of
the heat and the exercise our dance entailed and . . ."
He let the words fade, aware he sounded ridiculous.
Which was yet another new experience for him. He
cleared his throat, tried to think of something to say.
Anything to distract from his recent bumbling.

She came to his rescue. "Is it true that your brother
owns a popular club here in London?"

Thank God! A safe topic he could speak of with
ease. "Yes. He wanted to make one available for
gentlemen and ladies alike, so husbands would have
somewhere to take their wives. It's very exclusive and
tastefully done."

"A little strange, though, isn't it, for an heir to do
such a thing?"

Florian dipped his chin. "It's unusual for any aris-
tocrat to do so, not only for an heir. But it's Lowell's
passion, and although there was some resistance to
the idea and a fair bit of gossip in the beginning, it
has become a great success."

She gazed up at him, studying his face until

discomfort flooded his veins. "You're really proud of him," she said as if surprised by the fact.

"Of course I am. Lowell has worked extremely hard to make the Red Rose what it is today." He leaned back slightly, the heady scent of honey and jasmine making him slightly light-headed. "You should visit it one day. I'm sure you'd enjoy it."

"Why?"

The question threw him a little and for a second he was at a complete loss for words. They came to him in the next heartbeat and as naturally as a stream flowing through the woods. "Because of your easy ability to smile." A charming frown appeared above the bridge of her nose, forcing him to continue talking, lest he lose himself in the intricate detail it provided. "The Red Rose is a place of entertainment, my lady. There's card play, music, a fine restaurant and even singers who come to perform."

"I'll mention it to Raphe. Perhaps he and Gabriella can take me there one evening." She hesitated briefly, glanced away as if considering the crowd before returning her attention to him. She took a deep breath, expelled it slowly, and finally said, "Maybe you could come with us."

Florian's heart thudded hard against his chest. His skin tightened around his limbs and heat poured into his stomach. She wanted to see him again, to keep his company and . . . what? He was not in the market for a wife and had no intention of ever gaining one. So then what would be the point? The sort of friendship that was destined to torture him with lusty thoughts?

"Possibly," he said, promising nothing. She was lovely, the sort of woman a man like him would be fortunate to spend his days with. But his life was not as simple as most. He wasn't destined to be a husband, not only because of his dedication toward his patients, but because he would never lie to his wife about who he was. Telling the truth wasn't something he ever wished to endure.

Depressed by this thought, he wondered if it wouldn't be best for him to take his leave before he ruined the evening for Lady Juliette with the black mood closing in around him. He hesitated because her presence was the only thing stopping him from descending into the melancholic pit in which he so often found himself whenever thoughts of his "real" father rose to the surface.

He clenched his fists and fought the bitterness rolling through him, his gaze leaving Lady Juliette to wander across the crowd in search of escape. A group of women moved to the right and two older gentlemen stepped to the left, allowing a glimpse of a face that chilled Florian's blood. His heart slammed against his chest and a fist tightened around his lungs, cutting off air. He muttered an absent excuse to Lady Juliette and started toward the man he'd just seen.

Other people had hidden him from view once again, forcing Florian to weave his way toward the place where he'd seen him. His appearance was different from when Florian had last seen him, his hair color altered, his mouth and jaw concealed behind a neatly trimmed beard. Even his cheeks had taken a different shape. They were fuller, rounding off the features that had always looked so drawn. But his eyes, those ice blue eyes . . . They could only belong to one man.

Bartholomew.

It couldn't be him, not here in a Mayfair ballroom.

And yet, the similarities were there, small as they might be, and they made Florian wonder.

Nausea assailed him. The thought of sharing the same blood as the most notorious criminal in England turned his stomach. The possibility of it ever being made public filled him with dread. And the notion that he still lived, when everyone else believed he was dead, had resulted in many sleepless nights.

A judge had sentenced Bartholomew to death by hanging, but whatever justice Florian had hoped to find had evaporated when he'd come to witness the execution and examine the body afterward.

Whoever it was that had died that day, it wasn't Bartholomew. Just a man who looked a hell of a lot like him. Which meant the bastard was still out there roaming free, perhaps even knowing it was his own son who'd ensured his conviction.

Seeking a closer look at the man he'd just seen, Florian quickened his pace while clamminess crawled across his skin.

A pair of debutantes laughed to one side and a merry fellow with golden locks and a broad smile stepped into Florian's path while recounting a story to his friends. Muttering an oath, Florian stepped around him only to catch a fleeting glimpse of the man's hair. If it was Bartholomew, then he'd selected a color that matched Florian's.

Breathing hard, he pushed onward, apologizing as he increased his pace and brushed past people in an effort to reach the villain who should have died last year. It had to be him, as impossible as it seemed. Florian felt it in his gut and in the rapid beats of his heart. How dare he show his face in public? How dare he come here and taunt those he'd hurt?

Shoving past a few more people, he threw his gaze

around, frantically searching, knowing he couldn't have gotten far. A hand grabbed his elbow and he jerked away, knowing he had to keep looking.

"Florian?" Henry's voice ricocheted through his mind, pulling all thought into one fine point on which he was forced to focus.

"Not now," he said, spotting the man he sought and already moving to follow him up the stairs he was taking toward the front entrance.

But Henry held him back. "You seem distraught. What's going on?"

The man Florian was chasing paused halfway up the stairs and looked out across the sea of people, the edge of his mouth lifting the moment their eyes met. Dread and fury pooled inside Florian's chest. "Why is he here?" It was all he could think to ask.

"Who?" Henry asked. He followed Florian's gaze. "Mr. Mortedge?"

Doubt crept in once more, even as the man nodded ever so slightly in Florian's direction. Turning away, he took the remaining steps leading up to the door and disappeared out of sight. Blood roared in Florian's ears, the urge to make chase and discover if it really was his father straining his muscles until they burned. But it was futile. The man was long gone. And then Henry's words sank in and Florian turned toward him, aware of an empty void expanding inside.

"Mr. Mortedge?" Uncertainty cemented itself even further. Of course it had to be someone else. For Bartholomew to actually be here at Hawthorne House made no sense.

"He's an American investor. Came over about six months ago and bought a gorgeous town house on Bedford Square."

He'd been wrong then. It wasn't Bartholomew after all. Heat seemed to close in around Florian. He tugged at his cravat while trying to locate the nearest exit. Air. That was what he needed. Right now. This second. And perhaps a fortifying drink or two to calm his jangling nerves.

"Get me a brandy, please, would you?" he told Henry. Without waiting for him, he started walking away. "I'll meet you outside on the terrace."

Circumventing the cluster of people who stood in his way, Florian reached for the closest door and pushed it open. An uplifting breeze hit him, invigorating his senses and clearing his mind. He took a deep breath and crossed to the spot where he'd stood with Lady Juliette earlier in the evening. A wretched sigh escaped him and he muttered an oath. How things had changed since then, just in the course of the last five minutes.

He allowed his breath to float past his lips and escape into the night. Memories, so many he wanted desperately to forget, rose to the surface. The first of a beautifully bound encyclopedia he'd received on his eighth birthday and of his mother's stricken face when he'd read the inscription.

I hope this will help with your education. Study hard and there is no doubt in my mind that you and I will enjoy a decent discussion.

Until we meet in person,
B

She'd snatched it away from him without explanation and asked a maid to dispose of it while confusion, betrayal and loss overwhelmed him.

Later, when he was fourteen, there had been the incident in the park when a man had approached him during his afternoon ride. He'd complimented Florian on his horsemanship and asked a few questions about his interests and education. Florian could still recall the discomfort he'd felt and the panicked look in his parents' eyes when he'd mentioned it to them later.

Two more years had passed before he'd learned of his true identity, before his mother had felt the need to explain after they'd been approached by the same man again while taking a walk in the park. Nothing had been the same since, the life he'd known until then torn to shreds in a second.

"Is everything all right?"

He stilled in response to Lady Juliette's voice, almost too afraid to turn because he feared she'd want to know why he'd quit her company as quickly as he had. He couldn't be honest. Not without the risk of her discovering his connection to Bartholomew. Which was not the way he wanted to end the evening.

Christ, what a mess!

He swept his palm across his forehead and turned to find her standing a few feet away, beautiful as ever in her blue silk gown. The wind tugged playfully at the sheer fabric layers and at a few stray strands of her hair.

"Yes," he lied. "Everything is fine."

He couldn't even confide in Henry, he realized. Florian knew what it was to have the comfortable life you knew snatched away in an instant, and he refused to do that to his brother.

"You don't *look* fine," Lady Juliette said, her voice

dragging him out of the faraway place his thoughts had gone back to.

"The heat was too much." Another lie, but what else could he do? "It made me feel ill."

She studied him for a drawn-out moment and he realized he was holding his breath in anticipation of her response.

Eventually she took a step toward him and said, "Yes, it is a bit stuffy in there."

He breathed a sigh of relief and strove to be the gentleman he ought to be in her presence. "I hope you can forgive my hasty departure. It had nothing to do with you."

She smiled then, wide and lovely and without any pretense. "Thank goodness for that! For a moment there I feared you might have tired of my company, which would have been a pity since I've really been enjoying yours and—"

"Here you are," Henry said, announcing his arrival as he crossed to where they were standing. "Took me a while to acquire this. It's not as readily available in there as one might expect it to be." He handed Florian the glass of brandy.

Thanking him, Florian took a long sip, savoring the calming effect and the heat spreading out through his chest. And yet, as good as it felt, part of him regretted asking Henry to bring him the drink, because if he hadn't, he might have been able to enjoy his conversation with Lady Juliette a little while longer without interruption.

Her comment had squeezed his heart and made him feel . . . *more*. As strange as that was, it was really the only way he could think to describe it. And then there were her unspoken words, the ones she'd been about to say when Henry had arrived. Florian knew he would wonder about them later tonight and perhaps even for a few days after.

"Better?" Henry asked when Florian lowered his glass.

He nodded. "Yes. I think it was just what I needed."

His brother appeared on the verge of saying something more, then glanced at Lady Juliette and kept silent, for which Florian was grateful. He really didn't want to discuss what had happened. Not when he couldn't be honest about it.

"Will you be attending the Wilmington Ball on Friday?" Henry asked.

Florian shook his head. "I don't think so. The only reason I came here tonight was because our parents insisted on it."

Catching the fleeting look of disappointment in Lady Juliette's eyes, he shifted and straightened his spine. Whatever fanciful thoughts she was having, it was best she rid herself of them right now. He wasn't interested in courtship or marriage, no matter how compelling he found her. It was best if she realized that, so she didn't waste any more time on him.

"There are more important matters for me to attend to," he added while telling himself he felt no guilt over Lady Juliette's crestfallen expression.

"I see," she muttered, then turned her full attention on Henry. "Do you plan on going, Mr. Lowell?"

"I wouldn't miss it for the world," Henry declared. "Least of all if it gives me the chance to dance with you, my lady."

Lady Juliette chuckled in response to the easy flirtation while Florian dug his nails into the palms of his hands and forced down a growl. He would not be possessive. Not when he had no right to be. And yet there was no denying the way his muscles flexed and strained beneath his jacket and shirt or the way his heart ached in response to the emptiness stealing straight through him.

"She dances exceptionally well," he forced himself to say. "And Lowell isn't bad either, so I'm sure you'll both enjoy yourselves."

Henry gave him an odd look while Lady Juliette frowned, no doubt because he'd failed to keep the bitterness he felt from seeping into his voice.

"Considering how gracefully you executed the waltz with Florian," Henry told Lady Juliette, "I do believe I would like to try that particular dance with you myself. If you agree?"

"I'd be delighted," Lady Juliette replied without the slightest bit of hesitation.

Florian stared at her, the violent urge to step between her and his brother, to keep them apart somehow, so overwhelming it caught him completely unawares.

Thankfully, Liverpool arrived at that exact moment, ridding Florian's mind of the elemental compulsion to hit something. Like his brother. Which wouldn't do at all.

The prime minister's expression was bleak, his eyes filled with the burden of too much responsibility. The look did not bode well. It made Florian's heart rate escalate and his nerve endings scream with trepidation.

"Florian," Liverpool said, his eyes locking onto him and ignoring Henry and Lady Juliette as if they weren't even there. "A word, if you will." He swallowed and took a sharp breath. "Right away."

Liverpool's urgency and blatant disregard for proper manners increased Florian's unease tenfold.

"Of course." He glanced at Lady Juliette and at his brother. "Please excuse me a moment." He moved a few paces away from where they stood and gave them his back as he stepped as close as he could to Liverpool. "What is it?"

"I just received word from an apothecary surgeon in the Camden area. A Mr. Tibs?"

"I'm familiar with the name," Florian said, the unease he already felt now pricking at the nape of his neck.

"He believes we might have a serious case of typhus on our hands." Liverpool's words were hushed but firm. "He claims he's already seen two patients from St. Giles, both of whom were showing symptoms."

The unease became an all-encompassing numbness and the world seemed to still around him. A roaring silence echoed in Florian's ears while he thought of his previous encounter with the disease. He blinked, felt his chest contract against a deep exhalation of breath. And then the rush of music and chatter from inside the ballroom, the feel of the breeze against his skin and the keen awareness of imminent danger assailed him as his senses awoke to his surroundings.

His jaw tightened and medical intuition took over, banishing the fear. "Where are the patients now?"

"The message didn't say."

Florian gave Liverpool a hard look. "I need to see them immediately." Because if Mr. Tibs was right, then time was of the essence. Typhus was not the sort of thing to take lightly. It took several days for symptoms to show and often resulted in death.

With this in mind, he quietly said, "Let's keep this between the two of us for now. The last thing we want is unnecessary panic."

"Agreed," Liverpool muttered.

Florian glanced over his shoulder at where his brother and Lady Juliette were still standing. Although they were chatting amicably, he noticed that her attention remained fixed on him with the sort of tenacious curiosity he'd rather do without at the moment.

"Can you have a carriage readied?" he asked Liverpool.

"Of course. Give me ten minutes."

They parted ways and Florian took a deep breath, schooled his features and returned to his companions. "I'm afraid something has come up. A matter I must attend to right away."

"Nothing too serious, I hope," Henry said.

"No," Florian told him as easily as he would deny any connection to Bartholomew. "Just a couple of patients in need of treatment."

Lady Juliette's eyes narrowed and he sensed she didn't believe him. Not completely. So he hastened to bid her and his brother a continued good evening, and then strode away quickly, before she could question him further.

Bartholomew poured himself a large glass of brandy and took a seat in his favorite armchair. When he'd had to start over, he'd been prepared, killing the man he'd been for over three decades and claiming a new identity as William Mortedge. A humorless grin tugged at his lips. Bartholomew might be dead, but Mortedge was very much alive.

"Florian was there this evening, just as we predicted," Bartholomew said, addressing Mr. Smith, his most trusted employee.

"Did he recognize you?"

Bartholomew sipped his drink, savoring the spicy flavor as it trickled slowly down his throat. "Yes. I'm sure of it. Looked like he wanted to rip my throat out." He smacked his lips together and smirked. "I was lucky the crowd prevented him from getting to me."

Mr. Smith narrowed his gaze. "What's the next step?"

"We toy with him. Let him wonder if it really was me he saw. Keep him on edge." Bartholomew set his glass aside on a table. "And we try to uncover his weaknesses so we're ready to make him suffer when the time comes."

"You want his punishment to drag out then?"

"He deserves it." Bitterness made Bartholomew's chest tighten. "Had it not been for his interference last year, I would have gotten my hands on that house Amelia Matthews bought. We'd already pushed her hard. I doubt it would have taken much more to make her abandon her dream of opening a school there." He scoffed. "But Florian couldn't resist the urge to hurt me for something that's not even my bloody fault!"

"Perhaps you should tell him the truth," Mr. Smith suggested.

"It won't solve anything." Bartholomew sighed. "That house, located where it is on the edge of St. Giles, offered the perfect opportunity for me to start taking over Guthrie's territory." He clenched his jaw. "Florian ruined everything when he chose to tell Coventry about my tax evasion. God knows how he knew about that, but it was the only thing I could be charged with at the time. It gave Coventry the reason he needed to seek the king's help with my arrest. And after that everything fell apart."

"You were lucky to find a man who was willing to hang for you."

"He was dying anyway. Promising I'd look after his family once he was gone ensured his cooperation." Bartholomew glanced at Mr. Smith. "Most people can be bought at the right price."

Mr. Smith nodded. "Do you still want to win against Guthrie?"

Bartholomew tilted his head. "Why do you ask?"

"Because I've just heard that there might be a typhus outbreak in St. Giles. If we can ensure the disease takes its course and everyone dies, the entire area can be leveled and—"

"I could offer to purchase it." The prospect definitely appealed. And with the counterfeit bills they'd perfected during the last six months, he could afford any sum.

"As long as you tell the king you'll build some attractive properties, I'm sure he'll agree. Especially if part of the profit you make on selling those properties goes back into the Crown's coffers."

Bartholomew stared at Mr. Smith for a moment and then he suddenly laughed. "That's genius!" Guthrie wouldn't stand a chance—an idea that filled Bartholomew with pleasure. For years they'd been at odds. Ever since Guthrie had realized Bartholomew's whores came from St. Giles and that they didn't just include women and men.

There had been good money in catering to the perverse needs of those who were willing to pay. Which was yet another reason why he'd wanted that house Amelia Matthews had bought. His intention had been to turn it into an exclusive brothel for the elite— the sort of place that offered discretion and catered to every fantasy. But if he managed to secure the entire area, the possibilities would be endless, extending to opium dens and gaming hells. All under the guise of complete respectability.

Dipping his chin, Mr. Smith held Bartholomew's gaze. "As long as we stop your son from doing his job."

"Of course." If Florian started saving everyone, this plan would go to hell. "Let's wait and see what he does for now. Keep an eye on him and inform me of further developments." Picking up his glass of brandy again, Bartholomew swirled the amber liquid before setting the glass to his lips. If he played his cards right, he'd get his revenge on Florian *and* take over St. Giles. All in due course.

Chapter 5

When her sister, Amelia, came to call on her five days later, Juliette greeted her by the door and led her through to the parlor where their sister-in-law, Gabriella, sat waiting.

"It is so good to see you," Juliette said as she poured the tea. "How long has it been since the last time we did this? Two weeks or three?"

"I am not entirely sure," Amelia confessed. Her belly was larger than Juliette remembered, which was normal since her due date was only a little over a month away now. "It is surprising how time gets away from me these days. Having a husband and a child while running a business keeps me tremendously busy." She'd married Thomas Heathmore, the Duke of Coventry, the previous year, becoming stepmother to his then five-year-old son, Jeremy. It was a position she took most seriously.

"How is Jeremy doing?" Juliette asked.

"He is thriving. Thomas made the right decision, choosing to educate him himself instead of hiring more governesses. Spending additional time together has allowed father and son to bond in a new way. It makes me wonder if it is wise, leaving your children in other people's care for extended periods of time."

"I know what you mean," Gabriella said. She'd surprised everyone by giving birth to twins earlier in the year. "It is the reason why I have been nursing David and Rose myself. Mama and Papa were both horrified by the idea of it. I believe Mama said she had never heard of a lady doing such a thing. And I have to admit it is exhausting."

"With two hungry babies, I wonder you have time to rest," Amelia said.

Gabriella smiled. "I suspect it is easier than if I had triplets."

Juliette and Amelia both laughed. "Oh dear," Amelia sputtered. "I am not sure *that* would be manageable without a wet nurse."

"Truth is, I have been incredibly fortunate in my choice of husband," Gabriella murmured with a dreamy element to her voice. "Your brother is so devoted and loving. I honestly could not be happier."

"Me neither," Amelia said. "Knowing the man I fell in love with loves me in return is a true blessing. I hope you will experience the joy of it one day, Julie."

Taking a sip of her tea so she would not have to answer immediately, Juliette thought of Florian. She'd enjoyed his company tremendously the other evening and had missed him last night at the Wilmington Ball. Not that his ability to hold her interest or the occasional attraction she'd felt toward him meant anything at all. In fact, she wasn't really sure why she was thinking of him in the context of this particular conversation.

Unwilling to encourage any talk of courtship when the whole ordeal felt overwhelming and futile, she said, "I believe a similar kind of joy can be found in achieving one's goals."

Amelia and Gabriella shared a dubious look. "Doing so can be rewarding," Amelia agreed, "but it will not satisfy your soul in quite the same way."

"I suppose I shall have to take your word on that. But since I have no romantic feelings for any gentleman—"

"Are you sure about that?" Gabriella asked. "Considering Lord Yates's attentions, among others . . ." Her words trailed off as she glanced toward Amelia. "Never mind. You were saying?"

Taking the chance to avoid discussing potential suitors, Juliette spoke without hesitation. "Are you aware of the typhus outbreak in St. Giles?"

"Yes. I read about it in the newspaper this morning," Amelia said. "Thomas has suggested we close the school until further notice in order to stop contagion since it is located on the edge of St. Giles."

"That does make sense," Gabriella said. "The last thing you want is to get sick and then infect your own family."

"I still worry about the children," Amelia confessed. "If they are not in school they will be home and more likely to get into contact with other sick individuals."

"According to what I have read, children rarely die from the disease," Juliette said. "Fatality is much more likely in adults."

Both ladies stared at her. "Really?" They asked in unison.

Juliette nodded. The newspaper article had heightened her curiosity. So she'd gathered all the information she could find on the subject in the Huntley

House library and had spent the entire morning reading up on it. Which had made her think. Perhaps she could use her fortune to make a lasting difference, the way Amelia had done by opening a school and the way Raphe did every day by involving himself in politics. She took another sip of her tea. "But that doesn't mean something shouldn't be done."

"Well, at least the area has been closed off by the military," Gabriella said, "but the rate at which the disease is spreading is definitely worrisome."

"It's gone from only one or two people to more than ten in less than a week," Amelia said.

"Which is why I intend to offer Florian my assistance," Juliette told them.

"You do?" Amelia asked in an odd sort of voice.

Gabriella raised an eyebrow. "This is an interesting development."

Ignoring her, Juliette pressed on, determined to get all the facts out before she lost her courage. "I know St. Agatha's Hospital where Florian works already provides a lot of sponsored care, but with patient numbers increasing as rapidly as they are, I'm not sure if there are enough funds to cover the extra expenses." Even the *Mayfair Chronicle* had questioned this in one of its articles. "So, my intention is to help with the situation by covering the additional cost of treatment. There is no cure, mind you, but other things can be done to make the sickly more comfortable and prevent further contagion. It would be a specialized health plan of sorts, started with my donation and hopefully helped by others."

"What a wonderful idea," Gabriella said. "Are you considering a charity event?"

Juliette nodded. "Yes. Perhaps more than one even,

depending on the response. But if I begin by donating a large sum myself, it might encourage other people to do the same."

"How large a sum are you planning?" Amelia asked.

Juliette paused for a second before saying, "I want to do what you did and ask Raphe for an advance on my yearly allowance."

Silence fell and then Amelia said, "That is extraordinarily generous of you, Julie."

"I only hope it will make a difference." Juliette set her teacup back on its saucer.

Gabriella smiled with reassurance. "How can it not?"

"Any number of things can go wrong." Juliette chose to address the most immediate problem. "For starters, Raphe might refuse to help."

"He wouldn't do that." Amelia spoke with conviction.

Juliette glanced at her sister, finding strength in her confident expression. "He intends for me to make the most of this Season." She puffed out a breath. "I'm afraid he won't want me to get distracted by a project this size."

"Ensuring your future is certainly of great concern to him," Gabriella said. "He hopes to see you comfortably settled now that there's a chance to do so. You can't blame him for that."

"Of course not," Juliette agreed, "but it honestly feels as though I'm wasting my time doing nothing. I have met every eligible gentleman in the market for a wife, have spoken to all of them at great length but cannot for the life of me envision marrying a single one." An image of Florian's sober gaze flashed through her mind, no doubt because she suspected he was the sort of person who could sympathize with her plight. Amelia and Gabriella on the other hand . . . how could they possibly understand when each had made a perfect love match in no time at all? "I have the opportunity to do something significant right now. Surely getting married can wait awhile?"

"I can try to speak with Raphe on your behalf, if you like," Gabriella said, "but you should also consider that the Season is only just beginning. It's possible a gentleman or two who had no interest in marriage last year will want to find a wife this Season. I'm afraid disengaging from the marriage mart completely would be ill advised, Julie, and something you might come to regret."

Juliette straightened her spine. "I can still participate in some social functions." She certainly had no desire to disappoint Amelia or Raphe or to throw away the painstaking hours Gabriella had spent on teaching her proper comportment. "But consider my perspective for a moment. I have spent most of my life being coddled by Raphe because of my weaker constitution. I was never allowed to play with other children or even to speak with them. Whenever anyone came to visit, I was asked to keep my distance. Protected from the world, I suffered extraordinary loneliness because my brother feared I might get sick and die like Bethany did." Registering Amelia's pained expression Juliette immediately regretted reminding her of the sister they'd lost at much too young an age. "Forgive me. I—"

"Her death was incredibly hard on Raphe, Julie," Amelia said. "You have to understand that."

"Of course I do. But is it fair to punish me for what happened? To deny me *my* freedom because of it? Am

I not entitled to live my life on my own terms?" She sank back, unsure of how to continue. "I have always felt helpless, Amelia. Raphe was the one who earned a living. You made sure we were fed and that the house was kept in order. When Bethany got sick, the two of you nursed her and forced me to stay away. I have always been pushed aside or kept down on account of fear. But since coming to Mayfair, I have been healthier—stronger."

"You caught the measles," Amelia reminded her.

"And you probably would have too if you hadn't already had them when you were little." Juliette pushed out a frustrated breath. "I want to do this. I need to give my life some sort of meaning and purpose that goes beyond finding a husband. I want to accomplish something that I can be proud of and help the people who once helped us. The way you are doing with your school, Amelia."

"You're just as determined as I was, I think," Amelia said with a wry smile.

Juliette sighed. "I'm just so sick of aimless strolls in the park and sipping tea for hours on end without actually accomplishing anything." Noticing Gabriella's pinched expression, she hastened to say, "I don't mean to sound ungrateful or to imply that having tea with friends isn't fun. It's just—"

"I understand," Gabriella said. "You came from nothing, have acquired great wealth and would like to put your new advantage to good use."

"Precisely!" Juliette breathed a sigh of relief. "I know Raphe wants what's best for me, but—"

"But what?" Raphe asked as he strode into the parlor and dropped into a vacant chair. "Ladies." He greeted them all with a nod.

"You look like you had a refreshing walk," Gabriella said, the love she felt for her husband evident in her sparkling eyes and the rosy glow of her cheeks. "How about a nice cup of tea?" She was already reaching for the pot.

Raphe studied her with great appreciation as she proceeded to pour, his gaze lingering on her for a long moment. Then he blinked, as if remembering something, and tilted his head in Juliette's direction. "You were questioning whether I know what's best for you?"

Trapped by her own hasty words, Juliette decided to stand her ground. "There is no doubt in my mind that you *think* you know what that is."

"So I gather." Frowning, he took the cup Gabriella offered and sipped his tea.

"It's just, going from one ball to the other with carriage rides, social calls and shopping expeditions in between, has become incredibly tedious."

He set his cup down and eyed her with a hint of surprise. "As I recall, you were more excited than any of us about our change in status. It was like a real-life fairy tale, you said."

"And it was . . . *is* . . . but the novelty of this glamorous lifestyle has worn off a little." She bit her lip and told him as honestly as she could and with considerable regret, "The Season has barely begun and I'm already longing for it to be over."

Raphe studied her for a moment. "Is it Yates?"

"Of course not!"

"Because you don't have to marry him if you don't want to, you know. Just because he's a friend of mine and I happen to like him doesn't mean—"

"No, it's nothing like that," Juliette said. "I just

want to do something for myself for a change, and marrying isn't it. I'd be doing that for you."

"So . . ." He looked as though she was speaking a foreign language. "You don't want to find a husband?"

"Not right now and not with the pressure of having to do so within a certain time frame."

"Hmm . . ." Leaning forward, he laced his fingers together and rested his forearms on his thighs. "The only problem is that you *will* have to do so within a certain time frame, Julie. Considering your age, you have three Seasons, including this one, before you'll be on the shelf."

"That is true," Gabriella interjected, "but it isn't unheard of for matches to be made at other times of year. There are house parties and such, so perhaps she can meet her future husband at one of those."

Raphe gave her a censorious look. "I see you're on her side."

"Why must there be sides, Raphe?" Amelia asked with an exasperated sigh. "We're merely discussing the issue and taking every angle into consideration."

He didn't look happy about it as he gave his attention back to Juliette. "If you don't want to enjoy the Season," Raphe said in that resigned tone that suggested he'd given up trying to make sense of it all, "might I ask what you plan on doing with your time?"

Inhaling deeply, Juliette forged ahead. "As you know, there's a serious outbreak of typhus in St. Giles."

Raphe instantly stiffened. "I am not going to let you get involved with that, Julie. Not after what happened to Bethany." His voice trembled just enough to convey the heartache he still carried with him.

Sharing his pain, Juliette leaned forward and clasped

his hand. "All I ask is for an advance on my yearly allowance so I can donate the funds to St. Agatha's Hospital. I wouldn't be putting my life at risk in any way, Raphe. I promise."

He hesitated, his gaze darting toward his wife before returning to Juliette. "You won't go near St. Giles?"

"I have no reason to," she assured him.

Raphe seemed to consider. "I commend you for your kindness, Julie, but I doubt donating your allowance and walking away will give you the satisfaction you're seeking." He eyed his wife before saying, "I think Gabriella might be able to advise you on how to become more involved without risking your safety."

Gabriella gave her husband a knowing look before telling Juliette, "As a high-ranking donor, my mother has a seat on St. Agatha's committee. There are weekly meetings during which the distribution of funds is discussed. Perhaps if you could secure a spot for yourself you would have more influence on how typhus is treated and what the funds you procure are spent on."

Juliette blinked. "That is an excellent idea, Gabriella. I didn't even realize such a committee existed." She turned to Raphe. "So I have your support and permission to proceed?"

He sank back against his chair with a defeated sigh. "If it's what you really want, then, yes, you do."

Without thinking, Juliette flung herself into her brother's arms and hugged him tight while startled laughter was squeezed from his chest. "Thank you, Raphe." She closed her eyes and savored the comfort of his embrace. "You won't regret this. I promise."

Seated behind his cluttered desk, Florian tried to concentrate on what Lady Juliette was saying. Her arrival in the office he occupied at St. Agatha's Hospital had come as a surprise. Perfectly turned out in a dove gray gown trimmed with lilac ribbons, she'd been waiting for him when he'd returned from his rounds.

Sitting opposite him with her back perfectly straight and her chin set at precisely the right angle, she portrayed feminine comportment with extraordinary flair. Not a hint of her background could be detected by looking at her. Nor could it be heard in the soft sweetness of her voice when she spoke. One had to *know* she'd come from the slums of St. Giles to be aware of her meager upbringing. And now she was here, her intrusion on his private space throwing him slightly off balance.

He frowned, tried to focus, which was damnably hard when those warm brown eyes of hers were muddling his mind. The effect was not dissimilar to the one she'd had on him a week ago at the ball. Although he'd been terribly busy since then, thoughts of her had snuck their way to the front of his mind whenever he had a moment to himself.

Which was pointless of course and not at all helpful.

So he made a deliberate effort to focus on their conversation instead.

Something about raising funds to help with the typhus outbreak. It was certainly an interesting idea considering the cost of medical expenses.

"You make a generous offer. I will happily recommend it to the hospital's benefactor on your behalf. Donations are always welcome." He considered the graceful line of her jaw, the gentle sweep of her nose and the high cheekbones infused with a subtle blush of pink. Her complexion was flawless, her black lashes long and elegant, her lips—

"I think you misunderstand me."

The gravity of her voice sharpened his attention. "How so?"

She shifted slightly, her gaze sliding away from his for a moment. When their eyes met again, her resolve showed in the unforgiving hardness of her stare. "I do not wish to simply make a donation."

Confused, he darted a look at the maid Lady Juliette had brought with her. She offered no hint of what her mistress might be about to propose. So he shifted his gaze back to Lady Juliette. "The first thing you asked about when you arrived was for me to give an account of the situation in St. Giles."

She gave a firm nod. "Yes."

"But offering funds is not enough, is it?" He could see her eyes sharpen and knew he was on the right track. "You want to manage it—to ensure your donation is well spent, your idea executed to your liking."

"Exactly."

He hesitated, watching her closely while she chewed on her lower lip. "You want to be more than the average debutante." If their previous discussions had taught him anything about her character, it was that she possessed a desire to learn and to challenge ideas.

"What I want is to stop the typhus from spreading by whatever means necessary. My intention is to save those who can be saved, not by handing over a lump sum and then retreating to my comfortable Mayfair home. That is too easy, too selfish."

"Selfish?" He could not hide his shock.

She blew out a breath. "Donating vast amounts of

money to deserving causes is what rich people do to feel better about themselves. They do it because they want to help without actually helping, because it facilitates involvement at a safe distance, thus making it a selfish act of kindness."

Florian stared at her, confounded by the astute observation of such a young woman and her cynicism. She wasn't more than one and twenty. "Lady Juliette . . ." He wasn't entirely sure of what to say next. So he paused, schooled his features and tried to deduce her exact intent. Eventually, he asked, "Are you saying you want to nurse the sick back to health yourself?"

A gasp from the maid underscored the impropriety of such an idea. And yet, Lady Juliette showed no hint of outrage, though she did look at him as though he'd just fallen off the back of a wagon. "Of course not. I have no experience with such things, and besides, my brother would never allow it."

Her rebuff was so firm it almost overshadowed the relief flowing through him. Thank God he didn't have to persuade her to stay away. Apparently she was perfectly willing to do so on her own, which was good, not only for her own safety, but because the idea of having to work with her made his heart race in the sort of way that would only be an unwelcome distraction.

"Good to know," he muttered, sensing a need to fill the ensuing silence.

"I know the afflicted area has been closed off," she added with an extra bit of steel in her voice. "But that will only ensure the disease doesn't spread. It will not cure those who already suffer from it."

"Nothing will," Florian told her starkly. "There is

no cure for typhus, my lady. Surviving it is a matter of luck."

"Nonsense."

He blinked. "I beg your pardon?"

"Luck is an illusion created by man to explain the inexplicable." She narrowed her gaze on him, as if trying to see more than he wished her to see. "People survive diseases for a reason. Just because we haven't yet discovered the reason does not make it less true. But I believe you already know that. Don't you?"

Her mind was something to be admired. Florian knew he could easily lose himself in days' worth of discussions with her. So he stood and went to his bookcase, intent on ensuring her departure sooner rather than later so he could return to his work and stop thinking about the way her dress hugged the most perfect curves he'd ever seen.

Selecting a well-used copy of *Domestic Medicine* by William Buchan, he handed it to her. "You mentioned an interest in medical texts. This is one of my favorites. You're welcome to borrow it if you like."

She accepted the offering, her gloved fingers swiftly brushing his. Yet it was enough for a surge of energy to dart up his arm. "Thank you," she said, seemingly unaffected by the brief moment of contact. "I look forward to reading it."

He gave her an expectant look, willing her to leave.

Instead she remained in her seat. Her head tilted and he knew in that instant, before she uttered another word, that she was about to say something frightening. "I know you value honesty, so let me be blunt." Cold apprehension snaked down his spine. "The Duchess of Huntley has informed me of St. Agatha's committee and of her mother's seat on it."

Florian felt his stomach collapse and a rush of unease swirl up inside him.

"Since the donation I plan on making is substantial, and, keeping the additional funds I intend to raise in mind, I do not feel as though offering me a seat on the committee as well would be too much to ask." She folded her hands neatly across the book in her lap. "It will allow me to engage in the discussions regarding distribution of funds, which frankly, I think I deserve to be included in. Don't you?"

He stared at her, uncertain of how to extricate himself from this mess without causing offense or sounding unreasonable or giving up the money the hospital desperately needed. So he nodded and muttered an almost incoherent, "Yes," while trying to come to terms with all the time he would have to spend in her company.

Christ, it wouldn't be easy.

Not when she affected him the way she did. And it was all because of one stupid glance at a silly ball, which had led to a riveting conversation and a startling awareness he could not shake.

"Good."

She pushed herself out of her chair and stood. "My brother will arrange to have the money transferred as soon as possible." She smiled as though she'd won an award, her sense of victory affording her with a vibrant glow that made his chest burn and his fingers tingle with a curious need to reach out and touch her.

Restraint came to his rescue, strengthening his posture and tightening his features as he dipped his head in affirmation of her comment. "Thank you, my lady. I'll make sure you're informed of the next committee meeting."

Her eyes held his for longer than necessary before she turned away and went to the door. She paused there, glanced at him once again, but said nothing further before she slipped out into the hallway, her maid following close on her heels.

Florian stood as if nailed to the floor. What the hell had just happened? He stared at the vacant spot where Lady Juliette had been sitting moments earlier. Within half an hour, he'd gone from successfully keeping her at arm's length, to having to spend more time with her than ever before. Which wasn't the least bit wise. Because with the fight against typhus and the adjustment his new position as heir to a dukedom demanded, Florian had enough on his mind. The last thing he needed was for Lady Juliette to become an additional concern.

She was the sort of woman a man would have to marry if he seduced her, which meant that avoiding temptation was now at the top of his list of priorities. Right below saving people from certain death and figuring out how to run three estates.

Reaching for a nearby decanter, Florian poured himself a glass of brandy and set it to his lips. Trouble had come to call on him in droves and he knew the only way past it was to face it head-on.

Juliette left the hospital with a new sense of purpose. Her body still trembled with nervous trepidation though she'd done her best to conceal it in front of Florian. Instead, she'd forced herself to remain as rigid as possible, to meet his penetrating gaze with confidence, hopefully hiding the twisted mess her stomach had turned itself into while in his presence.

He was so intense and . . . inexplicably more handsome today with his hair in disarray and his cravat slightly askew, than he'd been the last time she'd seen him. How was that possible? She shook her head, unsure of the answer but keenly aware that his masculine presence was to blame for her turbulent nerves.

Her heart still beat a wild rhythm against her chest, not only because she'd so desperately longed for him to agree with her plan, but because of Florian himself. As usual, he'd been all seriousness without the tiniest hint of a smile, and although this had increased her awareness of him, it had also given her the opportunity to study the carved planes of his jaw and the sculpted shape of his mouth without the interference of laugh lines.

His nose was patrician, his eyes a deep shade of infinite blue. But what drew her attention the most—what had always drawn her attention where he was concerned—was the color of his hair. It was a beautiful shade of copper, the rich tones shifting in the light falling through the window behind him. Coupled with his features, he presented an image of virile beauty and uniqueness. Add his profession and the man demanded admiration. So much so it was a wonder he hadn't yet married—a puzzling notion she chose not to dwell on since doing so was likely to fluster her even more.

Reaching the carriage, Juliette climbed in and waited for her maid to follow. The door closed and she slumped back against the squabs. "That went so much better than I expected," she muttered on an exhalation of breath. She'd always spoken candidly with Sarah and appreciated her frankness in return.

"Really?" Sarah asked from her spot beside her.

"I thought he might be more resistant." But she'd been wrong. Although Florian had wanted to know the details of what she planned, he'd readily agreed to her involvement.

"He would have been a fool to turn you away, my lady."

"You're probably right and yet I'm still having trouble believing how simple it was to accomplish my goal. My nerves still haven't settled." Giving her attention to the passing street view, Juliette said, "My sister has found her purpose in the school she opened last year while Raphe makes a difference every day when he visits Parliament. I only want the same and this is important, Sarah. People will die unless something is done to prevent it."

"They will do so anyway, my lady. You heard what Florian said. Typhus is incurable."

"I know, but with the extra funds there's a chance that fewer will have to do so," Juliette murmured. "The thought of the people I grew up with not getting the treatment they deserve because they can't afford it is more than I can bear. Their suffering not only pains me, but compels me to try and do what I can in order to help."

"And so you will by offering up your allowance," Sarah said with the sort of admiration that could not be feigned. "No other lady would do so, I assure you."

"**Y**ou had a visitor earlier," Viola Cartwright, Dowager Duchess of Tremaine, said while Florian stitched his patient's wound shut.

The severely broken arm had required surgery. There was still no guarantee it would mend satisfactorily or that the young man to whom it belonged would ever be able to use it again. But Florian had done his best. He dropped the bloodied needle into the dish Viola held and went to wash his hands. "We'll need to dress that and bandage it well before he's taken up to the ward for recovery."

"I will take care of it. As soon as you tell me why the Duke of Huntley's sister came here to see you personally." As the founder of St. Agatha's and Florian's employer, the young widow had always made a point of knowing what went on at her hospital. Labeled an upstart on account of her hasty marriage to a dying old man, she was a woman with whom Florian had felt a connection from the start. Both had scandalous backgrounds, though hers was publicly known while his was not.

He sighed. "You would rather leave our patient on the operating table than let me avoid this conversation?"

"Mr. Peterson is fine. The morphine I gave him will keep him asleep for a while longer."

Seeing no dignified chance of escape, Florian took off his surgical apron and tossed it into a large basket so it could be taken out for laundering. "She wants to donate her yearly allowance to us. To the hospital, I mean."

"Well, that is marvelous!" Viola said. "Very generous of her."

"Yes. Except she wants to get involved."

"Can you blame her? It is her money, and as a duke's sister, I am sure the sum will be immense."

"I do not doubt it," Florian agreed. "But that is not the problem."

"Then what is?"

Florian hesitated sharing the details of his meeting

with Lady Juliette, then gave up when he realized his friend would never let the matter rest until he did. "She knows about the typhus outbreak in St. Giles, and since she grew up there, she wants to help save as many people as possible."

"And your issue with this is what, exactly?"

Still reeling from the idea of spending more time with Lady Juliette than he'd intended, he completely forgot himself and said, "It is naïve, Viola, perhaps even stupid for her to suppose that—"

"Florian!" Viola scowled. "That is unfair of you. Especially since you are always the first to get involved when a life needs saving. Don't think I do not know about your charitable visits to St. Giles in recent days."

"Would you have me turn my back on my patients?"

"No. Of course not. But you might have a lot more of them if you don't start acting responsibly." Crossing her arms, Viola boldly asked, "Can you imagine what would happen if you were to bring the disease back here with you?"

"You forget I had the disease years ago and survived it. I ought to be immune."

"Forgive me, but 'ought to be' is hardly reassuring."

"I am taking precautions."

"And doing so has served us well thus far, but—"

"God damn it, Viola! I took an oath and that means something to me!" Puffing out a breath, Florian raked his fingers through his hair. "Nobody deserves to be left to die, no matter how poor or neglected they may be."

"Agreed. Which is why I chose to support you when you wanted to donate treatment to those who cannot afford to pay. St. Agatha's has backed you, giving you all the necessary supplies. But there is a limit to how long we can afford to do so and that is discounting the risk."

He knew she had a point. The fortune her husband had left her had been put to excellent use in procuring and renovating the building constituting the hospital. But prosperous donors had been hard to come by lately. Other charitable organizations had started gaining more attention, like the Healing Hearts Orphanage in Holborne. Not that he thought the children there did not deserve donations, but it did mean St. Agatha's was struggling more than it ought.

"I wash my hands with soap while my peers laugh," he said, ignoring her reference to decreasing funds and focusing instead on the risk she'd mentioned. "I use alcohol to disinfect tools and I cover my mouth with a scarf to avoid breathing the same air as those who are ailing. Because of these rules and because we have also implemented them here at St. Agatha's, this hospital has the greatest survival rate in the country. You cannot tell me that is coincidence."

"Of course not." Viola looked thoroughly vexed. "But this is typhus we are talking about."

"And we are duty bound to protect the healthy while doing our best to save the sick. You know I am right."

"And yet Lady Juliette's involvement bothers you."

The mention of the woman who'd faced him earlier brought a recollection of creamy skin with it. Florian dismissed the alluring vision and focused on his friend. "Would it not bother *you*?"

"Why would I? We need the funds and it sounds like she is eager to provide them! If you ask me, her arrival is something of a blessing."

He grimaced. "She will want to decide things. You realize that, don't you?"

The dowager duchess seemed to ponder that for a moment, then said, "If she insists on helping, I think we should let her. And as far as her getting involved and you worrying about her wanting to decide things is concerned, I suggest you advise her. Be her mentor and teach her something useful the way you've taught me."

Unwilling to reveal his real protestations regarding Lady Juliette, which had little to do with her wanting to help and everything to do with the sparks rolling over his skin whenever he thought of how right she'd felt in his arms when they'd danced, he said, "I gave her a copy of *Domestic Medicine*."

"Well then. I am sure she will be fine."

The sarcasm wasn't lost on Florian but he chose not to respond. Instead, he left Viola to bandage Mr. Peterson's arm and made his way back to his office. The room was a mess, full of books and medical supplies he never had time to put away. There were even a few empty teacups and plates distributed on various surfaces. Lady Juliette hadn't seemed to mind, but that didn't stop him from wishing she hadn't witnessed the cluttered disorder. The impression it gave . . .

Blinking, he shook his head. Why did he care?

Unwilling to answer that question, he slumped down into his chair and pulled a blank piece of paper out of a drawer. Dipping his quill in a nearby inkwell, he proceeded to list all the ways in which Lady Juliette's donation could help.

He was just jotting down *improved nourishment for patients* right after *ability to afford more staff*, when a knock at the door brought one of the nurses into the room.

"Sorry to disturb you, Florian, but there is a man who needs your help." Her crisp tone conveyed the urgency even as she said, "He has a knife protruding from his back."

Florian dropped his quill and stood.

"He's been taken to operating room number three," she added as Florian followed her out into the hallway and fell into step beside her. Grateful for the chance to escape the rest of the world and all its complications, he quickened his pace.

Chapter 6

As it turned out, the surgery was not as simple as Florian thought it would be. The blade that had penetrated the man's back had pierced his lung, which required the evacuation of blood. For this purpose, Florian applied a flexible tube attached to a piston syringe and made a counter-incision on the man's back for additional drainage.

The procedure took a couple of hours, including the stitching of the wound, so by the time Florian was done and had finished detailing the surgery in his notes and checking up on the situation in St. Giles, he was exhausted.

He still had a house call to make, though, before he was able to return home.

Alighting from the hackney he'd used to reach Cowley Street, he paid the driver and climbed the front steps of the red brick mansion in front of him. The butler opened the door as soon as he knocked.

"Good evening, Irving." Florian stepped inside the impressive foyer and handed his hat over to the butler. "How is my uncle faring this evening?" He began removing his gloves.

"His melancholy is unchanged." Irving held the hat so Florian could drop his gloves into it. "But that is hardly surprising, all things considered."

"And my aunt?" Florian asked, hoping to get some additional insight from the aging servant.

Irving hesitated briefly, then quietly answered, "She suffers the knowledge that each passing second brings her closer to losing her husband."

Florian blew out a breath. Dealing with those who lay dying had become second nature to him since the day he'd decided to become a physician. Over the years he'd grown accustomed to removing himself from emotion since feelings of helplessness, despair and sadness were a hindrance to his profession. If there was one absolute certainty in the world, it was that everyone died eventually. And yet, the thought of losing his uncle before the man had reached his sixtieth year made Florian's heart ache in a way it had not done for as long as he could remember.

"I will show myself up," he told Irving, saving the butler from having to climb the steep staircase that led to the bedrooms.

"Very well. If you need anything, don't hesitate to ring the bellpull."

Thanking the man, Florian picked up the bag of medical supplies he'd brought with him and climbed the stairs. When he reached the landing he turned left and strode toward the door at the end of the hall-way. Hesitating briefly, he took a moment to compose himself before knocking. Entrance was immediately granted and he stepped swiftly into the dimly lit room with the pretense that this was just another regular visit.

"Good evening to you both." He cast a glance

toward the dishes still waiting to be cleared from a nearby table. "I trust the salmon was as good as always."

From her position next to the bed, Aunt Abigail rose weakly to her feet and came to greet him. Florian closed the distance and bent to kiss her cheek.

"It is good to see you again," Abigail whispered so only he could hear. "The pain he suffers is unbearable. I hope you can ease it a little."

Finding her hand, Florian gave it a gentle squeeze. "I shall do my best." It was all he could promise, though God knew it wasn't enough. It would not save his aunt from suffering the death of her husband in the weeks to come. Noting the dark circles under her eyes, he suggested she go and lie down for a while. "I will let you know when I leave, but an hour or two of sleep will do you good."

Reluctantly, she agreed and left the room after placing a kiss on her husband's brow.

"She worries too much," the duke said as soon as she was gone. "The whole ordeal is chafing her nerves."

Florian raised an eyebrow and approached the bed. "I would say she has good reason to be concerned, Uncle George. She loves you and fears your demise."

"It is not healthy, though. She ought to get out and socialize more."

"Her time with you is limited, Uncle. I doubt either of us can convince her to stay away. And you know I am right because you would do the same for her if the roles were reversed, would you not?"

Instead of answering, George winced, his face contorting for at least three seconds before he released a shuddering breath. Florian quickly opened his bag and retrieved the new bottle of morphine he'd come to deliver. He poured a measure into a thimble-sized glass and helped his uncle drink.

"Ah, you're a good lad," George murmured. "Your parents did a fine job raising you. I have always thought so."

The mention of his parents made Florian flinch. Fighting the vehement feeling that threatened to overwhelm him, he lowered himself to the chair his aunt had vacated and forced a grateful smile. "Thank you. They will be thrilled to hear you said so."

"Your brother's not bad either. More of a scoundrel, I suspect, but his heart is still in the right place, and as far as I am concerned, that's the most important thing."

"He would take a lead ball to the chest for anyone in the family," Florian said, agreeing with his uncle's assessment of Henry.

"I fear he may take one on account of a woman if he's not careful." George shifted against the pillows propping him up. "If the rumors I hear are true, he's likely to one day top a married one at the rate at which he is going. Simple odds, Florian."

"He wouldn't do that." Although Henry seemed to enjoy his reputation as a rakehell lothario, Florian knew he would never set his sights on another man's wife. "Opera singers, ballerinas and widows are more to his liking."

George grunted. "Either way, he is your father's heir." Florian stiffened in response to those words. If only he could return to that blissful time before he'd been made aware of his true paternity. "And one day he will inherit your grandfather's title as well," George continued, "and become the Earl of Scranton."

"That is how primogeniture works, Uncle." And thank God for that. At least Florian could take some comfort in the fact that Henry was the oldest and it was he who would inherit Armswell's title.

"Your father is a fortunate man, Jonathan."

Florian flinched at the use of his childhood name. No one had called him that in years, not even Henry. Since reaching adulthood, he'd chosen to go by his middle name and had continued to do so as a physician because it helped differentiate between himself and his brother.

"He has an heir and a spare." George spoke with increasing weariness. "His legacy is settled, while mine has always been so uncertain." He started coughing, and Florian quickly rose to help him sit up a bit more. Grabbing a glass of water that stood on the nightstand, he helped his uncle drink. "Thank you, my boy. You really are a good physician."

Florian grinned, amused by his uncle's brief attempt at humor. It was extraordinary that the man was able to find anything to joke about in his current condition. "I do try."

"I know you do." George settled back against the pillows once more, and when he looked at Florian again, seriousness filled his gaze. "Your determination is unparalleled. You persevere, setting goals and hunting them down until you reach them. It has been a pleasure to watch, and although I know there are those who question your medical methods at times, I want you to know that I have always admired you."

The compliment was almost too much to bear. It filled Florian with extreme discomfort, for he knew that what drove him came from a darkness that no man would ever approve of. As always, he considered revealing as much in a futile attempt to alleviate his guilt. Except doing so would likely cause more harm than good. So he kept silent and thanked his uncle instead.

"Which is part of the reason why I decided to make you my heir."

Florian froze. While Society seemed to have taken the news of his new position in stride, he was still having trouble getting used to the idea.

George offered a tight-lipped smile. "Lowell's future is settled. Yours, on the other hand, will be more promising with a title and all the funds and properties that come with it. Just think of all the good you can do."

"I only wish I could do so without gaining a title." He didn't deserve it and yet he had not been able to dissuade his uncle without revealing the truth.

Strong lines fell into place on George's forehead. "You are my only chance at leaving a legacy, Florian. You know that. And you needn't worry. My man of affairs has been thoroughly briefed. He will assist you with your new responsibilities. Additionally, there's an army of employees for you to rely on, leaving you free to pursue your career to your heart's content. As you have requested."

Although they'd already discussed this at length, Florian couldn't help but wince. "It is unheard of for a duke to have a profession. I shall bring scandal to the title."

"Unlikely, considering you will outrank anyone who dares to insult you. And your profession is a noble one. You have patients who would no doubt be sorry to lose you, which is why I insist you continue on as usual, in spite of the title."

"If it were only that simple."

George studied him a moment from behind a pair of droopy eyelids. "If I didn't know you better, I would think you were being ungrateful. But that is not the sort of man you are. Is it?"

Rising, Florian strode to the window and drew the heavy curtain aside so he could look out. It was dark now save for the yellow glow from a gaslight. "It is not that I am ungrateful, Uncle. It is just . . ." He drew a heavy breath and felt his chest tighten in response.

"You feel unworthy."

The words ricocheted through the room, forcing Florian away from the window. His eyes caught the look of deep understanding now etched on his uncle's face and realization finally sank in. "How do you know?"

"Because your moral compass has always been very precise and because I am also aware of your heritage. Your mother told me everything before you were even born."

The admission brought Florian back to the chair on heavy feet. He sank down and stared at the man who'd always been nothing but kind toward him—the man who insisted on making him heir and who'd gone through hell in order to do so. "Did she tell you who my father is?"

"As far as I and the rest of Society are concerned, Viscount Armswell is your father. He and your mother were married at the time of your birth so you are not the illegitimate son you insist on pretending you are."

Angered by that comment, Florian scowled. "I do not pretend to be anything I am not, but the fact is that I was conceived in a manner that I wish to this day I had never learned about. So call me what you will but there is no denying my blood is tainted."

Silence followed, the two men staring back at each other until George quietly asked, "How much did your mother tell you?"

"Enough for me to know where to lay the blame."

George nodded. "I would have killed the vile miscreant myself if I had been given the chance to do so, but the situation was complicated and . . ." His voice broke and he turned his head away. "Claire got no protection from me or from her husband. It is a wonder she was able to forgive us."

Feeling bile creeping up his throat, Florian closed his eyes and focused on deep inhalations. He hated being reminded of what had happened when Henry was two years old and his nanny had gotten sick. Claire had taken him to the park herself. It was there Bartholomew had seen her and decided to do what he'd since made a habit of doing: taking what he wanted. But being a selfish, heartless bastard, he'd chosen the cruelest path available. When Henry went missing a week later and Claire was summoned by Bartholomew, she immediately did what had to be done in order to save her son.

Florian shuddered.

"At least he is dead now," George said, filling the silence with an edge of gratitude. "There is some relief to be found in that."

"I quite agree." Florian would not take this small bit of solace away from a dying man by informing him that a doppelganger had died in Bartholomew's place.

"So you see, you need not worry about sullying the title. I know how you came into this world and I am sorry for it, but you are still my sister's boy and the only man able to continue my lineage."

Holding his uncle's gaze, Florian studied the man who'd known of his paternity long before he'd discovered it himself. George had loved him, championed him and offered support throughout his entire life and his career. Armswell had not had the capacity to do as much and it was not until Florian turned sixteen that he had finally understood why the viscount had favored his brother. It wasn't just that Lowell was his heir, but that Florian was the product of something Armswell wished to forget.

"Thank you, Uncle," Florian murmured. "You may rest assured that I will do my best to honor your wishes." He would deal with the problems it threatened to cause later.

Chapter 7

The Brighton ballroom was ablaze with light, the bright glow from chandeliers catching the facets of countless jewels and inviting them to shimmer. Finishing a reel with an eager gentleman who'd claimed the dance seconds after her arrival, Juliette went to join Gabriella who was presently conversing with her aunt, the Dowager Countess of Everly.

"Gabriella tells me you're joining the committee at St. Agatha's Hospital," Lady Everly said. She smiled slyly. "I wouldn't mind sitting at a table with Florian either."

Instinctively, Juliette glanced around, seeking the man in question. She hadn't seen him since she'd met with him in his office. He hadn't attended a single social event, and when she'd asked Lowell about his absence, she'd simply been told that Florian was busy.

"He has always fascinated me," Lady Everly continued.

Juliette blinked. "Who has?"

Lady Everly gave her a quizzical look. "Why, Florian, of course." A hint of mischief lit her eyes. "All that red hair, you know?"

"It is an unusual shade," Gabriella agreed.

Juliette didn't comment. She was not about to delve into a conversation about the exact shade of Florian's hair, which wasn't red at all. It was an intricate collection of color, mostly copper and bronze. "My reason for wanting to join the committee has nothing to do with him."

"Of course not, my dear," Lady Everly said with a sparkle to her eyes.

Despite her best efforts, Juliette couldn't stop from getting defensive. "He is an extremely skilled physician and surgeon." A far more impressive aspect than his looks, though she had to admit he was strikingly handsome.

Raising her fan to provide a private shield, Lady Everly leaned toward Gabriella and Juliette. "From what I hear, he has traveled the world, gathering all sorts of unorthodox methods from various places."

"His patients do not seem to complain," Gabriella said. "I personally believe he is the most skilled physician there is. I refuse to use anyone else."

"Do you know he advised against bloodletting and purging when I had the measles?" Juliette asked. "According to him, it does more harm than good."

"Yes. I do believe that particular opinion of his has been much debated in the medical community. He is not always popular with other physicians and has been widely criticized by some." Lady Everly snapped her fan shut. "If you ask me, one need only look to the success of St. Agatha's Hospital to know they are all mistaken. Florian is the genius behind that facility and it is doing very well indeed, without the bloodletting or the purging."

A couple of gentlemen approached at that moment,

asking Juliette if there was still room on her dance card. So she handed the card over and watched as they added their names before moving off. "I have almost filled it completely," she said, staring down at the long list of names. Her feet hurt and still four dances remained.

"Let me see," Lady Everly said. She peered at the card, nodding in response to the various names, each more formidable than the last. "Your popularity is growing. And yet, no one has claimed the waltz."

Juliette blushed. "I believe it may be because Raphe threatened to rip Mr. Newton's throat out last night when he pulled me closer than propriety allows." A new tune started and Juliette glanced toward the dance floor. "If you will excuse me, I must go and find my next partner."

She hurried off, engaging in a country dance with a handsome officer, then a minuet with a Mr. Somethingorother, followed by a cotillion and a quadrille. Her slippers pinched her toes by the time it was over and her last partner gallantly escorted her over to the refreshment table.

"You dance splendidly, Lady Juliette," the gentleman, who'd introduced himself as Viscount Euton, told her. He poured a glass of lemonade and watched her drink.

"Thank you, my lord, I do try."

For some reason he seemed to find that vastly amusing, chuckling while offering her a piece of cake. She declined and he set it aside. "Perhaps you will permit me to call on you tomorrow?"

"Tomorrow?" She couldn't think of what else to say except, "I have an engagement with my sister."

"Tuesday then? We could go for a ride in the park."

Juliette craned her neck and searched the room while speaking offhandedly. "I do not ride, and even if I did, I have promised my brother to offer advice on—" She spotted the man she sought and instinctively started to move in his direction while saying over her shoulder, "If you will excuse me, there is someone with whom I must speak."

Ignoring Euton's attempt at stalling her, Juliette left him behind and wound her way through the crowd. It was quite a crush with several attendees standing shoulder to shoulder on the edge of the dance floor. She would have to circumvent them somehow if she was to reach Florian, which meant speaking an endless series of excuse me's on her way toward her destination.

An ostrich plumed fan slapped her face and a gentleman elbowed her straight in the ribs while laughing in response to a joke. Cursing having to come here when she would so much rather stay home, Juliette focused on her purpose and continued onward, past a cluster of giggling debutantes and a similar, decades older, group of matrons who eyed her with undeniable censure.

It wasn't easy ignoring them or pretending their low opinion of her and her family did not matter. It did and it hurt, but there were more important things for her to think of right now. So she ignored her failing confidence and raised her chin even higher. Back straight and eyes on her target, Juliette approached Florian as if she'd been raised in a palace instead of in the slums of St. Giles.

Florian sensed her before he saw her. Engrossed in conversation with Moore, an acquaintance of his who'd recently returned from America, he hadn't spared a thought for any of the other guests attending the ball. Until now. It was as if his skin came alive beneath his evening attire, the scent wafting toward him so sweet, so captivating, so . . .

He instinctively turned and there she was, a vision clad in a gauzy concoction of blushing pink. Unlike the last time he'd seen her, she wore no bonnet. Instead her light brown hair, streaked with golden tresses, was piled up into an intricate mass of curls at the back of her head.

The sight made Florian want to unpin it and watch it fall over her shoulders. He frowned in response to the unbidden urge and deliberately pushed it aside so he could greet the woman with decorum. "Lady Juliette. What a pleasure it is to see you again. You look stunning as ever this evening."

Her cheeks filled with color until they matched the shade of her gown in the most delightful way. "Thank you, sir. I apologize for interrupting your conversation but I was hoping for a moment of your time." She glanced out across the sea of people. "It took some effort to get here."

He could well imagine. Addressing his friend, he said, "May I present the Duke of Huntley's sister, Lady Juliette?"

Moore bowed with all the gallantry of a well-schooled gentleman. "It is an honor."

Florian turned to Juliette. "Allow me to introduce Mr. Moore. He was just telling me of the last two years he spent in New York City."

"How exciting," Lady Juliette told Moore. She served him a radiant smile that provoked the most unsavory feeling in Florian's gut. He pushed that aside as well and clenched his jaw.

Moore's eyes brightened with appreciation. "The journey alone was thrilling. I shall never forget the wide expanse of endless water surrounding the ship. And then that moment when we finally caught sight of land! It was extraordinarily exuberating."

"What was your first impression of the city itself?" Lady Juliette asked. Her eyes were wide with interest.

"Oh, it is grand, thrumming with energy and filled with people all hoping to accomplish their dreams. And the layout of it is simply genius. The streets are straight and parallel, making it simple for anyone to find their way around."

"How fascinating." Lady Juliet threw a quick glance in Florian's direction—the sort suggesting she was either attempting to be polite by acknowledging his presence or trying to confirm he wasn't missing. Perhaps both. "I hope I have the opportunity to visit one day. Traveling abroad would be such an adventure." She turned to Florian in that moment, her sparkling eyes prompting him to hold his breath. "From what I hear, you are well traveled as well, are you not?"

It took a second for his brain to get his tongue working again, the effect of being the subject of her interest so astonishingly pleasant it momentarily robbed him of his mental faculties. "Mostly in Europe," he finally managed to say, "though my profession has taken me as far as St. Petersburg and even Persia."

"Goodness gracious! That is quite something."

Florian allowed his lips to quirk in response to Lady Juliette's unfeigned enthusiasm. Oh, who was he kidding? The truth was he could not help but smile, the effect she had on him so enchanting he was practically preening. Which promptly made him frown.

"It is indeed," Moore said. "Now, if you will

excuse me, I believe Lady Juliette wished to speak with *you*, Florian. I will allow her to do so without interfering any further." He sketched a quick bow and disappeared into the crowd.

Florian appreciated Moore's departure even though his nerves thrummed with uncertain anticipation. "Perhaps you would like to dance?" Even though he *detested* dancing since it never resulted in anything useful, he'd rather enjoyed partnering with her.

She met his gaze with a hint of mischief. "I would be delighted. Especially since I can think of no better place to address the subject at hand."

Thrown by her enthusiasm, it took a second for Florian to pull himself together and offer the lady his arm. Her arm wound snuggly around his own and her hand settled neatly upon his forearm. Acutely aware of her warmth and the way his body responded, he guided Lady Juliette toward the edge of the dance floor where a cotillion was presently coming to an end. The music faded and the rustling of silks, the hum of voices and the shuffling of feet filled the air as couples made their way off the floor. The introduction to the next set began to play and Florian dropped a look at his partner.

Her eyes were wide, her lips slightly parted as if by surprise, and everything stilled around him, shoved into the background by the hard beat of his heart and the woman who filled his vision.

She pressed her lips together and took a deep breath. "Another waltz," she said beneath her breath.

"Do you mind?" He didn't want her to. He wanted her to want it as much as he did right now. Even though he knew it was unwise and even though he shouldn't allow the attraction forming between them to flourish.

Her head tilted upward, her eyes sparkling with so much wonder and anticipation he felt his heart shudder and his chest grow tight. "Of course not, Florian. The waltz is perfect."

Unable to speak for fear of sounding as awkward as he felt, he escorted her onto the dance floor and took his position opposite, his hand clasping hers while the other settled snuggly against her waist. A swift exhalation of breath slipped past her lips. It was almost a gasp, though more subtle, coupled with wide-eyed dismay. Gone in an instant, she expertly hid her response beneath a cooler composure. But in the brief second it lasted, Florian realized that as nonchalant as Lady Juliette wished to appear, he affected her in the same way she'd begun affecting him. Which, as enticing as some men might find that, was rather something of a problem. Because if there was one thing Florian could not afford to do, it was getting tangled up in desire and, God forbid, love.

So he did as she did and schooled his features while trying his damnedest to ignore the sweet floral scent that clung to her body and the feel of said body beneath his touch. Spinning her around, he led her expertly between other couples, aware that it felt just as right as it had the last time they'd danced.

"What was it you wished to say?" Perhaps if he could focus on conversation he would not think of how well she fit in his arms.

"My brother met with his bankers the day before yesterday. My donation should be made available to you by tomorrow morning."

He held her gaze. She was the sister of a duke, so

the sum had to be substantial. Still, he had to know the details. "Forgive me for sounding vulgar, but how much exactly are you offering?" He'd never thought to ask until now.

Her eyes lit with the pleasure of knowing she was going to impress him. "Three thousand pounds."

Florian's heel hit the floor before it was meant to, forcing him to pull her closer in order to save them from stumbling. This time her gasp was unhindered, her pretty lips parting while the shock of awareness brightened her eyes. He felt it too and wasted no time adding distance once more. "That is quite a staggering sum, my lady."

She gave a curt nod to indicate she also wished to banish the inconvenient attraction blooming between them. "I know, but what I hope to accomplish will not come cheap."

He was well aware, but he still had not imagined she'd offer that much. "Is it the entire allowance you are giving up?"

"It is indeed."

"You have no wish to save some of it in case you need a new bonnet or—"

"Florian." Her voice was suddenly stripped of its usual softness. "I have survived without material things for most of my life. Since moving into Huntley House I have received more pretty trinkets and fripperies than any person needs. Doing without my allowance for a year will be no hardship, least of all when considering the good that will hopefully come of it."

She was fairly trembling with emotion, her nerves clearly on edge in spite of her efforts to convey complete calm. He admired her stalwart determination and her burning desire to help those in need. Though he knew it wasn't wise, that he shouldn't encourage a deeper attachment, he couldn't stop himself from wanting to know more about her.

"Have you always been so passionate in your pursuits?"

She tilted her head as he led her along the periphery of the dance floor, and he suddenly wondered what it might be like to be the subject of her dedication. The thought produced a provocative image of him submitting to her desire, of her mouth descending over his while her hands—

"I think so," she said, scattering the inconvenient fantasy. "When Raphe . . . Huntley, that is . . . insisted on teaching Amelia and me the Latin he knew, he brought home a book for us to study. With little else to keep me busy, I set my mind to learning every conjugation, reciting them several times daily while challenging myself to learn ten new words a day. Within a couple of months, I'd surpassed my brother's abilities and had started teaching him."

She smiled, not arrogantly, as some might have done, but with the pride of a woman who valued her achievements. Impressed and perhaps even slightly awestruck, Florian tightened his hand around hers as he spun her. He knew she and her siblings had faced the *ton*'s censure when they'd arrived, that there were still some who thought they didn't belong in high society—that they weren't good enough. But the truth was that Lady Juliette was better than most of the people who filled this ballroom. She had heart, the will to make a difference, not only to her own life, but to the lives of others, and this both fascinated and drew him like nothing ever had.

"Admiror te fortitudinem." *I admire your strength.*

A flicker of appreciation lit her eyes. "Et admiror tuam." *And I admire yours.* "Your accomplishments are impressive." She frowned slightly before saying, "Especially for someone as young as you."

He started a little, surprised as always by her candor. "Perhaps I'm not as young as you think."

This forced a grin to her lips, and once again the thought of kissing her pressed upon his mind. He tried to ignore it, but it persisted, heightening his awareness. It was more than a year since he'd last been with a woman. His work had buried his baser instincts and driven away all compulsion.

Until now.

"I would place you at roughly thirty years of age."

"And I suspect you've been studying Debrett's."

She made a face. "Guilty. Though studying it might be an overstatement. I only look up the families that intrigue me."

His heart expanded and for a lovely moment, all his concerns drifted away. It was only the two of them now, caught in a dance that he wished would last forever. He wanted to ask if *he* intrigued her, but was too afraid of breaking the spell and ruining the moment, though he could not stop his gaze from lowering to her lips.

"There wasn't as much information about you as I had hoped," she continued, then hastily added, "I thought it wise to learn as much about you as possible, considering we'll be working together."

The magic shattered, stabbing Florian straight in the chest. "I see." His voice was harder than he'd intended, but it couldn't be helped. Not when he'd been foolishly lost in a dream without her. "My education and accomplishments are outlined in the medical journals at the Royal College of Surgeons. I'll send a note over granting you access so you can look through them."

Her expression changed from confident to uncertain. "I'm sorry. I did not mean to offend you in any way."

"Why on earth would you suppose you might have done so?"

"I um . . . I don't know, except . . ."

"Except what?" Hurt by his growing suspicion that every interest she'd shown him had somehow been linked to her goals, he goaded her now with unforgiving insistence.

"You seem upset," she blurted. "Which isn't at all what I hoped to accomplish."

"No. I don't suppose it was." He managed to keep the bitterness from his voice as the music faded and relief swamped his body. Noting her stunned expression, however, he hastened to say, "I am not angry with you in the least, my lady. The only person at fault here is me."

For foolishly getting caught up in a fantasy.

Desperate to leave her company, he bid her a continued good evening and walked away while dreading the thought of having to see her again. Which would be sooner rather than later, considering the next committee meeting was scheduled to take place this coming week and she would now be there.

Chapter 8

Accompanying Gabriella's mother, Countess of Warwick, to Florian's town house three days later, Juliette braced herself when the carriage pulled to a jolting halt.

"You look worried," Lady Warwick said, "but you needn't be. Remember, you have donated more funds to St. Agatha's than the rest of the donors combined. Only the Dowager Duchess of Tremaine has offered a larger sum."

She reached for the door handle and paused. Her eyes met Juliette's. "Chin up. The last thing you want them to see are your nerves."

The only problem with this advice was that Juliette's worries had nothing to do with what the other committee members might think of her and everything to do with the way Florian's attitude toward her had changed as they'd waltzed with each other at the Brighton Ball. In an instant, the warmth in his eyes had died and the companionable mood they'd been sharing had lost its spark. Juliette had puzzled over it since, unsure of why he'd had such an adverse reaction to what she'd said.

Tamping down her reservations, Juliette followed the countess out of the carriage and up the steps to Florian's front door. It was opened by a servant the moment they knocked, granting them entry to a modest foyer. Handing over their shawls and bonnets, they continued through a hallway until they reached a door that was standing wide open. Beyond was a decent-sized room—the dining room—with a table fitted for twelve. Three chairs remained vacant while those already seated stood in response to Lady Warwick's and Juliette's arrival. It took but a second to notice that no other women were present.

"Welcome, ladies." The salutation was spoken by Florian who was now coming to greet them. He bowed stiffly, his countenance stark as he held his arm out toward the left side of the table. "Lady Warwick, your customary chair awaits." Lady Warwick strolled away in the direction he indicated, leaving Juliette alone with the physician. He studied her for a second, then turned toward the rest of the group. "Let us welcome Lady Juliette to our midst. Her generous donation to St. Agatha's promises to be of great significance."

The gentlemen dipped their heads in her direction and Florian introduced them each in turn. All were high-ranking peers, with the exception of Mr. Winehurst, whom Florian introduced as an affluent entrepreneur. The rest of the group included the Marquess of Stokes, Viscount Clearwater, the Earl of Elmwood, Baron Hawthorne and the Earl of Wilmington. To Juliette's dismay, Yates was there as well, which was slightly awkward since she'd been deliberately avoiding him for the past week and a half.

"Come," Florian said, offering her his arm and

pulling her attention away from Yates. "I have secured a seat for you next to me." When Juliette hesitated, he added, "It will make it easier for me to offer any necessary explanations if you are not at the other end of the table."

Nodding, she placed her hand carefully upon his arm. Warmth infused her veins as the length of her arm pressed into his.

Disturbed, Juliette tried to ignore the unsettling flutter in the pit of her stomach. It would be difficult enough having to address this group of high-ranking individuals without worrying over her progressively unsettling responses to Florian.

"Allow me," he murmured, his words breezing along the curve of her neck as he turned to pull out her chair.

Unable to breathe, let alone speak on account of the sudden leap of her pulse, Juliette gave a curt nod and quickly sat before the man could affect her further. Which of course was impossible to hope for since he would soon be sitting immediately to her left.

But rather than claim his own seat, he strode away to welcome another individual—a woman Juliette had never seen before. Once again, the gentlemen stood, as did Lady Warwick, so Juliette followed her lead and rose as well.

No older than Juliette, the woman, whoever she was, was plainly dressed in a practical-looking day gown cut from beige cotton. She wasn't particularly pretty, her hair a dim shade that fell between blonde and brown without being either. But her gaze was sharp as it swept the room, the fullness of her mouth curving into a welcoming smile the moment she locked eyes with Juliette. Addressing Florian with obvious familiarity, she exchanged a few words with him before making her way toward Juliette while he followed close behind.

"It is lovely to make your acquaintance at last," the woman told Juliette as soon as she stood before her. "I am Viola Cartwright, the Dowager Duchess of Tremaine and St. Agatha's patroness."

It took great effort on Juliette's part not to gape at the lady. A hundred questions formed in her mind all at once, the most prominent one being how a woman who appeared to be no older than herself had managed to become a dowager duchess and the founder of a hospital. And how was it that Juliette hadn't seen her or heard of her before? She was clearly going to have to ask Raphe to purchase an updated version of Debrett's.

Collecting herself, she quickly attempted a curtsey, which felt really strange on account of the duchess's age. But that was what one did, was it not? The only other duchesses she knew were Amelia and Gabriella, with whom she was always informal. It was as if all the training she'd undergone since arriving in Mayfair flew out the window, leaving her flustered and awkward.

"There is no need for that," Her Grace said. She spoke so low only Juliette and possibly Florian could hear her. "And since I do believe you and I are going to be friends, I must insist you call me Viola."

As relieved as Juliette was about not having to stand on ceremony, she could not help but wonder at Viola's complete departure from formality. It raised her curiosity. But with Viola already moving away to claim her own chair and Florian sitting down right between them, there was no opportunity for her to learn more about the dowager duchess at the moment.

Instead, she acknowledged Florian's closeness, the masculine fragrance of bergamot and sandalwood that hovered about his person. It tempted her to lean closer, the rich scent teasing her senses and producing the most peculiar yearning for additional nearness.

With him.

Juliette sucked in a sharp breath and held it. Heavens! What was happening to her? She must not have slept well or eaten enough breakfast to be having such puzzling observations. Except it wasn't so puzzling at all. She hazarded a glance at him as he addressed the committee. A nerve ticked above his right eye. Fascinating . . . She shook her head and gave herself a mental kick. This had to stop before she descended into madness.

But focusing on what he was saying became a little bit harder when he turned his head and regarded her with a frown. It lasted but a second, his attention returning seamlessly to the subject at hand, but it had been long enough for her to realize he'd become aware of her perusal.

Which only increased her discomfort.

She did not want him thinking she had a romantic interest in him. He was much too severe and standoffish for her to even imagine such a scenario, even if she did find him attractive and intriguing and . . . Heat rolled across her skin as she recalled the craving he'd incited in her when his gaze had dropped to her lips the last time they'd danced. She'd instantly wondered what it might be like to feel his mouth pressed firmly against her own, the thought so acute and so startling, she'd had to grasp for something to say.

She'd settled on the subject of his education because she'd thought it was safe. Instead, he'd made her feel as though she'd ruined what had until then been a promising friendship. She could only hope that wasn't the case so they could return to their engaging discussions.

"As you know," he was saying, "the typhus outbreak has become increasingly serious. In my opinion, our primary concern should be avoiding an epidemic. Because once that happens, thousands could perish."

"Are you suggesting that restricting access in and out of St. Giles won't be enough?" the Earl of Elmwood said. A heavyset man with bushy eyebrows dipping down in serious contemplation, he was the oldest member present.

"So far, only three deaths have been reported, but as infection spreads, that number will rise. Incubation is roughly ten to fourteen days, so it could be a week before we know how many additional people have caught it."

"But surely quarantining them in St. Giles will prevent the disease from spreading," Lady Warwick said.

Florian nodded. "It is a start. The problem arises when the sick begin outnumbering the healthy, because once that happens people will try to flee in order to avoid infection." He paused for a moment before saying, "We cannot allow them to do so, however. The risk is too great."

"Then what do you propose?" Viscount Clearwater asked.

"The military has, as of tonight, been ordered to shoot anyone attempting to leave St. Giles."

"Good God!" Juliette clasped her hand over her

mouth and stared at Florian in horror. Aware the room had gone utterly silent in response to her outburst, she glanced about hastily before turning her attention back to Florian. "You wish to murder people?"

A tic at the edge of his mouth conveyed his disapproval of her question. Well, too bad. What he was suggesting was absolutely preposterous and *wrong*.

"My lady." His voice was firm and direct. "I would advise against insinuating I or anyone else here would ever be guilty of such a crime."

The way he said it sent chills racing down Juliette's spine. She sat back, unsure of how to proceed. She shot a look at Lady Warwick for guidance but found no help there. Aware she was on her own in this, Juliette squared her shoulders. "Forgive me. I did not mean to cause offense, but surely you must agree that killing people is not the way forward. It is savage and . . . and uncivilized." Silence followed and the frowns grew deeper. Juliette began to wonder if she'd made a massive mistake by deciding to come here. Lowering her voice to a hushed tone, she said, "It is your duty to save people, Florian."

Florian stared at her for a long moment before he spoke. "No one is more aware of that than I, my lady." He clenched his jaw. His posture grew increasingly rigid and Juliette realized he fought to maintain control.

"Florian." Viola placed her hand over his in a comforting gesture that instantly sparked a detestable feeling in Juliette's belly. She fought to rid herself of it as the dowager duchess said, "Perhaps you ought to explain your reasoning more fully."

Florian seemed to relax a little, then finally nodded. "Very well." He turned his head so he could look more directly at Juliette. "You do not know the danger we're facing or how difficult it will be to fight this disease if it is not contained from the start. If it spreads, the entire city will be at risk." He was speaking slowly now, as if she were a child who failed to comprehend the simplest of things. It grated, but she made a deliberate effort to focus on his every word for the sake of the cause. "Since people also travel, contagion can easily spread to other parts of the country before we realize it has done so. It could even reach the Continent with devastating effect. Are you willing to risk such an outcome?"

"No. Of course not." It was absurd of him to think so.

"Then you agree that my proposal is the best way forward."

She instinctively shook her head. "No. There has to be another way that doesn't involve killing anyone."

"As long as the residents of St. Giles remain where they are, their lives will not be threatened."

"Except by the disease!" She glared at him, infuriated by his stubbornness and discomfited by the fact that he still possessed the ability to make her skin tingle even when the air between them was tense. Bolstering herself, she tried not to think of how scorched she felt when subjected to his assessing gaze, and forged ahead with her argument. "Surely the best approach would be to take those at risk of developing the disease to a safe location where they can be quarantined and, if it becomes necessary, appropriately treated. Can a floor at the hospital not be made available for this?"

Florian's eyes darkened. "You would place patients already at the hospital in danger?"

"They would not come into contact with these people, but considering the unsanitary conditions in St. Giles, remaining there does not seem like a feasible solution. That book you lent me . . ." She could feel herself grasping at straws but she could not seem to stop. "William Buchan clearly states that cleanliness is key when battling the spread of disease."

"She does make a point, Florian." It was the Marquess of Stokes who commented. "Thousands of pounds have been donated to this hospital. Lord knows it is not filled to capacity, so it ought to be possible to free up a floor for those infected by typhus. Choosing not to do so may be construed as wasteful and could result in the loss of future donations. In my experience, people do not wish to give money to a cause that fails to keep its promises."

It took enormous restraint for Florian not to march across the room and shake some sense into Stokes. Once he was done he'd be tempted to throttle Lady Juliette as well. This was all her fault. She failed to see the bigger picture. All because she wished to be kind. He winced at the thought of it. He knew better than anyone that it wasn't kindness that kept people safe. It was common sense and intellect. Those who wanted to be kind often got sick themselves because they used their hearts instead of their minds.

Forcing some sense of calm into his rigid muscles, he made an effort to relax. Anger would yield no results whatsoever. But when she'd accused him of wanting to murder people he'd almost imploded. The rage had been swift and acute, the suggestion that he and Bartholomew might have something in

common provoking a primitive urge to hit something. Especially when he'd had an inclination to
do so already—ever since he'd acknowledged the
yearning Lady Juliette inspired in him. He wanted
her, damn it, more than he'd ever wanted any other
woman before. And that, coupled with the chance of
her not wanting him in return, made him irritable.

Inhaling deeply, he tried to speak with a level
voice. "To be clear, I want to save as many people
as possible. Make no mistake about it. But when it
comes to deadly diseases, fatalities are inevitable.
My job is to minimize those fatalities as much as
I can. Even if that means making tough decisions
like ensuring that nobody leaves St. Giles, no matter
what."

Lady Juliette straightened in her seat. Her posture
was rigid, her face flushed and her eyes filled with
endless resolve. When she spoke, her voice was calm,
save for the slightest quiver. "I am not donating three
thousand pounds so I can stand idly by while you do
nothing for those who can be helped."

Jesus Christ and all his apostles!

Florian clenched his fist. "Sometimes," he grit out,
"sacrifices must be made for the greater good. And I
never said I would do nothing to help. Indeed, I have
every intention of tending to the sick, but I will be
damned if I am letting any of St. Giles's residents
near St. Agatha's or any other part of London for that
matter."

"What Florian and I would like to propose," Viola
said, taking over, "is setting up a clinic in St. Giles
itself so people there can be evaluated and treated
close to their homes. Any physician or nurse who
agrees to help with this effort will do so voluntarily.

But once again, it is our belief that risking the lives of a few is much better than risking those of many."

Florian considered Lady Juliette discreetly while Viola continued speaking. Her expression was set in firm lines that suggested she was trying very hard to control her emotions. Which was, of course, the problem. When it came to life and death, he never allowed emotion to interfere with his judgment. She, on the other hand, was new to all of this and could only focus on what he'd said about shooting anyone trying to flee St. Giles. But it could become necessary, and if she'd lived through a typhus epidemic like he had, she would understand.

She must have sensed he was watching her, for she suddenly turned to meet his gaze. It was then that he realized her eyes weren't an ordinary shade of brown as he'd initially thought, but hazel, the green flecks adding a fascinating degree of depth. Unable to stop himself, he dropped his gaze to her lips and immediately regretted doing so. For in spite of his increasing annoyance with her, that brief glance filled his mind with thoughts of kissing. It paved a path of desire so acute he was forced to look away, lest she be made aware of what he was feeling.

"On another point," Viola was saying, "we need to discuss this list of expenses." She proceeded to hand out pieces of paper to everyone. A discussion about the need for more staff and certain supplies ensued. "All of this will be costly. The clinic in particular will be a large expense, possibly exceeding Lady Juliette's generous donation and . . ." She paused. "While bringing those who are infected to the hospital is not an option, we must try to get them out of St. Giles somehow. I hope I can count on all of you to think of a way in which to do so as cheaply and efficiently as possible."

When Viola paused to glance around the room, Lady Juliette spoke up once more. "Perhaps a charity event with an auction would at least help bring in additional funds, which in turn could increase your options of relocating the typhus patients."

Viola turned to her. "We haven't had much success with such things in the past, but you're welcome to give it another try if you think you can make it work."

"I'll set my mind to it right away," Lady Juliette assured her.

The meeting was adjourned and the members pushed back their chairs.

"Your idea to set up a clinic in St. Giles is good," Lady Juliette was saying while gathering her reticule and rising to her feet. "And you will obviously need more staff to run it, as Viola says. There is also no denying that there are other costs incurred by the hospital itself and covering these is of course a necessity. That said . . ." Her voice, though quiet, was sharp enough to cut glass. "I was hoping I'd have more say in how my money is spent."

Florian rose as well.

"Of course." The surprised look in her eyes was priceless and fleeting. Florian took a moment to appreciate the effect of his geniality before pressing on. "But what you possess in ways of kindness and a desire to help, you lack in experience. As evidenced by your rash contrariness with my effort to save as many people as possible from a deadly disease. All because—"

"My rash contrariness?"

She was leaning toward him, allowing her sweet

fragrance to distract him from the outrage burning within her eyes. Hell, he rather expected her to jab at him with a pointed finger and for some peculiar reason he imagined he might enjoy such a heated display of anger on her part. It suggested passionate emotion, with him as the direct cause, which brought his mind straight back to his earlier thought of kissing.

Shoving the unwelcome notion aside, he stared her down. "You may have lived your life in the slums, my lady. Indeed, you have undoubtedly experienced your fair share of misery. But when it comes to saving lives, your naïveté is astounding."

Shock was the first emotion to cross her face but then she composed herself, like a warrior princess preparing for battle. Her features tightened, and if Florian wasn't mistaken, she even grew an inch in height. "I have admired you for your accomplishments and I have even enjoyed your company." Her breaths came in short little bursts of agitation. "I see now that I was wrong to do so, however, for although you may be an excellent physician and an interesting conversationalist, you are nothing but a cad, completely devoid of compassion."

His hand grabbed hold of her elbow before he could think of what he was doing. *Christ!* This woman was dangerous. She robbed him of common sense!

Ignoring that for the moment, he steered Lady Juliette a little further away from everyone else so he could give her a few choice words in private. Except he was not wearing gloves since he was at home, and the lady in question was dressed for the pleasant day that it was, her breezy muslin gown consisting of short cap sleeves that left most of her arms bare to his touch.

Her skin was smooth and wonderfully warm. He could feel the heat of her spilling through his palm and fingertips. The sharp inhalation she made, as he tightened his hold ever so slightly, forced him closer. His body nudging hers in an effort to raise her awareness of him just as she had raised his awareness of her.

"Compassion, as noble as it may be, has no place here." He placed himself between her and the rest of the room. Reluctantly he released her arm, but not without noting the way her breath quivered the moment he did so, as if she regretted the loss of his touch. Elemental appreciation tightened his chest and he suddenly longed to encourage such sentiment in her once more. *Later.* Right now, words had to be said. "Compassion doesn't save lives, my lady. Reasoning and solid medical experience do."

She shook her head as though not comprehending. "How can you be so devoid of emotion? How can you be so cold?"

He winced, aware of the callous man he presented. "To let my heart guide me in this matter could be detrimental." He softened his voice, willing her to see him for who he really was beneath the monster she saw. "That does not mean I do not have one or that I lack compassion. But for me to be the best physician I can be, I have no choice but to discount it in favor of making rational decisions."

She stared up at him as if mesmerized, her mind clearly working to process his comment. And then she asked, "Have you always been like this?"

The question squeezed beneath his ribs, constricting his lungs. And yet, he struggled to overcome the panic her question evoked. Because it wasn't an easy one for him to answer. At least not honestly. Even though he wanted to. For reasons he couldn't explain, he wanted to open up to her, if only a little.

Perhaps because of her hopeful expression or maybe because he wanted her trust.

"It's something I learned to do a long time ago," he revealed. After his mother told him about Bartholomew, he'd hated her, Armswell and himself for a long time. Until he'd banished the feelings shredding his soul and applied analytical thinking. "Objectivity is easier that way and heartache less likely to occur."

Her expression softened and she quietly whispered, "I'm sorry."

"For what?"

"For whatever it was that happened to you." Glistening with pain, her eyes locked with his. "It must have been awful."

Shuddering in response to the depth of her insight, he glanced away, pushing the negative memories back. By the time he looked at her again, he was back in control and able to speak in the same precise tone he always applied when discussing his work. "It has allowed me to excel at my profession."

He would not waste time wondering why he discreetly reached out to brush his hand with hers or why she allowed the gesture rather than pulling away. But in that moment, he felt he had no choice but to do so. She, on the other hand, had every chance and reason to add more distance between them. Instead she remained where she was, her shallow breathing suggestive of profound alertness.

Captivated, Florian dared to take a step closer so he could whisper close to her ear. "My lady, you are the only threat to my composure. And if I were indeed the cad you believe me to be, I would have no qualms about proving that to you."

"Sir." Her pupils were fully dilated, her lips parted with what could only be described as shock. "You forget yourself."

He stepped back and bowed his head. "Perhaps."

She swallowed and he noted the way her pulse fluttered rapidly against her neck and how her breathing grew more shallow. Maybe he did affect her after all. Maybe—

"I need you to help me put my money to good use as quickly as possible." She was suddenly completely serious, forcing him to wonder if he might have imagined her response to him. "The longer we talk, the more the disease is likely to spread with fatality rates climbing until we face a situation that is no longer possible to solve." When he opened his mouth to speak she cut him off. "Deciding to shoot people is not the answer, Florian. Resolution is."

This again? She was like a bloody brick wall refusing to budge. "Fine. But whatever the solution, it won't involve bringing typhus patients to St. Agatha's. And the soldiers stay where they are with their orders to act if necessary."

"But—"

"This is not a game. Lives are at stake and I intend to save as many as possible even if I have to fight your compassion every step of the way." Ignoring the flush that flooded her cheeks, he dipped his head. "Now, if you will please excuse me, I must attend to my other guests."

Without waiting for her to respond, he moved away quickly and went to join a conversation at the other side of the room. Because remaining in Lady Juliette's proximity was likely to make him go mad, not only from their differing points of view but from desire the likes of which he'd never experienced before. If only the subject of it were not so troublesome or un-attainable. But she was, and he would do well not to forget it.

Chapter 9

Even though Juliette had tried to convince Raphe that attending more social events would be a waste of her time, he insisted. Whether he hoped she would suddenly change her mind about marrying one of the eligible bachelors or expected some long-lost heir to make an unexpected appearance was unclear. But it did mean that, rather than spending the evening reading some additional books on medicine she'd found in the Huntley House library, she was once again forced to endure a crowded ballroom.

And since Amelia was in confinement and Gabriella had elected to stay home with Raphe and their children, that left her in the Warwicks' company. The evening was only tolerable because of the excitement Vivien had shown when Juliette had mentioned the charity event she planned to hold. They'd attended a few fund-raisers together the previous Season and when Vivien had hosted one herself for the benefit of the blind, Juliette had happily helped her organize it.

"Garden parties are all the rage," Vivien said. They were standing some distance from the dance floor where the crowd was slightly thinner. "If you set up a tent in the Huntley House garden with an area allocated for an auction, I think it could be very successful."

"Perhaps, but what if it rains?" Juliette asked. "It's only May, after all, so anything can happen. I rather think I'll ask my brother if I can use the ballroom for a massive tea party."

"Oh, how original!"

Running with the idea, Juliette said, "I'll have round tables set up with decorations on each one and frosted petit fours in bright, uplifting colors."

"A positive atmosphere will certainly help the bidding. What sort of items are you thinking of auctioning off?"

Juliette thought about that for a second. "The usual gift baskets, of course, but something else too . . . something bigger and more desirable, like . . ." A thought struck her and she couldn't help but smile. "A waltz with Florian."

Vivien's eyes widened. "Do you honestly think he'll agree to that?"

"I don't know." She recalled the panicked look in his eyes the night he'd arrived at the Hawthorne Ball and found himself surrounded by a horde of eager women. But on the other hand, he had promised to help, and it *was* for a good cause.

"Maybe other bachelors will agree to do the same," Vivien suggested with a playful touch of mischief. "You could even go so far as to auction off walks in the park or a boat ride on the Serpentine."

Juliette grinned. "The possibilities are endless when one puts one's mind to it."

A footman approached and both ladies snatched a glass of lemonade from his tray. "Do you realize how lucky you are?" Vivien asked while taking a sip of hers.

"Embarrassingly so," Juliette admitted. When Vivien showed surprise, she said, "I hope you don't think me ungrateful, but I sometimes hate the good fortune my family and I have had. We are judged for it, envied for it, criticized for it. While there are many who have welcomed us into Society, some have not. And although Raphe and Amelia have their titles to protect them from a great deal of censure, I don't."

Vivien took another sip of her drink. "You could change that, you know."

Juliette scoffed. "By marrying?"

"It is expected. And before you argue that point, allow me to tell you that growing old alone can be terribly lonely." When Juliette frowned, Vivien explained. "My aunt's husband passed away twenty years ago. Since then the only companion she's had has been me, a girl thirty years her junior."

"She could have remarried."

"Her love for my uncle would never permit that, which is a pity. Only five years of her life were spent with him by her side and . . ." She dropped her voice. "Once, after a bit too much wine before bed, she told me they used to have intimacy and . . . great passion." She coughed lightly before saying, "I have a feeling that marriage to the right sort of man could be a wonderful experience."

Juliette knew from the satisfied looks on Amelia's and Gabriella's faces whenever they saw their husbands that there had to be some substance to Vivien's point. "I suppose that might be true, but even if it is, what would you have me do? Marry someone on a whim in the hope of it all working out?"

"Of course not. But surely there must be someone you find attractive?"

"I can't think of anyone." Oh what a terrible lie that was.

Vivien gave her a dubious look. "Really?"

"In any case I would want more than physical attraction alone. I would want a husband who takes an interest in me, someone with whom I can talk at great length without either of us getting bored." Her thoughts turned to Florian and it took some effort to ignore them. "From what I understand, most peers marry for convenience and spend their lives apart. In which case, why bother at all?"

Rather than ponder that question as Juliette had expected, Vivien chuckled. "I believe most of them put in the effort so they can have children."

Which was certainly a compelling argument. Especially if Amelia's numerous insinuations were anything to go by. Juliette wasn't quite sure why her sister placed so much weight on *that* particular aspect of marriage since she refused to go into detail, insisting Juliette would have to discover the joy of it for herself.

A gentleman to whom Juliette had been previously introduced approached as if conjured by their conversation. Although she failed to recall the man's name, she knew him to be a peer. "Lady Juliette," he said by way of greeting. "I hope—"

"Allow me to present my dear friend, Miss Vivien Saunders," Juliette cut in. She knew it was rude to interrupt, but he was rude too for not acknowledging her friend.

"A pleasure to make your acquaintance, Miss Saunders. I am Lord Portham, the Earl of Fitzhewitt's heir." He addressed Vivien with the typical civility innate to his breed, but showed no overwhelming interest otherwise.

Vivien, on the other hand, beamed. The whole display bothered Juliette because, in her opinion, her friend was just as deserving of this man's attention as she was. The only difference was that Juliette could ensure a connection to a duke. That was all she was—a stepping-stone to more prestige.

Lord Portham turned to her again. "As I was about to say," he stated, deliberately pointing out Juliette's earlier faux pas in cutting him off, "I hope to secure the next dance with you, my lady."

"Thank you, but I have already engaged in several dances and wish to rest my feet for the remainder of the evening. Miss Saunders, however, is quite available." And more than willing to take her place considering the hopefulness pouring from her eyes. "I suggest you invite her to dance with you instead."

And just as Juliette had known it would, the man's innate civility ensured he would do as she suggested without any hint of disagreeability. Waiting until the pair was out on the dance floor, Juliette turned toward the terrace door. It would be a half hour before her friend returned, during which she would enjoy a much-needed breath of fresh air.

A cool breeze caressed her the moment she stepped out onto the terrace, provoking a sigh of pure pleasure. Lord, it was good to get out of the stifling heat and away from the chatter of voices. Out here silence reigned, soothing her senses and instilling calm. She moved forward, toward a group of ladies and gentlemen who were all engrossed in conversation. Passing them, she descended the steps leading down into the garden.

Torches punctured the darkness down there, the intimate illumination beckoning her to approach. So she did, even though it was starting to drizzle. But to go back inside seemed absurd. Out here amidst dormant flowers and trees she could finally breathe, forget Raphe's insistence she hunt down a husband and Florian's infuriating logic.

She'd thought of him repeatedly since the committee meeting a few days earlier and the deep underlying pain he'd revealed when he'd shared the truth about his emotions and his ability to hide them. Except where she was concerned. That thought had bounced around in her head ever since. The possibilities it posed had intruded upon her dreams when she slept, leaving her hot and breathless each morning when she awoke.

A rich fragrance of lilies infused the air as she started along a path leading off to the right. It was neatly paved with large stone slabs that allowed for a quiet tread, which was probably why, when turning the corner of the house, the person coming toward her failed to hear her approach. She collided with the individual at full walking speed and would have fallen backward if a hand hadn't found its way round her to keep her upright.

"Oomph!" The air was pushed from her lungs and for a quick moment she panicked. Her hands came up, grabbing the other person by the shoulders to steady herself even further. And then she froze, because her brain finally caught up with her actions, alerting her to the fact that she was *clinging* to a particularly sturdy man.

"My lady."

Oh God!

The man she was holding on to was not the stranger she'd hoped to walk away from without too much humiliation. It was Florian, his voice a strained murmur that brushed the curve of her neck. She shivered in response to it and her awareness increased tenfold. His hand was still at her back, the fingers splayed and pressing into her flesh while his chest made full contact with her breasts. In short, they were for all intents and purposes wrapped in a rather scandalous embrace. Neither one of them moved.

Juliette wasn't sure why Florian failed to release her. Perhaps he was too shocked to do so, his limbs frozen in place, rendering him immobile. For her own part, she could not understand why she did not simply jump back or push him aside or *something*, except for the utterly unreasonable reason that she wished to savor this moment for just a little while longer. It allowed her to explore certain aspects of the man that distance would not permit. Like the way his hair gently tickled her brow, how the spicy scent of him lured her closer and the strength with which he held her, letting her know she was safe in his arms.

What a deliciously alarming thought *that* was.

A strangled sound left his throat and she finally shifted, which prompted him to ease her away from him slowly. "My apologies." His level voice conveyed no hint of what he was thinking. "I hope you are unharmed."

"Yes. Of course. It is in fact *I* who ought to beg *your* forgiveness." When he raised an eyebrow, she explained, "Had I not been walking as fast as I was, there's a good chance we wouldn't have collided."

"What a pity that would have been."

His comment set her back, not because of what it

implied but because of the manner in which it was spoken. He sounded amused, which was very different from how he'd been when they'd last spoken.

"Since we did collide, as you put it, perhaps you would care to take a turn of the garden with me?" He offered his arm.

Juliette stared at the man who invariably made her insides twist into tight little knots, then glanced around. "Would it not be improper with nobody else around?"

"As long as we keep away from dark corners and don't stray too far from the house, I see no reason for anyone to disapprove."

Uncertain, Juliette struggled with the inner turmoil the situation evoked. She did not wish to insult Florian by turning him down. But her admiration for him could not be denied, nor could her increasing attraction toward him. And now that she knew what it was to be held in his arms, she longed to experience it again. Which was dangerous.

And yet, taking a private walk with him would allow for the perfect opportunity to discuss her idea for the fund-raiser she was planning. Which was important for her to do since she would require his agreement regarding the auction. So she set her hand on his arm and allowed him to lead the way forward, aware once again of the strength he emitted not only in his solid posture but in his stride.

When they'd gone a few paces and she'd worked out the best way to make her request, she said, "I've decided that the first charity event I host on behalf of St. Agatha's will be a tea party at Huntley House."

"Is a garden party not more common?"

"Maybe, but I think doing it like this will ensure the

event's success." She paused before saying, "Especially considering the items I'm considering for the auction."

"Oh?" His voice was low, sensual and terribly distracting.

She steeled herself. "In light of your increased popularity, I believe the promise of dancing with you would be great incentive for—"

"What?"

He'd drawn her to an immediate halt and was suddenly closer somehow. Her stomach flipped over and a shiver raced down her spine. "Well, um . . ." She struggled to regain composure, if only to get her words out. "I think many women will want to bid on the chance to partner with you."

"No."

"Especially if the dance in question is the waltz," she said, ignoring his refusal. "I dare say every debutante will covet such an opportunity."

Bowing his head, he murmured close to her ear. "Do you speak from experience, my lady?"

Flustered by his flirtatiousness and not entirely sure how to handle it, she held her tongue and continued along the path, distancing herself from him while trying to catch her breath. His footsteps sounded behind her, careful but certain upon the ground. Juliette's pulse raced.

The path up ahead split off in two directions, and when she started toward the left, he caught her by the elbow and steered her to the right, leading her toward the far end of the garden.

"I thought you said we should stay close to the house." Common sense warred with the thrill of anticipation.

"Will you answer the question?"

He spoke closer to her ear than she would have expected, causing her to shiver in response. "I enjoyed dancing with you tremendously, Florian." That was what he was asking, was it not? She could scarcely remember.

"And I with you. But that doesn't mean I'm eager to dance with anyone else."

Recognizing the compliment, but knowing she had to try and stay on point, Juliette said, "It's for a good cause."

"I realize that, but is it completely necessary?"

"No. Of course it isn't. If you really don't want to, I can think of something else. It was just an idea."

The path narrowed, so he drew her slightly closer—enough for her to enjoy the scent of him once again and to savor the feel of his arm pressing up against hers.

Silence settled between them for a moment before he said, "On second thought, I'll consider it and let you know by tomorrow afternoon."

"But—"

"We face great odds, my lady. Raising as much money as we can is important. So it wouldn't be right of me to ruin the chance of a successful event just because I don't want to waltz."

"Thank you, Florian." She couldn't help but smile. Hoping to give him ease, she tried for a bit of good-natured humor. "You know, for a man who claims he doesn't enjoy it, you're remarkably good. Even if your skill upon the dance floor is not your best quality."

He made a sound that could have been choked-back laughter. "It isn't?" he asked, his voice lighter than she'd ever heard it before.

Liking this playful side to him and appreciating his

willingness to let her see it, she smiled up at him as they walked and almost tripped when he responded with a smile of his own. The effect was dazzling, for as handsome as he was when he glowered, he was far more striking like this.

Her insides shivered and her limbs grew weak, and it took a moment for her to realize she hadn't responded. "No, um . . ." She glanced away, into the darkness, and said the first thing that came to mind. "You're an incredibly skilled physician." A pregnant pause made her realize she'd stated the obvious, so she hastened to add, "The way you saved those three boys from drowning last month, after another physician pronounced them dead, was remarkable. However did you do it?"

"By employing the methods advocated by the Humane Society. Their work pertaining to the resuscitation of drowning victims is incredible and has been effectively implemented for decades. One of their members even developed an electrical apparatus which can deliver a shock to the heart if breathing into the victim's mouth and adding pressure to their chest is insufficient."

Astonished and wanting to know more, Juliette asked, "Is that how you saved the boys? With such a device?"

"Partly." He paused before saying, "Only one of them needed it. The other two recovered quickly enough when I held their noses and set a billows to their mouths."

"They were fortunate to have you there," she said. "As fortunate as Lady Ingram was when you decided to cut into her womb and extricate her baby."

"I have performed several caesarian sections, my

lady." His tone suggested he was back to his signature frown. "The procedure is not very complicated."

"Then how about the operation you performed on a living man's heart a few months ago?"

Florian drew to a halt and released her arm so he could turn to face her. With the path as narrow as it was, his face was now but a few inches away, so close she could see the glow from the nearby torches casting his eyes in a dazzling display of color. "As much as I appreciate your admiration, you ought to know that I did not operate on the heart itself, but on the pericardium which surrounds it. All I did was copy the Spanish surgeon, Francisco Romero, who accomplished the exact same feat twenty years ago."

Juliette stared at him. "Why do you insist on belittling your achievements?" She truly wanted to know, because as far as she was concerned, he was amazing.

"Why are you so interested in my work?" he countered.

Disliking the shift in attention, she shrugged and lowered her gaze. "I read the newspapers. Articles relating to people I know are of particular interest to me." Glancing back up, she was shocked by the intensity with which he now watched her. She felt her cheeks warm with the sort of heat that could burn the sun. "I am not obsessive, if that is what you think, but the more I have learned about you, the more my esteem has grown. I—it is the reason why I wanted to make my funds available to you in the first place, because I believe you to be the best physician there is."

"Really?"

Worried he might misconstrue her meaning, even though he'd be right to do so, she pressed on, hoping to distract him from what she'd revealed. "I know you think me naïve and out of my depth with regard to the typhus epidemic." He opened his mouth as if to argue so she hastily said, "And you would be correct." He closed his mouth, which gave her the chance to continue. Needing to move while she spoke so she could escape the intensity of his gaze, she recommenced walking while he followed close by her side. "I lack your experience, so if you believe asking soldiers to shoot anyone who attempts to flee St. Giles is the best course of action, I will not argue that point any further."

"By the way, I never said they should shoot to kill."

"You're right," she agreed. "I made a foolish assumption."

His hand found her arm right above the elbow, and although he was wearing gloves, the contact still sent a wave of heat crashing through her. The tempered pace at which they were walking, the soft glow of torches and gentle evening air produced an intimate atmosphere ripe for romance.

Wait.

What?

Her heart stuttered in response to that unbidden thought, and yet there could be no denying the way she was feeling. Her entire body was humming with expectation and all because of his touch. Though, to be fair, this particular touch was rather startling with added pressure now as his fingers curled tighter, drawing her back up against him. The sensation only increased when he said in low tones, "I do not think you're naïve, my lady. At least not any longer."

She gazed up at him, momentarily stunned by the comment. "'That's very honest of you."

"Have you known me to be anything else?"

She shook her head. His hand still lingered against her arm as though he'd forgotten it there. "No."

His nostrils flared and he leaned in closer, crowding her with his much larger size. "I have always striven to be as practical as possible. When I work, I deliberately push emotion aside, allowing me to be critical, logical and ethical. It is a rare occasion when I lose my temper and yet you have managed to make me do so. Publicly, I might add."

"I am sorry."

He winced. "I am nothing more than a man, and like most men, I have my flaws, as I'm sure you've already realized. So, with this in mind, I urge you to ignore your compulsion to place me on a pedestal on which I do not belong. We are simply two different people, neither more nor less deserving of admiration than the other."

"I—"

"Allow me to finish." His thumb started stroking her skin in a manner no doubt intended to soothe. Instead it produced a series of sparks that skittered across her flesh.

Halting the motion, he recommenced walking, guiding her carefully onto a shorter path that would take them straight back to the house. "You haven't had an easy life," he said, "yet experience has not diminished your kindness. Rather, it has turned you into a woman who wants to save people with a desperation I have never witnessed before. Does this mean you do not need guidance? Of course not, but this can easily be acquired. What matters most is the drive with which you face adversity, for indeed this is something that cannot be learned. It is either in you or it isn't."

"Thank you."

They walked a bit more in silence before he added, "You ought to know that I have tremendous respect for you, my lady." Reaching the stairs leading back up to the house, he glanced up at the terrace as if to ensure they weren't being watched. He released her arm and took a step back. "You also ought to know that it's the only thing stopping me from kissing you senseless."

Juliette stared up at him, unsure if she'd heard him right.

Before she could ask he sketched a bow and bid her a good evening. He then strode away brusquely, leaving her utterly alone and more confused than she'd ever been before in her life.

Chapter 10

Florian left Brand House with haste. It was imperative that he arrive home as quickly as possible so he could lock himself away in his study and find solace in the bottle of brandy awaiting him there. Christ, what a mess his life had turned into!

Lady Juliette had been stunning this evening as usual, her white diaphanous gown hugging her delicate body in a manner that could only mean to entice. And it had. He'd scarcely been able to peel his gaze away from the fullness of her breasts or the delicate lace that held her gown up. How easy it would have been to pull it down over her shoulders and undo her stays . . . It had been impossible for him to think of much else after holding her in his arms. Pressed up against him, although by accident, she'd made him incredibly aware of her feminine softness and that alluring fragrance that always clung to her person.

And he'd held her close longer than necessary, alarmingly reluctant to let her go. To his dismay, he'd sensed she felt the same, her shallow breaths and the rapid beat of her heart keeping pace with his·own, alerting him to a shared sense of awareness and . . .

desire. It hadn't been clear at first, but later, when he'd impulsively—scandalously—touched her arm to stay her progress and stroked her skin with his thumb, he'd heard the slight hitch in her breathing, watched her gaze drop to his mouth and seen her lips part in preparation for a kiss that never came.

He wondered if she was even aware of how ready she'd been to accept his advances. It was unlikely, considering how young she was. Chances were she had no experience with being pursued in earnest. Especially when considering how protective her brother had been of her until now. Apparently he'd trusted the Warwicks to chaperone her for a change, except she'd somehow managed to elude their watchful eyes when escaping out into the garden. Neither one had come looking for her, perhaps because they'd thought she was keeping company with Miss Saunders. Florian had seen the two women together on his way out to the terrace and decided not to approach them.

Instead, she'd found him, even if it had been by chance.

But the intimacy they'd shared, not only through touch, but through conversation, had instilled in him a feeling of unity that he'd never experienced in anyone else's company before. He'd been surprised to discover how much she knew about him and he'd been flattered by the compliments she'd given.

Initially, he'd gone into medicine with the intention of undoing some of the harm his father had done in the world. He'd simply sought to balance the scales. But then he'd taken to it with uncanny ease, his fascination with medical discoveries and new surgical methods driving his thirst for additional knowledge. He'd applied himself and he'd studied hard, impressing his mentors with his dogged insistence to find the best treatment available for his patients.

Discovering Lady Juliette's appreciation for his accomplishments, that her interest in his field of expertise surpassed polite conversation, only made him want her more. She was temptation incarnate and a woman he had no business wanting, even after he claimed his title. Ironically, Society would claim she wasn't good enough for him. Especially not once he became duke.

But they would be wrong.

Those people knew him to be an earl's grandson, an upstanding member of Society and the physician most of them turned to when they were sick. They did not know of the monster who'd sired him or of the horrifying way in which it had happened. To subject an innocent woman like Lady Juliette to such a disturbing blemish would be beyond cruel. Best then for him to forget her before it was too late.

Which was easier said than done since they were now working together.

Groaning, he raked his fingers through his hair and hailed a hackney. Arriving home ten minutes later, he let himself in through the front door and shut it firmly behind him. He had three servants in total—Baker, his man of affairs who doubled as butler, Jillian, the maid, and Mrs. Croft, his cook—none of whom stayed overnight. A couple of letters littered the floor, one bearing his uncle's seal. Picking both of them up, Florian tossed his gloves on a nearby table and made his way to his study. He stoked the fire in the grate and sought out the brandy he'd been looking forward to savoring. Pouring a full measure, he threw it back, then refilled his glass and dropped down into the nearest chair.

Setting his glass aside, he stretched out his legs and picked up his uncle's letter, tearing open the seal and scanning the bold script on the crisp white paper.

> *Florian,*
> *My affairs are now completely in order. Funds have been set aside for your aunt, and my secretary has dispatched letters to my estates, instructing the caretakers and housekeepers there on how to proceed once I am gone. Hopefully, this will ease the coming transition for you.*
>
> *Sincerely,*
> *George Talcott*

Expelling a breath, Florian opened the second letter and froze.

> *Your intention to save St. Giles interferes with my plan to destroy it. Forget the people who live there, Florian, or those nearest and dearest to you will suffer the consequence.*

Righting himself, he leaned forward and reread the missive before crumpling it up in his hand so tightly his knuckles turned white. Rising, he tossed the ball of paper into the fire and hurled the rest of his brandy after it, producing a burst of angry flames. There was only one man he could think of who'd want to threaten him like this. Except it couldn't possibly be him. Could it? To suppose that William Mortedge, the American investor the *ton* had welcomed into their midst, and Bartholomew, were one and the same was ludicrous. Whatever similarities the two men shared had to be coincidental. Which made Florian all the more curious to know who'd sent the letter and why that person would want to see the people of St. Giles suffer.

Florian woke at precisely seven o'clock the following morning. Once dressed, he descended to the dining room where he devoured two eggs, some bacon, a fried tomato and a slice of toast, washing it all down with a strong cup of tea before heading toward his study. Perhaps he ought to confide in Baker about the threat.

The thought had barely formed when a loud knock at the front door halted his progress. Florian strode forward and opened it to find his brother with a cheerful expression upon his face. "Good morning, Henry." He opened the door a bit wider and stepped aside so Henry could enter. "I am surprised to see you this early. I would have bet a thousand pounds on you still being abed."

Henry grinned. "I have not yet slept." He began removing his gloves while following Florian into the study where Baker was busy with the ledgers.

"Would you please give us the room?" Florian asked his servant.

Baker was already on his feet and gathering up papers. A second later he was gone, leaving Florian and Henry alone in private. "Busy night at the club?" Florian gestured for Henry to sit.

"Running a business requires commitment. Surely you can understand that, considering how busy your work keeps you." Henry sat and so did Florian. "Besides, it was impossible for me to contemplate rest after reading the headline in the *Mayfair Chronicle* this morning. Have you seen it?"

"Not yet," Florian said.

Henry grinned. "You've officially been named the most eligible bachelor of the Season!"

Florian's throat began to constrict. "What?"

His brother's eyes danced with amusement. "Did you not think you would be after seeing how eager the young ladies are to dance with you now? You will soon be the only unmarried duke in the country. Add to that your youth and your"—Henry waggled his eyebrows—"dashing good looks, I believe you've already set numerous hearts aflutter. Frankly, it will be a relief to rid myself of some of the attention."

"Yes," Florian told him dryly. "What a burden it must be for you to be chased by all those women."

Henry sighed with exaggeration. "It can be quite exhausting, I must confess. But we digress. What I wish to know is what your plan might be from this point on."

"My plan?" Florian shook his head, befuddled by the urgency in his brother's tone. "I have no plan besides working on a solution to the problem of a potentially impending epidemic."

"Right." Henry nodded. "I agree that should take priority, but it doesn't mean you cannot start contemplating your progeny."

"I beg your pardon?"

Henry shrugged as if he hadn't just suggested Florian turn his whole life upside down. "You are Uncle George's heir."

"I am aware," Florian drawled. He did not like the turn this conversation had taken in the least.

"Then you also know that you have responsibilities

now that you did not have before. Uncle George obviously wants a legacy or he would not have bothered making the effort, which means you need to get yourself married and have some children so the favor he requested from the king won't be for nothing."

Shit.

Florian stared at Henry. He often forgot how astute his brother could be because he tended to hide it behind a façade of charming indifference. "Perhaps you should take some time to consider your own matrimonial future. You are older than I, after all. Should you not be hurrying off to the altar before me?"

"Right you are, Florian. Don't think I have not set my mind to it yet for indeed I have." This was certainly shocking. "The trouble is I want a love match and that, brother, is not so easy to come by."

Florian blinked. What the hell was happening? "You cannot be serious?"

"And why is that?"

"Because of who you are! You have taken deliberate strides to cement a certain reputation as one of London's most notorious lotharios. And now you say you want to fall in love and set up a nursery?" Had the earth been knocked completely off its axis?

"We must grow up at some point, Florian, and take responsibility. I will soon be three and thirty while you are steadily approaching your thirty-first year. Once you claim the title Uncle George is going to leave you, your world will change. You'll see."

Which was precisely what Florian feared. "I was assured that nothing would be different, that I would still be able to practice medicine while my staff takes care of the dukely business."

"What a charming delusion." Henry grinned while

Florian's chest grew tight around his lungs. The humor in Henry's gaze died and he was suddenly uncharacteristically serious. "You are a man of honor, Florian, which is how I know you will do your duty. And with the right woman by your side, it shouldn't be much of a hardship. Quite the contrary."

An image of Lady Juliette bathed in golden torchlight sprang to mind. As if reading his thoughts, Henry said, "I hear you've begun a working relationship with the Duke of Huntley's sister, Lady Juliette."

Schooling his features for fear of revealing even one speck of emotion, Florian served his brother the frankest stare he could manage. "That is correct."

"And?"

God! Henry could be worse than a gossiping old woman at times. The man loved intrigue and would not rest until he had enough information to sate his curiosity.

"And what?"

"Well, I've also seen you waltz with her twice."

"So what?" Florian decided the best way to tackle this situation was to feign ignorance.

Snorting, Henry shook his head as if Florian was the most impossible person he'd ever had to converse with. "You continued to keep her company once the dances were over."

"Only because I found her engaging."

"And stunning." Henry smiled with a knowing glint in his eyes. "Come now. You have to admit she is breathtakingly beautiful. To think you have the pleasure of keeping her company now on a regular basis almost makes me jealous."

Florian frowned. He didn't like Henry's comment because it suggested interest. Which could only mean . . . He steeled himself, careful not to reveal the sudden possessiveness darting through him while aiming for a nonchalant tone. "I will confess that she is pleasing to the eye but that is not sufficient when contemplating a permanent attachment."

Henry's eyebrows shot up. "Indeed, I wasn't even suggesting such a possibility. How intriguing that you would do so yourself." He leaned forward and Florian cursed himself for not guarding his words better. "So, you find her attractive and yet you indicate that there needs to be more to marriage than physical attributes. Could it be that you also hope for a love match?"

"No." Sufficiently annoyed, Florian stood and crossed to the window to look out into the street. He flexed his fingers and aimed to regain some measure of control of the discussion that had gotten quite out of hand. "If I were seeking a bride, Henry, which I can assure you I am not, Lady Juliette would not be a candidate on my list. She is too young at heart, her nature too gentle and unassuming for a man such as myself. She would be incredibly unhappy if she were my wife while I—"

"Yes?"

I would destroy her.

"It does not signify since this is nothing more than a hypothetical notion." And yet, speaking the words, voicing his thoughts, made the idea of actually courting her real. As impossible a concept as it had always been, it filled Florian with a deep sense of loss for what could never be. She was perfect in spite of her past, while he was tarnished in spite of his deeds. And that was without considering the potential ramifications of Bartholomew's eventual return. No. To pursue her would be selfish on his part.

"Well, it could be more." Henry's gaze was solemnly pinned to Florian's. "I have seen the way she looks at you when you talk."

Florian fought the urge to ask his brother to elaborate on that point and failed abysmally. "What do you mean?"

"She admires you."

"Ah. Well." Nothing new there. She'd admitted as much last night.

"Recently, however, something about her has changed. I noted it at the Brighton Ball."

Florian stared at Henry, who was looking most pleased with himself, and finally asked, "And what is that?"

Henry stood and faced Florian. He chuckled. "For a man who insists on having no interest, you do seem to be getting rather worked up about it."

Gritting his teeth, Florian shoved his hands into his trouser pockets and prayed for patience. "Let's just say you've heightened my curiosity."

Henry laughed outright in response to that acerbic comment and turned for the door. He paused there and met Florian's gaze. "She glows when she is in your presence, Florian. I have never seen another lady do that."

With a parting nod, he exited the room, leaving Florian utterly stupefied. He stared at the doorway through which his brother had departed and tried to come to terms with what he'd just told him. Although last night's encounter made him believe Lady Juliette responded to him just as easily as he responded to her, hearing Henry confirm it made it an indisputable certainty. Joy surged through his veins like rays of sunshine spilling between a pair of gray storm clouds.

He realized how much he looked forward to seeing

her again, to hearing her opinions and sparring with her. She had in very short time become the person he missed the most when they weren't together. Which gave him all the more reason to avoid her. Especially with the threatening note he'd received.

With that unpleasant thought in mind, Florian went to collect his things so he could head to the hospital. There was work to be done and he could not afford to let himself be distracted by anyone.

Trailing her fingers across several rolls of silk, Juliette relished the slippery feel of the fabric and all the vibrant colors in which it existed. On the other side of the room, her sister studied a cream-colored muslin.

"What do you think?" Amelia asked after getting one of the shop assistants to help her cut a few yards. The piece was now laid out on the counter along with a good selection of trimming. "Which of these would you choose?"

Juliette picked up a narrow piece of ivory lace ribbon and held it against the fabric. "This will be pretty."

With only three weeks left until her due date, Amelia was putting in an order for a christening gown. Being out and about in her condition was impossible without receiving a great deal of frowns that were often followed by whispered comments, but Amelia detested the idea of staying in bed or remaining at home. She wanted to be active, and since Florian had welcomed this idea with the assurance that women in most cultures outside the western world made no extreme alterations to their lives when expecting, Amelia had decided that neither would she.

"I agree," Amelia said in reference to Juliette's choice.

The dressmaker proceeded to cut the trim while Juliette watched. An idea came to mind and she bit her lip, wondering whether or not to ask the woman for help. Considering how many people relied on the hospital, she decided she had to at least try. "I was wondering," she began, then cleared her throat and raised her voice. "I'm hosting a fund-raiser in a couple of days to help the sick people of London. Would you by any chance be willing to donate an item for the auction?"

The dressmaker reached for a roll of fabric and paused. She considered a moment while Juliette held her breath. Finally, she smiled. "I have a gown in the back that one of my seamstresses made when I tested her skills for employment. You're welcome to have it as long as you say where it came from."

"Of course." Juliette thanked the woman profusely and left the shop with a new thrill of excitement. She would visit other businesses after seeing Amelia safely home and hopefully procure additional items of interest to the fund-raiser attendees.

"I know you have lots of energy, Julie, but can you please walk a bit slower?" Amelia asked as they headed toward Coventry House.

"Oh! Of course." Juliette deliberately slowed her pace and glanced at her sister. "How are you feeling?"

"I am more than ready to deliver this baby. My back has been aching for weeks at this point and there is something troubling about not being able to reach my feet."

Juliette smiled. "It will be wonderful to meet your son or daughter."

"Thomas will be a father again while I shall become a mother of a child I delivered myself. I am still not completely used to the idea."

"According to Gabriella, you will be the moment you hold your baby in your arms."

They turned onto Picadilly and Amelia linked her arm with Juliette's. "Do you not dream of experiencing the joy of motherhood one day?"

Juliette glanced at her. "Of course I do. I just don't like the *marry now or you'll be doomed* attitude everyone seems to embrace. It makes the whole experience unpleasant."

"I know what you mean. It makes me all the more grateful for the swiftness with which I managed to marry the man of my dreams." Amelia's eyes glowed with contentment. "But Raphe has agreed not to pressure you into making a hasty match, so that should make the Season more enjoyable for you. I would think."

"It has. Especially since I can concentrate my efforts on other matters without feeling as though I'm letting him down." She glanced at her sister. "Did you receive the invitation I sent for the fund-raiser?"

"I did."

"It's been a lot of work setting it up, preparing gift baskets and ordering flowers for the tables. Perhaps it would have been better if I'd chosen to hold it next week instead, but with the hospital's need for funds I rushed and . . . oh, I do hope it will be successful."

"I'm sure it will be." Amelia hesitated before asking, "Is Florian helping you organize it?"

"Not really. He's been too busy setting up a clinic in St. Giles and treating patients. But you needn't worry. Vivien has offered her assistance, and her experience with such things has proven invaluable. All we need are a few final touches before we're completely ready."

"So then, you don't see much of Florian?"

Alerted by her sister's interest, Juliette said, "Not more than one might expect under the circumstances."

"Hmmm . . ."

"What?"

Amelia shrugged. "I don't know. I suppose I was starting to think you might be engaged in an odd sort of courtship with him."

Juliette stopped walking. "You can't be serious." She tried to laugh in an effort to underscore the silliness of such a suggestion. "A courtship? Really?" And yet as she said it, she realized how much she wished her sister was right. Which froze her humor and filled her chest with a painful knot.

"It is not as ridiculous an idea as you are proposing," Amelia said. "Not when your interaction with him has not been limited to work alone. Gabriella says you've waltzed with him on two separate occasions. She also insists that you look very comfortable in his company."

"And? That doesn't mean anything, Amelia."

"When one considers the man in question, it ought to. He is not known for being the approachable sort, but rather intimidating. And yet, you have been seen in rapt conversation with him and—"

"I see Gabriella's account wasn't limited to my dancing alone." When Amelia gave her a firm look, she waved one hand. "You put too much emphasis on minor details."

"Really?" Amelia sounded dubious.

"Yes. Why must assumptions be made when a

woman speaks with a man at great length? Florian is simply more fascinating than any other man I've met. You know how I like to learn new things. I always have. So why should my interest in him be surprising?"

"It probably wouldn't be if you could talk about him without your cheeks turning pink."

Juliette stared back at her sister for a long moment. Eventually, she recommenced walking while saying, "It is a hot day." She cast a hesitant glance at Amelia and found her watching her with intense curiosity, which prompted her to add, "There is nothing more to it than that." Except the skittish sensations Florian managed to evoke in her when he was near, the quickening pulse and the shivering skin.

"Are you certain about that?"

Not at all.

"Absolutely."

"Hmm . . ." An expression that could mean any number of things. "I've been thinking."

"About what?" Something else, Juliette hoped. She was suddenly eager to move on to a different topic.

"Maybe you, Raphe and Gabriella should come for dinner tomorrow evening."

"That would be lovely."

"I miss the social interaction, you know. At least Thomas gets out. He has Parliament, even though he claims not to enjoy it, but the discussions there challenge his mind, while I . . . I just feel like a big lump most of the time."

Juliette laughed. "You carry it well, Amelia. The lumpishness, that is."

Amelia swatted her arm and grinned. "I'll invite Florian too." Juliette's heart did a little somersault. "It will give me a chance to get to know him better, which can only be a good thing since he'll be the one delivering my baby."

Juliette could only nod, and thankfully her sister did not pursue the subject any further. Instead, she began describing how the nursery had been decorated and what else needed to be done in preparation for the baby's arrival.

Juliette made a valiant effort to focus on this, but now that Florian had been mentioned, it really was quite impossible. Because all she could think of was how good it had felt to be held in his arms and how much she hoped to experience it again.

Chapter 11

"**Y**ou seem distracted." Viola tilted her head and regarded Florian thoughtfully.

He stared back at her, aware she'd been talking at length about something but unsure what that something might be. "Forgive me. There is much on my mind." He'd been honest with her about the threat he'd received. She was his employer and deserved to know if anything stood in the way of his work.

"I know. There is a lot going on in your life at the moment," Viola said. "How is your uncle doing?"

"As well as a man at death's door might be doing. It won't be long now. A week, perhaps less." He expelled a ragged breath. "I honestly cannot be sure."

"I am sorry. Losing the people you care for is difficult. No matter how prepared you think you are or how accustomed you may be to dealing with death. Florian—"

"Please don't. I would rather not talk about it."

A small pause followed. "What would you like to talk about then? It is clear that the question of whether or not to take on apprentices here is failing to hold your interest."

Was that what they'd been discussing?

"Forgive me. My mind is occupied with finding solutions for the typhus outbreak. With three people dead since the committee meeting and ten more showing symptoms, it goes without saying that it is rapidly spreading. Containing it is of the utmost urgency and will require my complete focus." He did not mean to sound irritable, but damn it all, he was finding it hard not to, all things considered.

Viola kept quiet as if waiting to see if he had anything further to add. When he said nothing more, she curiously asked, "And Lady Juliette?"

Florian's entire body responded to that simple name. No, not simple, far from it in fact. "What about her?"

"I worry she might prove more of a distraction to you than becoming a duke or receiving threats ever could. Don't think I did not notice the way in which you spoke to her after the last meeting. The heat in the room emanated solely from one particular corner."

"Don't be absurd!"

"Don't lie to yourself. Be honest."

Clenching his fists he stared back at the woman who'd inherited a family who loathed her, ridiculed her, shunned her. But instead of becoming the victim they wanted her to be, she'd raised her chin and used the funds her husband left her to cure the sick and save the suffering. She'd lost so much and yet she could not stop giving.

"She is not for me, Viola."

"Why?"

"You know damn well why." He was on his feet now, palms on his desk as he leaned toward her.

His intimidating stance had no effect on the

dowager duchess. "You are not to blame for your father's sins."

"I know that, Viola, but to drag a doe-eyed woman into my life would still be reckless."

"You speak of her as if she is a child when she is anything but."

As if he wasn't aware. The figure she'd put on display a couple of nights ago and the soft sigh of pleasure she'd made in response to his touch confirmed she was all woman. But that didn't make his wanting her any more right. "She has the opportunity to marry respectably. I will not ruin that for her."

"You are respectable and you'll soon be a duke. Any woman would be lucky to have you."

Bitter laughter was his first response. "Now who is being absurd?" When she merely crossed her arms and challenged him with a hard glare, he said, "My demons would tear her soul to shreds, Viola. You think me a good man, a kind man, because I chose to become a physician and because I always remember the oath I took to help those in need. But you forget that the reason I do so has nothing to do with kindness."

With a shake of her head she stood. "That's just a story you tell yourself because you insist you don't deserve better. But you are not Bartholomew. You are your own person and you have a right to some happiness in your life."

"I could say the same to you."

As he'd expected, her expression shuttered and she turned for the door, exiting his office without a backward glance. She'd spoken of her husband only once in the years Florian had known her. Saddened by the thought of her giving her life to the hospital alone, Florian blew out a breath and glanced at his pocket watch. Lady Juliette's sister and brother-in-law, the Duke and Duchess of Coventry, had invited him to dine this evening. If he hurried home now he'd have time for a bath and a much-needed change of clothes before going to meet them.

Juliette sipped her champagne while listening with half an ear to Amelia and Gabriella share their opinions on the education of children. Of far greater interest was the discussion taking place between Raphe and Coventry on the other side of the room for it involved the speech Florian had delivered to Parliament the previous day, outlining the symptoms of typhus, the progression of it and what he was doing in order to stop it.

Panic had apparently ensued among some, which was to be expected. They'd wanted to know the threat the disease posed to them and their families, but that wasn't something Florian was able to answer. He had instead advised them on how to practice proper hygiene, and his suggestion to inform the public of the same had been well received.

The parlor door opened, and Jones, the Coventry butler, entered. "Mr. Florian Lowell has arrived." The man made this announcement and stepped aside, granting Florian entry.

Juliette stared at him as he executed an impeccable bow and came to greet everyone. He was dressed as formally as he'd been when she'd stumbled into him in the Brand House garden. Instinctively, she darted a look in her sister's direction only to find Amelia regarding her with an unsettling degree of curiosity.

More unsettling were the butterflies taking flight in her stomach and the very obvious fact that the men and women were now evenly paired. She tried not to think of it, but a secret part of her—the part that had sprung awake with a jolt a few days ago when he'd held her—wanted to be close to him again.

And then he was standing before the women and she was rising to her feet, along with Amelia and Gabriella. Solemnly, he thanked his hostess for the invitation and apologized for his tardiness, then complimented Gabriella on how well she looked. Both ladies beamed with pleasure and thanked him for his kindness.

"If you'll excuse me," Amelia said, "I must have a word with my husband. Will you join me, Gabriella?"

A quick affirmation left Juliette alone with Florian. After all, it would be intolerably rude if she wandered off as well. So she stayed, battling the turmoil Florian's close proximity wrought on her nerves.

Slowly, he turned his dark blue eyes on her with such intensity she feared she might start smoldering. "Lady Juliette." There was a strange degree of sensuality to the way he spoke her name. Or perhaps her silly mind was merely playing tricks on her.

"Florian." She attempted a smile that he did not reciprocate, but the intensity of his gaze made her feel like the only woman in the world. Her heart leapt in response.

"You look . . ." He allowed his gaze to slide over her without apology, which in turn caused her skin to tighten around every limb. A muscle ticked in his right cheek. "Lovely."

She swallowed with a bit more effort than usual. "Thank you." For a moment they simply stood there staring back at each other until it became too difficult, and she hastily told him, "You look quite . . . good . . . yourself."

Oh how prosaic of her! She squeezed her eyes shut and cursed her lack of verbal proficiency in that moment and his ability to turn her brain to mush.

"My lady?"

Her eyes shot open to find him watching her with curiosity. But there was something else too that looked suspiciously like humor. It warmed her heart and gave her hope. Perhaps one day she'd hear his laughter. Intrigued, she studied him, surprised to find a definite easing of his features and even a sparkle to his eyes.

"Yes?" She finally spoke even though she knew she'd hesitated much too long in doing so.

He leaned a little closer as if intending to share a confidence. "There is nothing wrong with looking good. Indeed I strive to do so as often as possible." His lips twitched ever so slightly.

Juliette frowned. "Are you mocking me?"

His hand covered his heart and he was once again the face of seriousness. "I would never." Just then, Amelia announced that dinner was served and Florian offered Juliette his arm. "May I escort you through to the dining room?"

She nodded. Because she wanted to feel the strength of him beneath her hand once more, to savor the opportunity such nearness presented. So she took a step closer, heart pounding in her chest, and linked her arm with his. And as awareness captured her senses, intensified by the masculine scent of bergamot and sandalwood, she started to wonder what it might be like to have him by her side like this forever.

This thought, both startling and terrifying while equally refreshing, made her falter. He steadied her with seemingly little effort and drew her closer. So close she was tempted to lean right into the heat he emitted. Except that would be terribly scandalous and far too revealing. In any case, they were now at the table and he was already pulling out her chair.

"Congratulations once again on becoming the Duke of Redding's heir," Coventry said once all their wineglasses had been filled and the starters served.

Florian inclined his head.

"And no one deserves to have such good fortune bestowed upon them more than you," Raphe added.

The manner in which Florian stiffened and clutched his soup spoon as if the piece of cutlery might save his sanity was not lost on Juliette.

"You do not consider yourself worthy of being a peer?" she quietly asked when the rest of the party had become immersed in conversation.

Florian stilled and, for a long moment, said nothing. Then he set his spoon aside and reached for his wine. "You are very observant," he told her against the rim of the glass before taking a lengthy sip.

"I pay attention," she said, adding a chuckle.

"Hmm . . ." He set his glass aside and shifted closer, not enough for anyone else to take notice, but enough for her to know a boundary was being crossed. "Will you tell me what you see when you look at me?"

It was an unmistakable challenge—the dangerous sort from which she'd be wise to retreat. For the manner in which it was spoken made one thing quite clear: he wanted something from her, something that had nothing to do with the question he'd just asked.

Rising to the challenge, she licked her lips and

considered the man to whom she was so unequivocally drawn. "May I be completely honest?"

Glancing sideways, she noted the frown upon his brow and almost expected him to tell her she ought to forget the whole thing. Instead, he gave a curt nod. "Of course."

Taking a moment to gather her thoughts, she said, "Your life is devoid of pleasure and happiness. You rarely smile and I have never seen you laugh with abandon, which makes me want to poke you until you do." His lips twitched and her heart fluttered against her chest. Concealing her response to him with a small cough, she added, "You are an extraordinary man and physician, yet you never take pride in your accomplishments. Instead, you treat them like ordinary achievements, even though they are anything but." She met his gaze and held it, his blue eyes pulling her into their depths. "I wonder why that is and can only conclude that something must have happened to you in the past—something that affected your opinion of yourself so gravely that the light inside you was almost snuffed out. By what, I do not know, but it must have been extremely significant to influence you so strongly."

"So it was."

They were immediately distracted by footmen who came to clear the dishes, replacing them with plates filled with venison, creamed potatoes and caramelized carrots. Juliette picked at her food, eating slowly while pondering what to say next. She hadn't meant to criticize or pry, yet she felt as though she'd done so anyway.

Washing a piece of venison down with a sip of wine, she gave Florian her full attention once more.

"You are also extremely dedicated and loyal. You've proven this in the way you've helped Viola run St. Agatha's, in the attention you offer your patients and in the dignity with which you've accepted your uncle's legacy."

"I merely strive to do what is best."

"And I admire that. Especially your ability to know what the best thing is."

He harrumphed. "It's not difficult. I simply weigh the potential outcomes and choose the path that will lead to the most favorable one."

She stared at him and finally shook her head. "While that may be easy for you to do, it's not as easy for me. I am invariably ruled by my heart."

"Perhaps because you let different shades cloud your judgment. If you remove them, you'll see more clearly."

She chose not to argue even though she disagreed. To have that kind of objectivity would take extreme effort on her part and even then she doubted it would be possible.

The main course was finished, a sweet wine was poured and dessert, consisting of frosted cakes and marzipans designed to look like fruit, was brought in. Juliette carefully bit into one and immediately sighed with pleasure.

It took great restraint on Florian's part not to reach out and touch her. By God, the woman was tempting. He wondered if she was aware of it, if she knew how seductive she was being while nipping at her cake. Her dress this evening was chaste, less revealing than the ones he'd seen her wear at the balls, and he found it far more enticing. The wicked fantasies it evoked of pulling that extra fabric aside, preferably with his teeth, to reveal the soft swell of her breasts beneath, was starting to cause him physical pain.

It shouldn't have, after what she'd told him. The accuracy with which she'd homed in on the biggest influence in his life ought to have deterred him from having erotic musings where she was concerned. It ought to have jolted his senses, to force the same self-loathing he experienced whenever a connection was drawn between him and Bartholomew.

But it hadn't. Not this time. Rather, he'd found her analysis of him shockingly intriguing.

Shifting, he inhaled her scent and found he could stand it no longer. He simply had to know. "What perfume do you wear?"

Her throat worked with the effort of swallowing her food so she could answer, her eyes wider than ever before. Perhaps on account of the way he'd posed the question, whispering it as if answering him was forbidden.

His gaze dropped to her lips, parted now and quivering softly against her tremulous breath. Impossibly strong desire rushed through his veins without warning and in that moment, the only thing he could think of was how much he longed to press his mouth gently over hers and take the kiss he so dearly wanted.

And more.

As alluring as that thought was, he recognized the danger of it and deliberately eased back. Guarding his control, he looked at her with a bland expression, and waited for her response.

"Peonies," she told him simply. "We used to have

them in the garden when I was a child. I always favored the scent to that of roses and other fragrant flowers."

"I can understand why." His voice was once again level with no sign of intimacy, for which he was grateful. "It is an extremely pleasant scent." And since he wasn't sure what else to say on the matter without once again descending into a lust-stricken state, he returned to a far more comfortable subject by saying, "If you have finished reading *Domestic Medicine* and you're interested in the subject, there are other books I can lend you."

"I found a copy of *The View of the Theory of Medicine* by James Gregory at the Library, so I have been reading that for the past couple of days."

"Gregory is a fine physician. I was honored to meet him once."

"According to what I have read so far, his views appear similar to Buchan's, regarding hygiene, but what I found most interesting was his mention of poor food and drink as a cause for ill health. It made me wonder if this may have been the reason why I was always sick while living in St. Giles."

Florian pondered that thought. Her interest in medical texts, the fact that she'd read not only the one he'd lent her but sought out additional material on her own, pleased him immensely. "It is possible, considering how well you have been doing since moving to Mayfair."

"The nourishment here is much improved from the flavorless broth we were able to afford before. Not that I am complaining," she added with a hasty glance at Amelia and Raphe. "My siblings did their best to take care of us."

There was no denying the regret with which she said that last part. Understanding its meaning, Florian quietly reassured her. "You were a child. It was their duty to do so while it was your duty to allow it."

"I know."

But it was clear she didn't like it. "Now that you are older and your constitution has improved, you have the opportunity to do a great deal of good. Reading these books and educating yourself as much as possible on the subject you've chosen to get involved with is an excellent start."

Her eyes lit with pleasure and he would not have been able to tear his own gaze away from hers if someone had offered a million pounds for him to do so.

"You told me I am worthy of admiration," he said, "but so are you. The strides you are taking to help those in need are impressive."

Surprise touched her features, producing a charming blush.

"Thank you. I've done what I can to make the fund-raiser tomorrow as successful as possible, but I still worry something might go wrong."

"Like what?"

"I don't know, but I'm nervous." She averted her gaze with obvious shyness—the sort that produced an inexplicable feeling of protectiveness in the center of his chest. "Making a success of it is so important to me. You've no idea how hard it was to convince some of the businesses I approached to offer up prizes. And none of the other gentlemen I spoke to were willing to offer dances or even a walk in the park. Some even laughed at the suggestion."

"Relax, my lady. Take a deep breath. There is no doubt in my mind that this event of yours will be a triumph." The urge to take her hand in his was tempting, but he fought against it. His attraction toward her was one thing, a basic male instinct she'd likely inspire in most men. This immediate need to reassure her and make her feel safe was something else however. *Dangerous.*

Chapter 12

After dinner, the gentlemen adjourned to the library for a drink while the ladies took tea in the parlor. Although the discussion that ensued was an interesting one regarding responsibility toward one's tenants—a subject on which Florian would soon have to become an expert since he had no intention of leaving everything to his man of affairs like his uncle suggested—he could not seem to focus. Hazel eyes and blonde locks of hair occupied his mind to such a degree he was relieved when it was time to reconvene with the ladies in the music room.

Deliberately, Florian avoided crossing to where Lady Juliette was sitting. Doing so would only draw attention and prompt everyone to assume he had a deeper interest in her.

So he hung back and took a seat close to the door. It was the perfect spot really since it allowed him to watch her discreetly while enjoying the pleasing sound of the Duchess of Huntley's singing. Her husband, Florian noted, watched his wife with unfeigned adoration. It was clear their union was a happy one and that they loved each other a great deal, a notion compelling Florian to give his attention to Lady Juliette once more.

She was talking to her sister and Coventry, her occasional smiles and muted laughter producing an ache in his heart, and he was chagrined and somewhat mortified by the realization that he wanted it all to himself.

Her eyes caught his and in the next instant she'd risen, coming toward him like Thisbe drawn toward Pyramus. They had been an impossible pair as well, both suffering tragic deaths because of their love. Which wasn't very encouraging, as far as analogies went.

Florian stood and awaited her arrival.

"If you would rather sit alone, please say so and I shall not bother you further." She shot a look at the two available chairs with a small round table between them.

"On the contrary." He gestured toward one of the chairs. "Your company would be appreciated."

Rather than sit, she remained where she was. She even took a small step closer, which caused a riot of nerves to assault his chest. "Would it be accurate to say we are friends?"

His heart thumped wildly in response to the sweetness with which she posed the question. "Of course."

She nodded ever so faintly. "Good." Lowering herself to her chair, she waited for him to sit as well. "I'm pleased to know we're aligned."

The twinkle in her eyes denoting humor prompted him to smile, which not only felt like a foreign stretching of unused muscles, but also caused the lady to stare. This in turn made him laugh, which was even more peculiar, but her expression was too amusing to cause any other reaction.

She suddenly laughed as well. "You should allow yourself to smile more, Florian."

He tightened his features, returning them to their usual state of seriousness. "There is little for me to smile about, my lady. Pain shadows me wherever I go."

"But surely you must find joy in easing the suffering of your patients, in saving lives and also in bringing new life into the world."

"Of course I do, but the moment I allow such emotion to fill me, it is killed by the inevitable hand of death." And by the reminder that he was an imposter.

"I am sorry. It never occurred to me that your profession would be so trying, that it would take so much away from you."

Disliking the depressing tone of their conversation, Florian decided to make a deliberate effort to change it by attempting to get to know her better. "So aside from your keen attention to medicine these days, what other pursuits hold your interest?"

She folded her hands in her lap and turned to face him more fully. "I have always loved reading. Growing up, books were often my only companions. And with Raphe constantly exchanging them, there were always new ones available. It forced us to read things we never would have considered otherwise, like a discourse on Mediterranean fishing." Her expression grew pensive and she bit her lip before shaking her head and saying, "I suppose it will prove useful if I ever move to Spain."

For the second time that evening, Florian realized he was smiling, not out of politeness, but because of genuine amusement. Her effect on him at this point went beyond the carnal. She made him long for the sort of happiness he'd thought was out of his grasp. And he realized he might be able to have it as long as he kept her by his side, which was something of an astounding revelation, one which he would not spend too much time considering at present.

So he pushed the uneasy thought aside and asked, "And of these books, which were your favorites?"

A secretive grin made her eyes light up as if brought aglow by a thousand candles. "Andrew Marvell's *Miscellaneous Poems*."

Florian's heart stopped, or so it felt. Logic of course denied such a possibility since he knew he was still alive. "Really?" How much more could they possibly have in common?

"I simply adore *To His Coy Mistress*. Have you perchance read it?"

If someone had told him two weeks ago that he would discover he had more in common with Lady Juliette than with anyone else in the world, he would have called that person a fool. And yet, she studied people with his own sharp-eyed calculation, sought knowledge with unforgiving tenacity, fought tooth and nail for what she believed in and apparently had a penchant for Andrew Marvell. Who would have thought?

Unable to resist, he recited from memory. "'Had we but world enough, and time, this coyness, Lady, were no crime.'" His words were hushed beneath the musical sound of the piano, so low they would be lost to everyone else save Lady Juliette.

"'We would sit down and think which way,'" she continued, "'to walk and pass our long love's day.'" Pausing there, she met his gaze and bashfully pushed a stray lock of hair behind her ear.

Florian struggled to breathe. It felt as though she'd spoken directly to him instead of merely reciting the words he knew so well. Needing to quell the momentary awkwardness and save her the embarrassment he sensed she was feeling, he said, "It is a beautiful poem filled with vivid imagery and perfect metaphors. I have held a particular fondness for it since the moment I read it during my first year at Eton. In general, I prefer poetry to prose because of the talent it takes to convey a precise thought, concept or emotion within the confines of a predetermined structure. It is more difficult, I think, than writing a novel. At any rate I am rubbish at it myself."

She grinned. "So you have attempted it?"

He shrugged, not entirely eager to discuss his poetic failings. "I dabbled in my youth but it quickly occurred to me that I was better off concentrating on other pursuits and leaving the poetry to the poets."

"That has been my experience with watercolors." She produced a self-aware smile. "I enjoy it because there is something soothing about the experience of painting itself, but I cannot profess to have any talent."

"Then paint for the joy of it alone and forget the rest. It does not matter how good you are at painting when you have found another vocation at which you excel."

Lips parted on a stunned intake of breath, she stared at him with bewildered consternation. "You flatter me, sir."

"I speak the truth. Nothing more."

Pleasure softened her features while the dimmed light from the oil lamp between them brought a lovely glow to her cheeks. If she were captured on canvas right now the result would be reminiscent of an Adam de Coster painting. Regrettably, only his mind's eye would preserve her present appearance and not as eternally as she deserved.

She angled her head with a twitch of her lips, the motion animating her expression and destroying the mental painting. "You look trapped in thought," she told him gently.

An interesting description of his current state of mind.

With a shake of his head he leaned back while glancing sideways in her direction. "I almost did not come this evening. There is much for me to attend to at present, and dining out with friends seemed like an unnecessary distraction."

"More so than attending balls?"

He winced. "Social events can result in additional sponsors. I never attend them for my amusement."

"So why make an exception this evening?"

She'd stopped looking at him again, her entire focus on her family across the room, and he wondered how honest he ought to be, how much of himself he dared reveal. To say he was there because of her would probably make her wonder about his intentions. And rightfully so. But with no desire to start a courtship and no plan to marry, he shouldn't encourage her to do so. Which prompted him to say, "Caution has always guided me, my lady. I worry the truth might set things in motion that are better off left alone."

"I see."

Did she? He could not tell. "The hour grows late." It was time for him to add some distance between them. As it was, he'd already said too much, expressed too many emotions, allowed himself to touch her. Rising, he bowed low before her, then strode over to thank his hosts for a wonderful evening. His only regret as he went was looking back at Lady Juliette, who was watching his departure as if his impending absence would cause her personal pain.

He'd been charming. Wonderfully so. And he'd laughed, if only a very tiny bit. But the action had given her hope and instilled in her a warmth that lingered long after he was gone. Accompanying Raphe and Gabriella home in the Huntley carriage, Juliette settled back against the squabs and allowed their conversation to play back in her mind. A smile touched her lips when she thought of his compliments, and heat warmed her cheeks as she recalled the poem they'd recited. Parts of it were rather daring, like the mention of breasts and lust and the suggestion that it was best to give in to desire before time ran out. So she was glad he hadn't continued where she had left off since that would most likely have caused her entire face to catch fire.

"You spoke at great length with Florian this evening." Raphe's remark scattered Juliette's thoughts and brought her back to the present with a jolt.

"I enjoy his company."

"Is that so?"

Juliette rolled her eyes and sighed. "Yes, Raphe. He is an intelligent man and therefore more than capable of holding my interest."

"Hmm . . ."

"Was I mistaken or did I hear him laugh at one point?" Gabriella asked.

"Florian laugh?" Raphe asked before Juliette could answer. "Impossible. The man has the countenance of a marble statue."

"No, he doesn't," Juliette argued. Something deep

inside her revolted against such a bland description of a complex man. "While mostly serious, he conveys more emotion than marble ever could."

Gabriella and Raphe both stared at her in complete silence before Raphe quietly mused, "Your study of him is certainly intriguing."

"Hardly," she retorted. "I simply do what most people do when they are conversing. I look at the person to whom I am speaking. If I were to describe anyone else's expression I would do so with equal flair."

"Undoubtedly," Raphe murmured. His gaze lingered on Juliette for a few more seconds before looking away and turning the subject toward a boxing match he wanted to go and see the following week.

Juliette breathed a sigh of relief, grateful to no longer be the center of her brother's scrutiny. Because of course he was right. She *had* paid greater attention to Florian than she had ever done to anyone else. And her interest in him was founded in more than respect and admiration and a surprising number of shared interests. It was also the direct result of the way he made her feel, of this craving she had developed for his nearness. She could not explain it, save to say it went beyond the physical and the intellectual. It existed deep within her soul and, God help her, refused to be denied.

It also prevented her from thinking of anything else, distracting her from what Gabriella and Raphe were saying. And with each passing second, her thoughts grew more persistent. They chased her home and up into bed, crowding her mind until she grew restless.

"Florian."

She whispered his name to the darkness while savoring the kiss he delivered in the confines of her mind. Sparks ignited across her skin in response to the utter perfection of it, and heat filled her veins when he pulled her into his arms.

"Juliette," she imagined him murmuring close to her ear as he tightened his hold, imagined the palm of his hand sliding over her hip and the strength with which he held her.

On a sigh of exquisite pleasure, she allowed her most private desires to soar before following him into the land of dreams where additional kisses and slow caresses awaited.

Bartholomew gripped the fireplace mantel and leaned forward, allowing the heat from the blazing flames to kiss his bare chest. "Tell me you've found my son's weakness," he muttered, addressing Mr. Smith, who stood a few paces behind him, immediately inside the door to the room.

"Doing so is harder than we anticipated," Mr. Smith replied. "The drive with which he applies himself to his work is almost obsessive. As far as I have been able to tell, he does it mostly out of obligation."

"In other words, destroying his career would not ensure his suffering."

"It would, but not to the extent you hope. For that you have to aim at something he loves more than life itself. Which will be a challenge since Florian doesn't let anyone close enough to capture his heart."

Turning, Bartholomew considered the two naked women who slowly caressed each other on his bed. He'd been looking forward to sating his needs with their lush young bodies, but would regrettably have to wait now. "Leave us," he told them, his voice prompting both to exit the room in swift succession, the saucy smiles they sent his way encouraging him to make this conversation with Mr. Smith quick.

"What about the Dowager Duchess of Tremaine? I've heard rumors he's swiving her."

Mr. Smith's hard gaze met Bartholomew's. "Whether or not he is remains unclear. Either way, their interaction with each other is not suggestive of anything more than friendship and professional partnership. He speaks with her regularly, confides in her perhaps, but losing her would not cripple him completely. His mother, on the other hand, might—"

"No. You will have to leave Claire out of this." Not because he particularly cared for her, but because the history they shared had forged a peculiar connection. She was the mother of his child and guilty of doing no wrong. If anything, she'd always done precisely what he wanted, even if she'd claimed it had been for no other reason than to save her son.

"Perhaps you ought to reconsider going after him then," Mr. Smith murmured.

Bartholomew flinched. "No. Florian might be my blood, but he betrayed me. He brought the law down upon me and denied me the chance to take over Guthrie's territory."

"At least you have the opportunity to do so now."

"Yes. But not with Florian in my way. If he prevents typhus from spreading and the people of St. Giles from dying, acquiring the area will be just as difficult as it has always been."

"So what do you propose we do?"

Bartholomew spoke without even thinking. "It is

time to destroy Florian before he makes another attempt at destroying me."

"Lady Armswell will likely hunt you down herself if you touch one hair on his precious head."

"Which isn't something I find the least bit displeasing. Her anger with me resulted in truly high passion once. Perhaps it can do so again."

"Is that what you want?"

Bartholomew shrugged. "I don't dislike the idea of it."

"Then perhaps you should reacquaint yourself with her now. If Florian found out, the knowledge would probably drive him insane."

"Undoubtedly. But he's not the only one I would have to contend with then. Armswell might be weak, but Lowell isn't. I'm not sure I'm eager to incur his wrath." He took a moment to ponder that and eventually decided he was sure about this. "Find something else on Florian. There must be something about him you've yet to discover. And in the meantime, send the twins back in. All this talk about Claire has made me eager for a bit of vigorous bed sport."

Chapter 13

Hurrying from table to table, Juliette placed a silk rose upon every plate and made sure the real roses in the centerpieces looked as fresh as possible. "I think we need to switch this one out," she told Vivien, who was busy arranging gift baskets on a long table. Juliette pulled off a few miserable petals and took a step back to admire her work. "Never mind. I fixed it."

Vivien placed a large box wrapped in ribbon next to a series of cards. "Relax, Juliette. Everything looks perfect."

"Maybe," Juliette agreed, but she wanted to be sure. This was, after all, the first event she'd ever hosted, and with some people still not convinced she belonged in Society, she wanted to impress. Especially since she was sure there were many who doubted her ability to pull this off.

One hundred guests were expected to arrive in less than half an hour, and even though her family would be there to offer support, her nerves still quivered and quaked in anticipation.

And they didn't ease up when the first people walked through the door. Quite the opposite.

"You're doing well," Raphe murmured close to her. Since it was his house, he and Gabriella were helping her greet everyone, which was a relief. The thought of doing it alone . . .

"I cannot wait to bid on that waltz with Florian," an older woman declared as she made her way past Juliette and entered the ballroom where all the tables were set.

Her companion chuckled. "It's the best thing about this whole situation. Just be warned that I plan to outbid you!"

Juliette groaned. Perhaps she'd made a mistake by offering up such a prize. It had been done with the best of intentions, but from the looks of it, it threatened to be distasteful. Soured by this possibility, she wondered if she ought to pull the waltz with Florian from the bidding. There was still time. Except, it had been mentioned on the invitations as a means to encourage the women. Much as the promise of winning a cognac owned by Napoleon himself was supposed to reel in the men.

Judging from the turnout, it had worked, but at what cost?

"I have to say I'm impressed," Florian said when he arrived and accompanied her through to the ballroom. Heads turned to stare at them—or at him—and snickers permeated the air.

"You don't have to go through with this," she said, embarrassed on his behalf.

His jaw clenched as he studied the women who'd come for a chance to secure a dance. But then he dropped his gaze to Juliette and allowed a faint smile. "It's a small price to pay if it means we'll be able to afford proper quarantine." His smile vanished. "Your funds have already been well spent on the clinic we set up and on treating the patients back at the hospital. The extra funds you raise today will be most welcome."

Comforted by his willingness to help, Juliette pushed her concerns aside and showed him to his table. Amelia, Coventry, Raphe and Gabriella were already occupying the rest of the seats along with Lady Everly.

Before Juliette could turn away, Amelia caught her hand. "Good luck," she murmured. "I know you'll be a smashing success."

Hoping that was true, Juliette made her way to where Vivien was already standing. They waited while footmen served tea and refreshments. Conversation filled the air like a swarm of bees buzzing about their hive. Inside her tummy, Juliette felt the uneasy flutter of wings. Her heart began beating faster and she drew a long breath to steady her nerves.

"Are you ready?" Vivien asked when it looked as though all the guests had received their refreshments.

"No. But the faster I begin, the faster it will be over."

Vivien grinned. "Just look at one person and ignore the rest. That's what I always do."

Juliette looked out over the tables dotting the room and instinctively focused her gaze on the man whose serious demeanor served as a welcome anchor. She spoke to him, her voice cutting through the din and forcing the room into silence.

"Welcome, ladies and gentlemen. As you are aware, the lives of fellow citizens are currently threatened by a terrible disease, the funds to help them, too few to make a difference." She cast a quick look at Vivien, who gave her a nod of encouragement. Relaxing a little, Juliette turned back toward the crowd, surveying it slowly for added effect. "This is why I've invited you here today. Your presence is a testament to your kindness, your willingness to help those in need." She gestured toward the table behind her. "There are twenty wonderful donations to be auctioned off here today. Ladies and gentlemen, I encourage you to bid as much as you can afford and to do so with the assurance that your money will be spent on those who need it the most.

"First up, I offer two books written by Benjamin Franklin, donated to us by The Book Company. They are his autobiography and *Poor Richard's Almanac*. The latter is signed by the author himself and the combined works hold an estimated value of one hundred pounds." Juliette took a deep breath before asking, "Would anyone like to offer one hundred and ten?"

Hands began to rise, driving the bidding up. Juliette's pulse raced, increasing in speed when someone shouted, "Two hundred and fifty!"

"Three hundred!"

Overcome by the positive response, Juliette watched and listened with increasing awe as the number rose to a staggering 480 pounds before it was won by Lord Yates. He winked at her as he settled back in his seat, his goodwill implying that he held no grudge against her.

Grateful, she thanked him with a smile and moved on to the next items. The silk ball gown from Madame Lizette's brought in two hundred pounds, a cigar box with mother-of-pearl inlays ended up fetching 230 pounds.

The gift baskets were less successful. Containing

soaps and perfumes, most of them went for fifty pounds, except for the one with a puppy inside, which was won by Baron Hawthorne for six hundred pounds.

"I've been looking for a greyhound exactly like this one," he exclaimed with a burst of enthusiasm. "It reminds me of the one I had as a boy. The coloring is identical!"

Juliette grinned as she picked up the coveted bottle of cognac and held it up for all to see. A hush fell over the room, and then Lord Wilmington spoke. "I'll start the bidding at five hundred pounds, if that's acceptable to you!"

Juliette's fingers trembled in response to the shocking sum he suggested. Fearing she might do something awful like drop the bottle, she set it aside carefully and nodded. "Yes. That sounds more than reasonable." She'd intended to start at two.

"I'll give you six," another gentleman blurted.

Excitement increased as voices clamored for attention, driving the bidding up until Juliette felt somewhat dizzy. They were now at 1,000 pounds! She glanced at Vivien, who looked just as dumbfounded as she felt.

It wasn't until the sum arrived at 1,500 that the voices weakened as fewer people engaged. Eventually, Wilmington got the bottle he wanted for an astounding 1,600 pounds.

Juliette blinked, still dazed from what had transpired. She dropped her gaze to the spot on the table where the card promising a dance with Florian rested.

Hesitantly, she picked it up and turned it over in her hand, her chest squeezing her lungs as she wondered which of these women he would end up having to dance with. And not just any dance, but the waltz. Her heart thrummed with an almost unreasonable desperation. He wasn't her betrothed. He was simply a friend, perhaps a colleague, so for the idea of him waltzing with another to bother her so was ridiculous. And yet, she knew what it was like to be held in his arms, to have the intensity of his gaze fixed only on her, and the notion of sharing that experience with another woman broke something inside her.

Silence drew on as everyone waited for her to speak. Which she had to. Of course she did. Florian had told her so. The hospital needed the funds. She could not be selfish.

Bracing herself, she straightened her spine and hardened her resolve. She could do this. "Just as the gentlemen here were eager to bid on the cognac, I believe there are many ladies who would like to bid on the rare opportunity to waltz with Florian, the future Duke of Redding."

Whispers ensued and Juliette clutched the card in her hands even harder. "As with the cognac, I propose we start the bidding at five hundred pounds as well." She heard Vivien's gasp and glanced toward her.

"What are you doing?" she mouthed.

Juliette wasn't quite sure, except that it had occurred to her that a high enough sum might discourage anyone from bidding, which was really just as bad as telling everyone that the waltz was no longer available.

Desperate to steady her riotous nerves, she sought her anchor and found Florian's gaze intent on her. The flutter in her belly, which had long since subsided, returned with a vengeance, stealing her breath.

"Five hundred and fifty," someone called out.

Vivien gasped again, as did Juliette, her attention on Florian straying to the person who'd spoken. It was the older woman who'd told her friend about her intention to win.

Juliette bristled. "Five hundred and fifty pounds," she repeated. Just in case someone else had missed it.

"Five hundred and sixty," a lady said from across the room. Juliette recognized her as one of the debutantes she'd seen in the women's retiring room at the Hawthorne Ball.

"Five hundred and seventy," the older woman responded.

Her friend added an extra ten and other women joined in, sending the bidding higher and higher until it surpassed one thousand.

It was very strange, feeling happy and horrified at the same time.

"This is amazing," Vivien said as another hundred pounds was added.

Juliette had to agree. She stared at Florian and saw he was looking equally stumped. And then her gaze caught Amelia's right before she turned to whisper something in her husband's ear. Coventry frowned, hesitated a second and finally nodded.

"Two thousand pounds," Amelia said, her voice echoing through the room.

Juliette stopped breathing. Had Amelia lost her mind?

The stillness consuming the air illustrated the unified bafflement of those present.

Then someone spoke. "She can't do that! It isn't fair!"

Another woman could be heard saying, "The Duchess is already married. What need has she for a waltz with Florian?"

Disapproving murmurs ensued, silenced only by one proclamation. "Make that two thousand five hundred!" It was the older woman again, her voice carrying loud and clear.

Juliette reached for the edge of the table to steady herself. In her hand, the card shivered in concert with her trembling heart.

If only she had the funds herself, she'd happily offer them up on—

"Three thousand," Amelia said. She gave Juliette a pointed look, the sort compelling her to act quickly.

Feeling as though she was trapped in wobbly jelly, she spoke as swiftly as her tongue could manage. "Three thousand pounds by the Duchess of Coventry. Going once. Going twice. Gone."

Air rushed from her lungs as some congratulated Amelia and others simply took their leave with disgruntled mutterings.

"Did that just happen?" Vivien asked.

Juliette shook her head. The nervous tension inside her began to bubble, and then she laughed, the absurdity and shock of it all transforming into mirth. "Apparently so," she managed while still attempting to come to terms with her sister's extravagant gesture.

Looking toward her table, Juliette's gaze was drawn to Florian. She wondered what he was thinking about all of this, but it was difficult to discern since he was talking to Raphe and Coventry.

Knowing she had a few practical matters to see to before she could join them, she reached for a piece of paper on which she'd listed each prize. Grabbing a pencil, she wrote down the names of the winners and the final bids, tallying the sums at the end.

"How does it look?" Vivien asked.

Juliette set her pencil aside and looked at her.

Excitement buzzed through her veins. "Four thousand, seven hundred and sixty pounds."

Vivien stared at her. Her gaze dropped to the paper. "Let me see that." Juliette handed her the calculations and watched as her friend went over them. "Amazing," Vivien murmured. She met Juliette's gaze and smiled with wide abandon. "And to think you were worried." She shook her head and gave the paper back to Juliette, who carefully folded it before placing it in her reticule.

Juliette glanced toward the table where her family and Florian still sat. "Shall we have some refreshments to celebrate?"

"As much as I would love that, I really ought to get going," Vivien said. "I told my aunt we could go for a walk together this afternoon if I didn't get home too late."

"Will you call on me tomorrow then?" Juliette asked. Knowing she hadn't been spending much time with her friend lately except when she'd needed her help, she decided to try and give her some attention. "We could play a game of battledore in the garden if the weather is good and then have tea afterward. It will give us a chance to catch up properly."

"I'd like that," Vivien said.

Thanking her once again for all her help, Juliette told her to give her aunt her best regards. She then pulled an empty chair toward Amelia and Gabriella, who instantly scooted sideways and made some space so she could sit down between them.

"Congratulations on your success, Juliette," Raphe said as he raised his teacup in salute. "I am so proud of you."

"You did well," Florian agreed. He was looking

at her so attentively, her cheeks began to burn. "The funds you've made here today will be incredibly helpful."

Snapping out of the momentary daze his attention wrought, Juliette said, "In truth, I have Amelia to thank." She looked at her sister. "Whatever were you thinking to offer such a staggering amount? Not that a waltz with Florian isn't worth it," she hastened to add while her cheeks grew increasingly hotter, "but—"

"It's not the dance," Amelia said. "It's the cause." She then whispered, "Although I was also thinking of you. And Florian." Raising her voice while Juliette tried to make sense of that statement, she added, "Coventry and I decided to match your donation before coming here. But then when I saw how grasping those women were, like starved animals descending on a carcass, if you'll pardon the analogy, I couldn't sit and watch them continue. So I used the three thousand pounds at my disposal to bid."

"And I thank you for it, Duchess," Florian said.

"But considering the current state I am in," Amelia went on, "and the time it will take for me to recover after my child is born, I think I ought to donate the waltz to Juliette." She sipped her tea as if her comment was perfectly normal. As if her plot to put Juliette back in Florian's arms was not completely transparent.

Cringing, Juliette looked everywhere but at Florian. Until he said, "Once again, you have my utmost thanks. Dancing with Lady Juliette is always a delight."

It was impossible for her not to glance across the table at him. And when she did, she saw that he was smiling. At her. As if the rest of the world had vanished and nothing else mattered.

Her heart swelled and her stomach bounced, knocking the air from her lungs.

"Gabriella and I have also decided to match your donation, Juliette," Raphe said, ruining the moment with his wonderful declaration and forcing Juliette's attention to him and her sister-in-law.

As she thanked them, she looked at everyone sitting at the table and acknowledged how lucky she was to have them all in her life. Their support was invaluable, and with their help she had no doubt that she and Florian would be able to do what was necessary, not only for St. Giles, but for the rest of England.

"Will you call on us tomorrow then?" Gabriella asked Florian as they prepared to take their leave of each other.

"Of course. I will visit with you in the afternoon." He acknowledged the rest of the group and allowed his gaze to settle on Juliette. "It's been a pleasure." Touching the brim of his hat, he turned and walked away with a swift stride.

Juliette watched him go. "What was that about?" she asked Gabriella.

"Oh, nothing serious." Gabriella waved her hand dismissively. "David developed a cough right before we came here and his nose started running," she said in reference to her son. "It's probably just a cold, but I thought it wise to have Florian take a look at him just in case."

Juliette agreed. Asking Florian for help was a very good idea, even if it proved to be unnecessary.

Juliette raced after the shuttlecock Vivien sent her way, laughing as she almost tripped in order to hit it back toward Gabriella. It was a hot day, but the shade from an overhanging elm made the exertion the game provided bearable. "Pardon the interruption, Duchess," Pierson called from the terrace, "but Florian is here to see Master David. Shall I show him up to the nursery?"

"Please do," Gabriella told him. Panting, she swiped a hand across her brow and excused herself to Juliette and Vivien. "I must hear what Florian has to say about David's cold. I won't be long." She started walking away. "Why don't you have some refreshments on the terrace while you wait? Unless of course you prefer to carry on without me." She disappeared up the steps and through a pair of wide French doors.

Juliette glanced at Vivien. "Let's play a quick round first, shall we? The first to get five points wins."

"You don't stand a chance." Vivien grinned, tossing the shuttlecock into the air and whacking it hard in Juliette's direction.

"You're a devil in disguise," Juliette cried as she leapt toward her target, watching as it bounced off the edge of her battledore and onto the grass. Picking it up, Juliette put one hand on her hip and gave her friend a put-out look. "Does that count?"

"No. I just like teasing you." She laughed while Juliette plotted her revenge.

"Really?" Juliette glanced toward the garden gate and allowed her eyes to widen. "Oh my goodness! What on earth is that?"

Vivien turned and Juliette aimed the shuttlecock at her friend. It bounced off her shoulder and landed at her feet before she had a chance to realize what was going on. Her expression was comical and Juliette laughed, until she realized that Vivien was preparing to strike once more.

They were just taking their seats on the terrace after finishing their game when Gabriella returned, accompanied by Florian. He pulled out the vacant chair beside Juliette and sat. Doing her best to ignore his presence, Juliette picked up a biscuit and took a bite. She chewed carefully while trying not to focus on how intensely the man was radiating masculinity. It was in his scent, now so familiar her body came swiftly alive the instant she smelled it, and it was in the haphazard locks of copper falling across his brow, the broad set of his shoulders and the firm outline of his thighs beneath a pair of snug buckskin breeches.

Juliette drew a shuddering breath. Her gaze dropped to his hands and the long elegant fingers now taking hold of the lemonade glass Gabriella had served him. Tearing her eyes away by sheer force of will, Juliette looked up to find herself the subject of his regard. He raised an eyebrow and her mind went blank.

"Sir?" As if he deserved chastising.

"Forgive me, my lady, but there is a crumb where one ought not to be." He quickly abandoned his lemonade and picked up a napkin. "Allow me." And before Juliette could discern what was going on or what the man planned, he was gently dabbing at the edge of her mouth in a manner that might have been intended as an intimate caress if they'd been alone.

But they weren't. Gabriella and Vivien were both sitting across from them, seemingly undaunted by Florian's attention toward Juliette or the sound of her pounding heart which was, to her own ears, quite deafening.

"There." Florian turned away from her and addressed Gabriella. "As I mentioned, David will be fine." He reached for his bag and pulled out a piece of paper on which he proceeded to write with a pencil.

Juliette, her nerves all jumbled together, watched him with disappointed incomprehension. How was it that he could evoke in her a fiery response with so little ease while he himself remained seemingly unaffected? It wasn't fair! Not to mention that his effect on her was steadily increasing, leaving her horribly bewildered and overwhelmed.

"Have your cook prepare this for him," Florian said, handing the paper he'd been writing on to Gabriella. His manner was infuriatingly sober. Not a hint of emotion could be detected in either his features or his bearing. "It should soothe him and allow for better rest."

"Thank you, Florian." Gabriella handed the note to a nearby footman with instructions to pass it on to Cook immediately. "If only I were the one afflicted," she said once the footman had gone to tend to his duty. "Watching either of my children suffer is intolerable."

"At least you have had the foresight to separate them," Florian told her gently. "If you are lucky, Rose will not be infected by her brother's malady."

"Speaking of maladies," Vivien said, "I was thinking of putting some baskets together for the people of St. Giles. It's not much, considering what they are suffering through, but trapped as they are for the time being, I thought it might be nice to get some fresh produce to them."

"That is an excellent idea," Juliette said. She was surprised she hadn't thought of it herself. "Healthy sustenance may even encourage those who are sick to recover while saving the healthy from falling victim to the disease. Is that not so, Florian?"

He held her gaze briefly, but it was long enough for something tangible to pass between them, something Juliette thought might be respect. "It certainly can't hurt. If you let me know when the baskets have been completed, I will make sure they reach the people who need them the most."

Vivien beamed. "Thank you ever so much. It eases my heart to know I am helping if only a little." She picked up her reticule. "I must be on my way now. Thank you for a lovely afternoon."

"You are very welcome," Juliette told her. "I hope to see you again soon."

Agreeing, Vivien stood, as did Florian. She gave them each a swift parting nod and then left, promising to give her aunt their best wishes.

"She is very kind," Florian murmured upon resuming his seat.

"Unfortunately that is not enough," Juliette said. When Florian gave her a curious look, she explained. "Miss Saunders's greatest hope is to marry and start a family of her own. She longs for children to love, but with her limited funds and lack of status, most gentlemen ignore her. They're either too high in the instep or too poor to marry for anything other than convenience."

"It is the driving force behind most marriages," Florian said. "Choosing a spouse who's your friend or whom you might actually love is a luxury few can enjoy. There's no doubt in my mind that you and your sister-in-law are the envy of many young debutantes, Duchess. Your fortune cannot be denied."

"Perhaps," Gabriella agreed. "But what about you, Florian? If you were to marry, would it be for convenience or because you'd found the woman you cannot live without?"

Juliette didn't dare look at her sister-in-law or at Florian. She couldn't believe Gabriella had just asked such a forward question. And although part of her wanted to know the answer, another part dreaded hearing what he had to say.

"If I chose to marry, and I say this hypothetically, I would want my wife to share my interests."

"And would you make an effort to enjoy hers?" Gabriella asked while Juliette shifted uncomfortably in her seat.

"Naturally." He paused before saying, "I would enter the union expecting to spend the rest of my life with her, so it seems only reasonable for us to support each other, to engage in conversation and keep each other company. I would like for her to be my friend before all else, because I believe it to be a strong foundation from which love is likely to grow."

"I do believe you're more romantic than most people give you credit for," Gabriella said.

Florian didn't answer right away and Juliette finally hazarded a look in his direction, only to find his gaze riveted on her. "Perhaps," he murmured.

Feeling hotter than when she'd been playing battledore, Juliette snatched up her glass of lemonade and took a quick sip.

Gabriella chuckled as if completely oblivious to the impact Florian's response was having. "I'm sure you'll find the right woman, Florian. Maybe you already have."

Choking on her lemonade, Juliette sputtered ever

so slightly and took another sip while wishing she could go back in time to when Vivien left so she could go with her. But since that wasn't possible, she was stuck with hoping this conversation would soon be over so things could return to some sort of normal.

"Are you all right?" Florian asked, forcing Juliette to address him.

She nodded. "Mmm-hmm . . ." She coughed again. "The lemonade went down the wrong way, that's all."

"Well," Gabriella said when Juliette regained her composure. She glanced at Juliette and then at Florian. "The weather is lovely and there is scarcely a breeze. If you're not in a hurry to leave, Florian, perhaps you'd like to play a game of battledore with Juliette?"

Snapping to attention, Juliette threw a look of warning at Gabriella before saying, "That's really not necessary. I've already played a few rounds with you and Vivien and I'm sure Florian is terribly busy. Too busy to waste time on sport."

"On the contrary, I have time to spare."

Juliette gaped at him. "You do?"

He nodded. "I wasn't sure how long my visit here would take, so I made arrangements."

Befuddled, she wasn't sure how to respond, except to say, "I see."

"And besides, I haven't been getting nearly enough exercise lately. The exertion a game of battledore provides will do me good."

"Then it's settled," Gabriella said before Juliette could ruin her matchmaking plans. Which was obviously what this was. And since it didn't take much to see that, Juliette knew Florian must have realized it too, making her wonder all the more about his reason for choosing to stay.

He proved to be an excellent opponent. His skill and agility were impressive. Gripping the battledore, Juliette raced after the shuttlecock, almost falling over the hem of her gown in the process while stretching her arm out to send the feathery projectile straight toward Florian.

He caught it with ease and tossed it back with sharp precision. Juliette whacked it through the air, forcing him to chase it this time. Concentration showed on his brow as he studied the angle of the shuttlecock's descent and prepared to hit it straight back in her direction. He did so soon enough, and this time, Juliette lost her footing in her pursuit of it. She stumbled and went down onto her knees in the grass. From the terrace came laughter, not just from Gabriella but from Raphe, who'd come to keep his wife company.

"Well done, Juliette!" Gabriella shouted with as much encouragement as was possible under the circumstances.

Juliette blew out a breath and prepared to rise when an outstretched hand filled her vision. "Allow me to help you up."

Florian's hand was completely bare, which wasn't surprising considering the nature of their activity. With hers equally so, however, the thought of placing her palm in his sent a dart of heat shooting straight down her middle. Her pulse leapt and for a second she thought of denying him the courtesy. And yet, the secret thrill of surrendering to her own desire for increased contact was too great to be denied. Here was the perfect excuse for her to revel in it discreetly and without anyone thinking much of it.

So she reached up slowly and savored that moment

when her hand connected with his, the warmth of his skin pressing firmly against her own and the feel of his fingers wrapping tightly around hers. There was a pause during which he simply held on, and then, with a flinch, as if reminded of what he was meant to do, he pulled her up and released her as if she were a gemstone he'd just been caught stealing.

"Would you like to continue playing?" he asked.

"Yes," she said, her answer coming as naturally as it would have if he'd asked her if the grass was green. "Would you?"

Something indescribable surfaced from the depths of his blue eyes. It lingered for a second before it was once again gone. He inclined his head. "Yes. I like playing with you."

"Then you are in luck," she told him lightly while moving away and adding some distance, "for I am more than happy to continue playing until I win."

Florian grinned, his expression relaxing with humor. "Then I encourage you to do your best!"

She laughed, loving the banter and the sport while savoring the chance she'd been given to see him like this. Unwilling to let it end, Juliette picked up the shuttlecock and aimed it straight at him.

His battledore connected with it with a thwack and it shot back toward her. It continued back and forth, forcing them both to run left and right until she, catching him slightly off guard, managed to send it past his reach.

He shook his head and met her gaze. "Minx," he muttered, just loud enough for her to hear. And then, before she was fully prepared, he launched another attack.

They played until Juliette was gasping for breath

and he insisted they stop. "I said I was happy to play until I win," she complained.

He cut her a stupefied look. "Are you saying I should have allowed you to do so?"

"Of course not." She was having some trouble speaking on account of her ragged breathing. "I am merely saying that I do not need to rest."

Coming toward her, he took the battledore from her hand and offered his arm. "As your physician, I highly recommend a fair amount of exercise. I do, however, also ask that you do not push yourself to the point of collapse."

With happy reluctance—strange concept that— she looped her arm with his and allowed him to escort her up to the terrace where Raphe and Gabriella sat waiting. Keeping a slow pace, Florian said, "You played well. With practice, you may become quite proficient."

"I could say the same about you." She nudged his shoulder a bit with her own in a friendly way that made him turn to her with amusement. She smiled in response. "Thank you for playing with me. It was fun."

"You are welcome, my lady. And I agree. It *was* fun."

They reached the steps and started up. A thought occurred to Juliette and she decided to voice it. "Is it not time for you to dispense with the formalities? You have known me for almost a year and have seen me at my worst. Would it not be possible for you to simply call me Juliette?"

"I am not certain that would be wise." His voice was tighter than it had been all afternoon.

"Why?" She was genuinely confused.

He slowed their pace even further so they were

almost standing still, then quietly murmured, "Because doing so would place us on equal footing."

She blinked, astounded by what he'd just said. "But you will be duke. Your position as Redding's heir is already superior to my own."

"Only when it comes to social etiquette, but that is not the only aspect I must consider."

She turned her head and stared at him blankly. "I do not understand."

Unhooking his arm from hers, he clasped his hands behind his back and met her gaze with quiet solemnity. "The point is there are other facets at play, facets that make me unworthy of such familiarity."

Overcome by surprise, she laughed. "Surely you jest." When he remained completely grave, all humor died on her lips. She shook her head with incomprehension. "I grew up in the slums while you were raised by a viscount. All I have done is accept the wealth bestowed upon me by my brother while you have earned the respect of your peers by applying yourself to a noble profession. And now you will soon be a duke, and still you claim that you are not worthy of foregoing the honorific where I am concerned? It makes no sense, Florian. Least of all when I am forever addressing you by your middle name."

"Everyone does so. It is the only way to avoid confusing me with my brother."

She could only stare at him. "What if I insist on being simply Juliette?"

"I would advise against it."

"Why?"

He didn't respond immediately, but when he did, his voice was low and measured. "Because it would suggest a level of intimacy that I'm not completely ready for at the moment." He bowed before her, no doubt oblivious to the shiver his words evoked. "Thank you once again for a pleasant afternoon. I look forward to seeing you again tomorrow for the next committee meeting."

Leaving her side, Florian went to bid farewell to Gabriella and Raphe as he handed over the battledores and shuttlecock. Raphe escorted him out and Juliette watched their retreating forms until they were out of view, then claimed a vacant chair beside Gabriella. "Well that was enjoyable," she said with as much joviality as possible. "I did not expect him to be such a skillful player."

Gabriella smiled while pouring a fresh glass of lemonade for Juliette. "He has certainly taken a liking to you."

Juliette sighed and stretched out her legs. Lord, it was good to relax for a bit. "I don't know what makes you think so, when he has given no indication of such a thing."

Gabriella chuckled. "I dare say you are too involved in the situation to judge it with clarity. If you were to take a step back, however, and see how he interacts with you, you would know what I say is true. He favors your attention, Julie. The only question now is whether or not he'll allow himself to encourage it."

Chapter 14

After leaving Huntley House the previous day, Florian went straight to St. Agatha's where he immersed himself in work. He also made some house calls, including a visit to his uncle's, before returning home. There he discovered another unsigned letter, this time advising him that Armswell needed his help. When Florian arrived at his parents' home, he found the viscount in dire need of medical attention.

Thankfully, Florian recognized the symptoms of hemlock poisoning and was able to administer the necessary antidote. But the whole ordeal left him shaken and proved that the person behind the threats intended to act on them without remorse.

"Who would do this?" his mother demanded. "I cannot imagine any of the servants—"

"Did you recently hire a new employee?" Florian asked as he packed away his supplies.

"I . . . um . . ." She blinked. "Armswell hired a new footman about a week ago."

"Sack him," Florian advised. "I think he might be working for someone else."

"But—"

He reached for her hand while meeting her troubled gaze. "Someone wants to hurt me and I think they're attempting to do so through you, but you mustn't worry. I'm handling it."

Leaving her, he went to meet Henry. "I need your help," he said and gave a quick account of the threatening letters while Henry listened with increased concern on his face. "Tonight, I believe the person behind it attacked"—he swallowed, forcing the necessary words out—"our father."

"Christ, Florian!" Henry's eyes widened with alarm.

"He's all right," Florian added, "but I worry it's only the beginning."

It took a moment for Henry to relax and for Florian to convince him that hastening over to Armswell House was unnecessary. "Any idea who might be behind it?"

"No," Florian said. "Just be careful," he warned, "and maybe inform the magistrate of what has happened. I would do so myself but I fear it will only make matters worse if the villain finds out that I talked."

"Of course." Henry walked him to the door. "The footman will naturally be interrogated, but if he keeps silent, I'll launch a separate investigation with the hope of discovering who might stand to gain from St. Giles going under."

Florian thanked him for his help and headed back to the hospital to warn Viola.

When he finally returned home, he grabbed a pistol from his study for safety and a bottle of brandy for his nerves, before heading upstairs to bed. It had been an extremely busy day but it had provided him with a necessary distraction from his thoughts of

Lady Juliette and the physical craving such thoughts provoked.

As it was, she still managed to creep into his mind the moment he laid down to sleep. In spite of his best efforts, he failed to avoid the contemplations his mind was more than eager to provoke, of her body pressed against his, of what it might be like to undress her and how it would feel to slide his hands across every inch of her beautiful perfection.

Such thoughts took the toll they were destined to take, and he was left with no choice but to let himself succumb to the needy desire that followed. Guilt ensued, fast and swift. The manner in which he degraded her with lascivious imaginings was bad enough, but to actually indulge himself sexually while doing so was beyond reprehensible. He had no right. None whatsoever. And he was keenly aware that this was just one more reason for him to insist he address her formally, because she was a lady and he was anything but a gentleman when it came to her.

Now seated beside her at his dining room table, Florian conducted the committee meeting with professional aloofness. He kept himself stiff and precise, denying Lady Juliette any chance of excessive familiarity. She'd said they were friends but he knew better. They were balancing along a delicate boundary that threatened to send them both hurtling toward an inevitable need for seduction. Which was something he could not allow. So he'd kept his hands clasped behind his back when she had arrived, lest he inadvertently touch her, and he'd kept all conversation with her as brief as possible, which was easier now that the meeting was underway.

"Fatalities are rising in St. Giles, Florian," Lady

Warwick was saying. "People are worried that what we are doing isn't making much of a difference."

Florian felt the same, but he wasn't sure what else they could do besides treat the sick and keep them separate from the rest of the citizens. "The pamphlets that have been distributed and the articles in the newspapers should put them at ease. As long as they follow the advice on disease prevention, their chances of avoiding infection ought to be good."

"It's not enough," Baron Hawthorne said. "We need some means by which to reassure the public and prevent the panic I fear might be brewing."

"Any suggestions?" Viola asked.

"Yes." It was Lady Juliette who spoke. "After you asked us to think of a way to quarantine the sick, I have been trying to educate myself on the disease we face in order to better understand it and treat it." She paused for a second and Florian held his breath in anticipation of what she was going to say next. "What I have learned is that patients showing symptoms of typhus, or other contagious diseases, and who were admitted to the Edinburgh Infirmary toward the end of the last century, were ordered to surrender their clothes and take a bath. They were then given a clean hospital gown, shaved to remove all manner of vermin from their hair, and rubbed with a mercurial ointment."

"St. Agatha's would do so as well if such patients were brought in, but I am still concerned about the risk," Florian told her. He was well aware of the practices adapted by the Edinburgh Infirmary since James Gregory himself, the author to which Juliette was referring, had told him all about it, insisting it had prevented him from losing a single patient during the last five years of his practice in the clinical ward.

"Which is why I propose that we purchase a ship," Juliette said. Murmured interest hummed through the air.

Florian tilted his head. "A ship?"

Juliette nodded. "We ought to be able to afford it after the funds we procured from the charity event."

"Well, yes," Elmwood said, somewhat gruffly. "Especially if we can get our hands on a used East Indiaman. Production on those is relatively cheap. Shouldn't cost us more than five thousand pounds."

"Which is still within our budget," Clearwater said. He gave Lady Juliette a look that spoke of great admiration. "Quarantining the sick on a ship is an excellent idea. How did you come up with it?"

A lovely pink shade colored Lady Juliette's cheeks. "I found a reference to such a method being employed in one of the books in the Huntley House Library. It was written by a maritime surgeon, and although I initially dismissed it, thinking it wouldn't be helpful, I'm glad I took a closer look. Because in doing so, I learned something useful." She glanced around. "During the black death, for instance, ships arriving in Venice from infected ports were kept at anchor for forty days before landing. Surrounded by water without access to land, the people on the ships were not able to spread the disease." She paused before saying, "I believe it ought to be possible for us to contain the spread of typhus in a similar way."

Florian watched her as she spoke. The idea was not simply good, it was brilliant. And so simple he wondered why he hadn't considered this solution himself. Seeing that everyone waited to hear his opinion, he nodded and said, "Well done, my lady. You may have found the perfect solution."

She smiled then with pleasure and gratitude so dazzling he felt his heart thump quite wildly against his chest. Christ, she was lovely, and it suddenly occurred to him that he hadn't enjoyed anything as much in recent years as the act of making her happy. With that thought in mind, he added, "We will set about finding an appropriate vessel immediately. It will be thoroughly cleaned and prepared before a single patient is brought onboard. Since the Thames is narrow enough to allow a desperate man to swim across, we will have to sail it out to the Channel to ensure proper quarantine can be maintained."

"If the majority agrees, I will start working on the specifics immediately," Viola said.

Florian nodded. "Let us put it to a vote." They did so with everyone agreeing to this new proposal.

The meeting was adjourned with renewed hope, and several members stayed behind to discuss further details over tea and coffee in the parlor. Avoiding the torture of touching Lady Juliette, Florian denied himself the pleasure of escorting her by turning to Viola for a brief exchange. "This can work," he told her with certainty bubbling through his veins. "We actually stand a chance of minimizing the loss of life."

"And all because of Lady Juliette," Viola said with a smirk. "I bet you're happy you agreed to let her join the committee after all."

"She has a good head on her shoulders."

Viola grinned. "A true departure from your previous opinion of her as naïve."

Florian cringed at the reminder. "Opinions can change, Viola."

"Yes, Florian. They certainly can."

Juliette was trying extremely hard to focus on what Yates was saying. And failing miserably. She knew it had something to do with a painting he'd recently acquired, but with her mind occupied by Florian and his distant attitude toward her, she had no idea who the artist was or why Yates was so excited about it.

"My lady?"

Juliette blinked. "Hmm?"

Yates regarded her with a contemplative frown for a moment before offering a smile and saying, "The Vermeer painting I mentioned. It would be an honor to show it to you one day."

"Oh. Thank you." Juliette glanced across at Lady Warwick who was deep in conversation with Lord Elmwood, so she would find no help there.

"Enjoying your company has become my favorite thing," Yates was saying. "You cannot imagine how pleased I was when I learned you had joined this committee. It allows us to spend more time together while pursuing a common interest. This idea of yours to quarantine the sick on a ship is particularly intriguing. I am rather impressed if you must know."

"You flatter me, my lord."

"I only speak the truth," he told her while allowing his eyes to meet hers with alarming confidence. Apparently, her refusal to walk with him after their dance at Hawthorne House had not deterred him.

Juliette averted her gaze just in time to see Viola entering the parlor with Florian close behind her. The tightening of her chest dulled the beat of her heart until Viola went to join Lady Warwick and Elmwood while Florian continued toward the row of mullioned windows spanning the length of the room.

He stood there looking out with his hands clasped loosely behind his back.

"Please excuse me," Juliette told Yates. "There is something I need to discuss with Florian."

She wasn't sure what, but she did not wish to encourage Yates further and she also knew keeping her distance from Florian would be impossible. He drew her so powerfully she might as well go to him rather than make an attempt to fight it.

"Do you wish to be alone?" she asked once she'd crossed the room to stand beside him. Outside, the sunshine played upon the dense foliage of rhododendron leaves, creating an endless array of luminescent greens.

Florian dropped a glance in her direction before resuming his perusal of the garden. "Not if you are offering to keep me company."

The pressure around Juliette's heart eased. She drew a breath and savored the lightness now filling her body. Behind her, the conversations taking place faded until she felt she'd been spirited away to a private location where only she and Florian existed.

"I was starting to worry I might have done something to upset you," she said. "You've hardly spoken to me since I arrived."

A rumble rose from deep within his chest. "My dark mood has nothing to do with you. I simply have a lot of concerns."

"I know you do, which is part of the reason why I've been trying so hard to help."

"For which I am grateful."

"I'm just not sure if charity events and donations will be enough in the long run." It was a thought she'd been toying with for the past couple of days. "Ensuring a steady income would probably be better."

"You're right." He met her gaze. "Any ideas on how to accomplish that without charging the patients?"

She shook her head. "Not yet, but I will think on it."

Silence settled between them, and then with deep contemplation, he said, "Saving lives is a never-ending struggle against the evils of the world. The things I have seen have changed me in ways I am not always fond of. When I began my apprenticeship, I was sixteen years old and used to a life of leisure and luxury. Seeing a boy my own age lose a limb that first day was shocking. I confess I fled the operating room to cast up my accounts."

"And the boy?"

"He died three days later from infection." Florian's voice was strained with emotion. "I made it my purpose then and there to discover the best methods of medical treatment and surgery. Forced to complete my apprenticeship in order to be admitted into Oxford, I dedicated my free time to reading medical texts and interviewing not only other physicians, but anyone I could find who had traveled abroad and born witness to successful surgeries."

"I cannot be anything but impressed by your determination at such a young age."

He shifted, causing his arm to brush against hers. Skin pricking with awareness, Juliette fought the urge to move closer—the urge to experience his touch once again. "It was not unlike your own. This compulsion you have to do good is very similar to mine. I understand it completely."

She struggled against the flutter of nerves the intimacy of his voice provoked. "Would you be willing to teach me what you have learned?"

He held her gaze, and although he failed to smile, his expression was warm and inviting. It animated his eyes and did curious things to Juliette's body. Her knees grew weak while sizzling embers crept over her skin. "Will you allow me to think on it for a while before I make a commitment?" he asked.

"Of course."

The parlor door opened and Florian's servant entered. Without breaking his stride he crossed the floor and addressed his master in a murmur so muted it was impossible for Juliette to hear what he was saying despite her proximity. Whatever it was, however, caused Florian's features to set in rigid planes of severity. He thanked the man, exchanged a brief glance with Juliette, and turned to address the room as a whole.

"I have just been informed that necessary measures were taken by the military earlier today when three individuals attempted to flee St. Giles. A man and a woman were both fatally wounded."

Covering her mouth with her hands, Juliette tried to stifle her gasp. This was exactly what she'd been hoping to avoid. No matter how many times she told herself it was a necessary action taken for the greater good, she doubted she'd ever fully convince herself it was right. Because it wasn't. "They deliberately killed them when they could have chosen to injure them instead."

"Yes," Florian agreed. He showed no outward sign of remorse over what had happened, but when he spoke again his voice was troubled. "Unfortunately the third individual, described as a boy roughly six years of age, escaped. He could be anywhere."

And just like that it felt as though the ceiling was

falling down over her head. This was what Florian feared more than having to kill two people—the risk one child now posed to London's population at large.

"Oh God." Lady Warwick's stricken expression conveyed what everyone else in the room was probably thinking, namely that the typhus threat was no longer contained and that death was about to descend on the city with a vengeance.

"I have to go," Florian said. He was already striding toward the door while Juliette struggled to come to terms with the change of events. "Duchess," he said, addressing Viola, "I need you to come with me. Everyone else, please stay as long as you wish and let yourselves out. We will reconvene here in two days for an update."

He was gone the next second with Viola hastening after, the sound of the front door opening and shutting an acknowledgment of their departure. Juliette stared off into the space now stretching before her. The abandonment she felt was irrational and persistent. She could not seem to shake it or the unpleasant envy welling inside her. The moment trouble had come to call, Florian had turned to Viola for help, and the lady had come to his aid with remarkable swiftness. Rational thought reminded Juliette that the two were business partners of sorts, but she still couldn't stop from wondering about the degree of their involvement.

Especially when she had recently come to the realization that she wanted Florian for herself.

Chapter 15

Juliette climbed the steps of St. Agatha's hospital with the same degree of determination that had brought her to Florian's office for the first time three weeks earlier.

"I wish to see Florian," she proclaimed to the plump middle-aged woman who occupied the front desk.

"You have an appointment with him?"

"I am his patient."

And a concerned friend.

Three days had passed since Florian had stormed out of his home to collect the bodies of the shooting victims so they could be examined. The meeting he'd asked everyone to attend two days later had since been canceled by letter.

"That hardly answers my question." The woman gave Juliette a resolute frown.

"Perhaps not, but if he were not here you probably would have told me as much." Without further warning, Juliette marched past the gatekeeper with her maid on her heels and headed straight for Florian's office.

"Miss! Stop! You cannot intrude like this!"

Juliette ignored the hollering, turned down a corridor and strode toward the second door on her left. A quick knock was the only warning she allowed before shoving the door open and taking a look around the cluttered space. It was unchanged from when she'd last been there except for a stack of books now resting on the chair she had used.

"My lady." Florian struggled to his feet with weary movements. His features were drawn, his eyes rimmed with dark circles that bore proof of severe exhaustion while growth on his jaw suggested he'd been too busy to contemplate his own appearance.

Not that Juliette minded this aspect too much. She was in fact surprised by how much she liked him looking more rugged than groomed. What she could not accept was the manner in which he abused his health.

"You must forgive me," the front desk woman panted from behind Juliette. "I tried to stop her but failed."

"No need to trouble yourself, Mrs. Brown. Her ladyship is welcome."

Mrs. Brown retreated and Juliette took a step forward. She was very aware of Sarah hovering nearby and made a quick decision—a possibly ruinous decision—right then and there. Gripping the doorjamb to keep herself steady, she turned to Sarah and told her clearly, "I have a personal matter to discuss with my physician. Please wait for me here." Without giving her maid the chance to argue, Juliette stepped further into Florian's office and closed the door behind her with a click.

Florian watched her for a long, drawn-out moment before saying, "You are too bold for your own good."

"And you are no good to anyone in the state you are in." She strode forward and picked up the stack of books occupying the chair she wished to use and handed them to Florian, who placed them on top of another pile. "When is the last time you slept?"

His bleary eyes appeared to blink with great effort. "Not since I saw you last." He slumped down onto his chair, breaking protocol by sitting before she did.

"That was several days ago, Florian." She lowered herself to the edge of her seat and folded her hands in her lap. "You need rest."

"I need to find that boy and . . ." His words trailed off.

"Has it not occurred to you that you have no chance of doing so in your current condition? Besides, too much time has probably passed by now. All we can do is wait and see what happens, but if you do not take better care of yourself, you will be in no position to help anyone if it becomes necessary for you to do so. You cannot work effectively when you can scarcely hold yourself upright."

He grinned sedately. "You're being very bossy." There was something about the tiredness with which he spoke that she found incredibly soothing. "I think I rather like it." His eyes caught hers, holding her captive in the clear blue depths. A fuzzy feeling of warmth stroked over her skin, teasing and tempting. Enticing until her breath caught on the thrill of desire.

"Why have you come here?"

The question was far more complicated than it sounded.

Because I'm concerned about you.

Because I need to know you're all right.

Because I miss you and because . . .

"Because you did not give the committee the update you promised. You canceled the meeting, which naturally made me wonder about the reason for it. I see now that it was because you were incapable of attending."

The edge of his mouth lifted in acknowledgment of her comment. "So that is it, is it? You merely came to see what kept me away? To appease your own curiosity?"

"Yes." Juliette punctuated her answer with a firm nod.

The dry chuckle Florian returned conveyed disbelief. "I see." He covered a yawn with his hand before continuing. "Well, Viola and I have been hard at work since the shooting incident. When we weren't attempting to find the boy who got away, she was ensuring the patients here at the hospital were not forgotten while I went to visit and treat the people of St. Giles to the best of my abilities."

"And now?" When he seemed confused by her question she clarified. "Why are you not home in bed, Florian?"

Moving sluggishly, he leafed through some newspaper clippings and other scraps of paper on his desk. "When last we met, you suggested we acquire a ship for the purpose of quarantining the sick. The faster we implement this, the better. So I have been trying to find appropriate vessels. Several are listed in these advertisements but not all are large enough for our purpose." His words were spread out as if it took great effort for him to speak. "I have sent inquiries in response to a few but there are still several remaining."

"And you would like to get it done before you go rest." She understood him perfectly. His dedication was such that he would put himself last whenever it came to the well-being of others.

"This is a priority. It has to get done as quickly as possible."

"You are right. But succeeding in this will mean nothing if you sacrifice yourself in the process. Three days without sleep cannot possibly be healthy and will not see you at your best. What if someone arrives here requiring surgery? Can you be certain you will not make a mistake and cause more harm than good?"

Resting his elbows upon his desk, he placed his head against his hands and rubbed his eyes. "I am not the only surgeon here. Haines and Blaire are both available to anyone in need."

Juliette puffed out a breath. The man was too stubborn for his own good. "And what of the people of St. Giles?"

"I mean to go back and check on them later today."

She stared at him. "You are in no position to do so in your current condition."

Dropping his hands, he leaned forward with undeniable irritation producing a glower. "You speak as though I am foxed, which I am not."

"And yet your speech is slurred, your eyes appear bloodshot, your hair is in utter disarray and your clothes the exact same ones you were wearing the last time I saw you." This was something that had only just occurred to her now. "You are a crumpled and exhausted mess, Florian. Go home and sleep, take a bath, get changed, and you will accomplish more once you do."

"But—"

"In the meantime, I will take on the task of finding a ship. It is the least I can do since it was my suggestion to begin with." She glanced around, acknowledging the haphazard distribution of items around the room. "Raphe and Coventry can help me so you need not worry. We will figure this out and help ease your burden."

"And the missing boy?"

"You are no closer to finding him here than you would be from your bed. If we are lucky, he is either unaffected by the disease or hiding somewhere where he won't make contact with others. Children generally recover, so hopefully he will as well without infecting anyone else."

"I worry, Juliette."

Hearing resigned despair in his voice, she stood and went to stand beside him. Her hand found his shoulder, resting there in an effort to soothe away all his troubles. "I know. Truth is, we all do, but I suspect it is worse for you because you have seen the devastation typhus can cause."

"It has to be contained. It simply has to."

"Agreed. But you must also remember that you are not fighting it on your own." She gently squeezed the muscle beneath the wool of his jacket and savored the sigh he expelled in return. "You have friends, Florian—people who are ready to assist you with this." When he angled his chin so he could gaze up into her eyes, her body went still in response to the melancholy yearning she saw there. "Every day, you come to the aid of others. I think it is high time we repay our debt to you."

It felt as though he was hovering somewhere beyond reality, in a lovely place were Juliette's voice alone gave him endless comfort. He was well aware that his mind and body were weak with fatigue, but he had not felt able to take the necessary break he needed because so much remained to be done, it was overwhelming.

Her hand rested firmly upon his shoulder, occasionally squeezing it in the most agreeable way. And she was close, her hip no more than an inch from his face. He really shouldn't be seated while she stood, but he could not seem to bring himself out of the languorous state she'd put him in. Hell, he was sorely tempted to close his eyes and allow sleep to claim him right now, except doing so would deny him this moment of complicity.

"Take off your jacket, Florian."

His entire body jerked in response to her demand. Accompanied by the sweet scent of peonies, it lured him to surrender. Only a tiny speck of sanity reaching out from the back of his mind gave him pause. "To do so would be unwise."

She sighed with absolute frustration. "Seeing you in your shirtsleeves is hardly going to affect my sensibilities or cause me to swoon. I am made of sturdier stuff than that, you know." Her hands clasped hold of his lapels and began pushing the fabric back.

Florian, exhausted as he was, had no choice but to submit to her wishes. Or so he told himself, since the scoundrel in him was rather eager to see where her undressing him might potentially lead.

"When Raphe would return from his boxing matches," she said, "Amelia and I would often take turns rubbing his shoulders. It soothed his aching muscles and reduced the tension within so he could rest with greater ease."

Pulling his arms from the sleeves, Juliette laid the jacket across the back of his chair and began removing her gloves. The effect of her standing up while he submissively waited, of the slow unbuttoning and peeling back of the kidskin gloves, and of the knowledge that she would soon place her hands upon him, sent hot desire spiraling through him.

He knew he ought to stop her, that this couldn't possibly lead to anything useful since he couldn't act on his ever-increasing urge to claim her. But perhaps allowing himself a small indulgence would not be so bad.

She moved in closer and Florian held his breath in anticipation of what she might do next. And then her thighs connected with his back and her hands sank into his shoulders, and for one incredibly bright second it was almost as if the world exploded around him. Christ, it felt amazing. With a groan of unabashed pleasure, he leaned shamelessly into the gratifying pressure of her touch. "Thank you," he murmured, because he felt the need to speak in order to somewhat distract himself from the idea of sweeping one arm around her and pulling her into his lap so he could enjoy her body more fully.

He wanted to kiss her until she was boneless, he wanted to tear her bodice to shreds with his teeth and run his hands up the elegant length of her legs and drive her wild with pleasure. But he could not and would not act on such impulse. Not when she deserved better. Not when he ought to be focusing his energy on other things. Not when threats had been made to those closest to him.

"Is this good?"

Good?

He almost laughed since nothing in the world had ever felt better.

"Mmm-hmm." It was all he could utter without embarrassing himself and revealing the endless depth of his desire. Her thumbs worked a muscle and he groaned once again while impossible fantasies played out in his head. All of them involved her, each more scandalous than the last until all he could see was her, gloriously naked and waiting for him on his bed.

His breeches tightened with increased discomfort and he suddenly feared she might see the effect she was having. So he caught her hand and looked up and was instantly rendered speechless. Her cheeks were a deep shade of pink, her eyes reflecting the need he felt while the pulse at her wrist leapt violently beneath his thumb.

"Thank you, Juliette. That is enough."

Her gaze remained steady on his, and he knew in that moment that if he really wished it, he could kiss her right now without any resistance on her part. In fact, he knew without a shadow of doubt that she wanted him to do precisely that, perhaps more. But once he started down that path there would be no going back. And if her brother found out, he would likely insist they marry and possibly even throttle Florian for taking liberties with his sister. Which was as it should be.

So he released her, stood and reached for his jacket. Putting it back on, he then gathered the ship advertisements he'd managed to collect along with some information on a few people who might be persuaded to offer their vessel to a noble cause, and handed the lot of it over to Juliette. "Here. Maybe this will be of some use to you."

Her fingers trembled, but rather than lose her resolve, she held her ground with admirable boldness. "Promise me that you are going home to bed."

The nod he gave her was just as unwavering as her resolve to see him well rested. "I do." He followed her to the door and thanked her for all the help she offered.

"It is necessary for all of us to do what must be done if we are to succeed," she said. Opening the door she stepped out into the hallway where her maid stood waiting. "Come along, Sarah. There is much for us to accomplish." She sent Florian a final glance before striding away as if saving the world took nothing more than a bit of elbow grease.

Florian stared after her until she turned a corner and disappeared out of sight. She was incredible and worthy of great admiration, and his greatest wish right now was that he might one day deserve her.

With his heart pounding so hard his ribs hurt, Jack huddled behind some crates in an alley. When the shots had sounded, he'd run as fast as his feet could carry him, darting along the road and dodging passersby. It wasn't until he'd stopped for breath that he'd realized his parents weren't with him. Doubling back along side streets while taking care not to be seen, he'd looked for them, eventually spotting their sprawled-out bodies, lifeless, upon the ground.

A well of tears had choked him, silencing his cry of pain. He was alone in the world now and with nowhere to go. St. Giles was a death trap he'd be a fool to return to. So he'd turned away and started walking, taking shelter wherever shelter could be found. Starving, he'd pinched an apple from a street stall earlier, but the vendor had not been blind to his thieving and a friend of his had given chase.

So Jack did his best to keep silent, hoping he'd avoid discovery. When it finally felt as though an eternity had passed, he edged his way back out into the street and carefully glanced around. A cough started up his throat, wracking his body while pain poured into his belly. The apple, hidden away in his pocket, no longer held appeal. He coughed again as he stepped out onto the pavement with the conviction he'd managed avoiding capture.

"Hello."

Instinct told Jack to run but perhaps that would look too suspicious. After all, the voice was kind, so he chose to turn toward it instead. And coughed again.

"You poor dear, you look quite unwell." The woman who spoke was young with a pointy nose and brown hair. Both gave her a mouse-like appearance. She looked about. "Do you live far from here? Perhaps I can escort you home and suggest a remedy for that cough to your parents."

"I don't 'ave a 'ome, Miss." Not any longer at least.

Her eyes widened with dismay. "Heavens! You're a sickly street child. That simply will not do."

She looked utterly distraught, which Jack found surprising. Judging from her well-kept appearance and clothing, he supposed she had to be middle class at least, perhaps even gentry. It was rare that such people would even bother to speak with his kind.

"It's all right," he told her, hoping to ease her mind. "I'm used to it."

Her mouth flattened into a firm line, and before Jack knew what she was about, she'd grabbed hold of his arm and begun leading him along. "You are coming with me so you can have a healthy meal and recover from whatever it is that ails you. I shall even send for a physician."

"No. Please don't." Jack struggled against her grasp. The last thing he needed was some learned man asking questions about where he'd come from.

The woman stopped walking and frowned. "You do not care for physicians." He shook his head. "Very well. I doubt tending to you will be overly complicated, so I shall see to it myself then. Will that do?"

Jack hesitated for only the second it took him to contemplate the alternative, then nodded and allowed the woman, whoever she was, to lead him off to her home.

Chapter 16

Juliette parted ways with Sarah in the foyer of Huntley House and hastened upstairs to her bedchamber. Once inside, she closed the door firmly and leaned back against it on a shuddering breath. Good Lord! Her daring insistence to care for Florian in a manner most people would deem improper had left her feeling hot all over.

Frustrated, she released an agonized groan, untied her bonnet and flung it onto her bed along with her gloves and reticule. She didn't have time to daydream about a handsome physician who turned her head. Not when lives were at stake.

So she took a few fortifying breaths to regain her composure and hurried back downstairs in search of Raphe. After checking his study and finding it empty, she located him in the library where he was keeping company with Coventry. "Good afternoon," she said. "Mind if I join you?"

The men stood and welcomed her with partial bows. "Not at all, Juliette." Raphe gestured toward a vacant spot on the sofa. "We were just finishing our discussion."

Sitting, Juliette reached for the teapot and refilled Raphe's and Coventry's cups before filling her own.

"I have just come from the hospital," she said. "Florian was there." She took a sip of her tea. "He's in dire need of sleep, so I insisted he get some rest."

Coventry sighed. "He works too hard."

"He is doing what is necessary under the current conditions we face." Raphe frowned. "Typhus is not a matter to be taken lightly. Tell me, Juliette, has progress been made to stop it from spreading?"

"That is actually what I was hoping to speak with you about." Aware she had their full attention, she told them about the most recent committee meeting and her idea to procure a ship. "Florian was trying to do this but I promised I'd handle it for him."

"You did the right thing," Raphe said. "Are you certain he went home to rest?"

"He promised he would and I believed him." It was the best assurance she could give.

"Then let us do what we can to solve this problem so he can commence evacuation of the sick as soon as possible," Coventry said.

"I have these advertisements Florian gave me." Juliette placed the cutouts on the table so the men could take a look. "Perhaps they can be of some use?"

"It is a start," Coventry said. "I also have some merchant contacts. I will seek their counsel immediately." He stood, as did Raphe.

"See to the merchants and leave the advertisements with me," Raphe said. "Shall we reconvene here tonight at ten?"

Coventry nodded. He bid Juliette farewell, and Raphe escorted him out before closeting himself away in his study with his secretary.

Anxious for all their efforts to yield results and having nothing to do until they did, Juliette went to retrieve her next reading material from one of the shelves. She would continue her medical studies by delving into Cowper's *Anatomy of Humane Bodies* so she could impress Florian a little bit more the next time they met.

"**H**aving Armswell poisoned was not as efficient as I had hoped," Bartholomew said when he finished counting the bank notes Mr. Smith had printed for him that morning. "It got Lowell involved."

"Yes. That is an unfortunate turn of events, but at least he's chasing the wrong lead."

Bartholomew knew this. It was the maid Claire had taken on six months earlier who'd carried out his command, not the footman Lowell had had arrested. He was just a convenient scapegoat.

"Nevertheless, I'd like to make sure he doesn't discover this fact."

Mr. Smith nodded. "What do you propose?"

Leaning back in his chair, Bartholomew reached for a cigar, clipped off the end and lit it. He set it to his lips and inhaled deeply. Puffing out a ribbon of smoke, he considered his options. "Lowell has to go." He contemplated the best way to make this happen efficiently and discreetly. An idea emerged, stretching his mouth into a wide smile. "Find out who the best shot is among the peerage and make sure the man knows that Lowell is tupping his wife."

Chapter 17

Juliette knew the moment Florian arrived at the Stokes Ball because of the pompous announcement made by the majordomo. She hadn't seen him in almost a week, during which his life had changed forever. He was officially a duke now, and as such it took him an eternity to reach her, Gabriella and Raphe, even though they weren't standing far from the entrance.

"Your Grace," Raphe said by way of greeting.

Florian visibly flinched. "Please refrain from formalities, Huntley. If my friends stop addressing me in the manner to which I have grown accustomed, I truly believe I might hang myself."

Raphe nodded. "Understood. It goes without saying that my family and I would like to convey our condolences on the loss of your uncle."

"Thank you." Heartache marred Florian's features before he managed to rein in the emotion and bury it deep beneath his unflappable façade. "Thank you for helping me procure a ship, Huntley. Because of you, your sister and Coventry, we were able to quarantine everyone showing symptoms of typhus."

"I'm glad it suits your needs," Raphe said.

Florian nodded. "We had it readied three days ago and the patients brought onboard. They raised anchor this afternoon and ought to have reached the Channel by now."

"How expedient." It was all Juliette could think to say, considering the speed with which the solution had been implemented now that he also had funeral arrangements to make. In fact, it surprised her he was here instead of observing the customary three months of mourning the loss of an uncle usually required. But knowing he thought himself a physician first and keeping in mind his dedication to his profession, he must have decided he had no time for such consideration at present.

Alerted by her comment, he gave her his full attention. "I always strive to make the most of my time." The edge of his mouth rose. "With that in mind, I do believe I owe you a waltz, my lady. Unless someone else has already claimed it."

A flash of heat crept over Juliette's face, so she deliberately broke eye contact with the pretense of searching her reticule for her dance card. "We have only recently arrived so the waltz is still available." Retrieving the card, she held it toward him.

He took it from her, studied it closely and handed it back, the tips of his fingers brushing hers so swiftly and yet so completely it sent a fleet of shivers sailing down her spine.

"Did your sister mention her idea to create a steady revenue for St. Agatha's?" Florian asked Raphe, the calmness of his voice conveying not a single iota of what Juliette had just felt in response to his touch.

She envied him the ability to remain so collected.

Judging from his demeanor right now, it looked as though her effect on him was on par with how a single star might affect the cosmos—without particular notice.

So she pulled back her shoulders and decided to exude a similar degree of placidity. "I wanted to wait until I came up with a feasible solution."

"Maybe you could offer an exclusive service for the wealthy and use the income to fund the hospital," Gabriella said. "Like a luxurious spa-like retreat here in London, so people don't have to go all the way to Bath."

"A spa would require a mineral spring, but I think I see where you're going with this," Florian said. "The business would offer physical relaxation techniques and the client would leave with a sense of rejuvenation."

"It would require a good location," Juliette said, "and that will not come cheap."

"No, but I can afford to make such an investment now and I think it might be worth it." Florian's eyes shone with excitement. "The Swedes have recently developed a system of basic hand strokes intended to soothe the muscles and the Chinese have been applying finger pressure to relieve aching body parts for centuries. It's not entirely dissimilar from what you . . . um"—he caught Juliette's gaze—"suggested I try on that patient of mine with the pain in his shoulders . . ." He coughed, broke eye contact while Juliette's cheeks ignited, and quickly said, "We could also offer private saunas for the gentlemen and facial scrubs for the ladies."

"Why can't the ladies have saunas as well?" Gabriella asked.

Florian blinked. "Well, I suppose they can. The possibilities are endless really."

"There could even be a shop offering scented oils and soaps," Juliette suggested.

"Certainly," Florian said. "Ah! I believe that is our set starting." He offered Juliette his arm. "Shall we?"

Excusing herself to Raphe and Gabriella, Juliette allowed Florian to escort her out onto the dance floor where they took up positions across from each other. His eyes met hers, the blueness of his gaze reminiscent of a cloudless sky on a hot summer's day.

The music started and he pulled her into his arms. Her hand found his on a rush of wild embers, reminding her of the intimacy of his touch. It stole her breath, his fingers sliding gently across her back in ways that could not be accidental or innocent. And it occurred to her then that he craved the same closeness as she, even as he fought to prevent it.

"You are dancing a great deal these days, for a man who insists on disliking the activity," she managed to say after growing accustomed to the feeling of a thousand feathers tickling her insides. Something had to be said if she was to maintain her sanity.

"Only with you, in case you hadn't noticed."

Of course she had and of course the notion delighted her to no end, even though it would lead them nowhere. "Others might as well. If you are not careful, my brother might expect you to offer for my hand."

"You forget that I am a duke as well now. Your brother cannot insist on such a thing unless I were to compromise you. In which case I would naturally do the honorable thing."

He spun her around in a wide circle and Juliette

tried not to let his words hurt her. But it wasn't easy when he'd all but told her he'd only ever consider marrying her if circumstance forced him to do so. She would become his obligation, which was hardly something to aspire toward. So she raised her gaze to his and said, "You need not worry about such a thing occurring, Florian, for I shall do my utmost to prevent it."

Had she not spent as much time in his company as she had in recent weeks, she would most likely have missed his response to that statement. It was subtle, but it was there, the slightest tic at the edge of his mouth accompanied by the momentary tightening of his fingers against her hand.

Well good! It was high time the man felt a bit of the frustration shadowing her these days. She would have welcomed a courtship from him before they started working together. Now, after getting to know him better, nothing in the world would thrill her more than the prospect of one day marrying this man. He was clever and honorable. He knew what his priorities were and which of his duties came first. He would not permit any person to perish if he stood a chance of saving their lives. But beyond that, he was a serious man, alienated by his profession and confined to what Juliette suspected must be a lonely existence with only his work as his constant companion.

She wondered if he even realized what he was missing. It wasn't so different from what she'd been missing herself for most of her life. She'd had her siblings just as Florian had his family and colleagues, but she'd never felt as though she belonged with someone the way she knew she belonged with him or as though her heart might break if he chose to marry someone else. It was as if he'd reached inside her chest and jolted her heart into motion. And if he feared the increased closeness between them as much as he'd suggested, then it could only mean that he felt precisely the same. Which made his standoffishness all the more curious.

"Would you like a refreshment?"

The dance had apparently ended without her noticing, she'd been so caught up in her ponderings. "No." She glanced around at the thronging crowd. "I would rather get some fresh air."

"Then allow me to escort you." He led her toward a set of doors that opened onto a terrace. As they went, whispered words and stares followed, alerting Juliette to Florian's increased eligibility. He was a duke now, the only one available for marriage, and there was no shortage of women making him the subject of their assessment.

What a fine-looking man.
Have you ever seen such remarkable hair?
There is nothing more intriguing than a surgeon turned duke.
He has the handsomest bearing to grace the English isles in decades.

Juliette stifled the laughter that threatened to bubble up into a sputtering outburst. Handsome bearing? Such imaginative use of adjectives could only be attributed to his recent rise in aristocratic power.

Glancing up at the man in question as he guided her away from the whispered appraisals, she caught a troubled look in the corner of his eyes. "What is it?"

she asked while a breeze licked a cool path around her shoulders.

"Hmm?" He did not stop his progress as she had expected but kept on walking, taking her past the people who hovered in clusters and onward toward a fountain in the center of the garden.

"You looked worried just now." Instinctively, she glanced over her shoulder to see how many people had noticed he was taking her off to a private location. For a man who'd just told her he had no intention of compromising her reputation, he certainly had a funny way of showing it.

"It is nothing."

She blew out a breath and decided she wouldn't accept that answer. "I disagree. Not when you are trying to flee the ballroom as fast as possible."

"You are the one who requested fresh air."

"Which could easily be found on the terrace. Instead, you are pulling me along at a pace that is difficult for me to keep up with in my current state of dress. I cannot simply hike up my evening gown and lengthen my stride, Florian."

He slowed down immediately. "I am sorry, Juliette, I just had to get away from those people and all their jabbering."

"You heard that, did you?"

He cut her a look as if to say he'd have had to be deaf not to. "This is precisely what I wanted to avoid. Being the center of attention has never agreed with me, but now it has become an unavoidable hazard of my title."

Juliette sympathized, and yet, "It could be worse, you know. They could be sneering at you behind your back on account of your questionable background."

He released her so abruptly she almost fell into the nearby rosebushes. "What do you mean?" Shadows played across his features, evoking an image reminiscent of Pan or some other mysterious forest creature lurching about in the darkness.

His voice was hushed, the sharpness dulled by the gurgling water of the nearby fountain. And yet, the alertness with which he questioned her was telling. It suggested misunderstanding on his part, as if he suspected her of asking something she wasn't, though what that might be she honestly had no idea.

"When my siblings and I arrived in Mayfair, carving out a place for ourselves and gaining respect took time." This clarification seemed to calm Florian. His shoulders sagged beneath the weight of his black evening jacket. "There are still those who judge us harshly, who consider us social upstarts and imposters. It took time to learn to ignore them. Thankfully, we have more friends than foes these days, for which we are all incredibly grateful. Though none of us have ever been accompanied by as many compliments as you were just now."

"You must think me ungrateful."

He'd released her arm, leaving her feeling bereft, and was now strolling ahead of her at a casual gait. In spite of not wanting to risk getting compromised and married off to a man who did not want her, Juliette followed him as easily as Psyche would have followed her Cupid.

"Not at all." The torchlight dimmed as they approached the far corners of the garden. Deliberately, Juliette kept close to a group of trees in the hope of concealing herself if anyone happened to look their way and wonder about the two silhouettes straying from the rest of the party. "It is a sudden change for you, just as it was for me, and it will take time for you to adjust. That is all."

"Unfortunately there is so much more to it than that." He stopped and turned toward her with an abruptness that put them but an inch apart. And somehow, as with their previous encounter in a similar garden, his hand held her upper arm as if ready to either push her away or pull her toward him.

Juliette held her breath and waited while wishing against her better judgment that he would choose to do the latter.

It was dark. None of the torches lighting the garden reached the corner in which they stood; Juliette with her back against a tree and he with his hand wrapped gently around her arm. He wasn't sure how it had happened, only that it had. And he had no desire to release his hold on her but rather to savor the blessed intimacy of it.

She was close, so close he could smell the enticing scent of peonies, hear every breath she took and sense the rapid beat of her pulse which surely kept pace with his own. Damned if she wasn't the loveliest creature on earth and he wasn't tempted to take every liberty she would permit. But the consequences, ah, those blasted consequences always ruined the moment.

"I fear for your safety, Juliette." Whoever was responsible for the threats he'd been receiving, Florian would not permit the villain to use his fondness for Juliette as leverage. Or worse. The thought of anyone causing her bodily harm was enough to make him keep his distance even if scandal and his own tarnished entry into this world somehow failed. No matter what, he had to protect her.

Of course, she misunderstood his meaning entirely. "As you should." She leaned back as if seeking escape, yet the hitch in her breathing suggested a longing for more. "I cannot answer for what might happen between us if you do not walk away."

Christ, she was glorious! A tempting siren ready to lead him astray without any effort to pretend otherwise. Her admission stirred his blood to no end. It drew him to her so he was leaning in, his one hand still on her arm, the other one now at her waist.

"As regrettable as it is, you are a risk I cannot permit." He spoke the discouraging words even as he allowed his index finger to draw a line up the length of her torso. He did it with slow deliberation, reveling in the tiny little gasps she emitted when he finally reached the edge of her décolletage and, more daringly than he'd intended, stroked his way along it. "A treat I cannot savor." Flattening his entire hand across the lovely expanse of her breasts, he pressed himself into her warmth. A shudder rolled through her and then she arched, her hips seeking purchase while her breathing turned more ragged.

"Florian."

Damn him for letting himself encourage her needs. And damn him for loving the fervor with which she yearned for his touch. Somehow, he would have to put an end to this before they were found or before he did something foolish like strip her bare right here, right now and take her with every carnal need he possessed.

But first, he had to take something with him— something to treasure in the lonely nights that loomed before him. "Yes, Juliette. What do you want?"

"Everything," she sighed on parted lips that beckoned while reassuring him of her desire.

It quickened his pulse even as he pulled away, adding distance by stepping back and leaving her there, alone and without his reciprocation. But to tell her he felt the same would threaten his already thin control. "I am sorry." The incomprehension filling her eyes was more than understandable. And since he could offer her nothing else besides that pathetic apology, he turned away and headed for home while damning himself to the hell where he surely belonged.

"This evening's social function has offered some information that will be of great interest to you," Mr. Smith told Bartholomew. "Your spy has uncovered a weakness."

Sitting up straighter, Bartholomew angled his head and gestured for Smith to step closer. "Leave us," he told the woman who'd been licking her way up the length of thigh protruding from the opening in his robe. Reaching for his brandy, he asked her to wait for him upstairs in his bedchamber. "Pick a toy," he drawled, "and we'll have some fun." He watched her departure while sipping his drink. Once out of sight, he gave Smith his full attention. "You were saying?"

The servant smirked, which was always a good sign. "There is a lady whom your son seems to favor."

Bartholomew shifted, drawing his robe more tightly around himself. "Enough for a threat on her life to matter?"

"Possibly." Smith nodded pensively. "From what I gather he was spotted in a rather intimate embrace with her, though he made no actual attempt at seduction."

"Which would suggest he either fears attachment or cares about her too much to compromise her at a social event." Bartholomew's interest increased. "Who is this woman?"

"The lady's name is Juliette Matthews. She is the Duke of Huntley's youngest sister."

Bartholomew slowly lowered his glass and stared at Smith. "Isn't Huntley the fighter who leveled the Bull last year?"

In hindsight, the match had been a foolish undertaking, considering all the variables. But the Bull had been a champion and Bartholomew had been so damned certain of his success. Who knew that a duke would step up into the ring and best a man twice his size? Nobody could have predicted such an outcome, except for Guthrie, of course. He'd humiliated Bartholomew that day, forcing him to resort to other means by which to encroach on St. Giles. Securing the house that stood on the edge of it would have been a solid start, but then his own bloody son had interfered and the rest of his plans had gone to hell.

"The very same," Mr. Smith confirmed.

This was even better than Bartholomew could have hoped. "Then perhaps we'll kill two birds with one stone by targeting her." He hadn't intended to seek revenge on Huntley, but why the hell not? "Let's wait awhile and see how things develop. In the meantime, have Lady Juliette placed under constant surveillance. The more we know about Florian's love interest, the better."

"I couldn't agree more." Mr. Smith hesitated, shifted slightly and appeared to consider. Then, "What shall we do with Mr. Blaire?" he asked in reference to one of Florian's chief physicians.

The man had been tasked with checking on the quarantine ship, but Mr. Smith had intercepted Blaire's carriage en route to Brighton and offered him a better job as Bartholomew's private physician.

"Nothing, at the moment," Bartholomew said, in answer to Mr. Smith's question.

Mr. Smith arched an eyebrow. "What if he talks? It won't take long for Florian to figure out who you really are."

"Oh, I'm counting on it." Bartholomew chuckled. "I cannot wait to see the look on his face when he realizes I've destroyed his life."

Mr. Smith nodded. "I can understand that." He tilted his head. "Speaking of ruining his life, you'll be pleased to know that I've found the perfect adversary for Lowell." He pulled on the sleeve of his jacket and straightened his shirt cuff.

"Oh?"

"The Earl of Elmwood is reported to be a crack shot. He also has a very pretty wife who's twenty years his junior." Mr. Smith smiled. "From what I've been able to discover, Elmwood won't let her dance with anyone but him because he fears she might be led astray by a scoundrel."

Bartholomew grinned. "His insecurities will serve us well, Mr. Smith. Elmwood sounds like the sort of man who will reach for his pistol first and ask questions later. Which is precisely what we need."

Chapter 18

Seeing Florian again wasn't something Juliette looked forward to. Not after he'd left her in a state of utter bewilderment the previous evening. He'd been about to kiss her. She knew it deep in her bones. And yet the exasperating man had denied them both that moment of pleasure. Because he couldn't, or wouldn't, or whatever his unacceptable excuse had been at the time. She could not recall his exact words on account of the flustered state she'd been in. As it was, it had taken her a good fifteen minutes or more to gather her wits and return to the ballroom and a very impatient dance partner whom she'd forgotten about in the process.

But, when word arrived from Raphe, informing her that Amelia was having her baby, Juliette grabbed her reticule and hastened out into the street with the intention of finding a hackney, only to be met by Florian's carriage. "What are you doing here?" she asked as he leapt to the ground and made a quick bow. "Shouldn't you be at Coventry House?"

"I'm on my way over there now, but your home was en route, so I thought I'd make sure that you and your family were made aware of your sister's condition."

"Raphe and Gabriella are already there. They went for tea."

"Right . . . well . . ." Florian glanced back over his shoulder. "In that case, you can come with me." He stepped aside and offered his hand to help her up.

Juliette hesitated. "I should probably ask my maid to join us." Occupying a hired hackney alone was one thing, but sharing a carriage with an unmarried gentleman was quite another.

"I'm sorry, but I can't afford to wait. And besides, there'll be no harm to your reputation as long as the windows remain uncovered so people can see us."

Assured by his comment and propelled into action by the urgency of the situation, Juliette stepped forward and placed her hand in his. Her heart immediately leapt and her skin began to tingle. Since ignoring it was no longer possible, she accepted her body's response to his presence and climbed into the conveyance.

"About last night . . ." Florian began as soon as they'd taken off. He sat across from her, not touching her at all, yet he could still prompt flames to lick their way along her limbs with nothing more than a glance.

Juliette expelled a breath. The man had apparently no intention of leaving her in peace. "Must we discuss it?"

"I think we ought to. You see, as a gentleman, I would like to convey my sincerest apologies for the way in which I treated you. It was disrespectful and . . ." He paused while Juliette squeezed her eyes shut. His voice deepened as he continued, heightening her awareness. "You drive me to the brink of madness, Juliette. Your beauty, your boldness, your courage and your kindness . . ." His hand caught hers and she opened her eyes to the face of desire. "You encourage me to lose all reason."

She stared at him in disbelief. "Am I to blame for the manner in which you led me into the darkness then? For the way in which you chose to touch me? For pressing your body up against mine and forcing me to confess my most intimate thought?"

"I beg your pardon, I truly do." He released her hand and leaned back. At least he had the decency to look thoroughly chastised, which was a rare departure from his usual poise. And then his expression filled with regret. "Abstaining from you has proven a chore. You cannot possibly imagine how much I want you. To walk away from you every time there is an opportunity for more between us is no simple feat. On the contrary, it is torturous to say the least."

As angry and hurt as she was by his stupid denial of what they could share, she sympathized with his plight. Which made her ask, as his friend, rather than the woman who wanted him with every fiber of her being, "Why won't you let me help you? If you confide in me, perhaps together we can destroy the obstacle in your path."

He huffed out a tired breath. "You are sweetness itself, Juliette, and I am fortunate to have won the admiration of a woman such as yourself. Which is precisely why I cannot possibly share my reasons for why we cannot be together. Because your opinion of me is too important. I will not risk it."

It was as if a part of Juliette's heart died in that

moment, for he spoke with more conviction than she'd ever heard before—the sort that would brook no argument. "So then there is no hope for us at all?"

"No."

"And you will give me no acceptable explanation."

"Suffice it to say that you deserve better."

Crossing her arms, Juliette clenched her jaw and glared at him. "You are insufferable. Do you know that?" When all he did was raise a brow, she went on, bolstered by the pain he'd caused by denying her the future she wanted. "How dare you decide such a thing without consulting me? I will be the judge of what I deserve, not you or the fear that prevents you from sharing the truth." She was suddenly unbelievably furious. "If anyone ought to deserve better, it is you! You are educated, well-traveled, respected, and now a duke! For heaven's sake, Florian. I am nothing more than a viscount's grandchild, the daughter of a woman who abandoned her family and a man who killed himself for it. I may be the sister of a duke, but I have spent the majority of my life in the slums. Putting fine clothes on me and teaching me manners is never going to change any of that and yet you're the one who worries I might be too good for you! Are you completely cracked in the head or have you lost your mental faculties by some other means?"

Florian was actually gaping at her now as if she'd just escaped Bedlam. Eventually, he closed his mouth, shook his head and said, "I know it seems unreasonable, but you must trust me in this. There are things you do not know about me that you would surely find distasteful."

"Such as?" When he failed to respond she asked, "Are you a highway robber by night?"

He shook his head. "Don't be ridiculous."

She ignored his comment. "Have you committed a heinous crime?"

"Of course not. Juliette, this questioning will lead us nowhere."

"It will allow me to ascertain the extent of your supposed unworthiness. So tell me, what is it?" An awful thought struck her. "Is it the French disease?"

He looked as though he might choke and promptly proceeded to cough. "How the devil would you know about something like that?" The question was swiftly followed with an apology for the expletive which Juliette waved away without much thought.

"Raphe mentioned it once or twice after hearing of someone who contracted it." She felt oddly smug about having surprised the good surgeon so thoroughly he'd actually lost his composure. "If this is what ails you, your reluctance to marry begins to make sense."

"I do not have syphilis," he clipped. "Practically speaking, I am in perfect health."

"Hmm . . ."

He stared at her. "You don't believe me?"

"I might if you were to kiss me."

Crossing his legs, Florian pulled his bag onto his lap and met her gaze. Undeniable heat loomed there, the fire stoked inside him by that simple statement as blatant as her own. It sparked and sizzled in the air between them until the carriage drew to an unfortunate stop, signaling their arrival.

"I will not kiss you," he murmured as he opened the door and alit so he could help her down.

Juliette clasped the hand he offered and stepped

down onto the pavement with a smile. "We shall see," she told him slyly.

Whatever his demons might be, she suspected they weren't as difficult to slay as he believed. All she had to do was find the obstacle in Florian's way and destroy it.

Chapter 19

Picking up the nearby rattle, Juliette shook it gently above Peter's face. The baby, snuggly nestled in her arms, chortled and waved his arms with amusement. It was two days since he'd been born and both he and his mother appeared to be thriving. As for Florian . . . Juliette tried to force all thought of him from her mind. She hadn't seen him since the birth, deliberately allowing him the space she'd suspected he needed after their discussion.

Frankly, she still wasn't sure what had possessed her to be so outspoken toward him, but it had been necessary. She'd wanted to clear the air and give voice to all her frustration. Bringing up the French disease had been a bit much, but her tongue had gotten away from her, and so, here they were.

She set the rattle aside and offered Peter her finger, which he happily clutched in his tiny hand. "He's so strong."

"And handsome," Amelia said with a smile. Sitting beside her, she sipped her tea while watching her sister and her son form a bond. "I cannot wait to meet *your* children one day."

The honesty resonating from Amelia's voice produced a lump in Juliette's throat. Her eyes were suddenly stinging and she was having difficulty drawing breath. "If I will ever be so lucky." She forced the maudlin mood aside since it had no place here in this room. Instead, she managed a smile while adding sincerity to her voice. "To marry a man who loves you and bear his children is truly a blessing."

"Such a man exists for you as well, Juliette. You only have to open your heart to him and he will have no choice but to love you."

A bitter bit of laughter stole past Juliette's lips before she could stop it. "I would like to think so."

Amelia reached for her son, pulling the baby into her arms so she could place a tender kiss upon his forehead. "Florian could be that man." Her voice was quiet, crooning even and so contradictory to the point she raised.

"Perhaps," Juliette agreed. If she could convince him. "Perhaps not. It is a complicated situation."

Amelia chuckled. "People will invariably make a mess of their emotions when in truth, love is a simple thing. You either feel it or you don't. But if you do . . . well, I am of the opinion that it is worth fighting for."

Juliette could not deny sharing that sentiment. But Florian would not be an easy man to convince. Talking to him and attempting to reason with him had yielded no results thus far. But something else had . . . something Juliette might be wise to use to her advantage. Because if there was one thing he seemed to have trouble resisting, it was her closeness. She tempted him. He'd confessed as much. So if she truly wanted to win him, she might have to speak to his desire instead of to his brain.

After helping the Duchess of Coventry deliver her son, Florian had left her and the rest of her family to marvel over the newborn baby. Returning to St. Agatha's, he'd resolved to keep his distance from Lady Juliette by avoiding all social events in the coming weeks and focusing on his work.

"Did the footman you questioned yield any results?" he asked Henry when he came to call two days later.

"None," Henry said with a downcast expression. "I'm starting to think he's innocent."

"Then we'll need to look at the other servants," Florian said.

"There's something else." Lowell pushed his hands into his pockets. "Elmwood has called me out."

"What!" Florian stared at his brother.

"He thinks I'm bedding his wife."

"Jesus!" Although he knew Henry had better sense, he still had to ask, "You're not, are you?"

"Of course not, but good luck convincing Elmwood of that. He demands satisfaction."

"You could apologize," Florian suggested.

"That would imply I'm guilty, which I'm not."

Fair point. Florian tapped his fingers on his desk and considered his brother. "When are you supposed to meet?"

Henry sighed. "I'm not sure. Apparently Elmwood has left London on business. He didn't say when he'd be back, but he insisted I be ready."

"Good. That gives us some time to get to the bottom of this—find out who started the rumor and put an end to it."

"Do you think it has something to do with the threats

against you?" When Florian didn't reply, Henry said, "I thought perhaps the person behind it might have learned of my investigation into Armswell's poisoning and forged a plan to remove me from the picture."

"Well, if that's true, then it means we're following the right lead by questioning Armswell's footman."

Henry nodded and stood. "I know you have a lot of other things on your mind besides all of this, so I'll head over to Armswell House and take a closer look at the rest of the servants."

"What about your club?"

Henry paused in the doorway. "It doesn't open for another couple of hours, so I have time."

As soon as he'd gone, Florian wondered if he ought to tell his brother about the resemblance between Mr. Mortedge and Bartholomew. He shook his head. The more he thought about it, the more absurd it seemed. Perhaps the similarities he'd observed at the Hawthorne Ball had simply been the result of too much champagne. But if that was the case, Florian couldn't for the life of him understand the threats. He had no other enemies that he knew of, so it made no sense.

A knock at the door brought a nurse into the room. "This just arrived for you," she said, handing him a letter and departing once more.

Florian tore open the seal and read the missive.

Blaire never arrived. We're in dire need of help. Please come quickly.

Haines

Florian's nerves twisted into a riotous mess as in-comprehension took hold. It was followed by anger and a jarring need for answers. Pushing himself to his feet, he snatched up his jacket and shoved his arms into the sleeves. If Mr. Blaire, the physician who'd been tasked with reporting updates from the quarantine ship, had betrayed him, the man would have to pay.

"He's not here," Mr. Blaire's manservant told Florian half an hour later. "He and his wife have gone out for the evening."

"Where to?" Florian asked, aiming for a sense of calm he did not feel in the slightest.

"The King's Theatre."

Thanking the man, Florian rushed back to his waiting carriage and gave the driver directions before climbing in. The carriage lurched and began rolling forward. Staring out at the starting rain, Florian tried to think of one single way in which Blaire's actions might be acceptable. And failed. The physician had turned his back on his duty without bothering to inform anyone, which was unforgiveable.

When the carriage pulled to a halt minutes later, Florian leapt from the conveyance and entered the theater. Without breaking his stride he marched across the foyer and took the steps two at a time. He was furious—absolutely livid—so much so he feared the blood vessels next to his eye might pop if he did not calm himself soon. But doing so was going to be damnably difficult. So he hastened onward until he found the box he sought and tore open the door without knocking. The second half of *The Marriage of Figaro* was already underway, the soprano and baritone of the singers rising and falling in waves.

Not pausing to listen, Florian bent close to Mr. Blaire's ear and spoke with the chilling venom he felt in his veins. "Where have you been?"

The man did not even deign to look him in the eye, his attention fixed on the stage below. "Out of town."

"Where?"

Blaire's wife, who sat beside him, served Florian a disgruntled look. He tilted his head in her direction and swiftly apologized for the intrusion before returning his attention to one of the best physicians in St. Agatha's employ. "Well? You were supposed to check on the ship and did not do so. I just received a letter from Haines postmarked three days ago. In it, he asks for assistance that should have arrived if you had been doing your job."

Blaire's face turned a brilliant shade of red. "It comes down to money, Florian. Mr. Mortedge offered me the sort of salary a man like me cannot walk away from."

Florian's head began to spin. He'd been wrong to doubt his instincts. Mortedge *was* Bartholomew. He had to be, because no one else would go to such lengths to ruin Florian's plans for St. Giles.

"And you didn't think to tell me?"

Blaire frowned. "It happened so fast I barely had enough time to pack. Mortedge needed me to accompany him on a business trip. He suffers from terrible pain because of his gout."

For a second, the idea of reaching out and strangling the man presented itself until Florian managed the resist the urge. "People have probably died because of you," he hissed.

"I'm sorry," Blaire muttered.

"The devil you are," Florian clipped.

Straightening, he glanced out over the crowded theater, his gaze drawn directly toward a spot on the far side where Lady Juliette sat staring back at him. He deliberately held her gaze, allowing her presence to bolster his strength before telling Blair, "I hope I never have to speak with you again."

The insufferable man muttered something which Florian did not wait to hear.

Instead, he exited the box as swiftly as he had entered it and made his way along the hallway and toward the stairs. Heart hammering on account of his rage, not only with Blaire and Bartholomew, but with himself for not realizing sooner this had happened, he clicked his heels angrily against the marble floor as he went. Christ, what a fool he was to entrust such a vital task to another. And Haines . . . What the hell would he say to him when next he saw him? No apology was good enough to suffice.

"Florian!"

He almost turned on his heel with the intention of fleeing in the opposite direction the moment he saw her. Dressed in a golden gown and with her hair loosely fastened at the nape of her neck, Juliette looked like a dream. Which was not a good thing at all if he was going to continue resisting her charms.

"What is it?" His tone was harsher than he'd intended, brought on by his anger and his increasing need for her.

Slowing her pace, she approached him more hesitantly. "I saw you arguing with someone and came to see if you were all right. You look extremely distraught, Florian."

He gritted his teeth and glanced around. The hallway was empty, so they could speak privately, but he feared the moment someone appeared and spotted them there together without a chaperone. "You should not be here, Juliette. Your reputation is at stake."

When she stubbornly remained where she was, he caught her by the hand and urged her toward an alcove where sofas provided theatergoers with a comfortable place to relax during intermission. Entering ahead of Juliette, Florian ensured the space was empty before pulling her inside and away from the immediate gaze of anyone who happened to go in search of the retiring room.

Once inside, Florian released her hand and gestured toward the sofa. "Would you like to sit?"

"Not especially." Her eyes were wide with unappeased curiosity. "Will you tell me what happened?"

Florian puffed out a breath. "The man with whom you saw me speaking is Mr. Blaire."

"The physician you charged with checking up on the quarantine ship."

"Yes." He felt all the muscles in his face contract with displeasure. "Except he did no such thing. Instead, he went to work for someone else. I received a letter from Haines earlier this evening, informing me of Blaire's absence, except several days have already passed since he sent it, which means any number of things could have happened by now."

"Good Lord!" Juliette's concern was visible. "He asked for help, didn't he?"

"He did indeed, except none has been provided." Conscious of the failure for which he was responsible, Florian pushed his hand through his hair, scattering his locks while accommodating himself to the situation at hand. "I have to go to him at once."

"But—"

"No, Juliette, you will not try to dissuade me from this."

"I wasn't going to try. I was merely going to point out the late hour and suggest you leave in the morning instead."

"As wise as that might be, I am reluctant to do so when Haines may be in dire need of assistance. Making haste is the only reasonable course of action. If I leave now, I ought to arrive there by dawn and save a day in the process."

Understanding filled Juliette's eyes, bringing out the green in them. "You are a good man, Florian. Your patients are lucky to have your commitment." She glanced away for a second before meeting his gaze once more. "I shall worry about you endlessly, however, until you return home safely."

The confession was the closest she had ever come to admitting an emotional attachment to him, and the knowledge that she cared for him deeply enough to concern herself about his well-being was touching. It filled his heart with warmth and something foreign he could not define.

"You needn't." It was all he could think to say in response to the strange discomfort her words had evoked. Because alongside the gratification of knowing she was fond of him, he worried where such feelings might lead. "As you already know, I ought to be immune."

"*Ought to be* does not reassure me." Her expression had gone from calm to panicked. "If there is any chance you could get infected, then . . ." She dropped her gaze and turned her shoulder toward him.

"You were going to suggest I not go?" The concern she was expressing, the angst and the visible pain, made it impossible for him not to reach out and touch her. His hand settled gently upon her shoulder, startling her enough for her to look up at him with watery eyes that undid him in a heartbeat.

Without considering consequence, he drew her

into his arms and held her. His face pressed softly against the top of her head so the slightest movement she made caused her hair to tickle his nose. It smelled as though freshly washed with chamomile soap, the herbal scent mingling with her signature peony perfume. The concoction was potent yet calming and so very her.

"To do so would be futile," she murmured against his chest. "I know this and yet I still wish you did not have to be the one tasked with putting your life at risk."

Her honesty was humbling. If only he could be equally honest with her. But the fear of what Bartholomew might decide to do, the threat he posed to her safety, held him back. "While I can offer you no guarantees, I do believe I would have contracted typhus by now if I wasn't immune. My close contact with the sick people of St. Giles while examining and treating them prior to their evacuation should have ensured it."

She relaxed against him as he spoke, which meant he'd had the calming effect he'd hoped his embrace would evoke. It was time to pull back. Except she still held him tight, as if she dreaded letting him go.

"Juliette?" Unsure of what else to do, he smoothed his hand along her back, reminding himself of her femininity and the extent of his need for her the moment she purred in response.

Damn, but this was not going to end well. Least of all if someone saw them like this. So he lowered his hands to her waist and tried to ease her away, only to have her tilting her head back and looking up. They were close, so close he could see flecks of gold

shimmering in her eyes. Her lips parted and only one
thought echoed through his brain.

For God's sake, lower your mouth and kiss her!

A myriad of overwhelming emotions had assailed
Juliette during the last few minutes. She'd gone from
curiosity, to despair, to insatiable need. The urge to
convey how she felt about Florian, the physician, the
duke, the man, welled up inside her with inescap-
able force. Since seeing him last she'd prepared to do
whatever it took to make him understand how much
easier life would be, if they only allowed their attraction to bloom.

Whether or not he would ever care for her, as
deeply as she cared for him, was uncertain, but she
knew one thing: she'd met and danced with every
eligible bachelor in London and none had provoked
the depth of emotion she felt for Florian. She wanted
him, even if she had to make him surrender to the
ever-present desire glowing in his eyes when they
were together. It was there right now, bright and impossible to ignore even as he did his best to fight the
course she insisted on taking.

"Whatever your doubts," she whispered while
looping her arms securely around his neck, "whatever your reasons for always pushing me away, I
cannot let you go without this." Rising up on her
toes, she prepared to steal the kiss she longed for,
but not without giving him the chance to end things
between them for good. "If you truly want to avoid
this, then now is the time to stop me."

His breath came roughly as he placed one palm
to her cheek and spoke with gruffness. "My

power to do so has fled me, Juliette. You are like the sirens Odysseus feared." Upon which he closed the distance between them and captured her mouth with his.

The feel of his lips against hers was soft and warm, the sensation both unfamiliar and wonderful at once. Relief swept through her, bringing pleasure in its wake. It felt . . . incredible. More so when he pulled her around and away from the entrance to the room, his body maneuvering hers until she was pushed up against the wall. Pressing into her, his hands roved over her shoulders, her arms, her waist and her hips. "Dear God, Juliette." The murmur vibrated through her, provoking a sigh that parted her lips and gave him access.

Shivering tendrils of heat shot through her the moment he deepened the kiss, the sensation so utterly exquisite she had to cling to him for support lest she lose the strength to stand. She was in his power, surrounded by his masculinity and answering to it in ways she would never have thought possible. The yearning to feel his hands all over her body was likely to drive her mad. As was the increasing need for more than what a kiss could offer.

"Yes." She whispered the word when he disengaged from her mouth and kissed his way along the length of her neck. Instructed by instinct, she arched toward him, offering herself to him like a pagan princess on a sacrificial altar of desire.

"You push the bounds of my restraint." The words ghosted across her skin, erased by the heat of another kiss. "The things I would do if we were elsewhere, preferably ensconced behind locked doors."

Her hands clasped at his head, her fingers threading

their way through his hair with the frantic fervor of a woman in whom awareness of carnal pleasure had just been awoken. "Tell me."

Muttering an oath, he met her mouth again with greater insistence. The act drew a wanton moan from deep inside her chest, the intimacy of his uninhibited effort to taste her, encouraging her to squirm against him. Trailing a smoldering path toward her ear, he carefully tugged at her lobe with his teeth, sending a flare of heat all the way to her toes.

"I would worship every inch of you until you would not recall your own name." His hands gripped her hips, holding her to him with firm deliberation. "You play with fire, Juliette. Best stop now lest one of us gets burned."

Before she was able to adapt to what he implied, he'd released her and stepped away, leaving her feeling deprived and horribly unsatisfied.

"I must be off." He spoke the words as if trying to remind himself of what he'd intended to do before she'd distracted him. "Go back to your family, Juliette. Enjoy the rest of the opera."

Gathering some semblance of control over her still-quaking limbs, she quietly asked, "Will you call on me when you return?"

He stared at her for a long hard moment, then said, "It would probably be best if I sent you a note. This . . ." He clenched his jaw and glanced away, and in that moment, Juliette's happiness crumbled in response to the obvious regret he attempted to hide. "We cannot keep letting this happen."

"Of course not." Her words were marred by irritation and unrelenting sarcasm. "Why on earth would we allow ourselves to succumb to mutual desire?"

"Because there is much you do not know," he said with equal amounts of aggravation. "You think I choose to save you from marrying me on account of some silly, pointless reason, no doubt. But I tell you my reasons are real and noble and only intended to keep you safe." He was breathing fast, his hair falling over his forehead in distraught disarray. "If I were someone else, someone better and someone purer, I would ask for your hand in a heartbeat. But to trap you in a union you are bound to regret would be heartless."

"How can you possibly know I would regret it, Florian, and how am I to make an informed decision with regard to my future when you refuse to disclose all the facts?" Reaching out, she placed her hand on his arm. "Confide in me. Please."

His chest rose and fell with agitated movements. "Once I do, there is no taking it back. It could change your impression of me forever, and for that reason, I cannot allow myself to do it."

"Not even if I promise not to judge you?"

He winced and she dropped her hand. "You cannot do so, Juliette. It isn't possible."

Watching all hope slip away between her fingers, she made one last attempt to grasp it. "Of course it is. My affection for you would not allow for anything else."

His eyes met hers with vast degrees of heartache and, worst of all, pity. "If only I could believe that." He bowed before her even as her heart was breaking. "Good evening, my lady."

He was gone before she could wish him a safe journey, the sound of his footsteps fading into the background until only silence remained. She'd gathered her courage and risked both her heart and her pride by telling him how she felt. In return, he'd spurned her for reasons she could not begin to comprehend. All she knew was that it hurt, more than anything else ever had.

Chapter 20

Juliette paced back and forth in the parlor while Gabriella looked on. She was agitated for numerous reasons, the least important one being Florian's response to her declaration of affection and his subsequent departure from London.

"She should have arrived an hour ago," she said in reference to Vivien, who still remained absent. "It is unlike her to break an appointment like this without sending word."

"Calm yourself, Juliette, or you will wear a hole in the carpet." Gabriella poured some tea into Juliette's recently emptied cup. "Come sit with me for a while. I am sure there must be a reasonable explanation."

Like the possibility of Vivien succumbing to any number of accidents on her way over. "Perhaps we should send someone to inquire about her?" Juliette dropped down onto her chair and reached for her tea. It was remarkably soothing.

Gabriella frowned. "You are not the sort to expect the worst without cause, making me wonder if there might not be some other reason for this mood you're in. Especially since I feel it began last night after you returned from the ladies' retiring room at the theater."

Blast her sister-in-law's observational skills. "I banged my toes on a door by accident if you'll recall." At least that was the explanation she'd given for the peevishness she'd exuded upon returning to the Huntley box.

"Because it could not possibly have had anything to do with a run-in with Florian. Could it?"

Stripped of all ability to speak, Juliette simply gaped at Gabriella.

Eventually, the duchess took pity. "I saw him arguing with someone in one of the opposite boxes and when he left, so did you. Meeting him in the hallway would have been inevitable, whether you intended to do so or not."

"Did Raphe notice?" She didn't want her brother to figure out what she'd been up to. If he did, he might encourage a courtship that Florian, at least, would be very opposed to.

"I think you would have known by now if he did. But, you were gone for a very long time, so I do feel I ought to address the issue, delicate as it may be." She watched Juliette with careful consideration before asking, "Did he take liberties with you?"

Giving the carpet her full attention, Juliette shook her head.

"Very well. Allow me to rephrase that. Did you give him leave to do anything that might be construed as scandalous or ruinous?" Juliette's gaze snapped onto Gabriella's, conveying everything her sister-in-law needed to know. "I see."

"Not that it matters. The wretched man does not want me, and since there were no witnesses, no harm was truly done." Except to her heart which remained in ruins.

Gabriella stared at her for a moment and then, to her amazement, she laughed. "I am sorry, Juliette, for I know this is no laughing matter, but either Florian is completely ignorant of his own feelings or determined to ignore them." All traces of humor vanished as she turned completely serious. "Either way, he has been dishonest, for which I shall have to chastise him later. It is obvious to everyone with an ounce of common sense that he is mad about you."

"Perhaps, but not in the way I want him to be."

"In every way, I assure you." Gabriella reached for Juliette's hand. "I have known him most of my life, Juliette, and I have never see him look at another woman the way he looks at you. Rest assured, his feelings for you run deep, which may be why he is so determined to resist your charms. If he is like most men I know, he is likely terrified of the impact you're having on his otherwise orderly life."

It was possible, though Juliette was reluctant to let herself hope. She'd experienced too much disappointment lately to start asking for more.

"Ladies," Pierson said upon entering the room and distracting them from the subject at hand. "The Dowager Duchess of Tremaine has come to call. Shall I tell her that you are at home?"

"By all means, show her in." Gabriella turned to Juliette as soon as Pierson had quit the room. "I believe she must be here to see you more than me. Would you rather I take myself off to another part of the house so you can speak with her in private?"

"Only if she says she would like to address me alone. If not, I see no reason why you should not stay and enjoy the rest of your tea with us."

Viola entered immediately after Juliette had finished whispering to Gabriella. She stood at once and welcomed the young woman into her brother's parlor. "Are you acquainted with my sister-in-law, the Duchess of Huntley?" she asked Viola with a glance toward Gabriella.

"Regrettably not," Viola said. "My lack of participation in social events has prevented me from making anyone's acquaintance. It is a pleasure to meet you, Your Grace."

Gabriella smiled. "Likewise, Your Grace."

Try as she might, Juliette could not refrain from laughing. "Excuse me, but can we not permit ourselves to be less formal? We are friends and family if only recently introduced, and if I am to listen to you two Your Grace-ing each other for the remainder of the afternoon, I will likely succumb to a permanent bout of giggles."

Viola grinned. "I quite agree." She looked at Gabriella. "If you will permit?"

"Of course. Allow me to introduce myself properly. My name is Gabriella Matthews."

"And I am Viola Cartwright."

"A pleasure," Gabriella said. She indicated a nearby armchair. "Please join us for some refreshment."

Thanking her, Viola sank down onto the proffered seat and watched while Gabriella poured the tea. "With Florian away at the moment, I thought I'd stop by and give you an update on how things are going at the hospital." She reached for a biscuit, took a bite and set it aside on her plate. "In addition to purchasing the quarantine ship and stocking it with supplies, the funds you raised have enabled me to hire two new physicians and three nurses, which is especially helpful now that Blaire's no longer with us."

"He wasn't very loyal," Juliette said. "His decision to leave when he did may very well have harmed a great many people in the process."

"Ah." Viola sipped her tea and turned her gray eyes on her. "So you have been apprised of the situation. I was not sure Florian would manage to speak with you before leaving town."

"I believe he did so last night," Gabriella murmured. There was mischief in her gaze accompanied by the knowledge of what had transpired the previous evening at the opera.

Juliette blushed while Viola assessed her with an inquisitive stare. "I see." She paused for a moment, took another sip of her tea, then said, "You need not worry, Juliette. He will be quite all right, I assure you."

Realizing her anxiety must be painted all over her face, Juliette could only ask, "How can you be so certain?"

"Because he is the best physician there is." She paused before asking, "Did he ever tell you how he contracted typhus?"

Thinking back, Juliette realized he hadn't. She shook her head. "No."

Viola paused for a second. "He witnessed the devastation wrought on Napoleon's troops when he invaded Russia, and, in his efforts to save some of those men, Florian caught the disease himself."

"He helped Napoleon's army?" Juliette leaned forward, eager to learn more.

Nodding, Viola continued. "His path crossed with the soldiers when he was on his way back from St. Petersburg in 1812." She paused before adding, "It wasn't possible for him to turn his back on those men, no matter what the political climate was like between Britain and France at the time."

"He did a brave thing, risking his own life like that," Gabriella said.

Juliette couldn't speak. She knew he'd risked a lot more than that—the possibility of being labeled a traitor if it became publicly known that he'd helped the enemy. She wondered if this was what he was keeping from her, if this was what he feared would alter her good opinion of him.

If it was, then he was wrong.

"Turning his back on those in need is not in his nature," Viola said. "No matter the circumstance."

Juliette knew this. It was in fact one of the reasons why she thought so highly of him. His selfless dedication to others was most impressive and worthy of everyone's admiration. "I only wish it did not have to be him."

"Because you care for him." It was a blatant statement spoken with the utmost certainty.

"Does everyone know?" Juliette asked, directing her question to both Gabriella and Viola.

Gabriella grinned. "It is rather obvious."

A moment of silence passed between them and then Viola quietly spoke once more. "You would be good for him, I think. There is no one more deserving of happiness or love than Florian." Juliette blushed and Viola cleared her throat as if to cover the awkwardness just as Pierson returned to the room, carrying a letter on a silver salver.

"This has arrived." He handed it to Juliette, who tore it open the moment she saw who had sent it. Her eyes scanned the page. "It is from Miss Saunders's aunt. Apparently Vivien has caught a chill, which explains her reason for missing our meeting this morning. Her aunt believes she ought to be well in another couple of days, provided she gets enough rest."

"Oh dear. Poor Miss Saunders." Gabriella's brow knit with concern. "Perhaps you ought to send a care basket her way? She and her aunt are not in the best financial state, so I am sure some good food, tea and honey would be welcome."

"That is an excellent idea," Juliette agreed. She would deliver the basket herself so she could check on her friend and maybe offer her help.

Rolling up his sleeves, Florian plunged his mop into a pail of vinegar solution and spread it across the deck, drenching the wood planking. The air, heavy with the putrid stench of human suffering, had also been filled with the pungent smell of tar water fumigating the air. Around him, stretched out on cots, were the people who continued their fight for survival, two of the five nurses who'd been brought onboard to care for them, and Haines.

The physician had been tending to patients when Florian had arrived, the poor man barely keeping himself upright while he coughed and sputtered his way around. A sheen of sweat had been visible upon his brow, his eyes red from exhaustion and fever. Florian had promptly thanked the man for his commitment and then ordered him to get some rest and focus on his own recuperation.

Sloshing more of the vinegar solution onto the floor, Florian cursed Blaire again and then chastised himself for not taking Haines's place. But the man had told him he'd had the disease as a child so

Florian had thought him immune. Unless of course Haines was wrong and he hadn't had typhus at all but some other ailment instead, like measles. Both produced similar rashes and could be confused with each other if the physician diagnosing the illness lacked competence.

In any case, there was no denying the gravity of the situation currently facing everyone onboard this ship. With only himself and two nurses to care for the sick, they lacked the necessary workforce, which could potentially lead to worsening conditions. As it was, Florian had been horrified to find lice present in some of the bedding. He'd promptly demanded that every scrap of fabric recently used be boiled in hot water and replaced by fresh ones. This had required the undressing of the thirty people who remained onboard, rubbing them down with mercurial ointment and providing them each with clean gowns and clothing—something which had not been done in days.

"I am sorry," Haines told him as Florian passed by his cot. "The infection progressed so fast I"—he coughed—"could not keep up. My negligence—"

"You are not at fault here," Florian told him sternly. It was difficult for him to hide all the anger he felt, all the fear for these people now under his care. "Blaire was meant to offer support. He is to blame for what has happened. Not you."

Haines closed his tired eyes on a groan. "What will you do?"

"Whatever I must." Florian glanced toward the deck where one of the nurses was hanging the recently washed clothing to dry. "Right now I am going to finish cleaning the floor, and then I intend to prepare some food. Soup will do everyone good, I should think."

Haines's only response was a sigh and a nod. He turned his head away as if preparing to sleep, so Florian left him in order to see to his chores. Twenty people had perished so far while only five had experienced a full recovery. They had returned to land the same day Haines spotted his first symptoms.

"Another life lost," one of the nurses whispered close to his ear so nobody else would hear. She pointed toward the unmoving figure some short distance away. "Will you help me remove him so he can be buried?"

What a delicate way of describing how the man would be wrapped in his sheet along with a weight and then dropped feet first into the Channel. There would be no priest to say a prayer, no loved ones to shed a tear.

The depressing thought brought to mind his last encounter with Juliette. He missed her, he realized, her radiant laughter and the way she took charge. She was like a shining star in the darkness, showing him the way home, and he couldn't help but wonder how many tears she would shed if the worst were to happen to him.

She'd be devastated.

He felt it in his gut without even thinking. And the truth was that he'd be crushed too if anything bad were to happen to her. He'd grown accustomed to having her in his life, to sharing his thoughts and ideas with her, to the excitement he felt whenever they met. It was what he looked forward to most right now, the prospect of returning to London so he could share his experiences with her, so he could confide the fear he'd felt for his patients and let her soothe and comfort his soul.

What he'd said to her at the theater about sending a note when he got back was absolute rubbish. It wouldn't do at all. Not when he longed to be near her.

His muscles flexed. He'd treated her poorly by keeping her in the dark for this long. It felt dishonest in light of how truthful she'd been, all because he feared losing her even as he refused to claim her. It kept them apart, prevented them from moving forward, which wasn't fair to either of them.

Witnessing the burial, he stared down into the rolling waves for long moments after and clutched the railing. The salty air licked his face and pulled at his hair, and as he stood there, it occurred to him how much he not only wanted Juliette in his life, but how much he needed her. She pushed him when he needed pushing, showed him that there was more to life than work, that he was allowed to enjoy himself too. She wasn't just good for him. She was right for him, and as this sank in, cementing itself in his core, he knew he had to be brave. Sharing an honest future with her depended on it. Which meant he would have to start by telling her everything.

This decision brought some measure of ease with it. It loosened the tightness that had been constricting his chest since their parting. It gave him additional purpose. Because the truth of it was she'd been right when she'd said she deserved to make her own choice. Life was fleeting. He was surrounded by the evidence of it. So if there was a chance he might share some happiness with her, perhaps it was time he decided to grab it.

Taking a large basket of goodies with her, Juliette went to check on Vivien. In addition to the food, tea and honey Gabriella had suggested, she had also included a bottle of red wine, a pile of clean handkerchiefs and a copy of *The Female Quixote*, which had been given to her by Lady Everly for her birthday and which Juliette was sure Vivien would enjoy. Since she did not want to subject Sarah to Vivien's cold, she'd left her behind at Huntley House with some mending.

The carriage ride was not particularly long. Juliette arrived at Lady Arlington's modest home without incident, paid the driver and strode toward the front door, basket in hand. She rapped the knocker three times, waited and then rapped it again before Lady Arlington herself finally appeared, as was expected since she had long since let her entire staff go in order to save the expense.

"Good afternoon, my lady." Juliette offered her most polite smile. "After receiving your letter, I thought I would come to pay a call. Vivien could use the distraction and the food I have brought along. As could you, no doubt."

Lady Arlington opened the door wider and stepped aside so Juliette could enter. "That is very kind of you, Juliette. Vivien is fortunate to have such a good friend, especially now when she is feeling so horribly unwell."

"You mentioned a chill, so I trust she must have a cough and a runny nose." Juliette reached inside her reticule and pulled out a length of linen.

"Indeed the cough has proven quite a nuisance for her, poor thing. But I do not recall a runny nose." She invited Juliette to leave her basket in the small parlor just beyond the entryway. "If you ask me, she caught the ailment from that scruffy child she brought home with her a week or so ago. The lad had the same sort of cough, and naturally, Vivien insisted on caring for him herself once she learned he had no parents. Honestly, her heart is too big for her own good sometimes."

Juliette considered this information. A cold without a runny nose was quite unusual. "Are there any other symptoms besides the cough?"

"I do not think so."

"And the boy?"

Lady Arlington sighed. "He was gone from this house the next morning. Took a silver candlestick with him, ungrateful thief."

A thread of unease wound its way through Juliette. Lady Arlington had described the boy as scruffy and thieving, which meant he was likely poor. Very poor. And sick. She shook her head, unwilling to accept the possibility she faced. London was filled with such children. The chance of him being the one who'd escaped getting shot as he fled St. Giles was unlikely. And yet, he'd passed on a cough.

Covering her mouth with the linen she'd brought with her while Lady Arlington looked on with hesitation, Juliette tied it securely in place. "Please show me up to her room so I can check on her."

The lady did as Juliette bid, ushering her into a darkened room that smelled of sweat and disease. A cough raked the air, and Juliette turned her attention toward the bed where her friend's flushed face was illuminated by a nearby candle.

Oh, Vivien!

Juliette approached her friend with increasing

despair. Her eyes were barely open, her breath wheezing past her lips as she offered a weak smile in greeting. "I would rather—" A cough made her body shudder for an agonizing length of time. "You should not see me like this."

"Nonsense," Juliette told her as calmly as she possibly could. She placed her hand upon Vivien's burning brow and expelled a fragmented breath. "Will you let me examine you?"

"I didn't think her condition warranted a physician, but I can send for one if you think it necessary," Lady Arlington spoke from the door.

Juliette feared that doing so might be too late. "There is no need," she said with as much positivity as she was able. "I believe I know what this might be, but I cannot be sure unless you allow me to take a closer look."

"It's all right," Vivien whispered. "Go ahead."

Carefully, Juliette peeled back the covers and helped Vivien sit so she could pull up her nightgown. As she feared, a rash had started to spread across Vivien's abdomen which, when combined with the fever and hacking dry cough, suggested a sickness more serious than a cold.

"Have you experienced any nausea lately?" Juliette drew back to hide her distress as much as possible.

"Some. Mostly, my back and my limbs really ache and I have a terrible headache."

"That's probably because of the fever." Juliette reached for Vivien's hand and gave it a gentle squeeze before picking up the glass that sat on the bedside table and holding it to Vivien's lips. "I will fetch some more water and some cloth so we can make a cool compress for you. Rest awhile until I return."

"I hope it is not too serious," Lady Arlington said

once she and Juliette had left Vivien's bedchamber. "She does look worse than she did this morning."

Steadying herself against the banister, Juliette followed the dowager baroness down the stairs. Suppressing her fear would not be easy. Already, panic was building inside her, growing and expanding with each passing second.

"Your niece is indeed quite ill." The voice that spoke sounded foreign, completely devoid of all the emotions assailing her body. Her eyes began to sting, but since crying would serve no purpose, Juliette deliberately pushed back the tears and ignored the aching lump in her throat.

By the time they arrived in the kitchen, she had squared her shoulders and accepted what had to be done. And that brought a strange sense of peace to her mind, which was something she would not have expected under the circumstances.

Steeling herself, she gave her prognosis. "Although I am not an apothecary surgeon or a trained physician, I believe Vivien has typhus."

Lady Arlington, who'd begun pouring water from a large jug into a smaller one, went utterly still. She shook her head, alarm creeping into her eyes. "No. It cannot be."

"Of course there's a chance I might be mistaken, but according to what I have read, Vivien's symptoms are in accord with this disease and . . . considering the outbreak in St. Giles and the boy she brought home, I fear she may have contracted it."

"Dear God in heaven!"

Juliette nodded. "If I am correct, measures must be taken to prevent further spread." She paused for a second before saying, "No one can enter or leave this house for the next two weeks."

Lady Arlington stared at her, the jug in her hand completely forgotten. "But . . . You cannot be serious! We shall need food and any number of things that I cannot seem to think of right now."

"I am sorry, but quarantine is necessary. At least until we can be sure not to pass the disease on to others." Resolve gripped Juliette's body. "Since you may already be infected and there is no guarantee that covering my mouth is enough to keep me safe, it goes without saying that I shall remain here until this has passed."

"Juliette . . ." Lady Arlington looked thoroughly distraught, which was understandable, all things considered. After all, Juliette had just delivered the closest thing to a death sentence she possibly could.

"Putting my family at risk by returning home is out of the question. Besides, you might need my help."

"I scarcely know what to say." Lady Arlington's voice broke, and the corners of her eyes began to glisten. "But what if you have not yet caught it? Staying here with us could ensure that you do."

Juliette nodded. "Yes, but to leave here, without knowing if I am carrying the disease with me, would be highly irresponsible. I cannot do it, though I will need to inform my brother of what has occurred. If you would be so kind as to lend me some writing utensils when we return upstairs, I will pen him a note." She bit her lips while pondering the best path forward. "Perhaps I can toss it to a passerby from one of the upstairs' windows and ask them to deliver it."

"It seems as though you have it all figured out." Lady Arlington's lips began to tremble, and when she spoke again, she sounded weak and defeated. "I am frightened by this. I cannot deny it."

"I know." Juliette softened her voice and told her gently, "We must be strong, however, for Vivien and for ourselves. If we are lucky, we will avoid the suffering she has succumbed to, but if we are not, then we must endure it without inflicting this ailment on others."

"How you can be so calm in the midst of such dire circumstances, I do not know."

Juliette wasn't sure she understood it either. Perhaps it was her experience with being sick that made her so, or perhaps it was knowing that typhus was survivable. Florian had lived through it, which meant there was hope. That thought alone was soothing, as were the endless thoughts of the man himself. She wondered how he was faring and prayed she would live to see him again.

The possibility she might not sent a tear rolling down the side of her cheek. She swiped it away before Lady Arlington had a chance to see it. Strength and courage would get her through this and hopefully . . . *hopefully* . . . allow her to tell the man she loved how sorely she had missed him.

Chapter 21

The last week had passed with infernal slowness, but at least Florian had watched most of the remaining people onboard the quarantine ship return to shore. They would be well on their way back to London by now while Haines, the only remaining patient, was showing excellent signs of improvement.

"Your symptoms were surprisingly mild compared to everyone else's," he told his colleague. "Perhaps you did have typhus as a boy and suffered a reoccurrence."

"I would not have thought it possible." Reclining in a chair placed out on the deck in the sun, Haines watched while Florian mopped the spruce planking for the last time. Circling the ship while hunting for fish, a cheerful flock of seagulls kept them company.

"Nor I." It was curious how diseases worked, and Florian was wise enough to acknowledge he did not know everything about them. Far from it. "We were lucky," he said. "This outbreak would undoubtedly have claimed more lives had it not been for Lady Juliette's suggestion about this ship."

"And her help in procuring it." There was a tiny

pause before Haines said, "She will make some lucky fellow an excellent wife one day."

Florian shot the man a look. "Are you thinking of trying to court her?"

"No. I would not dare encroach on another man's territory."

Straightening, Florian stopped mopping for a second and frowned at Haines. "What are you saying?"

At this point Haines rolled his eyes and sighed with excessive amounts of exasperation. "You are obviously interested in her. It is in the way your eyes light up whenever you speak her name."

Florian's cheeks grew hot, and he realized to his horror that he was probably blushing. *Damn!* He quickly turned away and gave his attention to sloshing more water onto the deck. "I confess I find her appealing."

"Is that all?"

"Very well. She is a woman of pleasing anatomical configuration whose ability to find solutions in a crisis deserves any man's admiration."

A loud snort was Haines's immediate response. "You sound like an equine breeder showing off the merits of his favorite mare."

Expelling a sigh, Florian set the mop against a barrel and crossed his arms. "I do not excel at sharing my feelings with people. Hell, I rarely share them with myself, so you must forgive the clinical way in which I describe my affection."

"At least you are able to call it affection, which would suggest emotional attachment."

Florian groaned. "Precisely what I have been trying so hard to avoid."

"Why?"

He could not possibly reveal that much, so he merely shrugged and walked to the railing and looked out over the water. The air was blessedly fresh out here, such a pleasant departure from the filthy city air.

"With all the pain and death that surrounds me, shutting it out is easier than letting it in." And since he'd no desire to continue this conversation with a man he wasn't particularly close to, he quickly snatched the mop back up and resumed his task. "It will be good to return to some proper lodgings soon. I, for one, am looking forward to sleeping in a real bed and eating a fine piece of meat."

"As am I."

Florian glanced at Haines who looked like he might be drooling at the very idea of such luxury. "A good glass of wine would be welcome too. And an ice! I have been craving a visit to Gunther's for the last two days."

Florian grinned and gave his attention to completing his chore. If all went well, they would leave the ship and return to London in another couple of days and he would finally . . . *finally* . . . be able to tell Juliette how much she'd come to mean to him.

"**Y**ou ought to be in bed yourself," Vivien said. Her voice was so weak Juliette was forced to lean in closer so she could hear.

"I will be fine." *I hope.* A rawness within forced a cough from her throat even as she spoke. Since showing symptoms of the disease the day before, Juliette had stopped covering her mouth and nose with the linen, which made it easier for her to breathe. "You are the one I am most concerned about, Vivien. You—" The words caught and cracked with the desperation she felt on account of her friend's deterioration.

During the course of the past week, Vivien's fever had lingered. When it had suddenly subsided, Juliette had been overjoyed, only to have her hopes crushed when it had returned, stronger than ever before and throwing Vivien's mind into an often delirious state. Today when Juliette had come to check on her, she'd been distraught by the sight of gangrenous sores on Vivien's fingers and toes and by the cadaverous stench she emitted. Washing her had tested Juliette's composure when all she had wanted to do was succumb to the sobs knotting tightly inside her chest.

"Juliette . . ." Vivien reached out, and Juliette caught her hand, cradling the frail thing as if it might break. "I fear Lord Portham has lost his chance to court me."

Tears brimmed in Juliette's eyes, and unlike her previous efforts to force them back, she failed this time. Heat had begun creeping over her own forehead last evening and her weakening constitution apparently made her exceedingly weepy.

"Don't be silly." She coughed again and pressed a hand to her aching belly. "That pompous man never stood a chance with someone as wonderful as you." She forced a smile for Vivien's benefit. "You deserve an earl at the very least."

"Perhaps one awaits me in heaven." Vivien's eyes closed on that thought. "Would such a thing not be lovely?"

Unable to speak for fear she might choke on the misery of it all, Juliette simply sat, coughing from time to time while offering Vivien companionship. Lady Arlington had taken to her own bed three days earlier, so Juliette had made it her mission to care for these women as best as she could.

A clink against the windowpane drew her attention. Rising, she assured Vivien she would be right back and then went to look out. As expected, it was Raphe. He had been stopping by every day since she'd informed him of her decision to isolate herself with Vivien and Lady Arlington. Just as on those previous occasions, he'd brought a basket of food which would be placed on the front step so she could fetch it later, once he was gone.

"How are you?" His voice called up to her from below with such vitality, she could not help but envy the energy he possessed. And yet, in spite of his positive tone, there was no denying the layer of concern covering his eyes.

"As expected," she rasped while curling her fingers around the window frame for support. "I've a fever, my body aches all over and I am exhausted by fatigue. Compared with Vivien, however, I am in excellent condition."

Compassion settled upon his face, but beneath it, she saw the dread he struggled to hide from her. "I am sorry, Juliette." His voice fractured on her name and he glanced away for a second before looking back up with renewed determination. "I have written to Florian, but have not heard back. The Dowager Duchess of Tremaine has once again offered to come and check on you herself or to send another physician if you prefer."

"No." Juliette shook her head. "Florian is the only one who might resist infection. I will not allow anyone else near us."

"But . . ." Words seemed to fail him. He shook his

head and raked both hands through his hair. "I do not know what to do. It wasn't supposed to be like this, Julie. You are my sister, and I swore I would always protect you and now . . . Why did you have to come here? Why—"

"You know why." The effort it took to raise her voice enough so he could hear was starting to wear her down.

Pressing his lips together, he offered a jerky nod. "Yes. You are goodness itself, Juliette, and I love you. We all love you."

"As I love you." Another bout of coughing overcame her, scraping over her throat until it felt raw. "Give my best to Gabriella and Amelia."

"I will come again tomorrow," he promised before offering his best ducal bow and turning away. One hand rose to his cheek and gave it a swipe as he climbed into his carriage, waving one last time before the conveyance took off and rolled out of view.

"We have fresh food," Juliette told Vivien while offering the window her back. A strange stillness greeted her, creeping through her veins and shaking her heart. "Vivien?"

Not a single sound emerged from the bed, not even the hint of slumber. Approaching slowly while alarm took hold of her body, Juliette forced her feet steadily forward until she was able to see her friend clearly. An uninhibited sob rose from her throat at the sight she beheld, of Vivien's glassy eyes staring up at the ceiling, her lips slightly parted upon her final exhale.

She'd died alone, in that brief moment in which Juliette had left her side.

Pressing her knuckles to her mouth, Juliette muffled her grief while tears spilled over her cheeks. With trembling fingers she reached out and carefully lowered Vivien's eyelids. She then proceeded to smooth the sheets around her while trying to come to terms with what came next. She had no idea what to do, truth was. To let another person into the house could prove detrimental and yet, leaving Vivien's body here for more than a day was not an option either. Overwhelmed by sickness, tiredness and the hopelessness she faced, Juliette felt her last bit of stubborn determination evaporate. This was it. Before long, she would be following Vivien into the beyond. And before she did so, she was going to have to inform Lady Arlington of her niece's passing.

After dropping Haines off at his lodgings, Florian continued toward his own home. Having a bath and getting a change of clothes would be necessary before he headed over to the hospital or even considered meeting with Lady Juliette.

"Welcome home, Your Grace," Baker said the moment he opened the door and offered to take Florian's bag, hat and gloves. "We are all extremely relieved to have you back safely."

"It was a trying ten days, I have to admit, but it was necessary." Florian shrugged out of his jacket and hung it on a hook on the wall.

Baker set Florian's hat on the hallway table. "Some correspondence awaits your attention in your study, and the Duke of Huntley stopped by earlier in the week. He said to call on him as soon as you return."

Florian nodded. "Did he say what it was in regard to?"

"No. He refused to mention it."

Well then, it would simply have to wait until Florian had put himself to rights. "If you could please ask Jillian to help you bring up some hot water from the kitchen, I would be much obliged." He would usually have offered to lend a hand, but he was too bone-weary to do much of anything besides climb the stairs.

He did so slowly, reaching the landing only minutes before Jillian and Baker arrived with the first pails of water. The small brass tub that permanently stood in an adjoining chamber was expeditiously filled, the servants departing swiftly so Florian could bathe in private.

Lord, it felt good to slide into the soothing bathwater. The warmth of it lapped against his tired body from all sides, producing a deep calm. He had not gotten a proper night's sleep in weeks, but now, with the typhus under control and the threat of further contagion drastically minimized, he would finally be able to enjoy some much-needed relaxation.

Closing his eyes he leaned back and allowed a tentative smile. It would be wonderful seeing Juliette again. Of course there was still Bartholomew to consider. He'd have to meet with Henry as soon as possible to see if he'd discovered anything new about Armswell's poisoning and the false claims about him seducing Elmwood's wife. Proof of Bartholomew's involvement would be essential when trying to bring him down.

With this in mind, Florian washed himself, dried off and got dressed. Selecting a clean handkerchief from the top drawer of his dresser, he placed the piece of monogrammed fabric in his pocket and left his bedchamber.

"You've a visitor," Baker said when Florian arrived downstairs.

He handed him a calling card and Florian instantly froze as he read the twirling script. Mr. William Mortedge. Invisible pins pricked at the nape of his neck while apprehension flared out across his skin.

Steeling himself, he closed his hand around the calling card, crushing it in his fist. He then entered the parlor and saw that he'd been right in his deduction.

Mr. Mortedge *was* Bartholomew.

His father.

"Ah! There you are." Sitting casually with his legs stretched out before him, Bartholomew took a sip of the brandy he'd helped himself to.

A chill gripped Florian's spine. "What. Do. You. Want?"

Bartholomew eyed him over the brim of his glass, grinned and set the piece of crystal aside. "Why, to see you of course! It is not every day a father has the honor of greeting the son who sent him to the gallows."

The reminder that they were so closely related disgusted Florian to no end. Gritting his teeth, he glared at the man before him. "I did what was right." Ignoring Bartholomew's comment would serve no purpose, and to suppose he did not hold a grudge would be equally futile. The only question now was what else Bartholomew intended to do about it.

A smile slid across Bartholomew's face. He was the perfect portrayal of a man at leisure and yet to presume he was not a dangerous predator ready to pounce would be a mistake. Many men had suffered before on account of his wrath.

"You betrayed me," Bartholomew told him with eerie calmness.

"I cannot see how, since one must feel some sense of loyalty toward a person in order to do so." Florian inhaled slowly, forcing himself to relax. "Since I feel nothing for you but revulsion, betraying you was never a real possibility."

"A fine comeback, I must say." Bartholomew drummed his fingers lazily against the armrest, his hawkish eyes trailing Florian as he went to pour himself a much-needed drink. "You appear sturdier than I remembered—more masculine."

Florian glanced at him as he finished pouring himself a brandy. "And you look entirely different."

Bartholomew chuckled. "A bit of pig fat surgically stuffed into my cheeks has worked wonders in altering my appearance."

"Doesn't sound like a healthy procedure," Florian muttered.

"It seemed a touch safer than risking the rope."

A grunt was the only response Florian would offer that comment. Downing his brandy, he poured another and considered the man who'd raped his mother decades ago. The full cheeks were not the only changes he'd made. He'd also grown an impressive beard, colored his hair to a shade not so different from his own, and procured a pair of spectacles.

"I have to say that I'm a little surprised by your unwillingness to heed my warnings," Bartholomew said. "You put Armswell and Lowell in danger. You're lucky you don't have to bury either one of them yet."

Florian stared at him. "What are you talking about?"

Bartholomew scoffed. "You saved Armswell yourself, didn't you? As for Lowell . . . It was fortunate

Elmwood sprained his wrist on his way to the duel. Bloody bastard missed your brother entirely."

Surprise was dismissed by relief. Apparently Lowell had met with Elmwood while he'd been away on the ship, and he'd survived. "Thank God."

"I wouldn't celebrate just yet if I were you," Bartholomew said. "There are other ways to make you pay for what you did to me."

"I am a duke now," Florian felt compelled to remind him, "and far beyond your influence or control."

The smirk forming on Bartholomew's lips was not the least bit reassuring. "You think so, do you?" He gave a snort. "For years I've been trying to take control of St. Giles and push Guthrie out only to fail because of the information you gave Coventry about my taxes. Clever, I'll grant you that, but if you think I will ever forgive you for working against me, then you are quite mistaken."

He stood and walked toward Florian much like a panther might prowl toward its prey. "Armswell thought he could wheedle his way out of my clutches as well." He grinned, the beastly sort of satisfied grin one might expect from an evil genius. "It cost him his wife, you know."

Every particle of Florian's body began to stiffen, from his toes all the way to each strand of hair. "What do you mean?" He asked the question not knowing if he truly wanted an answer. From what his mother had told him, Bartholomew had taken what he wanted because he'd threatened Lowell's life. She had complied with his wishes and Armswell had allowed it because they'd felt they had no choice.

"Do you honestly believe I would have done what I did on a whim?" The edge of Bartholomew's mouth lifted ever so slightly, lending a secretive air to his countenance. When Florian failed to respond, he answered his question himself. "I never act without good reason." The half smile transformed to a grin. "Nothing is random. I am not insane, and although you have clearly been led to believe so, I did not beget you on your mother simply to satisfy my lust. Ha! A man so easily swayed by any woman would not have been as successful as I."

Florian gaped at him. It was all he could do seeing as the life he'd come to know and trust was being picked apart before his very eyes. Nothing made sense, least of all the part about him wanting to hear what Bartholomew had to say next.

"Armswell was weak, perhaps he still is, though he has had the sense to steer clear of me since our previous dealings."

"Previous dealings?" *Dear God.* What the hell had Armswell done?

Bartholomew gave Florian a pensive look before nudging him aside so he could get to the brandy behind him. "He was young." Speaking over his shoulder as if they were having a casual discussion, Bartholomew refilled his glass. He turned, paused to take a sip and then crossed the floor to reclaim the armchair he'd vacated earlier. "His father had tasked him with proving his worth by refusing to give him more than five hundred pounds of the family fortune. Sink or swim, he no doubt told him. Trouble was, Armswell had no sense for investment or any other means by which to replenish his coffers. Marrying your mother was an excellent solution to his financial troubles, albeit a temporary one. And since keeping up appearances was of the utmost importance . . ." He spread his arms and it all came together.

"You lent him money." The notion was too awful to contemplate and yet so obvious, Florian wondered why he'd never suspected it before. An answer came swiftly: because his mother had fed him a story that he'd believed without question—a story in which Bartholomew would be the only villain.

"And since I do not appreciate it when those indebted to me refuse to pay, I must find some means by which to punish them properly. So . . . I took your mother and did my very best to ensure that Armswell would have to lay claim to a cuckoo."

"You ruined so many lives."

"And yet I am not the one to blame. Armswell is." Bartholomew finished his drink and set his glass aside. "Had it not been for his stupidity, greed and lack of honor, none of this would have happened. You would not have been born, a fact I have largely ignored, though curiosity did compel me to seek you out on occasion. But, I would have left you alone, the victim of Armswell's lapse in judgment and your mother's fierce determination to do whatever she had to in order to save your brother. Now that you've crossed me, not once, but twice, I can no longer pretend you do not exist."

He'd proven this by hurting Armswell and Lowell. "What will you do?" Florian asked while doing his best to hide his concern.

Bartholomew's eyes sparkled with amusement. "Excellent question." The amusement faded until he remained the face of all seriousness. "Pushing Guthrie out of St. Giles and claiming the territory for myself proved unsuccessful, but perhaps I should make one final attempt." He gave Florian a pointed stare. "Have Carlton Guthrie arrested tomorrow by noon, and I promise I'll leave you alone from this point forward."

"But I cannot simply—"

"You're a duke now, Florian. Congratulations, by the way. A man as powerful as you can no doubt see that this deed is done in a satisfactory manner." Rising, he brushed his shoulders with his fingers, as if removing lint, and strode to the door. "I expect you to meet with success, or face the consequences."

"And if I refuse?" Florian tried. "As you say, I am a duke. As such, I could decide to use my power on you."

Turning just enough to meet his gaze, Bartholomew sniffed and opened the door. "You might want to consider what the world will think of you if they discover how you were conceived. And if that's not enough to convince you to help me with this, perhaps I'll decide to be a little harsher with your loved ones. Just to dissuade you from issuing threats, hmm?"

Bartholomew closed the door to the parlor as he left, leaving Florian alone in the silence that followed. Scandal would be unavoidable, the gossip and the social destruction relentless if the truth about him ever came out. Florian's reputation would be destroyed while everyone related to him would bear the stigma of his disgrace, or worse, suffer annihilation at the hands of Bartholomew.

Chapter 22

A soothing piece of piano music sifted through the air, lending an atmosphere of casual elegance to the Red Rose. The exclusive club was one of few allowing both men and women to acquire memberships, but as Henry had said when he'd opened the place, "In my experience ladies enjoy spending money more than men. It would be foolish of me to deny them entry."

Arriving at the door to his brother's office, Florian gave it a couple of raps and entered without bothering to wait for a response. Henry, seated behind his desk, stood the moment he saw him. "Florian! Thank God you're back. I cannot tell you how relieved I am to see you looking well."

Florian nodded and met his brother's gaze. "We need to talk," he said.

On the way over, he'd decided the best course of action from this point forward was absolute unwavering directness. Cutting across the floor, he dropped onto one of the black velvet chairs across from where Henry sat and regarded him closely. His handsome face, comprised of smooth princely lines, a full lower lip and raven-black hair, ensured he looked nothing like Florian. That no one had ever suspected they might only be half brothers was actually rather strange.

"I'm still not sure who's behind the attack on our father or—"

"I am," Florian said, cutting him off.

"Really?" Surprise was evident in Henry's expression.

Inhaling deeply, Florian clutched the armrest, ignored what his revelation might lead to and spoke with absolute candor. "It is time for you to know the truth about me, Henry." He paused, aware that this was his last chance to avoid the facts. Now was not the time for cowardice, however. Not when his family's reputation and possibly even their lives were at stake. He needed council and after what he'd just learned from Bartholomew, he wasn't sure he trusted his mother or Armswell to provide it. "You and I are only half brothers, Henry. Armswell is not my real father."

A moment passed, one in which awkwardness swept aside any lingering feelings of comfort.

"What do you mean?"

The disbelief in Henry's voice was overpowering. He blinked, grinned as if Florian had to be joking and then, realizing he wasn't, produced a thunderous expression so at odds with his characteristically charming one that Florian instantly cringed.

But since there was no taking back the words now, the best way forward at this point was through explanation and apology. "Our mother was forced to lie with Bartholomew years ago."

"The villainous blackguard who allegedly lured the innocent into prostitution and had the Duchess of Coventry stabbed last year?" Henry's voice rose, accompanying his increasing outrage. "*That* Bartholomew?"

"I am afraid so. Yes."

Henry stared at him for a long, drawn-out moment before heaving a sigh and sinking back into his chair. "If the bugger was not dead already I would kill him myself."

"If you don't mind, I would like to have the honor of doing so." When Henry gave him a quizzical look, Florian explained, "Bartholomew wasn't executed last year. Some other poor bastard was hanged in his place."

Henry stared at him, eyes shadowed by darkness. "Tell me this is a joke."

"I am no more pleased by the truth of it than you are, I assure you." Sliding his palm across his face, Florian blew out a breath. "Claire did what she felt was necessary in order to save you when Bartholomew threatened your life."

"So this is my fault?" There was no denying the affront Henry felt at such a prospect.

"God no!" That wasn't at all what he wanted to suggest. "If anything, I fear it might be Armswell's. He borrowed money from Bartholomew to cover his debts and then refused to pay it back."

"He's always been lousy at keeping his affairs in order," Lowell muttered. "I discovered as much when I came of age and he showed me the books. Didn't take me more than a good half hour to see our family fortune was in dire straits. Hence my investment in this." He spread his arms to indicate the business he'd built. "It was more than a flight of fancy, Florian. It was a necessity—my own personal safeguard against Papa's mismanagement of the family assets."

"I had no idea. You never said."

Henry snorted. "Between the two of us, I rather think you're more guilty than I of keeping secrets. How long have you known you weren't Armswell's son?"

"Since my sixteenth birthday."

"Fourteen years and you never thought to tell me?" Disappointment filled Henry's eyes along with a look of distinct betrayal. He shook his head as if in disbelief.

"Discovering what Bartholomew did and that I was related to him was humiliating," Florian tried to explain. "It tore me up inside, Henry, especially since I knew how others might judge me. I feared you would scorn me if you knew, and I dared not risk that."

"Christ, Florian. You're my brother, no matter what." Rising, Henry went to fetch a decanter from a nearby side table. He grabbed a pair of tumblers as well and brought everything over to the desk. "I only wish you'd confided in me sooner. But since you have chosen to now . . ." He poured a large measure of brandy into each glass and handed one to Florian. "I cannot help but wonder what prompted you to do so."

Tossing back his brandy for fortification, Florian told Henry about Bartholomew's visit earlier in the day. "He threatened to expose me unless I have Carlton Guthrie arrested before noon tomorrow."

"Which might be possible," Henry murmured. "The man has been suspected of all sorts of criminal behavior over the years, but the authorities have never found anything incriminating enough to lead to his arrest."

"Which probably means it won't be possible for

us to do so either unless we commit forgery or fraud, and I simply refuse to lower myself to such levels for any reason."

"So you're preempting the inevitable by ensuring the family is warned and prepared."

"Precisely."

"I don't suppose there's a chance Bartholomew might be bluffing?"

Florian shook his head. "No. I've just learned that *he's* the one who had Armswell poisoned. He also arranged the duel between you and Elmwood. So I'm sure he'll follow through on his threat if I fail to meet his demand." He hesitated before saying, "There's something else."

Henry eyed him warily. "Tell me."

"Bartholomew and Mr. Mortedge are one and the same."

"What? But that can't be possible. I mean, he's been out in public without anyone taking notice!"

"The man is transformed. I hardly recognized him myself."

Henry shook his head. "It doesn't seem possible." Sighing, he gave Florian a serious look. "Anything I can do to help?"

"Maybe. Bartholomew lost his fortune last year when he was arrested and yet he's able to afford an exclusive town house. Something's not right. If you can figure out how he's financing his home and his investments, it might reveal that he's guilty of fraud or theft, either of which could help with his arrest."

"We need absolute proof before we go to the authorities," Henry said, following his brother's thought process. "The last thing we want is for him to go free again."

Florian stood and went to refill his glass. "I am sorry it has come to this." He downed yet another brandy and set the glass on the sideboard next to the decanter. "I have to get over to the hospital now so I can warn the Duchess of Tremaine about the potential impact on St. Agatha's."

"Any chance I might meet her one day?" Lowell asked in a pensive tone that denoted great interest. "Hardly seems fair of you, keeping her all to yourself."

"You're welcome to join the committee if you like. Otherwise, you've little chance of seeing her unless you suffer an injury. She has a severe aversion to Society and rarely ventures out in public because of it."

"Hmmm . . . I wonder why."

"And I could tell you if I had the time, but I really ought to be on my way." He bid a hasty good-bye and thanked his brother for the drink before dashing out of the Red Rose and heading toward the hospital.

Arriving there, he climbed the front steps and entered the foyer where he almost collided with the Duke of Huntley, who was on his way out. "Florian!"

"Your Grace." Florian steadied himself with one hand on Huntley's shoulder, dropping it as soon as he'd regained his balance. "My manservant said you wished to see me, so I was planning to call on you after checking up on things here." He registered the duke's expression which suggested a state of grief-stricken despair, and immediately stiffened with concern. "What is it? What has happened?"

The haunted look in Huntley's eyes was beyond disconcerting. "It is Juliette. I believe she may be dying."

There were times in Florian's life, moments he could look back on in which he'd lost all hope, and moving past the bleakness had seemed impossible. One such moment had arisen when he'd experienced death as a child—the quiet passing of Roland, a beloved family dog. It had come again when he'd lost one of his own patients for the very first time. But it had never hollowed out his insides as much as it did right now.

"No."

Huntley dropped his gaze and spoke to the floor. "She went to check on a friend of hers and became infected with typhus. Unwilling to spread the disease, she quarantined herself, her friend and her friend's aunt. I see her only through the window, but I can tell she is getting worse."

Steeling himself in an effort to gather his strength, not only for Huntley's benefit but for his own, Florian squared his shoulders, determined to put all emotion aside so he could focus on the problem at hand. "Allow me to fetch my bag and then you must take me to her at once." Without wasting a second, he hurried off to his office, scribbled a note to Viola, and went to accompany Huntley, all the while praying Juliette would recover with unprecedented swiftness.

After leaving Vivien's room, Juliette had staggered toward Lady Arlington's chamber only to find the lady sleeping. Unwilling to wake her only to cause her tremendous amounts of grief, Juliette had chosen to seek her own bed and get some rest. Only then, when sleep overcame her, did she find peace. It fled as quickly as it had come when she awoke to the sound of pounding on the downstairs door. If only she could gather the strength to rise and see who it was. But the very idea of having to stand on her own two feet was too debilitating to allow for the effort. So she stayed where she was, breathing the raw air and occasionally coughing while heat blanketed her forehead.

A loud crack roused her once more, and she realized she must have fallen asleep again. It was followed by the thud of feet climbing the stairs and the sound of doors opening and closing nearby. Distraught, Juliette gathered what strength she could manage and stumbled from the bed, crossing the floor and throwing her weight against the door just as someone on the opposite side attempted to open it. Several bangs followed in an effort to make the door budge.

"Go away," she groaned. "You cannot be here. It is not safe."

All sound on the other side ceased, filled seconds later with a voice she'd feared she might never hear again. "Juliette." Florian spoke as though the world was ending and the only life he cared about saving was hers. "Please open the door."

"Are you alone? I will not put anyone else at risk."

"I told your brother to wait outside while I came to check on you."

Relief swamped her, bringing on fresh tears as she unlocked the door and fell into Florian's arms. "Vivien died this morning," she cried. "I tried to save her but . . ."

He stroked his hand over her hair. "It is not your fault, Juliette. You did what was right and your friend at least had the comfort of knowing you cared."

A torrent of tears overflowed from her eyes, wetting Florian's jacket and closing off her throat until she could scarcely breathe.

"Hush now," he whispered against her ear. "You

must calm yourself so you can get well." Without warning, he gathered her up in his arms and headed toward the stairs. "I am taking you to my house so you can receive proper care."

"But Lady Arlington . . ." Fighting the heat that burned in her eyes, Juliette looked toward the dowager baroness's bedchamber as they passed it. "We cannot leave her here."

As if he refused to listen, Florian marched on. "I am sorry," he told her tightly, "but it is too late for her as well."

With that ominous remark, the remainder of Juliette's energy failed her and she sagged against Florian's chest, allowing his vigor to carry her forward. Arguing over where they were going or how her staying in a bachelor's home would affect her reputation was futile at this point. She was in his hands now and doubted any amount of resistance on her part would sway him from his determination to see her fully restored. Which was just as well, since the only thing she wanted to do was sleep.

Having placed Juliette inside Huntley's carriage, Florian spoke to the duke. "You cannot ride with us, Huntley. The risk is too great."

Huntley nodded. "I understand."

"And I intend to have this conveyance burned once we have finished with it." Considering the rampancy with which typhus could spread, Florian dared not let anyone else use it later.

"My biggest concern is Juliette's propriety." Huntley winced. "I know it sounds ridiculous under the circumstances, but I had hoped to offer her a respectable life and an advantageous marriage. She cannot have those things after spending so much as a single night in your home."

"I know. But I dare not take her to the hospital or anywhere else. At present, I am the only person I know who seems to be immune, which makes this the logical course of action. I shall care for her, Huntley, and do my utmost to ensure her survival."

"And your servants?"

Florian knew the scandal of what he proposed was immense, but he could not think of another choice. Not when it came to ensuring everyone's safety. "They will remain belowstairs for the duration of your sister's visit."

Distinct discomfort colored Huntley's cheeks. "I know you are a physician, Florian, but still, I cannot pretend to be in favor of this idea."

"None of us are, least of all Juliette, I suspect. But if the situation calls for it in the end and you think it necessary, I will do what must be done to save her reputation as well."

Clenching his jaw, Huntley stuck out his hand and Florian shook it. "Thank you. My sister is lucky to be in your care, but as much as I appreciate your offer, you ought to know I would never insist she marry for reputation alone." He withdrew his hand and crossed his arms in a solid display of dukely authority. "My family has braved scandal before and shall do so again before sacrificing happiness for the sake of appeasing Society."

"I will keep that in mind." Even though Florian knew all too well that they might not have any choice in the end. If the gossipmongers chose to be malicious, Juliette would be ripped to shreds by their wagging tongues. The only positive outcome—the one that would truly give her the chance to decide what she wanted for herself—was the one in which no one found out she was staying with him as his patient. Especially since he knew she had long since become so much more than that.

Chapter 23

The first thing Juliette registered when she woke was the blessed coolness upon her skin, covering her body in the most incredible way imaginable. It wasn't until she moved that she realized she was submerged in water, the liquid shifting around her, offering weightless bliss and endless amounts of comfort.

Which was thoroughly enjoyable when compared to the aching weight she'd been feeling the last two days. Until she started wondering about how she'd arrived in a tub. The last person she recalled speaking with was Florian, but beyond that, she remembered nothing.

Curious, she opened her eyes just enough to discern she was in a room darkened by tones of gray. A candle flickering somewhere nearby cast dancing shadows across the walls. Dropping her gaze, she saw the tub had been covered by a white sheet in an effort to protect her modesty, for which she was grateful.

Her eyes slid shut once more even as the dryness in her mouth, informing her of her need to drink, pushed a groan from her throat. The impulse to use what little strength she possessed in order to procure a glass of water was suddenly uncontrollable. She grabbed at the sheet, determined to pull it away, her arms and hands splashing about in the process.

"What is it?" Florian was beside her in an instant, crouched down with his lovely blue eyes so close she imagined swimming right into his gaze. "What do you need?"

"Drink." The effort it took to say that one word was astounding, and once it was spoken, it sounded like wood crackling in an open fireplace.

A glass was promptly produced and set to her lips, the wine she tasted upon her tongue easing away much of her discomfort. It was followed by something else—something bitter—and then by wine again. She muttered her thanks, as inaudible as they were. Her eyes, impossible to keep open, drifted shut, and she allowed herself to succumb to slumber.

When she woke again she was lying on a bed and dressed in her favorite nightgown. Feeling light pressure beneath her chin, she reached up and touched the fastening of the nightcap that had been firmly secured to her head. Expelling a breath she dropped her hand. The room was unfamiliar, which meant she wasn't at home. Turning her head with some effort, she observed the man who snored ever so softly from his position in a nearby armchair. Strands of copper fell in absolute disarray around his handsome face—a face far more relaxed in sleep than it had ever been while awake. He looked . . . at peace, she decided; free from all the worry and concern he otherwise carried with him.

Further study drew her attention to his torso. He'd shucked his jacket, vest and cravat and rolled up the sleeves of his shirt, revealing the fine dusting of golden ginger hair upon his forearms. Allowing her gaze to drift lower, she followed the length of his long legs until she arrived at his feet. Both were bare, which for some absurd reason made her smile. In spite of her sickliness, there was something utterly charming about Florian's informal state of undress. She appreciated it and liked the fact that he'd had the good sense to let propriety slip in favor of comfort.

Unwilling to wake him, Juliette tried to rise from the bed as quietly as possible. Which wasn't easy since she required a chamber pot with extreme urgency. She practically tumbled from the bed with a thud in her desperation to reach it, all the while trying to figure out how she would see to her business without Florian bearing witness.

"Juliette." Her name spoken with hasty alarm sent all such hope flying out the window. Before she had a chance to protest, Florian had ascertained her requirement, procured the chamber pot from under the bed and helped her use it. "Hush," he whispered while stroking his thumbs across her cheeks. "There is no need for tears. All of this is perfectly normal to me. I have experienced it hundreds of times before."

As true as that might be, Juliette was mortified. Only Amelia and Raphe had seen her like this before, and even then it had not been quite so bad. To find herself reduced to this infirm state, while the man whose admiration she craved bore witness, was beyond awful.

After helping her back to bed, he propped her up and helped her drink more wine. "Sustenance is vital to your recovery." His voice was firm. "I brought some chicken and fruit for you. Try to eat a little."

He handed her a small plate before going to pick up the recently used chamber pot. "I will be back soon."

Juliette groaned but did as he asked and made a deliberate effort to push food down into her belly. To her surprise, it wasn't as much of a struggle as she had expected, and by the time Florian returned, she only had one small piece of plum left.

Florian glanced at the plate and gave her a nod of approval. "Your appetite is excellent. If you can continue eating and sleeping like this, I do believe you will get well again soon."

"Where . . . am I?" She wanted answers while she could get them.

"In the guest room of my house." He moved closer, removed the plate from her hands and placed it on the bedside table before perching on the edge of the bed. "Your brother agreed it was for the best."

Closing her eyes, she chose to ignore the impropriety and the possible scandal this might cause. There would be enough time to worry about that later if she survived. So she reached for his hand instead and squeezed it. "Thank you." It was all she could manage to say.

His thumb brushed across her cheek. "Please don't cry."

She hadn't realized she was. "Thank you," she told him again, since she could think of nothing else. Her brain felt like a big wad of cotton. Forming coherent thought and then voicing it was proving a chore, and the small amount of effort she'd made to leave her bed and then eat had drained her completely.

"Get some rest," she heard him say, the comforting sound of his voice accompanying her as she drifted away once more.

Pulling back his cue, Bartholomew peered across the green felt topper of his billiards table. Taking aim, he struck his target with swift precision. The ball rolled smoothly forward, knocking another ball into the corner pocket.

"It's time for me to be merciless," he told Mr. Smith as he straightened his posture. Reaching for his nearby glass of claret, he took a sip and savored the sweet flavor against his tongue.

"What are you proposing?" Mr. Smith asked.

Bartholomew sighed. "I'm tired of playing games and of not finding satisfaction. I gave Florian a chance to redeem himself by ensuring Guthrie's arrest and still he refuses to comply with my wishes!"

"I believe he's been a bit busy tending to Lady Juliette."

Bartholomew pinched the bridge of his nose. He could feel a headache coming on. "I don't care what his reasons are. The point is, he needs to be taught a bloody lesson, which means I have to follow through with my threat this time no matter how it might affect Claire."

"You want me to contact Harper?"

Recalling the journalist whose loyalty Mr. Smith had paid for, Bartholomew nodded. "I want Florian's reputation ruined. And when that's been accomplished, I intend for him to watch the woman he's saving suffer and die so he'll understand what it truly means to lose everything. The way I did."

The gentling of Juliette's breathing as she fell asleep chased away some of the panic Florian had been feeling for the last seventy-two hours. She didn't appear as restless as she had when he'd brought her home three days ago, her body shifting about in a constant attempt to seek comfort. She'd been pale with red-rimmed eyes and a cough that never boded well. Employing the strict rules he'd used on the ship which were equal to those he'd put into place at the hospital, he'd stripped Juliette of her clothing and given her a thorough bath, which had proven more necessary than he had expected after having discovered the lice in her hair.

What he had chosen to do because of this wasn't something she would forgive him for soon, even though he was sure she would understand his reasoning.

Sighing, he stood. The worst was yet to come, but for now at least she was able to rest and forget what he had witnessed. She hadn't wanted him to see her like this and it clearly pained her that he had. Which was why he'd felt compelled to remind her of his profession when she'd needed to use the chamber pot for the first time. He'd reasoned that if she thought of him as a physician instead of a man, she would not mind his help quite as much. And it must have worked, because she'd seemed more accepting of his assistance since then. For which he was grateful.

Tending to Juliette like this made him feel more connected to her than he'd ever felt toward anyone else. The disease denied her the chance to dress her hair in a pretty coiffure or to put on a perfectly cut gown, and yet to Florian's eyes, no woman had ever looked lovelier than she did right now.

Which probably meant he was losing his mind since there was no denying her cracking lips, sweaty forehead or puffy eyes.

Shoving his hand through his hair, he wondered when it had come to this. When the devil had this woman slipped beneath his skin and taken up residence in his heart? She was all he could think of—indeed she had been for some time—but where lust had initially driven his desire to seek her company, he knew there was more to it than that. There was the gut-wrenching knowledge his life would be over if she did not pull through this.

He'd meant what he'd said when he'd told her brother he would do what he could to save her reputation. In spite of all the resistance he'd felt toward marriage, the idea of vowing himself to Juliette had become increasingly appealing. Whether she felt the same, he could only hope. What mattered the most right now, however, was her imminent recovery, not the story that had appeared in several prominent newspapers after Florian had failed to see to Guthrie's arrest.

He recalled with perfect clarity the words originally written by Dorian Harper from *The Gentleman's Daily Gazette*. They had been damning and horribly precise.

Each Season has its scandal. Last year it was Raphe Matthews's unexpected elevation in status from bare-knuckle boxer to Duke of Huntley. This year, it seems to be the new Duke of Redding's parentage.

More popularly known as Florian, until he claimed his uncle's title, this physician turned peer has managed to deceive us all. He was, as rumor has it, not fathered by Viscount Armswell at all, but by the murderous traitor, Bartholomew.

While law dictates that Florian is Armswell's legitimate son, since the earl and his countess were married at the time of Florian's birth, one cannot help but wonder what role Bartholomew may have played in Florian's life. The two are regrettably bound together by blood and since it is common knowledge that certain traits will invariably be passed from parent to child, one has to ask: To what extent does the new Duke of Redding resemble his real father?

As expected, a note had arrived this morning from Huntley, who naturally worried about how all of this was going to impact his sister. Unsure of how to respond, Florian had not written back yet. Instead he focused his attention on ensuring Juliette's well-being.

Which became more of a struggle when her fever rose two days later, prompting nonsensical mutterings while she turned her head from side to side as if hoping to somehow escape the pillow, the bed, her body. He'd known this would happen and yet it still tore at his chest and made him feel more helpless than he'd ever felt before in his life. Because this was Juliette and . . . With trembling hands he forced some laudanum past her lips. Half of it dribbled down over her chin but he hoped she drank enough for it to soothe her nerves.

"Florian."

He barely heard her, she sounded so weak. "Yes, Juliette." He placed a new compress upon her forehead and took her hand in his. "I am right here and I am not going to leave you."

Her body shook. "Not ever?" She clutched at the bedding as if it could save her.

Considering her delirious state, he doubted she spoke of a permanent attachment, and yet as he gave her his answer, he pretended this was precisely what she asked for. "That's right, Juliette. I will always be with you."

A lengthy bit of silence followed and he almost thought she'd fallen asleep. Until she spoke one word with greater insistence than anything else she'd said since he'd taken her into his care.

"Love."

It wasn't perfectly pronounced but there was no mistaking what she'd said. He understood and his heart swelled with gladness and hope and a torrent of powerful emotion. It was as if all sentiment had been locked away deep inside him forever and she had released it from its confines, allowing it to roam free.

"I love you." She pushed the words past her lips with impressive stubbornness, her determination and honesty in the face of her suffering prompting tears to gather at the corners of his eyes.

He had not cried since he was a boy and yet Juliette caused him to do so now, the fear he might lose her when he had barely won her tightening his throat to the point of severe discomfort. It was only made worse by the knowledge that her love for him wasn't real. It couldn't be when she did not know the most vital thing about him. And with this awareness came additional fear, of how she would respond when she learned his real father had almost succeeded in killing her sister the previous year when he'd been trying to stop Amelia from buying the house on the edge of St. Giles—the one she'd since turned into a school. Would Juliette be able to forgive Florian for keeping this from her? He wasn't sure, but since doubt wasn't helping, he did his best not to dwell on it extensively. There would be plenty of time for that later after she recovered.

So with this in mind, he bowed his head over hers and touched her brow with his lips. "I love you too, Juliette." The words were as clear as could be, and God help him if they weren't the truest he'd ever spoken.

Juliette wasn't sure if she was awake or if she was dreaming. It felt as though she was drifting beyond the confines of her body, yet somehow aware of the aches sliding through her and the shivering chill that caused her to shake. Whatever the case, she felt at peace, safe in the knowledge that her feelings had been reciprocated.

Terrified she might die without telling Florian how she felt, she'd delivered the message as well as she'd been able. And he had answered, ensuring her that he loved her in return. She was certain he'd said so while kissing her forehead, though it felt so surreal now she'd started to doubt if it had in fact happened or if it was the fever playing tricks on her brain.

Then he'd brought her additional food, mostly meat, accompanying each serving with a full glass of red wine. He'd changed her nightgown more than once, an act she'd become increasingly used to since he always did it briskly and without appearing to pay any interest in her nudity. Caring for her comfort seemed to be his priority now, completely overshadowing the blatant desire he'd shown for her before she'd succumbed to the illness.

The effect was calming, for it allowed her to ignore the initial apprehension she'd had about him seeing her so disabled.

She relinquished herself to his ministrations, sitting limply in the bath while he bathed her and leaning on him for support while he dressed her. All without a single inappropriate touch. His professionalism was such a stark departure from the passionate man who'd whispered scandalous suggestions in her ear that she began to wonder if she had indeed fabricated his declaration of love. And because of this doubt, she refrained from repeating her own, lest he respond contrary to how she hoped.

"How long have I been here?" she asked one morning when he brought her a larger plate of food than usual. She truly had no idea how much time had passed since he'd taken her away from Lady Arlington's house and brought her here to his home.

"A week."

His response surprised her. "It does not feel like that long."

He watched while she ate a slice of ham. "Losing track of time is expected considering how much you have slept." He offered a tentative smile. "I am relieved to see you looking better."

"I feel better, though not quite myself just yet." Allowing herself to think of all that had happened, she quietly asked, "What about Vivien and her aunt?"

"Funeral arrangements have been made. Your sister-in-law took care of it." His eyes filled with the sympathy of knowing how much this probably meant to Juliette. "They will be buried in the Grosvenor Chapel churchyard."

"I wish I could have done more for them. Vivien did not deserve to have her kindness toward a sickly child repaid with such devastation."

"No, but you did what you could to help—more than most would have done, I dare say. And rather than flee her home in fear, you did the right thing and controlled the contagion by staying. That cannot have been easy."

Reminded of how awful it had in truth been, she shook her head. "It is the worst thing I have ever experienced, looking on helplessly while those around me perished."

"I know precisely what you mean."

Her eyes locked with his to share a lengthy moment of silent propinquity.

A thought struck her. "I know you put the nightcap on my head to keep my hair away from my face when I . . ." She bit her lip, blushed a little and said, "This must sound terribly vain to you, but do you think we can take it off so I can have my hair combed out and dressed? I'm sure you're not an expert on such things but it would mean a lot to me and—" The look of regret that surfaced in his eyes stopped her. "What?"

"I kept wondering when you might notice, but you never did." Crossing the floor, he allowed his gaze to linger on hers before saying, "Your hair was infested with lice, Juliette. I had to cut it off."

Disbelief poured through her as she reached up and tugged at the bow beneath her chin before clawing the nightcap away. Her fingers trembled as they slowly touched her scalp. "No." She patted her head, desperate to negate reality.

"I am sorry, Juliette, but I had no choice."

It was too much, the crippled state he'd seen her in lately and now this. "Get out." She looked away, hiding him from her view and pretending that if she could not see him then he would not be able to see her either.

"This doesn't change my—"

"Please go, Florian." She couldn't even begin to imagine how awful she probably looked—much worse than she'd ever thought possible. "I want to be alone."

"Juliette—"

"Please."

A long moment of hesitant silence followed, and then she heard the soft snick of the door closing as he left the room. The moment he did so, Juliette threw back the covers and climbed out of bed. Fearing the worst, she crossed the floor to the cheval glass standing off to one side in a corner, inhaled deeply and stepped before it.

The image reflected therein was of a woman so foreign to her she had to remind herself it was she. Her body, which had always been slim, looked highly malnourished now in spite of the food she'd been eating. Her collarbones stuck out and her face appeared gaunt while her hair—her beautiful lustrous hair—had been reduced to stubble. In short, she looked like a starving boy dressed in a woman's nightgown. Not exactly the level of attractiveness she hoped to present to Florian.

"I will overcome this." She muttered the promise out loud, giving power to the words. "I will rally and I will get better." Already Florian's doctoring had helped her regain much of her strength. She was able to stand at least without feeling as though she risked falling over, and she no longer felt the urge to cast up her accounts or make a desperate grab for the chamber pot. Florian was to thank for this and he deserved her appreciation rather than the bitterness she had shown him when she'd told him to leave her alone.

Chapter 24

Florian had left her in peace for over an hour and had used that time to put himself to rights. Having slept in the armchair close to her bed for a week meant that he was in dire need of a bath, a fresh set of clothes and a shave. Since he'd yet to call the upstairs safe and free of possible contagion, he chose to bathe belowstairs where Baker could help him shave. Dressed in a clean pair of trousers and a newly ironed shirt, Florian finally felt a bit more like himself.

"How is she faring?" Mrs. Croft asked while stirring the soup she was preparing for dinner.

"Better. I think." When this reply was met with curious stares, he added, "It is my belief she will make a full recovery, though I fear her pride may have taken a hit in the process. She did not like finding out I cut off her hair."

"It will grow back," Jillian assured him. "She will realize that soon enough."

"But in the meantime, there isn't a woman in the world who wants to look dreadful." Mrs. Croft sampled the soup and added a bit more salt. "Least of all in front of a handsome young man like yourself, Your Grace."

"Perhaps you should give her a compliment of some sort," Baker suggested. He helped Florian don his waistcoat and jacket. "It might boost her confidence."

Thanking his servants for their advice, Florian returned upstairs. He hadn't bothered saying that he'd attempted to do precisely that only to have Juliette cut him off and demand he leave her alone. Perhaps now, after having some time to herself, she would be ready to hear him out. Especially since he did have a whole lot more to tell her than compliments alone.

Reaching the door to her room, he stopped to gather his thoughts. Ordinarily, he would have given a quick knock, entered and stated his business. He'd always been a direct man, had never really given much thought to what people might think of what he said. Getting to the point as quickly as possible was paramount in his line of work. Efficiency mattered. Yet now, standing here in his own bloody house, he worried over how to proceed. For one thing, he wanted to make Juliette happy—as difficult as that was for him to admit since he wasn't accustomed to such concern—and for another, her opinion mattered. He did not want it to do so, but damn it all, it did. She was purity, untouched innocence and goodness to which he had no right. Yet he wanted her with a fierceness he'd never felt before.

Reprimanding himself for his ridiculous indecisiveness, he did what he should have done five minutes earlier and knocked. A welcoming answer granted him entry, so he drew a fortifying breath and went inside the bedchamber. She was sitting much as he'd left her, propped up in bed against a pile of cushions. Immediately, the physician in him began ascertaining the animated look in her eyes, the faint glow to her complexion and the pink shade of her lips.

"You look as though you are on the road to recovery." *And on your way out of my house.* That thought did not sit well.

"I feel much improved, thanks to you." She smiled and it was that wondrous smile that lit up the world. "Thank you for all you have done, for sacrificing your own comfort in order to take proper care of me." Her smile faded a little and her eyes grew serious. "I regret the way I treated you earlier. It was rude of me and I am sorry for it. After all you have done—"

"You were upset and understandably so." He approached the bed but paused and glanced toward the nearby chair he'd been spending a great deal of time in lately. Veering off course, he proceeded to pull it toward the bed so he could be close to her without actually sitting on the bed. Now that her health was improving, he did not dare allow quite so much nearness. "But the lice are gone and your hair will grow back," he said as he took his seat and leaned forward slightly. "From this point onward, you ought to improve a bit more each day."

"So then . . . I will be returning home soon?"

He nodded. "Yes." It was unavoidable, and yet . . . "But there is no need to rush. In fact, I would like to be perfectly certain a remitting fever isn't looming on the horizon before we risk exposing you to your family."

"Of course." A couple of lines creased her otherwise perfect forehead. "That sounds quite reasonable. Shall we give it another week?"

Her wish to stay so long surprised him, and he could not resist. His hand found hers, his thumb carefully caressing the smoothness of her skin. "Juliette . . . there are things I must tell you, explanations you deserve to hear."

"If this is about my reputation, you need not worry. My brother and brother-in-law are both powerful men. They will see to it that Society understands the necessity of my staying here."

He held her gaze and felt his heart ache. Her certainty in this, her belief in the goodness of others and that all would be right in the end was devastating. "I fear you may be wrong in that regard."

She produced a chuckle and shook her head. "Considering all my family has been through, the disapproval we faced when we first arrived in Mayfair, I am confident my sojourn here will be overlooked. Especially if people are told how essential it was, not only to my health, but to everyone else's as well."

It was time to face his fears head-on. So he drew a deep breath and forged ahead. "And that might have been the case except for the fact that I am not the man you think me to be. As a consequence, staying here in my home, for even a single night, will have wrecked any chance you ever had of redeeming yourself in the eyes of the *ton*."

"What do you mean?" A hint of nervousness threaded its way around every word.

Florian withdrew his hand from hers and steeled himself for what was to come. "I am not Lord Armswell's son." Ignoring the instinct to gainsay this admission, he forged ahead. "Bartholomew is my real father, the sort of man one doesn't cross without facing the consequences." He paused. "He gave me an ultimatum and when I didn't respond, he made sure my connection to him became publicly known. The newspapers have had a wonderful time writing about it for the last few days."

Juliette stared at him as if he'd fallen off the back of a wagon and begun doing acrobatics.

"My reputation, not only as a peer but as a respected physician has been decimated by this while yours . . . the fact you have been living with the son of a known criminal, confined in his house for extensive periods of time, will not be easily forgiven. Least of all when taking your own past into consideration."

Realization dawned in her eyes, more brown now than green. "People will think the worst in spite of our good intentions to save them from typhus."

Florian nodded. "And they will say it and print it in every gossip column there is. Of that I am certain, considering the harm that has already been done. It is only a matter of time before they attach your name to mine." Expelling a breath, he fell back against his chair and watched her process this information. "I am sorry, Juliette. Truly I am."

She blinked as if startled out of a reverie by his apology. "Why?" Confusion knit her brow and she slowly shook her head. "You have done nothing wrong, Florian."

"Of course I have, Juliette." Why was she being so stubborn? "I took you into my home without chaperone and—"

"Because you were trying to save my life while keeping other people safe."

Her placating tone was too forgiving for him to bear.

He frowned. "Not once in all the time I have known you did I inform you of the risk you faced by keeping my company. Not at Hawthorne House, Brand House or Stokes House, not in my office or at the opera." She blushed, a deep shade of pink that had nothing to do with her recent illness. "I kissed you as if I had the right, as if I could promise you the future you deserve when all I can give you now is a tarnished name."

"You forget that kissing takes more than one person and that I was equally involved." Too embarrassed to look at him, she spoke to her lap. "I wanted that kiss, Florian. Indeed, I dreamed of it for a long time before it happened, so you have nothing for which to apologize. Truly."

Her honesty slayed him, for although he'd seen desire and longing in her eyes and had known she wanted the same as he, hearing her say it roused a primitive beast within him. It made him want to grab her and hold her and kiss her again until she was breathless, until she forgot time and place and until the only word on her lips was his name.

But to do so could easily destroy her. Already, he feared it might be too late. "My fault was in letting you think I was the man you saw, the man the whole world knew me to be, when I was someone else entirely."

Biting her lip, she shot a glance in his direction. "As if your parentage, over which you have no control, would have kept me away." She raised her head so she could look at him more fully. Sparkles surfaced in her eyes, producing an ethereal effect. "You are still the same noble man, intent on saving others no matter the cost and often too serious for his own good."

Her assessment of him was accurate, but her dismissal of all his concerns made him angry. "Our society is built on reputation and pedigree. Losing one of these might be survivable, especially for a man, but to lose both is unpardonable. My name has been slandered! Viola sent word today that Elmwood, Stokes and Winehurst have all left the hospital committee, which ought to impress upon you the gravity of this situation."

Silence passed in the wake of his outburst until her gentle voice told him, "It is not that I fail to comprehend the gravity of what has occurred or of what this revelation about you means. I merely want you to understand that it does not affect my opinion of you in the slightest."

Her acceptance of him was disarming. He hardly knew how to respond except with one last attempt to make her see reason. "My father is the most renowned criminal in England."

"Yes," she agreed. "He is. But that doesn't mean you should let his actions define you."

Sage advice from someone so young. "I became a physician because of him, not because I wanted to do good but because I needed to prove I was better than him, that the tainted blood in my veins would not decide who I would be."

The edge of her mouth lifted to form a sanguine smile. "And yet you described your profession as a vocation when you spoke of it during the Falconrich Ball last Season."

"I suppose it became one." He'd had a natural flair for it and had consequently applied himself without second thought.

"So then what does it matter how it all began?" She bunched the coverlet in her hands and held on tight. "What is important is where you are now, the man you have become and the fact that the world owes you a debt of gratitude for your unfailing dedication."

The way she saw him was more than enlightening;

it was simple, cutting through rank and profession and delving beyond façade to where only truth existed. It was humbling and gratifying all at once, but it did not make reality any easier to deal with. Least of all when he could think of only one way in which to lessen the damage to her reputation, but since she was still on the mend and he wished her to focus all energy on improving her health, he refrained from making the suggestion. It was enough that he had to worry about taking away her choices and of her never knowing if he made his offer in earnest or because he felt honor bound to do so.

"You are a godsend, Juliette." He spoke without thinking, saying the first thing that came to mind. Her eyes, when they met his, appeared less alert than earlier, so he took that as his cue to leave. "Get some rest. It is the best thing you can do for yourself right now."

Closing her eyes on a nod, she rolled her head to the side and snuggled deep into the pillow. "Thank you for taking such excellent care of me, Florian."

He fought the urge to bow down and kiss her and went to the door instead. "You are most welcome." His chest was tight as he quit the room, his every nerve ending screaming for him to stay with her. But he also needed to clear his head in order to think, which was something he could not do as well as he ought when he was near her. The distraction she offered was simply too great, the temptation to let his gaze linger upon her eyelashes, the tip of her nose, the curve of her ear . . . He truly was losing his mind over this woman.

No.

He had lost his mind over her when he'd succumbed

to the urge to kiss her. Until that moment, he'd maintained some semblance of sanity and control, but there was now a precise instant in time—a second he could literally point to—in which he had lost it. His heart was in her hands now, which wasn't as frightening as he had feared. In fact, for a man who'd done everything in his power to avoid falling in love, he had to admit that there was something remarkably pleasant about it.

It was two days before Juliette decided she was well enough to venture out of bed. Sitting in the armchair Florian had occupied whenever he'd come to check on her, she tried to concentrate on the book she was reading. It was difficult. *Very* difficult. In fact, she had already reread the same page three times, which was not a criticism of Ann Radcliffe, whose novels she adored, but a testament to her preoccupation with a certain gentleman.

Florian was wrong to castigate himself for being Bartholomew's son. She certainly had no issue with it. But since he was the one directly affected by it and she sensed it cut a deep wound in his soul, she understood that saying as much would not be enough. She would have to show him that he was deserving of love no matter who his father was or what he had done. But to do so would take time—time spent together—time for him to realize she would always choose him, no matter what.

A knock sounded at the door and her "Enter!" brought the man in question into the room. He was just as casually attired today as he had been all the other days he'd tended to her. The domestic appearance warmed her heart, but the breadth of his shoulders and the hint of skin peeking out from behind his open shirt collar made a flush creep over her cheeks. Yes, she had recovered, enough to appreciate Florian's physical attributes and enough to long for him to kiss her again.

"Your beauty never ceases to astound me." His words were soft and yet they crashed over her with delightful force. Since registering the distress she'd felt upon discovering her hair had been sheared, he'd been complimenting her as often as possible. "I am not just saying that," he added hastily. "I honestly mean it."

"I know you do and I thank you." The new uncertainty with which he had started addressing her was endearing. She wasn't sure what caused it, but she liked him like this, a bit out of sorts. It matched the way she'd always felt in *his* presence. "Will you join me?"

He glanced across at the bed, hesitated a moment and then went to sit on the edge of the mattress. "I ought to have Jillian tend to you for the remainder of your stay." His voice was thoughtful. "All gossip aside, having me visit you in your bedchamber like this, now that you are almost fully recovered, is highly inappropriate."

Juliette's heart sank. She did not want to lose his attention or the chance to make him see how right they were for each other. Setting her book aside, she pondered her options. He had been raised with a strict concept of how to treat a lady. Rules and etiquette had been drilled into him all his life, so it was only natural for him to insist the closeness they had shared during her illness come to an end. Unless she was able to speak to the part of him that had tossed propriety aside at the opera and kissed her with abandon. That part of him existed, no matter how much he tried to restrain it.

With this in mind, she told him simply, "I do not wish for Jillian's ministrations. I wish for yours."

His eyes, those deep blue eyes, drove into hers with hot intensity. "Juliette."

Her name was spoken in warning and with encouraging roughness. "I still feel slightly faint." *Faint because of you, not because of fever.* Rising to her feet, she forced him to stand as well. "You are my physician, Florian. I am here because of you, so I think it only proper that you should be the one to ensure my full recuperation."

His posture had gone completely rigid, his stance suggesting he was caught between the urge to run and the duty to stay. "Helping you dress and undress, assisting you with your bath, is no longer something I must do, Juliette. Indeed . . ." His expression had turned tumultuous. "It is not something I *should* be doing any longer."

Tilting her head, she took a step closer to where he stood. "Why not?"

"Because I am no longer a mere physician, Juliette. I am a man who desires you in every way imaginable." His breath was ragged, his words coming in quick succession as if they were bricks in a wall being built to protect him from her advance. "It was easy to ignore it while I was struggling to save your life. But now that you are well again, I am embarrassed to admit I cannot see you unclothed without betraying my professionalism."

"Of all the compliments you have ever given me,

I do believe that is the best." For it wasn't spoken in an effort to pamper her ego or soothe her spirit, but as a real warning of what might occur if she chose to ignore him. Brazenly, she continued forward, not stopping her progress until she was but a hand's width away. "Would it trouble you if I were to tell you that I rather like the idea of you betraying your professionalism?"

When on earth had she started sounding so wanton? And when had she gotten the courage to say such outrageous things? It had to be her determination to win him that made her do so. For in truth, she was sure she would say what was necessary, no matter how improper or undignified, if it meant she would meet with success.

"We are in a bedchamber, Juliette. You cannot say such things to me without consequence." His voice was raw, his chest rising and falling heavily while his eyes studied her with infinite longing.

"If the consequence is a kiss like the one we shared before, then it shall be worth it." She looked up at him from beneath her lashes, praying for his surrender. He was tall, his masculine presence crowding her with its physical power. Energy hummed between them, a living thing writhing and thrashing against its chains until she placed her hand on his arm.

The action, tentative as it was, seemed to unravel his finely held control. Without warning, he wound his arm around her, pulling her close as his mouth met hers with desperation. It was rough and un-forgiving, elemental in its urgency and thoroughly effective in feeding the cravings of Juliette's mind, body and soul. She reveled in it, in the force with which he held her and the diligence with which he accommodated her need for him to surround her, caress her, taste her.

The skill with which he applied himself dressed her in sparks that pricked at her skin until she trembled. Her legs grew weak, forcing her to cling to him while an unfamiliar sigh was wrenched from deep within. He responded with a guttural growl and by flattening his hand against the curve of her lower back.

"Juliette." Her name tickled the edge of her mouth and was quickly succeeded by a trail of kisses along the edge of her jaw.

Angling her head, she allowed him greater access while arching more boldly against his embrace. "Yes." Her fingers pushed through his hair and clasped at his head, holding him close while he licked a path along her neck.

"You're mine." His teeth nipped her flesh, marking her in a way that made her feel claimed. It was basic, the action thoroughly male, perhaps even a little barbaric. But rather than put her off, it made her insides sizzle with increased passion. Until he drew back with a ragged breath and set her aside as if he'd been scorched. "We should not be doing this. I . . . I have taken alarming liberties with you and I—"

"Apologize and I shall never forgive you."

He stared at her in utter stupefaction. "But—"

"I encouraged you because *this* is what I want." She swallowed, braced herself by straightening her spine and squaring her shoulders. "Because I want *you*, Florian. If you will have me, that is."

Florian's eyes almost bulged from his head and his mouth fell open. Juliette could not recall a man ever looking more shocked than he did right now, which prompted her to smile even though she'd never felt more nervous in all her life. This was his chance to deny her, to say he did not want her in return. Because if there was one thing he'd been adamant about from the start, it was his reluctance to marry—more notably, his reluctance to marry *her*. So she stood, still as a statue, and waited for him to gather his wits. Part of her wished she'd had more sense than to lay her heart bare without even the slightest finesse while another part sighed with relief. They would finally determine where they stood with one another. Or so she hoped.

Chapter 25

Facing Juliette, this force of nature who stood before him with fearless and honest abandon, was mesmerizing. *I want you, Florian. If you will have me, that is.* The words had besieged his mind. He could not think of anything else besides this wild declaration and all the possibilities it laid out before him.

Heart hammering in his chest and still reeling from the perfection of the kiss they'd just shared, he waded past his fears. Of course he wanted her. The question was whether or not he would make her happy and if he'd be able to keep her safe. "Just to be clear," he stated slowly, "you want me to ask for your hand?" He had no wish to misunderstand her and to propose they marry before she was ready to accept such an outcome.

"Yes."

She did not even flinch. The certainty with which she delivered her response was unwavering and, he had to admit, thoroughly arousing.

Banking that thought for a moment, he contemplated the path before them. "My disinclination to consider courting you was never on account of disinterest. It is imperative that you understand this,

Juliette, because of what I am about to tell you."
Uncertain apprehension stole into her eyes, but she
nodded, encouraging him to continue. "I have been
attracted to you from the start, but I did not think
us well suited until I got to know you better. And
then my connection to Bartholomew held me back.
At first, because I was ashamed to tell you about it,
and later because I feared what he might do to you if
he learned we'd formed an attachment."

"I understand your reasoning completely." Not a
hint of censure clung to her words, only flagrant acknowledgment of fact. "But do you really want to let
fear deprive you of happiness and love?"

"*Love*." He tested the word and all it implied.

"I love you, Florian. I cannot deny it or run from it
any more than I can change the course of the stars in
the heavens or turn back the hands of time."

This was what he wanted. Astoundingly, it was
what he had always wanted, he acknowledged with
some surprise—to be loved for who he was in spite of
his flaws, no matter what the rest of the world might
think of him. There was no obstacle in his path, save
his own apprehension, but perhaps even this could
be put to rest if Bartholomew could somehow be removed from the equation.

"He was supposed to hang." He murmured the
words.

"What?"

Blinking, Florian registered Juliette's bewildered
expression. "Forgive me. I was merely voicing a
thought." He moved toward her, intent on returning
to the discussion of marriage.

But she stepped back and held up her hand, halting
his stride. "I hope you're not contemplating murder."

The possibility had been pressing upon his mind

for a while, though not in quite so dishonorable a way. "A challenge, rather."

"On the field of honor?" She looked appalled. "Nothing good can come of such a thing. Surely you know that."

"I could rid the world of a cur and live happily ever after." The thought was a rather appealing one.

"No. You would forever be the man who took his father's life." The disappointment that flared in her eyes was as real as the passion she'd shown moments earlier. "Consider how difficult it has been for you to forgive yourself for actions you weren't to blame for, and ask yourself if you will truly be able to absolve yourself of all blame and find the peace you seek if you proceed with such a plan."

Clenching his jaw, Florian damned her insightfulness and his own reluctance to walk away and do as he wished. He cared too much about her, however, to ignore what she said. Instead he listened and grudgingly offered his agreement. "Very well." He could not keep the disgruntled tone from his voice even though he knew she was right.

Her voice drew nearer, curling around him as she took a step in his direction. "But as duke, your power is not insignificant, no matter the shame Bartholomew brings to your name. If you join forces with Coventry and Huntley, inform the king of what has transpired, then surely the error regarding Bartholomew's punishment shall be corrected and justice served."

He gave an absent nod. "I must return you to your brother's care sooner than I intended. Until this matter has been resolved and you and I are married, you need to be under his roof."

The disappointment marring her features made him

wish it weren't so, but the truth was that he'd already kept her here longer than necessary. So he moved to pass her, pausing next to her shoulder so he could whisper in her ear. "It is the only way to prevent me from acting dishonorably." Her sharp intake of breath confirmed she knew what he meant and he couldn't resist. His hand found hers, his thumb brushing gently over her palm. "Don't worry," he assured her. "Everything will work out in the end." Turning his head, he placed a tender kiss upon her brow. She responded by nuzzling closer, her breath falling warmly against his neck.

It was intimate and it was perfect and he regretted having to walk away. But there were matters he had to attend to if they were to marry as fast as he hoped.

Putting on one of the dresses Gabriella had sent over, Juliette studied her reflection in the cheval glass. Jillian had been sent up to help her prepare for her return to Huntley House since Florian was apparently quite serious about adhering to proper etiquette. He would not allow the two of them to spend more time together alone. Not when she was well enough to go back home. Which meant she had not seen him since he'd left her the previous evening, hungry for more of his kisses but grateful for his restraint. As much as she longed for them to be together, she would have regretted relinquishing the sanctity of their wedding night.

With this in mind, she tied her bonnet in place and made her way downstairs to the foyer where Florian stood in quiet conversation with Sarah. He must have heard her upon the stairs for he turned to greet her, his expression characteristically serious while his eyes . . . his eyes conveyed warmth and such depth of emotion Juliette felt a wild urge to fling herself into his arms.

Instead, she nodded politely, observed wryly that his hands were clasped behind his back so he could not touch her, and went to greet her maid, who welcomed her with a happy smile.

"I intend to call on your brother later today," Florian murmured for Juliette's ears alone while leading her out to the awaiting carriage. "If he approves of my intentions, we shall soon be betrothed." He handed her up behind Sarah and shut the door swiftly, as if fearing he might otherwise follow her into the conveyance.

If only.

Rather, he took a step back and signaled for the driver to set the horses in motion. Juliette moved in order to look out the window. She watched his somber form until he vanished from sight and then fell back against the squabs with a sigh.

From beside her, she heard a chuckle and glanced up to meet Sarah's dancing eyes. "You truly are besotted, my lady."

Juliette smiled in return. "As well I should be when glancing at my future husband." The carriage rolled on, picking up speed.

"Indeed?" Sarah grinned. They rounded a corner. "I am relieved to hear that all will be set to rights. Considering all the nasty rumors circulating the City, I feared—"

A jolt and a pistol shot halted the carriage along with whatever Sarah had been meaning to say. "My lady." Sarah's hand touched Juliette's arm in alarm.

Beyond the carriage, voices arguing, presumably

with the coachman, followed until another shot pierced the air and all went silent. Juliette's heart leapt frantically against her chest. Steadying herself with a deep breath, she tried to remain as calm as possible. She would be fine. She had to be. Her future with Florian awaited.

The carriage door was wrenched open and a tall man with a thick white scar running right beneath his left eye came into view. His gaze went directly to Juliette. "Get out." He pointed a pistol in her direction to ensure she complied.

"Take me instead," Sarah offered with a wobbly voice. She was already leaning forward, her arm stuck out in front of Juliette in an effort to hold her back.

The man glared at Sarah for one fleeting second before returning his attention to Juliette. "We've no need for your friend there. It's you we want. Now get out or suffer the consequence."

"I will go." Juliette pushed Sarah's arm aside. She had no idea who the men were or what their motive was for insisting she come with them, but she would not allow them to harm Sarah.

"No! You cannot!" Sarah's voice was desperate.

"Return home," Juliette told her as calmly as she was able. "Tell my brother what has happened." She began climbing out but paused in the doorway just long enough to give Sarah a meaningful look. "And make sure Florian knows as well."

Sarah responded with a jerky nod. Her eyes were wide with fear.

An arm came around Juliette's waist. "That's enough." Her kidnapper hauled her down into the street so Juliette could see that each end had been closed off by workers, or men pretending to be workers. They'd diverted traffic and trapped them without anyone taking notice. "Time to go." The man who held her grabbed her wrist so tight her skin twisted and burned beneath his fingers.

Pulling Juliette along, he dragged her toward another carriage, taking her past Raphe's driver, whose lifeless body lay sprawled out next to the whinnying horses. *Dear God!* They'd actually killed a man without second thought! Blood pooled beneath his chest, staining the road in a morbid shade of glistening red.

Fearing she might be sick, Juliette turned her head away and allowed herself to be shoved up into her assailants' carriage. She would comply without complaint lest they choose to punish her by murdering Sarah as well.

So she told herself to keep a tight leash on her composure. Succumbing to tears would serve no purpose beyond annoying these men who'd already proven themselves quite merciless. There was no telling what they might do if she proved too difficult for them to manage. Instead, rational thought and a clear assessment of the situation at hand was the only chance she had of escape and perhaps even of survival.

The man who'd grabbed her got in and sat down beside her while his companion made himself comfortable on the opposite bench. Black curtains blocked out all light, casting them in grimy shadows. A dull object pushed into her side.

"Don't do anything stupid," the man beside her muttered.

"I wasn't planning to," Juliette told him sharply. Across from her the other man aimed his pistol straight at her chest.

"Smart girl," the man beside her said, his weapon nudging her hard in the ribs as the carriage rolled forward. "You wouldn't want to risk a shot going off by accident, would you?"

"No." She said nothing further, remaining silent as the carriage moved onward, her greatest fear being the lack of clues left for Florian and Raphe to follow.

To Florian's relief, everything seemed fine at the hospital when he arrived to make his first rounds after more than a two-week absence. His patients had been well taken care of by the new physicians Viola had hired, and even Haines was there, back at work without a hint of his recent bout with typhus.

"I asked the chief magistrate to press charges against Blaire," Viola said as the two of them strolled through the wards while assessing the standard of care that was being provided. "He will go on trial next week for severe negligence and if found guilty, could go to prison for up to a year."

"It isn't enough, but at least it is something." All Florian could hope for was that the case would set a precedent, reminding other physicians, surgeons and apothecaries of their duty toward their patients.

They walked a few steps in silence before she hesitantly said, "About your reputation . . ."

Florian winced. He'd been wondering when she would bring that up. "The committee has suggested you take a leave of absence for a while. If the situation escalates, you will in all likelihood be asked to resign your position." Her expression was apologetic. "This decision was not made lightly, Florian, but the members felt it was necessary to act in the hospital's best interest and I . . . I do not have enough power alone to go against their wishes."

"Nor should you." As much as he hated having to abandon his work, he understood why it was necessary for him to do so. "The hospital takes priority, Viola. It comes before my pride and whatever duty we have toward each other."

"I knew you would accept the decision, though I do regret that it had to come to this."

"It was Bartholomew's doing. When I failed to meet his demands, he punished me by making my fears a reality." Allowing a humorless grin to surface, he said, "What he probably didn't expect was for me to find comfort in the outcome. For years I have lived with this burden, this abject anxiety, wearing me down. He chose to crack it wide open and release it out into the world, and frankly, the experience has thus far been rather liberating."

"What about Juliette?" Viola gave him a coy glance. "How does she feel about all of this?"

"She loves me for who I am." It still felt miraculous, to have met a woman of her social standing who did not give a fig for appearances, titles, prestige or anything besides core values and character. "To think she will be my wife is . . ." He contemplated the best possible adjective and eventually gave up. "Words cannot describe it."

Viola chuckled. "I am so incredibly happy for you. Everyone deserves to be loved, and I am pleased to know you have found a woman who was able to convince you that you are worthy of such affection."

His cheeks grew uncomfortably hot so he made a hasty attempt to divert attention away from himself. "What about you, though? Is it not time for you to dip your toes into Society and perhaps make a match of your own?"

Viola rolled her eyes right before preceding him through a doorway. She paused on the other side at the top of a wide landing and faced him. "Your kind is too hungry for scandal. They devour it as easily as children devour their sweets—in quick succession and without pause." She shook her head and expelled a wistful breath. "My entire life was lived in private until I accepted Tremaine's proposal. The moment we married everything changed. I was written about in the most unfavorable terms because of my age and background. To meet the people willing to read these articles, and use them as fodder for all sorts of rumors, has never appealed. I prefer to keep away and to focus on something larger than myself, rather than on those looking to see me fail the moment I enter a ballroom." She smiled with the assurance of a woman who knew her own mind. "This is my domain, Florian. This is where I stand a chance of success. Not out there in public and certainly not with some aristocratic snob of a husband by my side."

When he raised an eyebrow, she relaxed her expression and chuckled while hitting him lightly on the arm. "You know what I mean, Florian, and besides, you are as different from that lot as I am."

He was well aware of the fact. They started down the stairs at a steady pace. "Still, I always imagined you settling down one day and having children." She was so protective and nurturing it would be a shame if she didn't.

"*This* is my child." She spread her arms wide, encompassing the entire hospital in her statement. "I have pledged my life to it, Florian. I do not have the time or the energy for the responsibilities of marriage and motherhood."

Viola's words resonated deep within. It was precisely how he had felt until recently, until Juliette had become more important to him than anything else in the world. He still wanted his career, of course, if keeping it was possible. One of the things he loved about Juliette was knowing she would support him in this and that she would show him how to have both.

Reminded of this, he told Viola, "I have an important call to make. Will you let me know what the committee members decide?"

"Of course." She smiled at him warmly. "I will continue insisting that no one can take your place."

Pleased to know he had her unwavering support, Florian left the hospital quickly, hailed a hackney and directed it to Huntley House. "I wish to speak with His Grace," he told the butler as soon as the door to the massive residence was opened. He handed the man his card even though it was a superfluous effort considering the number of times he'd come here in the past. The butler knew precisely who he was.

"Wait one moment." The butler departed down a corridor.

To Florian's surprise, however, it wasn't he who returned, but Huntley himself, his creased brow, chaotic hair and quick stride affording him with a wild appearance that instantly alerted Florian to the man's distress. "Thank God you're here. I was ready to go and find you myself."

Ice began to form in Florian's gut. It shivered through his veins until cold panic was all he could feel. "Juliette. Is she not well?" If she had suffered a relapse, it could prove fatal in her already weakened state.

"This has nothing to do with her health." Huntley said, but the dread in his eyes lingered. Florian held his breath, fearing the worst and expecting his life to be torn to shreds within seconds. "She was taken at gunpoint, evicted from the carriage I sent to collect her."

The ice expanded, pushing its way into Florian's heart and filling it with a pain so acute he almost clutched at his chest. "We have to find her." Dear God, if something had happened to her, if these villains had harmed her in any way, he'd rip their heads from their bodies and—

"Her maid described a tall broad-shouldered man with a thick white scar beneath one eye," Huntley said, scattering Florian's bloodthirsty thoughts of revenge. "She said his hair was black and his eyes an odd shade of amber."

Coherent thought returned, pushing his panic aside and allowing him to assess what he knew with the same precision with which he'd always applied himself to everything. The information led to only one possibility, one in which fear turned to outrage, then anger and finally fury.

Meeting Huntley's gaze with the determination of a man setting out on a hunt, he told him crisply, "It sounds like the man who took her was Mr. Smith, Bartholomew's manservant."

Huntley frowned. "What the hell does he want with Juliette?"

"I'll explain on the way," Florian promised, already striding back toward the carriage. He held the door open for Huntley who climbed in without further question. Florian leapt in behind him and fell back against the bench as the carriage lurched into motion. "The truth," he said after righting himself, "is that Bartholomew's still alive and hell-bent on seeking revenge."

Chapter 26

The room Juliette had been brought to was without a doubt the most garish she'd ever seen. Red velvet drapes flanked each window, the excess fabric pooling richly upon the glossy parquet. Gilded furniture clad in plush brocade matched the drapes and the gold braided ties that held them. Thick carpets stretched across the floor, decorated by lavish designs of flowers in full bloom. Most unsettling were the paintings hung side by side on the walls, each depicting scenes of nude men and women engaging in explicit acts of sexual congress.

Perched on one of the chairs, Juliette deliberately gazed at her feet. She had yet to be informed of why she'd been brought here, though she had begun to suspect who was behind it since the only criminal she could think of with this sort of wealth was Bartholomew. After all, this was precisely what Florian had feared, that his father would use his loved ones to seek revenge.

A door opened and footsteps approached with a soft tread. Juliette refused to look up, refused to give her captor the satisfaction of her curiosity, her interest. So she kept her eyes stubbornly on her feet until a black pair of fine leather shoes, freshly buffed, came into view. Silence followed, keeping her escalating heart rate company. And then, the distressing stroke of a finger sliding firmly over her jaw.

"My, my, my . . ." A low chuckle followed. "You certainly are a pretty one, even though I suspect you look much better with hair."

A palm crept under her chin, tilting it back and forcing her gaze up until it collided with blue steely eyes. The nose between said eyes was narrow and delicately shaped, the mouth beneath well hidden behind a finely trimmed beard.

"Do you know who I am?" His silky voice made her shudder. She clenched her jaw, thought of Florian and tried to ignore the ripples of fear flowing through her. "My name is Mr. Mortedge, but perhaps you know me best as Bartholomew."

So she was right. This was Florian's father, and he had deliberately taken her in order to hurt his son. A fine plan, one that would likely work as long as Bartholomew thought she was Florian's weakness.

"What do you want?" She forced as much venom into her tone as she could muster.

Bartholomew gave her a syrupy smirk. "Retribution." He withdrew his hand and took a step back, his gleaming eyes sliding over her body until she felt dirty and violated. "First, Florian betrayed me, then he ignored me. Informing the world of his heritage isn't enough. He needs to suffer and learn that I must be heeded."

Dread slithered through her, curling around her insides and snapping at her sanity. She had to stay calm, no matter what. "You assume any harm you inflict upon me will have the effect you desire, but Florian isn't a man prone to deep emotion. He is guided by logic alone."

"Except when he is with you." Bartholomew spoke with the confidence of a man who was well informed, and that made Juliette's confidence wither. "His affection for you has been made quite clear. The look in his eyes when you are together is oh so touching. And let's not forget the risk he took on your behalf."

"He would have done the same for anyone else."

Bartholomew looked at her with condescension. "Unlikely. He gave up everything he held dear in order to save you, Juliette. I bet he would do so again by offering marriage . . . yes . . . I see I'm correct. He hopes to salvage what remains of your reputation!" A dull bit of laughter tumbled from his chest. "Ha! Imagine how upset he will be when I take away his chance to do so—that incessant need he has to be a knight in shining armor, waving his noble sword in the wake of my destruction."

"You're mad."

"No." All trace of humor vanished from his face as he leaned in close, his light blue eyes driving straight through her own. "I am fueled by hatred and severe disappointment and I have suffered my son's disobedience long enough. The time has come for me to teach him a lesson, by making him watch you die."

Juliette's stomach dropped. A cold shiver scraped her spine. "He will not come."

"Hmm . . ." He studied her closely, then lowered his gaze to her breasts and allowed it to linger. "Perhaps not. Perhaps . . ." His hand was suddenly between her legs, pushing them apart so he could stroke along her inner thighs. "I could teach you a thing or two about pleasure."

She tried to clamp her legs together while wriggling back in her seat. Bile rose in her throat. "My brother will kill you before you have the chance."

He straightened himself and seemed to consider her warning with calculated care. Eventually he grinned, wide and mockingly. "You underestimate the speed with which I am able to accomplish the deed."

She stared at him in horror. "You're a monster!"

"No. I am wronged!" He bellowed the words, letting them bounce off the walls with violent fury. Glaring at her, he squared his shoulders and smoothed his jacket. "I believe our guests will arrive soon—it's a gift, you know, sensing your child's nearness." Moving away, he went to the door and paused there to smile at her as if all was well and he was the most incredible host in the world. "You may want to start praying if you're the religious sort." And with that ominous piece of advice, he left her to do precisely that.

"**A**re you absolutely sure we shouldn't alert the authorities?" Huntley asked. Sitting opposite Florian in a hired hackney, they'd been discussing the situation at hand and their approach to it during their drive over to the Red Rose. Unsure of what they were up against, Florian wanted as much support as possible and intended to ask Henry for help.

"Absolutely. Doing so would only put Juliette in additional danger."

"Because Bartholomew might decide to take her down with him if he starts to feel threatened," Huntley reasoned.

Florian nodded. "Let's not forget how easily he murdered your driver. And he is not the only man Bartholomew's killed over the years, I assure you." Why the devil were they moving so infernally slowly? Shifting, he glanced out the window and saw to his relief that they were almost there. "The worst part is we're not dealing with a lunatic who belongs in Bedlam, but with a calculated evil-doer whose mind is sharper than most. Our only chance is to try and reason with him, though I can assure you it will not be easy."

"Because he believes he is right and you are wrong."

"Precisely."

The carriage drew to a halt and Florian sprang out, not waiting for Huntley, whom he sensed was following close behind. Without breaking his stride, he almost ran through the Red Rose's entrance and down the hall to his brother's office.

The door stood open so Florian entered without knocking, greeting Henry with a quick nod before getting straight to the point of his visit.

"Bartholomew has her." Florian strode forward until he stood face-to-face with Henry. "The bloody bastard has taken Juliette and we need your help in getting her back."

"Christ!" Henry's eyes sharpened, lit by a kindred fury. He stood, rounded his desk and followed Florian from the room, talking as they went. "If we had only alerted the authorities when you discovered he poisoned Armswell then—"

"What?" Exasperation gripped Florian with full force. "Bartholomew looks entirely different from the man he once was. How would you have proven he was one and the same when everyone thinks him dead?"

"I would have found a way," Henry insisted.

They exited the Red Rose. "Unlikely, considering how good he has always been at deception." Climbing into the waiting carriage, Florian paused while Henry and Huntley followed him inside before adding, "He would have dismissed all accusations and made you look a fool, Henry. Especially since his new persona is that of an upstanding citizen."

"He is liked and respected," Henry agreed. "More than that, he is needed. I know several people who've welcomed his investments in recent months."

"I don't suppose you were able to find the source of his wealth?" Florian asked.

Henry shook his head. "I would have told you if I had."

"Which validates my argument," Florian told him. "As Mortedge, Bartholomew was reborn. There was nothing we could pin on him, no means to take him down once and for all."

"Until now," Huntley pointed out with a glower.

Florian nodded. "Precisely." He clenched his fists and turned a stiff gaze out the window. The carriage started forward with a brisk lurch, carrying them all toward Bedford Square and the town house where England's most renowned criminal now resided, unbeknownst to his wealthy neighbors.

Time was a curious concept. Even when Juliette had been confined to a bed and ought to have felt it drag on, the days had flown by because Florian had been there. Now, with a nearby clock telling her only one hour had passed since she had arrived in this room, it felt like she had been there for an eternity.

To her surprise, she had not been restrained in any way, most likely because Bartholomew did not think she stood much of a chance against him and his men. Which was probably true. But if Florian came for her—*when* he came for her—she wanted to be ready to help.

So she strolled around the room searching for something to use as a weapon. To her disappointment, the room did not contain a single sharp object. Not even a misplaced pencil. The infernal clock ticked the monotonous passing of seconds. Juliette eyed a vase. If she broke it, perhaps she could claim it an accident while hiding away one of the shards? She shook her head. It was much too obvious a ploy.

Tick-tock, tick-tock . . . If only the damn thing would stop! She glared at it, at the gold casing, the mother-of-pearl dial and all the little Roman numerals neatly placed upon it. Gradually, like a dream invading reality, an idea began to take shape. Juliette blinked. Yes. This could work. Maybe. She went to the clock and made a quick study of it, then carefully opened the glass door.

Voices approaching the room made her hasten her movements. Swiftly, she closed the front of the clock back up and hurried across the floor, dropping into an armchair just as the door to the room swung open. Bartholomew strolled in as casually as if he were having guests over for tea. He was followed by three welcome faces, Raphe, Lowell and Florian, with the same men who'd kidnapped her bringing up the rear. Both were holding pistols at the ready.

"You see," Bartholomew purred as he came toward her. Taking her by the hand, he pulled her to her feet. "Your ladylove is perfectly fine, Florian." He flung his arm around Juliette's waist and pulled her close. "For now."

Florian bristled. "Get your filthy hands off her." He spoke between clenched teeth while Raphe and Lowell accompanied his words with venomous scowls.

Bartholomew clucked his tongue. "Where are your manners?" He squeezed Juliette until revulsion snaked through her. "You see she is unharmed and yet you choose to insult me. In my own home, no less."

"Let her go." Florian's voice had cooled to a tone far more threatening than his previous one. "I am the one you want to punish. Me. Not her."

"And what better way to do so than through her?" Bartholomew moved, as did Florian. "Ah, ah, ah! Stay right where you are lest one of my men there produces a twitch and accidentally fires his weapon."

Something sharp made contact with Juliette's neck. A blade, the fine edge of it grazing her skin. Instinctively she sucked in a breath. Her gaze met Florian's and held it. If she died here today it would be with his dear face filling her vision.

"Bartholomew," Florian warned, hands raised in surrender. "Put the knife down. Please."

"Or what?" Bartholomew paused for a second. "You came here unarmed, expecting to what, convince me to show compassion when you would grant me no such thing? Or have you forgotten that you are the reason why I had to go into hiding? I lost thousands of pounds in my business while having to pretend I was dead. All because you couldn't keep your bloody mouth shut!" The blade pressed harder against Juliette. "You just had to thwart me."

"Do not pretend you did not deserve it," Florian countered. "I know better than anyone what you are capable of. If anyone deserves revenge, it is I, not you."

"As if you have the bollocks for it." Sneering, Bartholomew tightened his grip on Juliette. His men moved around, their weapons aimed only at Raphe and Lowell.

Intuitive realization dawned on Juliette. No matter what happened, Bartholomew would not harm Florian. He might cause him grief and misery by killing her, Lowell and Raphe, but Florian was his son. In spite of everything, he would not be able to take his life.

The relief this knowledge gave her was profound. It meant not only that the man she loved would live, but that she had one less person to worry about. Biding her time, she eyed Bartholomew's men. Their eyes were fixed on their targets, ready to fire if Raphe or Lowell made any sudden movements. But if she distracted them . . .

Florian took a step forward. Juliette felt a sharp sting as the blade pressed even closer. It must have broken her skin. She tried to focus on where it made contact and deliberately turned her body more fully toward Bartholomew. "Regarding your earlier suggestion," she whispered, all the while moving her critical veins out of harm's way, "I accept."

The blade lost contact with her neck entirely as Bartholomew met her gaze. "Be more specific."

"Kill me and you could hang. In truth this time." Distracting him as she spoke, she positioned herself just so . . . "Bed me and you will exact your revenge without risking your neck."

Greedy lust, abhorrent in it proclivity, captured his every feature. A grin spread wide across his face while laughter spilled from his mouth. Juliette struggled to hide her disgust while pulling a long piece of spindly metal out from under her sleeve. Gripping it, she listened while Bartholomew claimed she was his, bragging of how he would take great pleasure in making her a party to his every deviance.

"When I'm done, I'll toss her lifeless body out onto your doorstep, Florian." He shook with the humor he found in that statement. "Imagine the joy I shall find in knowing I took her from you and tainted her with the filth you've been so ashamed of all these years."

Behind her, Juliette heard Florian curse Bartholomew with words that would shame the devil himself. Taking her chance, she held on firmly to the clock hand she'd stolen and plunged it deep into Bartholomew's leg. He cried out in pain and a thud sounded from somewhere behind Juliette right before a shot shattered the air.

All laughter ceased.

Bartholomew's eyes bulged and he bared his teeth like a rabid dog.

As expected, the blade sliced her neck.

"No!"

Another shot fired followed by a grunt.

"Juliette!" Florian's voice told her he lived and would be all right while she on the other hand had to finish what she had started. Especially if Raphe or Lowell had just been killed.

Retracting her hand to unblock the wound, she followed Bartholomew down to the floor. "You fucking bitch!" Bartholomew writhed beneath her and Florian was suddenly there, pulling her off him, his hand pressed over the side of her neck.

"Jesus." He drew her into his arms, surrounding

her trembling body with his strength while she came to terms with what she had done. "I thought I lost you," Florian whispered against her cheek. "I thought he cut too deep. Thank God it is just a graze." Unwinding his cravat, he carefully tied it around her neck to stanch the bleeding.

Tears welled in Juliette's eyes. "Heavens, what have I done?"

"What was necessary, sweetheart." Florian's hand smoothed over her hair. "He threatened to kill you so you had no choice. You did the right thing."

Pulling back, Juliette forced herself to look at the body beside her. "Do you think you can save him?" Blood pulsed from Bartholomew's thigh. His face was already paling.

"You punctured his femoral artery with surgical precision, Juliette." Florian's voice was packed with amazement for only a second before turning serious. "How on earth did you know how to do so?"

"Cowper's *Anatomy of Humane Bodies*. I've been studying it in great detail."

He stared at her as if she were the most incredible woman who ever lived. "Of course you have." His knuckles brushed her cheek. "So full of surprises and always ready to astound me with your interest in learning." He glanced sideways to where Bartholomew lay. "There is nothing I can do for him at this point."

Juliette's insides twisted. "I'm sorry. I know you deserved your own vengeance and I . . ." She gulped, sucking air into her lungs. "I took that from you, but—"

"You made the right decision, providing us the distraction we needed to take out his men." Nudging her chin, he turned her gaze toward his own. "There is absolutely nothing for you to be sorry about. Do you understand?"

She nodded even as the severity of her actions sank deeper into her consciousness. Florian might forgive her, but would she ever forgive herself? She'd taken a man's life after all, even if he was guilty of heinous crimes and had been sentenced to hang. Getting over that would not be easy. It would take time, and even then she feared she might never fully recover from the shocking awareness of her own capabilities.

Helping her to her feet, Florian clasped her head between his hands and held her gaze. Compassion darkened the blue in his eyes, speaking volumes of his affinity with her. "I am so incredibly relieved to know you are safe." He bent to kiss her, thoroughly and desperately and without caring about Raphe's or Lowell's presence. A tight hug followed, infusing Juliette with warmth and steadfast calm before he released her and took a step back. "Give me a moment to say a few words before it is too late."

She nodded and went to stand next to her brother whose solid embrace was a welcome support against all that had happened. Behind where they stood were Bartholomew's men, one dead, the other held at gunpoint by Lowell.

"What happened?" She could not believe the speed with which they'd been taken out.

"When you stabbed Bartholomew and he cried out in pain, his men's attention was directed away from us," Raphe told her. "Florian must have realized they would not shoot him, so he made a grab for one of the pistols. Lowell and I followed suit, which was when the men fired, one of them hitting the other in the fray."

"I'm glad it wasn't you, Lowell or Florian." It was sobering to think how lucky they were since the situation could easily have played out differently.

Raphe squeezed her against him and kissed the top of her head. "Me too." His voice, always so strong and certain, was weak with emotion. "These past few weeks have been hellish for me. Had it not been for Florian's stalwart dedication toward you, I fear . . ." Words failed him for seconds on end before he managed to draw a deep breath and say, "He loves you so much, Juliette. The dread in his eyes, first when he realized how sick you were and then when I told him that you had gone missing, left no doubt about it."

Peace settled deep in Juliette's chest, spreading warmth through all her veins. "I love him too, Raphe. I love him so much my heart's bursting with it."

Raphe chuckled faintly. "I know what you mean and so does Amelia. The three of us have been truly blessed."

Not by the wealth they'd secured but by the people who longed to spend their lives with them. It was dizzying, Juliette decided, knowing Florian wanted to make her his wife—that in spite of his strict aversion to marriage, he welcomed it now. Because of her.

With this in mind, she looked up at her brother and smiled. "Blessed doesn't even begin to cover it, Raphe, and I am not really sure if anything does."

Chapter 27

It was peculiar, the melancholy Florian felt as they left Bartholomew's home. The chief magistrate had been called to the scene, and they had spent an hour or so thereafter explaining what had transpired. Naturally, the magistrate had not been pleased to discover the wrong person had been hanged while the true criminal went on with his life as if nothing had happened. It would likely result in lengthy apologies having to be made, unfavorable articles in the papers and the public questioning the justice system's efficiency.

Climbing into a hired hackney, Florian sat down across from Raphe, who'd claimed the seat next to Juliette. This was expected and yet it still grated. After all that had happened, the only person he longed to be near—to hold and to touch—was her. Yet he was being denied such liberty because of a long list of truly annoying rules. So he folded his arms across his chest and tried not to miss her.

She was right there, after all, alive and well, no more than a few feet away. But it still felt like a wide expanse had been placed between them.

"Do you mind if I accompany you to your home instead of returning to my own, Huntley?" he asked as they plodded along. "There is something I wish to discuss with you as soon as possible. I would rather not wait."

"I'm sure you would not," Huntley said with raised eyebrows. He sounded amused while Juliette's cheeks, Florian noted, turned a charming shade of pink. "There is an excellent brandy in my study that I would be happy to share with you."

Satisfied with this answer, Florian spent the rest of the carriage ride thinking of what lay ahead. It was curious how drastically his life had changed. He'd gone from being a physician, with no intention of seeing himself wed, to a duke who could scarcely get married quickly enough. All because of the good-natured woman who'd entered his life with purpose and shown him he could have so much more than he'd ever dared dream.

With Juliette in his arms, he'd realized what he'd been missing, what he had been willing to throw away. She'd humbled him with her kindness, her generosity and steadfast resolve to do more than what was required of her.

They were good together. Their common interest in caring for the sick had forged an initial bond that had steadily deepened as they'd become better acquainted with each other. And then there were the kisses. Daring a glance in Juliette's direction, Florian could not help but study her lips. They were perfectly shaped and capable of delivering the most passionate responses.

Huntley cleared his throat and Florian's gaze darted to his. The duke shook his head ever so slightly, though his eyes showed a touch of humor. Chastised with the reminder that he had no right to be ogling Juliette, Florian turned to look out the window. The meandering progress he was presently forced to endure was not the least bit conducive to the haste with which he was hoping to become affianced.

When Juliette climbed out of the carriage in front of Huntley House, Raphe ushered her straight up the front steps, preventing Florian from offering escort. "I wish you would stop being so fussy," she murmured.

"Impossible," her brother replied, "considering all the rumors surrounding your extended stay in Florian's home. And besides, you are my sister. It is my duty to safeguard your reputation to the best of my ability."

She supposed that was true, however inconvenient such safeguarding happened to be.

The front door was opened by Pierson, who instantly remarked on how glad he was to see her safely returned. Behind him stood Gabriella, who'd come from the parlor as soon as they'd entered the foyer.

"We were so worried about you, Julie. I cannot tell you how good it is to see you are safe from harm," Gabriella said. She turned to Pierson. "Would you please ask one of the maids to bring up some sandwiches and a fresh pot of tea?" She eyed Florian briefly before adding, "And have my husband's valet pick a cravat for the Duke of Redding to borrow."

"Yes, Your Grace." Pierson went to take care of the refreshments.

As soon as he was gone, Raphe gave Gabriella a

quick account of what had happened before addressing Florian. "I believe our brandy awaits," he told him. To Gabriella he said, "If you will excuse me, dearest, this ought not take long. But I fear Juliette and Florian are both very anxious for certain matters to be resolved, and considering all they have been through, they deserve a positive turn of events. I dare not delay them further." Leaning forward, he pressed a kiss to his wife's cheek and then waved for Florian to follow him down the hallway and into his study.

The door closed, leaving Juliette alone with Gabriella. A moment of silence passed while Juliette fumbled with the ribbon holding her bonnet in place.

"Well?" Gabriella stared at her expectantly. "Will you tell me what that was about?"

A length of satin slipped between Juliette's fingers, undoing the bow. She tried to refrain from smiling too broadly but failed miserably. "Florian intends to ask for my hand."

"Oh but that is wonderful news!" Gabriella was suddenly hugging her. "I always knew the two of you would end up together."

Juliette stepped back. "You did?"

"The air always seemed to spark when you and Florian were in the same room." She hugged Juliette again and grinned. "I am so incredibly happy for you. For both of you."

"Thank you. I . . ." She swept the bonnet from her head. Gabriella gasped, and Juliette suddenly remembered how she must appear. She raised her hand to stroke the downy softness of her head. "My lack of hair must be shocking for you."

"No." Gabriella's initial surprise seemed to vanish. "Sarah did mention it but I had forgotten." She gave a sly smile. "It is not exactly fashionable, but since turbans are in vogue—"

"I will not be wearing a turban!"

"Very well." She linked her arm with Juliette's and led her toward the parlor. "Mama raves about them, but frankly, I find them hideous."

"Besides, my hair will grow back in no time at all."

"Of course it will," Gabriella agreed in the most unconvinced voice ever.

Juliette grinned in response. The only thing that mattered to her was how Florian saw her. And there was no doubt in her mind that he found her beautiful no matter what.

"**T**here is something I need to be absolutely certain about before I allow you to marry my sister," Raphe said while pouring two glasses of brandy. He handed one to Florian and gestured for him to take a seat.

Apprehension nipped at Florian's neck but he shrugged it aside, telling himself he was able to answer anything Huntley asked him. "I love her, if that is your concern." Ordinarily, he would never have shared such feelings so openly, but where Juliette was concerned, he felt compelled to give them free rein. His affection for her had grown so vast that containing it was no longer possible.

Huntley eyed him while taking a seat behind his desk. "It is not. The distress you showed when her life was in danger has left no doubt in my mind that your feelings for her are profound. What worries me is her reputation."

Florian understood. "Marrying me will not be

enough to save it." Not when his own social standing had been torn to shreds.

"I feel as though I have spent most of my life trying to protect her only to fail for the silliest of reasons, because of a social class that places appearance above all else." Huntley took a sip of his brandy. "Juliette's well-being has been in my hands since she was five years old. I cared for her and worried over her, even though I was just a child myself. And since her constitution was always weak, she caused me greater concern than Amelia, who was always so much stronger."

"And yet Juliette has been doing much better since moving to Mayfair."

"Undoubtedly." Huntley swirled his tumbler while studying Florian with forthright pensiveness. "I owe you a debt of gratitude for what you did in order to save her."

A knock at the door was swiftly followed by the arrival of Huntley's valet who came to deliver the cravat Gabriella had requested. Helping Florian don it, the valet tied the length of fabric with expert flair and stepped back to examine his work. With a quick nod, he gave his approval and took his leave.

As soon as he was gone, Raphe said, "I want your assurance that you will treat Juliette as your equal and that you won't ever keep secrets from her again. I know that legally a wife belongs to her husband and has few rights, but when it comes to my sister—"

"I promise," Florian told him. "I will never force my will on her and I will always be completely forthright."

Huntley nodded and set his glass down. "In that case, if she wishes to marry you as much as you wish to marry her, you have my blessing."

A sigh of relief swept through Florian's body. He expelled a breath, even as he realized it would not be quite so simple. "As far as her reputation goes, there is little I can do besides trying to salvage my own. But if I can convince Society that it was wrong to believe what the papers have written, then perhaps I have a chance of regaining my reputation and hers by association."

Huntley met his gaze with interest. "How would you accomplish such a thing?"

"By asking Armswell to deny the story and insist I am his actual son." He'd not yet had a chance to speak with the viscount after everything he'd learned about his dealings with Bartholomew. It wasn't a conversation he looked forward to having, but it was a necessary one, under the circumstances.

Huntley nodded. "In the meantime, I will talk to Coventry. Perhaps the two of us can help by reminding everyone of what an excellent physician you are."

"I appreciate your support, Huntley." Florian set his empty glass aside. "Now, if you do not mind, I would like to speak with Juliette in private."

Huntley grinned. "I will allow it. The parlor is at your disposal, as long as you leave the door slightly open."

When Florian entered the parlor and his gaze met Juliette's, she felt her entire body relax. It was as if his increased nearness helped restore harmony to her soul. And to her own fanciful way of thinking, she imagined her spirit stretching toward his from across the room and pulling him closer until he'd reached the sofa on which she sat.

"Gabriella." Raphe's voice intruded from the doorway. "Might I have a moment of your time?"

As if propelled into motion by her husband's words, Gabriella stood. "Of course." She gave Juliette a quick nod before leaving the room.

The briefest pause followed before Florian lowered himself to the vacant spot beside Juliette and reached for her hand. He swallowed audibly while brushing his fingers gently over hers. A frown creased his brow, and his eyes, those stunning blue eyes, were more reserved than she'd ever seen them. A knot squeezed her heart as awareness crept in, alerting her to his apprehensiveness. Hoping to ease it, she offered a smile and placed her free hand over his, trapping it there while meeting his gaze with every bit of warmth, gratitude and devotion she felt for this man who had come to mean everything to her.

"Juliette." The sound of her name on his lips was like tonic. "So much has happened these past few weeks I scarcely know where to begin."

"May I suggest the part where you officially ask for my hand in marriage?" Blood trembled in her veins, pulsing with enthusiastic expectation.

His characteristic severity shattered, giving way to an unexpected grin. "I do not plan on proposing more than once in this lifetime, so I prefer not to rush it."

Biting back the teasing retort that tempted, Juliette forced herself into silence even as her stomach tightened and her heart beat more rapidly than ever before.

"You are like a ray of sunshine spreading light on a dreary world." As far as beginnings went, Juliette had to concede that this was an excellent one. She held her breath while he continued. "Becoming a husband was never something to which I aspired. Until I met you." His hand squeezed hers. "Your kindness, your dedication to ensuring the well-being of those around you and your devotion when pursuing your goals is incredibly admirable. You made your way past defenses no other woman has ever managed to scale. You burrowed your way inside my chest and took up residence in my heart." Leaning forward, he pressed a kiss to her brow with so much reverence, an emotional tear spilled from her eye. "You have become my entire world, Juliette. I have never felt as lost as I did when your life was threatened."

"Florian." She could scarcely reply she was so overcome by the beauty of his declaration.

"Now that you are healthy and safe and here for me to see and touch, I feel restored, as though the part of me that was missing has been returned." He flattened his hand against her cheek and swiped away the fallen tear with his thumb. "To lose you again is unthinkable. Marry me, Juliette. Be mine and let me be yours. Love me as I shall love you, until my dying breath."

Unable to speak on account of the painful lump that had wedged itself in her throat, Juliette could only think of one way to convey her answer. Without hesitation, she closed the distance between them, pressing her lips to his in a kiss wrought from endless depths of affection. It was hungry but sweet, an aching portrayal of true devotion wrapped up in yearning.

Winding her arms around his neck, she shifted closer until their thighs touched. His hand stroked over her back, holding her to him while he followed her down the steep path of desire, catching momentum as he deepened the kiss until thoughts of all else were whisked from her mind.

It wasn't until his teeth nipped her earlobe and sent several sparks dancing over her skin that she recalled time and place. "Yes." She was finally able to offer a verbal response to his question. "Yes, I will marry you, Florian. Nothing in the world would make me happier than spending the rest of my life with you."

His mouth captured hers once again, stealing her breath until she felt dizzy. She was almost in his lap he'd pulled her so close, the joy she found in his ardor making her giggle even as she did her best to keep up with his kisses.

"I love you, Juliette." Pulling back, he met her gaze with unwavering sincerity. "And I promise you that I will always strive to make you happy and that you will never regret your decision to be my wife."

"I have never looked forward to anything as much as I do my wedding day." She gave him her best smile, the one that conveyed how much she longed to be his. "Do you think a special license might be possible?"

"I hope so." Unwinding his arms from around her waist, he took her hands in his and lowered his gaze to that intimate point of contact. "My intention is to call on the archbishop immediately after visiting Armswell."

"You do not sound pleased about having to speak with him, Florian." She could hear it in the dry crispness of his voice. "Have the two of you had a falling-out?"

He winced. "No. It has merely come to my attention that he is to blame for all that has happened. And since that is the case, I mean to ask him to right the wrong he has done my mother and me, even you by association."

Unsure of what exactly Armswell was guilty of,

Juliette shook her head. "How will you accomplish that?"

"By insisting he tell the newspapers they were wrong and by publicly renouncing the idea of me being Bartholomew's son." Florian withdrew his hands and raked his fingers through his hair, scattering copper and gold in every direction. "I do not care how many lies the viscount has to tell to convince everyone that I am his blood, but he will do it or so help me I shall—"

"Florian." She did not like seeing him like this, so consumed by anger it seemed to turn his face to stone while pushing all light from his eyes. "Threatening Armswell is not the answer." She stood and walked to the window, looking out on the street for a moment before turning to face him. "What does it matter what people think of us as long as we have each other?"

He expelled a defeated sigh and came toward her. "It may be of great importance one day to our children."

This was not something she had considered. She bit her lip and did so now. "You are right. It might. Unless we manage to defeat the stigma we have both fallen prey to by then. There is time, Florian. Years, in fact, for us to regain our positions. And let's not forget your impressive title. It means something, no matter whose son you are."

"Very well." His hand reached out and drew her into his arms. Holding her close, he pressed his mouth to hers in a slow and reverent kiss. "I must confront Armswell, though, for my own peace of mind, but I will make no demands. You and I will do what we can to improve Society's opinion of us. And if we fail—"

"We still have each other, our dignity and the love and support of two other dukes and duchesses."

Thoughtfulness puckered his brow. "Our connections are quite impressive."

"They are certainly better than what most people can hope for." Rising up onto her toes, she kissed him with adoration before leaning back and meeting his gaze. "Perhaps we can go on an extended wedding trip right away. I might not care what people think of me, but I would like to look respectable when I make my first public appearance as your wife."

"Of course. Now that I am out of work there is nothing keeping me in London. We may go wherever we please, Juliette. To Paris or Rome, if you like."

"Or we could simply enjoy a peaceful visit to a countryside cottage in the Lake District."

"Quiet walks and picnics sound like the perfect remedy for what we have been through."

She grinned up at him, and in that moment her heart overflowed with warmth and tenderness. "I could not agree with you more, Florian. Now be on your way, so you can return here as quickly as possible. I find that I am increasingly impatient to become your wife."

With one final kiss he stepped back and gave a quick bow. "When I see you again, I will have a vicar with me." Upon which he strode from the room leaving Juliette behind with a fluttering heart.

Chapter 28

When Florian arrived at Armswell House, he took a moment to study the façade that held so many turbulent memories, of a father who'd always seemed reluctant to offer affection, even though he had no such qualms when it came to Lowell. Growing up, Florian had always thought it related to Lowell being the firstborn heir. It wasn't until his sixteenth year that he'd learned the truth.

Florian climbed the steps and steeled himself for the conflict waiting on the opposite side of the front door. The butler granted him entry, as expected, and directed him through to Armswell's study.

The viscount looked up from the ledgers spread out on the desk before him and set his spectacles aside. "Florian!" He stood and gestured for Florian to have a seat across from him. "I was not expecting to see you so soon. With everything that has been going on, I thought you would be too busy for family visits."

Florian crossed to the proffered chair and lowered himself down onto the plush velvet cushion. "This is not a social call," he said while doing his best to sound cordial. "My coming here has everything to do with what has transpired."

Armswell gave a swift nod. "Yes." He nodded again, then turned and went to the sideboard. "Brandy?"

"No, thank you. I prefer to keep a level head for this conversation."

Armswell grabbed the nearest decanter and poured a quick drink, spilling some of it on his way back to his chair. He sat and took a long sip. "We were very sorry to hear about Lady Juliette's illness, but it is our understanding that she is much improved now?"

Word really did spread like a virus. "Yes. She has recovered from her bout with typhus."

Armswell expelled a breath. "What a relief." He set his glass aside and seemed to relax his posture. "The papers were most unkind about her lengthy quarantine in your home without chaperone, but your mother and I believe you did what was best."

"I did not come here to discuss Lady Juliette's health with you or to inform you of our intention to wed." Armswell's eyebrows rose and he prepared to speak, but Florian cut him off. "The reason I am here is because Lady Juliette was kidnapped this morning by Bartholomew. Her life was threatened because I failed to meet the demands of a man who would never have paid our family any mind, if it had not been for you."

Armswell's jaw tightened before going slack. Admirably, he did not avert his gaze but held Florian's with visible determination. "You are right. I was young and stupid and have struggled with my conscience over what I did many times over."

"Does Mama know?"

He shook his head. "No. She told you the truth.

At least her version of it but I . . . I was too ashamed to tell her or anyone else that I had squandered my fortune. Foolishly, I allowed my cowardice to determine my actions and begged a loan from Bartholomew."

"And then refused to pay it back."

"Had I done so, I would have been no better off than before he gave me the necessary funds. I needed time to secure a steady income but he would not allow that."

Disgust churned in Florian's belly. "So you whored away your wife instead."

"Not willingly!" Wild insistence sparked in Armswell's eyes. "Damn it, Florian. The bastard took Lowell and demanded your mother's compliance!"

"Something he would not have done if you had not sought his help in the first place." Contempt had long since weeded out all sympathy. "Instead, Mama lost her pride, her dignity, her reputation, now that the truth is out. Have you even considered what people will think of her?"

"Of course I have. Which is why I have visited every paper that printed the damn story and demanded a retraction with an apology included."

"Really?" Florian had to admit he had not expected the viscount to do so.

"Of course." He expelled a deep breath and folded his arms on the table. "In spite of what you may think, I love your mother a great deal. Allowing the world to think the worst of her, because of something I am to blame for, is not an option."

"So you lied for her?"

A quick nod confirmed this. "The retraction and apology will be printed tomorrow."

Which was excellent news. And yet . . . "You should also make a public statement at the next social function, preferably with one of the journalists backing you up, if that's possible."

Armswell nodded. "I think I can handle that."

Florian didn't return the smile Armswell offered. Instead, he gave a curt nod. "Thank you." He stood and went to the door.

"I do not know if you can ever forgive me for the choices I made, but I want you to know that I am glad something good came out of it." When Florian turned with a raised eyebrow, Armswell said, "Had your mother not gone to him, you would not have been born and the world would have lacked an extraordinary man and physician."

Unsure if such a trade was worth the cost, Florian chose not to comment, turning away instead and leaving Armswell House in favor of grasping his future with every bit of strength he possessed.

An hour later, he was admitted into the archbishop's chambers and one hour after that, he was back at Huntley House with a special license, Henry, and a vicar agreeable enough to perform a service on short notice.

It felt like a dream. Dressed in her best muslin gown and with a wide length of stunning silk gauze draped over her head, Juliette repeated the words the vicar spoke and then listened with tears in her eyes while Florian did the same. Behind them stood Raphe, Gabriella, Coventry, Amelia and Lowell, all bearing witness to their heartfelt exchange of vows.

Florian kept his eyes trained on Juliette the entire

time, just as she kept her gaze on him when it was her turn to speak.

"Do you have the ring?" the vicar asked Florian when Juliette had finished making her vows.

"I do." Reaching inside his jacket pocket, Florian produced a simple gold band which he placed upon the vicar's Bible.

The vicar gave a satisfied nod, then picked up the ring and handed it back to Florian. "Please put this upon the fourth finger of Juliette's left hand and hold it there while repeating after me . . ."

Juliette's heart leapt the moment she felt the cool piece of metal slide comfortably into place. Her eyes met Florian's once again and saw in them the same degree of love she herself was experiencing. Her soul was verily overflowing with it, her body humming with infinite joy and excitement.

Laughter bubbled up inside her with such force she could barely contain it. The vicar added a prayer, a blessing and a piece of scripture, but she failed to focus in her eagerness for all of this to be over so she and Florian could proceed with their newly wedded state. He conveyed his own exuberance with the wide smile that had crept into place on his handsome face several minutes earlier and with the fierce kiss he gave her the moment the vicar had finished speaking.

It was passionate and warm and probably lasted a great deal longer than what was considered acceptable, but Juliette did not care. In fact, she could think of nothing better in all the world than kissing Florian back while he held her securely in his arms.

"Congratulations," Raphe said moments later when they'd pulled apart and faced their family. He'd stepped forward so he could give Juliette a brotherly hug. "I am so incredibly happy for you."

Everyone seconded this sentiment, embracing both Juliette and Florian in turn before calling on Pierson to serve some champagne.

"We will host a ball in your honor once you return from your wedding trip," Amelia said. She stood with Coventry's protective arm around her waist. "How long do you expect to be gone?"

"At least until the scandals pertaining to Florian's lineage and my extended stay in his home without chaperone have blown over," Juliette replied.

"Huntley and I intend to use our influence to fight the scandal hanging over your heads," Coventry said.

"As will I," Lowell told his brother. "Between the lot of us, I have no doubt we will meet with success."

"Thank you," Florian said. "We're extremely grateful for your help."

Juliette glanced at him and met his gaze while reaching for his hand and giving it a tight squeeze. The only thing that mattered now was the future, the love they shared for each other, and the incredible support their family was willing to provide.

Later, when Florian and Juliette returned to the home they now shared, he felt like a green lad about to kiss a girl for the very first time. He was desperate to get it right. Having to inform his servants of his wedded state and accept their congratulations was actually a welcome distraction from the increased tightening of his nerves.

"You may take the rest of the evening off," he told Baker, Jillian and Mrs. Croft. "We will manage on our own. But please be here tomorrow by noon as we plan on departing for the Lake District and may need your help packing."

The servants readily agreed and quickly dispersed, leaving Florian and Juliette alone in the silence that followed. He glanced at her, eager to proceed with their wedding night but uncertain of where to begin since he did not wish to cause her unease or discomfort. And since he was the most experienced one of the pair, it fell to him to guide them both through this new experience, which added a surprising amount of pressure—more than he would ever have imagined. But he desperately wanted their first time together to be pleasant for her and unencumbered by shyness or fear.

With this in mind, he reached for her arm and linked it snugly with his own before proceeding toward the stairs. "I have an excellent port for us to enjoy." The sweet liquor would help calm them both. They climbed a few steps in silence before he dared ask, "Are you worried about the sexual act?"

She jerked her head around so she could stare up at him while they walked. Much to his relief, she shook her head. "No. I am familiar with the basics, and Gabriella was kind enough to offer some enlightenment while you took care of the special license. She assured me that it can be very pleasurable indeed as long as I relax and participate with enthusiasm."

Coughing so he would not choke in response to that bit of blunt information, Florian made a mental note to thank his new sister-in-law later. "She is correct."

He escorted his wife the rest of the way to his bedchamber and ushered her inside, watching as she took her time to survey the space. A four-poster bed draped with a dark blue canopy occupied the center. It was matched by a comfortable armchair that stood beside a low table in front of the fireplace. A tall armoire flanked the white wall next to the door while a solid chest of drawers and a washstand rested beneath the window looking out onto a small courtyard below.

"It is simple but elegant. No flourish." Juliette turned to face him. "I like it a lot."

It was silly how much that compliment pleased him. Abashed by it, he went to pour them both a glass of the port he'd mentioned earlier. "To our new life together as husband and wife." He clinked his glass with hers and drank while she did the same.

"I should probably examine your wound," he said while eyeing the piece of linen still wrapped around her neck.

When she nodded, he set his glass aside on the nightstand and reached for the fabric. A gentle tug and a bit of unraveling revealed a blotch of red smeared across her neck, but it was dry now and the graze itself was no longer bleeding.

"I'll clean it a bit," Florian murmured, his pulse so rapid it made the tips of his fingers tremble.

Grabbing the pitcher from his washstand, he poured a measure of water into the washbowl, located a clean handkerchief and wet one corner of it. He then returned to where Juliette stood and dabbed the handkerchief against her neck.

"There," he said when no more traces of blood remained. Blowing out a shuddering breath, he put the handkerchief in his pocket, recalled it was wet and retrieved it again so he could hang it to dry.

Juliette surveyed his every move, which did nothing to ease the tension inside him.

"You seem . . . unmoored." She placed her glass next to his and watched him with glittering eyes. "Is it possible you might be more nervous about our joining than I am?"

Her forwardness was both welcoming and admirable. "I believe I may well be. Making it perfect for you has put me in a state of uncommon apprehension."

"Which must be disconcerting for a man who is otherwise accustomed to being confident, methodical, certain." She moved toward him. "Stop worrying." He must have looked dubious, for she suddenly gave him a very reassuring smile and said, "I want this, Florian. I want to be with you in this way and considering how we feel about each other can only ensure that—"

He didn't let her finish, stealing the words she might have spoken with a kiss that instantly fueled his desire. She was stunning, self-assured, perfect in every way and the very personification of goodness itself. And she was kissing him back as though her life depended on it. Her arms were around his neck, her mouth moving in perfect concert with his, tasting and exploring with unrestrained fervor.

Hands on her waist to hold her steady, he walked her back until she came up against the bedpost. "Juliette." He whispered her name against her lips and slid his hands upward, stroking her torso, the sides of her breasts, until little whimpers rose from her throat.

Still, she kissed him, arching her back to press herself closer. "Florian." His name was a gasp, an elixir heightening each of his senses and strengthening his arousal.

"Turn around." He deliberately infused the demand with the promise of pleasure and to his delight, felt her shiver beneath his touch.

She did as he bade without question, allowing him to unbutton her gown and draw it over her shoulders. It slid down her body to pool at her feet, followed swiftly by her stays and her shift. She stepped away from the clothes, removing her shoes in the process so all she was left with were her stockings.

Florian drew a shuddering breath while allowing himself the delicacy of perusing his wife's nudity. He'd seen it before, of course, but that had been different. She'd been sick then, whereas now . . . Christ, the look she was giving him over her shoulder . . . A timid display of innocent lust so tempting he had no choice but to reach for her with unsteady hands and plant a row of kisses along the length of her spine.

The sigh with which she responded was decadent indeed and quickly had him divesting himself of his own clothing. She turned to watch, her eyes devouring every part of the process as she leaned against the bedpost. Apparently, she felt no shyness, perhaps because she'd become accustomed to him seeing her naked during the week when he'd cared for her. Whatever the case, he was grateful, for it allowed him to admire her body without her trying to cover it up, his eyes lingering on the places where his touch would give her most pleasure.

Juliette could only stare as the man she loved shucked his shirt to reveal a chest defined by rippling muscles. Kicking off his shoes, he removed his hose and straightened himself to his full height. As if enjoying her perusal, he met her gaze boldly and held it for a second before allowing it to fall away. She followed it down, her mouth going dry as she watched his hands move to his waistband. Unfastening buttons, he opened the placket and pushed his trousers and smalls down over his hips and all the way to the floor where he kicked them aside.

She inhaled sharply when he rose again to stand before her. His arms were strong and beautifully shaped, his belly completely flat with a thin strip of copper hair darting down toward . . . She swallowed as she considered that part of him. It was larger than she'd expected and—

"I won't hurt you," he said as if reading her thoughts. "Your body will accommodate mine, Juliette. Of that I can assure you."

She nodded, determined to regain her confidence from earlier. "I know." He must have sensed that she wasn't quite certain, for he instantly closed the distance between them and lowered his lips to her ear, whispering all manner of wicked intentions while his hands wandered over her curves.

When she was almost undone by need and ready to beg him for more, he picked her up in his arms and lowered her onto the bed. Frantic for his caresses, she reached for him and he was there, his body hovering over hers while his questing fingers brought anticipation to a peak. "Please." Her hands clasped at his shoulders, insistent on bringing him closer.

"Yes, sweetheart." His kiss was accompanied by the briefest pain and then by endless amounts of bliss. Gently, he moved against her, teaching her the timeless rhythm that would send them both right over the edge.

She caught on quickly, her body adjusting to each

new sensation until the initial discomfort was over-shadowed by a ravenous need for more. Without warning, it barreled toward her with sudden speed, sweeping her up in euphoric pleasure and carrying her higher until she burst like one of the fireworks she'd once seen at Vauxhall.

"Juliette . . ." Her name torn from his chest spoke of promise and hope, the deep kiss he gave her con-veying his love while his body found its own satis-faction. "Mine." He murmured the word against her ear in the moments that followed. "You are finally mine."

A boneless languor overcame her. It lingered as she gazed up into his deep blue eyes. Her hand reached up to stroke his cheek. "Yes." And then, knowing he'd likely appreciate the assurance, she gave him a smile and told him sincerely, "I have never enjoyed anything more than what we just did."

His eyes seemed to darken. "In that case, allow me to show you another way I can give you plea-sure." Lowering his head, he kissed his way down the length of her body while Juliette sighed in response. Whatever her expectations of the marital act had been, this was so much better than she could ever have imagined. Her husband was just as attentive and loving as she planned on being. But more than that, she looked forward to sharing her life with him as his equal and of simply conversing with him over break-fast, which was more than she'd ever dared dream might be possible.

Chapter 29

Rolling onto his side, Florian smoothed Juliette's hair away from her forehead. It was still very short, having grown only about an inch and a half in the three months they'd been away. As had become their daily routine during their escape to the Lake District, they'd taken a morning walk and spread out a blanket on one of the hillsides overlooking a valley. There, bathed by the August sun, they'd made love to each other until their sighs of pleasure whispered across the bright green landscape.

"I love you." He spoke the words that were constantly in his heart.

The smile she returned was dazzling. "As I love you."

Kissing her had become as necessary to him as breathing. So he bowed his head and captured her lips with his. As always, she tasted delicious. "I could easily kiss you forever," he told her, nuzzling the side of her neck with his nose.

To his immense satisfaction, she wound her arms around his torso and pulled him back between her thighs, shifting slightly so her pelvis met his. "How about doing *this* forever?"

He grinned, free from all the worry that had shadowed his life for so long. With Juliette he felt like the lad he'd been before his mother had pulled him aside and confessed he was really Bartholomew's son. His soul had lightened, and his heart, influenced by her kindness, had filled to overflowing with the sort of love that cleansed the soul.

"I do believe I'd enjoy that," he told her while she in turn offered a cheeky smile.

When they returned to the cottage they'd rented for luncheon, they found a letter waiting. "It is from the Duchess of Tremaine," he told Juliette, recognizing her seal.

"Open it."

He paused for only a second before doing as Juliette suggested, tearing the seal and unfolding the foolscap. His eyes scanned the page, absorbing every detail. Blinking, he raised his gaze to Juliette. "The hospital wants me back."

Juliette beamed up at him with encouraging zeal. "That is wonderful news!"

"Apparently, some of my patients refuse to be treated by anyone else and demand to know where I am and what is keeping me away."

"Raphe did write a month ago letting us know there are only a few people left who seem to question your heritage and what transpired between the two of us while I was living beneath your roof."

"True." He set the letter aside on a nearby table. "But there was no rush to return, especially since you would like for your hair to grow out before venturing back into Society."

Trumpeting her lips, her face took on an adorably pensive expression. "You are right," she eventually told him, "but your patients are more important than my vanity."

His heart felt like bursting. "Are you sure?"

"Absolutely. My only regret is having to leave all of this behind. You and I have been gifted with a wonderful retreat. With you going back to work, that will be over."

"I know. I am just as sorry for that as you are." He drew her into his arms. "Perhaps we should make it a rule to come back here once a year, for a month at least."

"If the hospital can spare you."

He drew a deep breath, inhaling the scent of peonies that would always remind him of home. "I will make it conditional upon my return." Drawing her close, he sealed this promise with a kiss, grateful for the day when her unfailing tenacity had brought her into his office on a mission. That day had changed his life and would always remain a fixed moment in time when their lives had collided, shifted and continued on together toward an endless series of happy tomorrows.

Chapter 30

Henry Atticus Lowell was convinced he was going to die. After all, that was what one generally did when one had been shot in the chest. The pain of it was excruciating, an experience he could have avoided if he'd only fired his pistol faster. But he hadn't wanted to hurt the young baron who'd called him out after Henry had advised the man to change his tailor if he wanted a better result on the marriage mart. This had led to a heated discussion, a muddy morning on the field of honor and a solid reminder to stay out of other people's business.

Groaning, Henry considered the people bustling about all around him. His brother, Florian, was there, thank God. At least he would be entrusting his life into the hands of a man who knew what he was doing.

"I am going to give you some morphine for the pain." Florian spoke concisely. "It will probably knock you out."

"Sounds wonderful," Henry muttered. An escape from the agony would be most welcome.

His brother grimaced and briefly placed his hand

over his. "I am going to get you through this. You are not going to die today, do you hear?" He did not wait for Henry to respond. "Now drink this."

Henry did, swallowing every last drop of the bitter concoction his brother held to his lips. He felt something cool on his skin but could not figure out what it was. A compress perhaps?

Metal clattered like fine silver cutlery placed on a tray. His eyes closed and the words exchanged between Florian and someone else grew increasingly fuzzy. The pain began to subside and he mercifully drifted off into a blissful state of unconsciousness.

When he awoke later, the first thing he became aware of was the gentle tread of someone moving carefully about. He flexed his fingers and felt the soft cotton of a sheet draped over his body. Well, it would seem he was still alive, thanks to his brother's miraculous efforts. And the pain . . . it was more of an ache now, which was a definite improvement.

Hesitantly, he opened his eyes just enough to let a bit of light in. It was blinding, the sunshine spilling in from a nearby window with unforgiving brightness. He winced and immediately closed his eyes again.

"Mr. Lowell?" The voice that spoke was feminine, soft and soothing, a mere whisper almost. Henry grunted his response and sensed the woman came nearer. "I hope I did not disturb you." A soft hand settled upon his brow for no more than a fleeting second. "You do not seem to have a fever, which is excellent news."

He drew a deep breath, focused on the tightening effect it had on his chest, and gradually expelled it. "No." Again he tried to open his eyes, to see the nurse who'd come to attend him. She sounded lovely and . . . The light was no longer as bright as it had been. It shone at the woman's back, surrounding her in a halo of gold. She was fair, with dark blonde tresses catching the sun and tossing it back. Her face, however, was perfection itself, a pair of warm chocolate eyes and full lips portraying the deepest shade of rose he'd ever seen.

Perhaps he had died after all.

Henry closed his eyes on that thought and allowed himself to drift off again, certain he'd just caught a glimpse of heaven and one of its prettiest angels.

Author's Note

Dear Reader,

As you can probably imagine, writing this story required a great deal of medical research, especially pertaining to the early 1800s.

Although epidemic typhus was a known disease at the time, it was not until 1903 when Charles Nicolle, a French bacteriologist, traveled to Tunis to research an outbreak, that its connection to lice was discovered. Incidentally, Nicolle received a Nobel Prize in medicine for this accomplishment.

But even though Florian would have lacked Nicolle's knowledge, he was still able to implement the successful treatment used at the Edinburgh Infirmary throughout the late 18th century. Fumigation was done daily there using tar water or muriatic acid, the tiled floors were mopped and the walls periodically whitewashed. Additionally, those who were admitted were ordered to surrender their clothes. They were then washed, their heads shaved, and their skin rubbed with mercurial ointment, a process Florian applies onboard the quarantine ship and also when treating Juliette.

It was known that dirt, poor air conditions and lack of proper food could spread and/or exacerbate disease. Typhus patients were therefore given hearty meals, especially meat and fruit, with diluted wine to accompany it, preferably eight ounces of wine in four ounces of water. For more serious cases, undiluted wine was called for, as much as a half to one and a half pints per day.

For the description of the disease's progression, I relied on "Typhus Fever in Eighteenth-century Hospitals" by Guenter B. Risse since this provided a period accurate account. *Domestic Medicine* by William Buchan, which some of you may recall me referencing in *There's Something About Lady Mary*, was once again an excellent source on contagion attentiveness from the late 1700s onward. It proves that awareness of hand-washing and general cleanliness in disease prevention existed even though it did not become a requirement for medical practitioners until much later. In fact, in spite of Buchan's book, which was originally published in 1771, Ignaz Semmelweis, a Hungarian physician, is credited with discovering the benefits of hand-washing in 1847 when he noted a connection between physicians handling corpses, then delivering children without cleaning their hands first, and mothers contracting puerperal fever.

Not to diminish Semmelweis's findings, but Buchan's were made eighty years or more earlier and would have been known to a well-read man like Florian.

Although morphine was not commercially used until the mid-1800s, a German pharmacist named Friedrich Wilhelm Sertürner had managed to isolate the crystalline compound from crude opium by 1816. During his experiments, he discovered that the pain relief effect of this compound was ten times that of opium and named it morphine after Morpheus, the Greek god of dreams.

Considering how well traveled and open to new medicinal discoveries Florian was, he would have wasted no time in acquiring this new narcotic and administering it to his patients when performing surgeries.

As with every piece of medical information I've used to flesh out this story, The Humane Society is a real organization which still exists today. Modeled after the Amsterdam Society for the Rescue of Drowning, it awarded a silver medal to one of its members, Charles Kite, in 1788. Kite not only advocated the resuscitation of victims in cardiac arrest with bellows as well as oropharyngeal and nasopharyngeal intubation long before CPR is commonly known to have been discovered, but also developed his own electrostatic revivifying machine. This device used Leyden jar capacitors in a similar way to the DC capacitive countershock of the modern cardiac defibrillator.

Other historically accurate facts and characters include James Gregory, a Scottish physician whom Florian recalls having met, and the Spanish surgeon, Francisco Romero, who is indeed credited with performing the first heart surgery in 1801, even though, as Florian correctly tells Juliette, the surgery was on the lining of the heart and not on the actual heart itself.

I hope you have enjoyed this story. As you already know, Henry and Viola are destined to fall in love in the fourth installment of *Diamonds in the Rough*. It will be interesting to see what obstacles they encounter on the way to their own happily ever after, so please join me again soon to find out.

Until then, happy reading!

Acknowledgments

It takes more than an author to grasp an idea and transform it into a book. My name might be on the cover, but there's a whole team of spectacular people behind me, each with their own incredible skills and experience. Their faith in me and in my stories is invaluable, and since they do deserve to be recognized for their work, I'd like to take this opportunity to thank them all for their constant help and support.

To my editor extraordinaire, Nicole Fischer: your edits and advice have helped this story shine. Thank you so much for your insight and for believing in my ability to pull this off.

To my copy editor, Libby Sternberg; publicists Caroline Perny, Pam Jaffee and Libby Collins; and director of marketing, Angela Craft, thank you so much for all that you do and for offering guidance and support whenever it was needed.

A special thank-you goes to the Royal College of Surgeons in England for the articles they sent me upon request and for their willingness to delve into eighteenth and nineteenth century medical education on my behalf. The information your library provided has helped me tremendously.

To my author friend Katharine Ashe, with whom I've enjoyed sharing facts that can only be found when one is willing to search the haystack, discussing medical research with you has been an absolute pleasure!

I would also like to thank the amazing artist who created this book's stunning cover. Chris Cocozza has truly succeeded in capturing the mood of *The Illegitimate Duke* and the way in which I envisioned both Florian and Juliette looking—such a beautiful job!

To my fabulous beta readers, Jacqueline Ang, Maria Rose and Jennifer Becker, whose insight has been tremendously helpful in strengthening the story, thank you so much!

Another big thank-you goes to Nancy Mayer for her assistance. Whenever I'm faced with a question regarding the Regency era that I can't answer on my own, I turn to Nancy for advice. Her help is invaluable.

My family and friends deserve my thanks as well, especially for reminding me to take a break occasionally, to step away from the computer and just unwind—I would be lost without you.

And to you, dear reader—thank you so much for taking the time to read this story. Your support is, as always, hugely appreciated!